Harry Collingwood

The Pirate Slaver

Harry Collingwood

The Pirate Slaver

ISBN/EAN: 9783743313309

Manufactured in Europe, USA, Canada, Australia, Japa

Cover: Foto ©Andreas Hilbeck / pixelio.de

Manufactured and distributed by brebook publishing software
(www.brebook.com)

Harry Collingwood

The Pirate Slaver

THE PIRATE SLAVER

A STORY OF THE WEST AFRICAN COAST

BY

HARRY COLLINGWOOD

AUTHOR OF

"THE CONGO ROVERS," "PIRATE ISLAND," "THE LOG OF THE 'FLYING FISH,'"
"THE CRUISE OF THE 'ESMERALDA,'" ETC., ETC., ETC.

ILLUSTRATED BY W. H. OVEREND

PUBLISHED UNDER THE DIRECTION OF THE GENERAL LITERATURE COMMITTEE

LONDON
SOCIETY FOR PROMOTING CHRISTIAN KNOWLEDGE
NORTHUMBERLAND AVENUE, W.C.
43, QUEEN VICTORIA STREET E.C.
BRIGHTON: 129, NORTH STREET
NEW YORK: E. S. GORHAM

THE PIRATE SLAVER

CHAPTER I

THE CONGO RIVER

" LAND ho ! broad on the port bow ! "

The cry arose from the look-out on the forecastle of her Britannic Majesty's 18-gun brig *Barracouta*, on a certain morning near the middle of the month of November, 1840 ; the vessel then being situated in about latitude 6°. 5' south and about 12° east longitude. She was heading to the eastward, close-hauled on the port tack, under every rag that her crew could spread to the light and almost imperceptible draught of warm, damp air that came creeping out from the northward. So light was the breeze that it scarcely wrinkled the glassy smoothness of the long undulations upon which the brig rocked and swayed heavily while her lofty trucks described wide arcs across the paling sky overhead, from which the stars were vanishing one after another before the advance of the pallid dawn. And at every lee roll her canvas flapped with a rattle as of a volley of musketry to the masts, sending down a smart shower from the dew-saturated cloths upon the deck, to fill again with the report of a nine-pounder and a great slatting of sheets and blocks as the ship recovered herself and rolled to windward.

The brig was just two months out from England, from whence she had been dispatched to the West African coast to form a ·portion of the slave-squadron and to relieve the old *Garnet*, which, from her phenomenal lack of speed, had proved utterly unsuitable for the service of chasing and capturing the nimble slavers who, despite all our precautions, were still pursuing their cruel and nefarious vocation with unparalleled audacity and success. We had relieved the *Garnet*, and had looked in at Sierra Leone for the latest news ; the result of this visit being that we were now heading in for the mouth of the Congo, which river had been strongly commended to our especial attention by the Governor of the little British colony. Our captain, Commander Henry Stopford, was by no means a communicative man, it being a theory of his that it is a mistake on the part of a chief to confide more to his officers than is absolutely necessary for the efficient and intelligent performance of their duty ; hence he had not seen fit to make public the exact particulars of the information thus received. But he had of course made an exception in favour of Mr. Young, our popular first luff ; and as I—Henry Dugdale, senior mid of the *Barracouta*—happened to be something of a favourite with the latter, I learned from him, in the course of conversation, some of the circumstances that were actuating our movements. The intelligence, however, was of a very meagre character, and simply amounted to this : That large numbers of African slaves were being continually landed on the Spanish West Indian islands ; that two boats with their crews had mysteriously disappeared in the Congo while engaged upon a search of that river for slavers ; and that a small felucca named the *Wasp* —a tender to the British ship-sloop *Lapwing*—had also disappeared with all hands, some three months previously, after having been seen in pursuit of a large brig that had come out of the river ; these circumstances leading to the inference that the Congo was the haunt of a strong gang of daring slavers whose capture must be effected at any cost.

It was for this service that the *Barracouta* had been selected, she being a brand-new ship especially built for work on the West African coast, and modelled to sail at a high speed upon a light draught of water. She was immensely beamy for her length, and very shallow, drawing only ten feet of water with all her stores and ammunition on board, very heavily sparred—*too* heavily, some of us thought —and, as for canvas, her topsails had the hoist of those of a frigate of twice her tonnage. She was certainly a beautiful model of a ship—far and away the prettiest that I had ever seen when I first stepped on board her—while her speed, especially in light winds and tolerably smooth water, was such as to fill us all, fore and aft, with the most extravagant hopes of success against the light-heeled slave clippers whose business it was ours to suppress. She was a flush-decked vessel, with high, substantial bulwarks pierced for nine guns of a side, and she mounted fourteen 18-pounder carronades and four long nine-pounders, two forward and two aft, which could be used as bow and stern-chasers respectively, if need were, although we certainly did not anticipate the necessity to employ any of our guns in the latter capacity. Our crew, all told, numbered one hundred and sixty-five.

I was in the first lieutenant's watch, and happened to be on deck when the look-out reported land upon the morning upon which this story opens. I remember the circumstance as well as though it had occurred but yesterday, and I have only to close my eyes to bring the whole scene up before my mental vision as distinctly as a picture. The brig was, as I have already said, heading to the eastward, close-hauled, on the port tack, under everything that we could set, to her royals; but the wind was so scant that even the light upper sails flapped and rustled monotonously to the sleepy heave and roll of the ship, and it was only by glancing through a port at the small, iridescent air-bubbles that drifted astern at the rate of about a knot and a half in the hour that we were able to detect the fact of our own forward movement at all. We had been on deck just an hour—for two bells had barely been struck—when the first faint suggestion of dawn appeared ahead in the shape of a scarcely-perceptible lightening of the sky along a narrow strip of the eastern horizon, in the midst of which the morning star beamed resplendently, while the air, although still warm, assumed a freshness that, compared with the close, muggy heat of the past night, seemed almost cold, so that involuntarily I drew the lapels of my thin jacket together and buttoned the garment from throat to waist. Quickly, yet by imperceptible gradations, the lightening of the eastern sky spread and strengthened, the soft, velvety, star-lit, blue-black hue paling to an arch of cold, colourless pallor as the

dawn asserted itself more emphatically, while the stars dwindled and vanished one by one in the rapidly-growing light. As the pallor of the sky extended itself insidiously north and south along the horizon, a low-lying bank of what at first presented the appearance of dense vapour became visible on the *Barracouta's* larboard bow; but presently, when the cold whiteness of the coming day became flushed with a delicate tint of purest, palest primrose, the supposed fog-bank assumed a depth of rich purple hue and a clear-cut sharpness of outline that proclaimed it what it was—*land*, most unmistakably. The look-out was a smart young fellow, who had already established a reputation for trustworthiness, and he more than half suspected the character of the cloud-like appearance when it first caught his attention; he therefore kept his eye upon it, and was no sooner assured of its nature than he raised the cry of—

" Land ho ! broad on the port bow ! "

The first luff, who had been for some time meditatively pacing the weather side of the deck from the binnacle to the gangway, with his hands clasped behind his back and his glance directed alternately to the deck at his feet and to the swaying main-royal-masthead, quickly awoke from his abstraction at the cry from the forecastle, and, springing lightly upon a carronade slide, with one hand grasping the inner edge of the hammock rail, looked long and steadily in the direction indicated.

"Ay, ay, I see it," he answered, when after a long, steady look he had satisfied himself of the character of what he gazed upon. "Wheel, there, how's her head ? "

"East-south-east, sir ! " answered the helmsman promptly.

The lieutenant shut one eye and, raising his right arm, with the hand held flat and vertically, pointed toward the southern extremity of the distant land, held it there for a moment, and murmured—

"A point and a half—east-half-south, distant—what shall we say—twenty miles? Ay, about that, as nearly as may be. Mr. Dugdale, just slip below and let the master know that the land is in sight on the port bow, bearing east-half-south, distant twenty miles."

I touched my cap and trundled down to the master's cabin, the door of which was hooked back wide open, permitting the cool, refreshing morning air that came in through the open scuttle free play throughout the full length of the rather circumscribed apartment in which Mr. Robert Bates lay snoring anything but melodiously. Entering the cabin, I grasped the worthy man by the shoulder and shook him gently, calling him by name at the same time in subdued tones in order that I might not awake the occupants of the contiguous berths.

"Ay, ay," was the answer, as the snoring abruptly terminated in a convulsive snort: "Ay, ay. What's the matter now, youngster? Has the ship tumbled overboard during the night, or has the skipper's cow gone aloft to roost in the main-top, that you come here disturbing me with your 'Mr. Bates—Mr. Bates'?"

"Neither, sir," answered I, with a low laugh at this specimen of our worthy master's quaint nautical humour; "but the first lieutenant directed me to let you know that the land is in sight on the port bow, bearing east-half-south, distant twenty miles."

"What, already?" exclaimed my companion, scrambling out of his cot, still more than half asleep, and landing against me with a force that sent me spinning out through the open doorway to bring up prostrate with a crash in the cabin of the doctor opposite, half stunned by the concussion of my skull against the bulkhead and by the avalanche of ponderous tomes that came crashing down upon me as the worthy medico's tier of hanging bookshelves yielded and came down by the run at my wild clutch as I stumbled over the ledge of the cabin door.

"Murther! foire! thieves! it's sunk, burnt, desthroyed, and kilt intoirely that I am!" roared poor Blake, rudely awakened out of a sound sleep by the crashing fall of his pet volumes upon the deck and by a terrific thwack across the face that I had inadvertently dealt him as I fell. "Fwhat is it that's happenin' at all, thin? is it a collision? or is it a case of sthrandin'? or"—he looked over the edge of his cot and saw me sitting upon the deck, ruefully rubbing the back of my head while I vainly struggled to suppress my laughter at the ridiculous *contretemps*—"oh! so it's *you*, thin, is it, Misther Dugdale? Bedad, but you ought to be ashamed of yoursilf to be playin' these pranks—a lad of your age, that's hitherto been the patthern of

good behaviour! But wait a little, my man—sthop till I tell the first liftinint of your outhrageous conduct——"

By this time I thought that the matter had gone far enough; moreover, I had in a measure recovered my scattered senses, so I scrambled to my feet and, as I re-hung the bookshelf and replaced the books, hurriedly explained to the good man the nature of the mishap, winding up with a humble apology for having so rudely broken in upon what he was pleased to call his "beauty shlape." Understanding at once that my involuntary incursion into the privacy of his cabin had been the result of pure accident, "Paddy," as we irreverently called him—his baptismal name was William—very good-naturedly accepted my explanation and apology, and composed himself to sleep again, whereupon I retreated in good order and re-entered the master's cabin. The old boy had by this time slipped on his breeches and coat, and was bending over the table with the chart of "Africa — West Coast" spread out thereon, and a pencil and parallel ruler in his hands. He indulged in one or two of the grimly humorous remarks that were characteristic of him in reference to my disturbance of the doctor's slumbers; and then, pointing to a dot that he had just made upon the chart, observed—

"If the first lieutenant's bearing and distance are right, that's where we are, about twelve miles off Shark Point, and therefore in soundings. Did *you* see the land, Mr. Dugdale? What was it like?"

"It made as a long stretch of undulating hills sloping gently down to the horizon at its southernmost extremity, and extending beyond the horizon to the northward," I replied.

"Ay, ay, that's right; that's quite right," agreed the master. "It is that range of hills stretching along parallel with the coast on the north side of the river, and reaching as far as Kabenda Point," indicating the markings on the chart as he spoke. "Well, let us go on deck and get a cast of the lead; it is time that we ascertained the exact position of the ship, for the deep-water channel is none too wide, and although there seems to be plenty of water for us over the banks on either side, I have no fancy for trusting to the soundings laid down here on the chart. These African rivers are never to be depended upon, the shoals are constantly shifting, and where you may find water enough to float a line-of-battle ship to-day, you may ground in that same ship's launch a month hence."

He rolled up the chart, tucked it under his arm, gathered up his parallel ruler, pencil, and dividers, and together we left the cabin and made our way up the hatchway to the deck, where we found the first luff still perched upon the carronade slide, anxiously scanning the horizon on either bow under the sharp of his hand.

As we reached the deck a spark of golden fire flashed out upon the horizon on our lee bow, and the sun's disc soared slowly into view, warming the tints of a long, low-lying broken bank of grey cloud that stretched athwart his course into crimson, and fringing its skirts with gold as his first beams shot athwart the heaving water to the ship in a tremulous path of shimmering, dazzling radiance.

The lieutenant caught a glimpse of us out of the corner of his eye as we emerged from the hatchway, and at once stepped down off the slide on to the deck.

"Good-morning, Bates," said he. "Well, here we are, with the land plainly in view, you see; and I am glad that you have come on deck to tell us just *where* we are, for all this part of the world is quite new ground to me. We are closer in than I thought we were, for just before the sun rose the horizon ahead cleared, and I caught sight of what looked like the tops of trees, both on the port and on the starboard bow—you can't see them now for the dazzle, but you will presently, when the sun is a bit higher—and there seemed to be an opening or indentation of some sort between them, which I take to be the mouth of the river."

"Ay, ay," answered Bates, "that will be it, no doubt." He sprang on to the slide that Young had just vacated, took a long look at the land, and then, turning to the helmsman, demanded, "How's her head?"

"East-south-east, sir," answered the man for the second time.

With this information the master in his turn took an approximate bearing of the southernmost extremity of the range of hills, after which he stepped down on to the deck again and, going to the capstan, spread out his chart upon the head of it, calling me to help him keep the roll open. The lieutenant followed him, and stood watching as the master again manipulated his parallel ruler and dividers.

"Yes," remarked Bates, after a few moments' diligent study, "that's just about where we are," pointing to the mark that he had made upon the chart while in his own cabin. "And see," he continued, glancing out through the nearest lee port, "we have reached the river water; look how brown and thick it is, more like a cup of the captain's chocolate than good, wholesome salt water. We will try a cast of the lead, Mr. Young, if you please, just to make sure; though if we are fair in the channel, as I think we are, we shall get no bottom as yet. Nor shall we make any headway until the wind freshens or the sea-breeze springs up, for we are already within the influence of the outflowing current, and at this season of the year—which is the rainy season—it runs very strongly a little further in."

The lead was hove, but, as Bates had anticipated, no bottom was found; whereupon the master rolled up his chart again, gave orders that the ship was to be kept going as she was, and returned to his cabin, while the watch mustered their buckets and scrubbing-brushes and proceeded to wash decks and generally make the brig's toilet for the day.

Our worthy master was right; we did not make a particle of headway until about nine o'clock, when the wind gradually hauled round aft and freshened to a piping breeze before which we boomed along in fine style until we came abreast of a low, narrow point on our port hand, protected from the destructive action of the Atlantic breakers by a shoal extending some three-quarters of a mile to seaward. Abreast of this point we hauled up to the northward and entered a sort of bay about half-a-mile wide, with the low point before-mentioned on our port hand, and a wide mud-bank to starboard, beyond which was an island of considerable extent, fringed with mangroves and covered with thick bush and lofty trees. On the low point on our port hand were two "factories," or trading establishments, abreast of which were lying two brigs and a barque, one of the brigs flying British and the other Spanish colours, while the barque sported the Dutch ensign at her mizen peak. We rounded-to just far enough outside these craft to give them a clear berth, and let go our anchor in four fathoms of water.

It was a queer spot that we now found ourselves in; queer to me at least, who was now entering upon my first experience of West African service. We were riding with our head to the north-west under the combined influence of wind and tide together, with the low point—named Banana Peninsula, so the master informed me, though *why* it should be so named I never could understand, for there was not a single banana-tree upon the whole peninsula, as I subsequently ascertained. Let me see, where was I? I have gone adrift among those non-existent banana-trees. Oh yes, I was going to attempt to make a word-sketch of the scene which surrounded us after we had let go our anchor and furled our canvas. The sea-breeze was piping strong from the westward, while the tide was ebbing down the creek from the northward, and under these combined influences the *Barracouta* was riding with her head about north-west. Banana Peninsula lay ahead of us, trending away along our larboard beam and slightly away from us to the southward for about half-a-mile, where it terminated in a sandy beach bordered by a broad patch of smooth water, athwart which marched an endless line of mimic breakers from the wall of flashing white surf that thundered upon the outer edge of the protecting shoal three-quarters of a mile to seaward. The point was pretty thickly covered with bush and trees, chiefly cocoa-nut and other palms—except in the immediate vicinity of the two factories, where the soil had been cleared and a sort of rough wharf constructed by driving piles formed of the trunks of trees into the ground and wedging a few slabs of sawn timber in behind them. The point, for a distance of perhaps a mile from its southern extremity, was very narrow—not more than from one hundred and fifty to two hundred yards wide—but beyond that it widened out considerably until it merged in the mainland. On the opposite side of the creek, on our starboard quarter and astern of us, was what I at first took to be a single island, but which I subsequently found to be a group of about a dozen islands, of which the smallest may have been half-a-mile long by about a third of a mile broad,

while the largest was some nine or ten miles long by about t1 ree miles broad. These islands really constituted the northern bank of the river for a distance some twenty-four miles up the stream, being cut off from the mainland and from each other by narrow canal-like creeks running generally in a direction more or less east and west. The land all about here was low, and to a great extent swampy, the margin of the creeks being lined with mangroves that presented a very curious appearance as they stood up out of the dark, slimy-looking water, their trunks supported upon a network of naked, twisted roots that strongly suggested to me the idea of spiders' legs swollen and knotted with some hideous, deforming disease. The trees themselves, however, apart from their twisted, gnarled, and knotted roots, presented a very pleasing appearance, for they had just come into full leaf, and their fresh green foliage was deeply grateful to the eye satiated with a long and wearisome repetition of the panorama of unbroken sea and sky. Beyond the belt of mangroves the islands were overgrown with dense bush, interspersed with tall trees, some of which were rich with violet blossoms growing in great drooping clusters, like the flowers of the laburnum; while others were heavily draped with long, trailing sprays of magnificent jasmine, of which there were two kinds, one bearing a pinky flower, and the other a much larger star-like bloom of pure white. The euphorbia, acacia, and baobab or calabash-tree were all in bloom; and here and there, through openings between the trunks of the mangroves, glimpses were caught of rich splashes of deep orange colour, standing out like flame against the dark background of shadowed foliage, that subsequent investigation proved to be clumps of elegant orchids. It appeared that we had entered the river at precisely the right time of the year to behold it at its brightest and best, for the spring rains had only recently set in, and all Nature was rioting in the refreshment of the welcome moisture and bursting forth into a joyous prodigality of leaf and blossom, of colour and perfume, of life and glad activity. The forest rang with the calls and cries of pairing birds; flocks of parrots, parrakeets, and love-birds were constantly wheeling and darting hither and thither; kingfishers flitted low across the placid water, or watched motionless from some overhanging branch for the passage of their unsuspecting prey ; the wydah bird flaunted his gay plumage in the brilliant sunshine, where it could be seen to the fullest advantage ; and butterflies, like living gems, flitted happily from flower to flower. Astern of us, some three miles away, lay Boolambemba Point, the southernmost extremity of the group of islands to which I have already alluded. where the embouchure of the river may be said to begin, the stream here being about three and a half miles across, while immediately below it abruptly widens to a breadth of about five and a half miles at the indentation leading to Banana Creek, in the narrow approach to which we were lying at anchor. Of course it was not possible for us to distinguish, from where we were lying, much of the character of the country on the southern or left bank of the river, but it appeared to be pretty much the same as what we saw around us ; that is to say, low land densely covered with bush and trees along the river margin, with higher land beyond. About half-a-mile beyond us, broad on our starboard bow as we were then lying, the anchorage narrowed down to a width of less than half-a-mile, the western extremity of the group of islands already referred to there converging toward Banana Peninsula in a low, mangrove-wooded point. Beyond this, however, could be seen a stretch of water about a mile and a half wide, which I subsequently learned ran for several miles up at the back of the islands, between them and the mainland, in the form of a narrow, shallow, canal-like creek that Bates, the master, seemed to think might well repay the trouble of careful inspection, since the narrow maze of channels to which it gave access offered exceptional facilities for the embarkation of slaves, and a choice of routes for the light-draught slavers from their places of concealment into the main channel of the river.

CHAPTER II

WE RECEIVE SOME IMPORTANT INTELLIGENCE

WE had barely got our canvas furled and the decks cleared when we saw a fine, handsome whale-boat, painted white, with a canvas awning spread over her stern-sheets, and the Portuguese flag fluttering from a little staff at her stern, shove off from the wharf and pull toward us. She was manned by four Krumen, and in the stern-sheets sat a tall, swarthy man, whose white drill suit and white, broad-brimmed Panama hat, swathed with a white puggaree, caused his sun-tanned face and hands to appear almost as black as the skins of his negro crew. The boat swept up to our gangway in very dashing style, and her owner, ascending the accommodation ladder, stepped in on deck with a genial smile that disclosed a splendid set of brilliantly white teeth beneath his heavy, glossy black moustache.

" Good-morning, sar," said he to the first lieutenant, who met him at the gangway. " Velcome to Banana," with a flourish of his hat. " Vat chip dis is, eh ? "

" Her Britannic Majesty's brig *Barracouta*," answered Young. " You are the Portuguese consul here, I suppose?"

" No—no ; I not de consul," was the answer. " Dere is no consul at Banana. I am Señor Joaquin Miguel Lobo, Portuguese trader, at your savice, sar ; and I have come off to say dat I shall be happie to supply your chip wid anyting dat you may require—vattare, fresh meat, vegetabl', feesh, no fruit—de fruit not ripe yet ; plenty fruit by an' by, but not ripe yet —parrots, monkeys—all kind of bird and animal, yes ; and curiositie— plenty curiositie, sar."

Here the skipper, who had been below for a few minutes, reappeared on deck, and, seeing the stranger, advanced toward him, whereupon the first lieutenant introduced Señor Joaquin Miguel Lobo in proper form.

" Glad to see you, señor," remarked the skipper genially. " Will you step below and take a glass of wine with Lieutenant Young and myself? "

" Ver' happie, captain, I am sure," answered the señor with another sweeping bow and flourish of his Panama ; and forthwith the trio disappeared down the hatchway, to my unbounded astonishment, for it was not quite like our extremely dignified skipper to be so wonderfully cordial as this to a mere trader.

" Ah, I'm afraid that won't wash," remarked Bates, catching the look of astonishment and perplexity on my face as I turned my regards away from the hatchway. "The captain means to pump the Portuguese, if he can, but from the cut of the señor's jib I fancy there is not much to be got out of him; he looks to be far too wide-awake to let us become as wise as himself. I'll be bound that he could put us up to many a good wrinkle if he would; but, bless you, youngster, he's not going to spoil his own trade. He professes to be an honest trader, of course—deals in palm-oil and ivory and what not, of course, and I've no doubt he does; but I wouldn't mind betting a farthing cake that he ships a precious sight more *black* ivory than white out of this same river. Look at that brig, for instance—the one flying Spanish colours, I mean. Just look at her! Did you ever set your eyes upon a more beautiful hull than that? Look at the sweep of her run; see how it comes curving round to her stern-post in a delivery so clean that it won't leave a single eddy behind it. No drag *there*, my boy! And look at her sides: round as an apple—not an inch of straight in them! And do you suppose that a brig with lines like that was built for the purpose of carrying palm-oil? Not she. I should like to have a look at her bows; I'll be bound they are as keen as a knife—we shall see them by and by, when she swings at the turn of the tide. Yet if that brig were overhauled—as she probably will be—nothing whatever of a suspicious character would be found aboard her, except maybe a whole lot of casks, which they would say was for stowing the palm-oil in. Well, here we are; but we shall have to keep our eyes open night and day to weather upon the rascally slavers; they are as sly as foxes, and always up to some new circumventing trick."

With which reflection, followed by a deep sigh at the wily genius of the slaving fraternity in general, the worthy master turned upon his heel and retired below.

The Portuguese remained in the cabin for over an hour; and when he came on deck again, accompanied by the captain and the first lieutenant, I thought that the two latter looked decidedly elated, as though, despite the master's foreboding, they had succeeded in obtaining some important information. The captain was particularly gracious to his visitor, going even to the length of shaking hands with him ere he passed out through the gangway, the first luff of course following suit, as in duty bound.

"Then we may rely upon you to send us off the fresh meat and vegetables early this afternoon?" remarked Young, as he stood at the gangway.

"Yais, yais; dey shall be alongside by t'ree o'clock at de lates'!" answered the Portuguese. "And as soon as you have receive dem you had better veigh and leave de creek. Give dat point"—indicating Boolambemba Point—"a bert' of a mile and you veel be all right."

"Yes, thanks, I will remember," returned the first lieutenant. "And where are we to pick you up?"

"Hus-s-s-h! my dear sair; not so loud, if you please," answered Lobo, hastily leaving his boat and coming half-way up the gangway ladder again. "Dere is a leetl' creek about two mile pas' de point, on de nort' bank of de river. I vill be on de look-out for you dere in a small canoe vid two men dat I can trus'. And you mus' pick me up *queevk*, because if eet vas known dat I had consent to pilot you my t'roat would be cut before I vas a mont' oldaire."

"Never fear," answered Young. "We will keep a sharp look-out for you and get you on board without anybody being a penny the wiser. Good-bye."

The Portuguese bowed with another flourish of his hat, seated himself in the stern-sheets of his boat, gave the word to his Krumen, and a few minutes later was on the wharf, walking toward his factory, into the open door of which he disappeared.

"Come," thought I, "there is something afoot already. The captain and the first luff have, between them, evidently contrived to worm some intelligence out of the Portuguese. I must go and tell Bates the news."

Before I could do so, however, the captain, who had been standing near the gangway, listening to what was passing between Young and Lobo, caught sight of me and said—

"Mr. Dugdale, be good enough to find Mr. Bates, and tell him that I shall feel obliged if he will come to me for a few minutes in my cabin."

I touched my hat, dived down the hatchway, and gave the message, whereupon the master stepped out of his cabin and made his way aft. He was with the captain nearly half-an-hour; and when he reappeared he looked as pleased as Punch.

"I'll never attempt to judge a man's character by his face again," he exclaimed, as he caught me by the arm, and walked me along the deck beside him. "Who would have thought that a piratical-looking rascal like that Portuguese would have been friendly disposed towards the representatives of law and order? Yet he has not only given the captain valuable information, but has actually consented to pilot the ship to the spot which is to serve as our base of operations, although, as he says, should the slavers get to know of his having done such a thing, they would cut his throat without hesitation."

"Yes," said I, "I heard him make that remark to Mr. Young just before shoving off. And pray, Mr. Bates—if the question be not indiscreet—what is the nature of the expedition upon which we are to engage this afternoon?"

"Well, I don't know why I shouldn't tell you," answered Bates, a little doubtfully. "Our movements are of course to be conducted with all possible secrecy, but if I tell you I don't suppose you'll go ashore and hire the town-crier to make public our intentions; and all hands will have to know —more or less—what we're after, very soon, so I suppose I shall not be infringing any of the Articles of War if I tell you now; but you needn't go and publish the news throughout the ship, d'ye see? Let the skipper do that when he thinks fit."

"Certainly," I assented. "You may rely implicitly upon my discretion."

"Oh yes, of course," retorted the master ironically. "A midshipman is a perfect marvel in the way of prudence and discretion; everybody knows *that!* However," he continued, in a much more genial tone, "I will do you the justice to say that you seem to have your ballast pretty well stowed, and that you stand up to your canvas as steadily as any youngster that I've ever fallen in with; so I don't suppose there'll be very much harm in trusting you. You must know, then, that there's a bit of a creek, called Chango Creek, some fourteen or fifteen miles up the river from here; and in that creek there is at this moment lying snugly at anchor, quite unconscious of our proximity, and leisurely filling up her complement of blacks, a large Spanish brig called the *Mercedes*, hailing from

Havana. She is a notorious slaver, and is strongly suspected of having played the part of pirate more than once, when circumstances were favourable. Moreover, from what our Portuguese friend Lobo says, she was in the river when the *Sapphire's* two boats with their crews disappeared; and according to the dates he gives, she must also have been the craft that the plucky little *Wasp* was in chase of when last seen. There is very little doubt, therefore, that the *Mercedes* is the craft—or, at all events, one of them—which it is our especial mission to capture at any cost; and we are therefore going to weigh this afternoon for the purpose of beating up her quarters. Lobo has undertaken to pilot us as far as the mouth of the creek; and as he tells us that the brig is fully a hundred tons bigger than ourselves, is armed to the teeth, and is manned by a big crowd of desperadoes, every man of whom has bound himself by a fearful oath never to lay down his arms while the breath remains in his body, I shouldn't wonder if we find out before all is done that we have undertaken a pretty tough job."

"It would seem like it, if Señor Lobo's information is to be relied upon," said I, an involuntary shudder and qualm thrilling me as my vivid imagination instantly conjured up a vision of the impending conflict. "But I suppose every precaution will be taken to catch the rascals unawares?"

"You may be sure of that," answered the master, peering curiously into my face as he spoke. "Captain Stopford is not the man to court a reverse, or a heavy loss of life, by unduly advertising his intentions. But you look pale, boy! You are surely not beginning to funk, are you?"

"No," said I, a little dubiously, "I think not. But this will be my first experience of fighting, you know—I have never been face to face with an enemy thus far—and I must confess that the idea of a hand-to-hand fight —for I suppose it will come to that— a life-and-death struggle, wherein one has not only to incur the awful responsibility of hurling one's fellow-creatures into eternity, but also to take the fearful risk of being hurled thither one's self, perhaps without a moment of time in which to breathe a prayer for mercy, is something that I, for one, can hardly contemplate with absolute equanimity."

"Certainly not," assented Bates

kindly, linking his arm in mine as he spoke; "certainly not; you would be something more or less—*less*, I should be inclined to say—than human if you could. But, as to the responsibility of hurling those villains into eternity, do not let that trouble you for a single moment, my lad; in endeavouring to put down this inhuman slave-trade we are engaged upon a righteous and lawful task—lawful and righteous in the eyes of God as well as of man, I humbly believe—and if the traffickers in human flesh and human freedom and human happiness choose to risk and lose their lives in the pursuit of their hellish trade, the responsibility must rest with themselves, and in my humble opinion the earth is well rid of such inhuman monsters. And as to the other matter—that of being yourself hurried into eternity unprepared—it need not occur, my boy; *no one* need die unprepared. What I mean is, of course, that *all* should take especial care to be prepared for death whenever it may meet us, for we know not what a day, or an hour, or even a moment may bring forth; the man who walks the streets of his native town in fancied security is actually just as liable to be cut off unawares as are we who follow the terrible but necessary profession of arms; the menaces to life ashore are as numerous as they are afloat, or more so; the forms of accident are innumerable. And therefore I say that *all* should be careful to so conduct themselves that they may be prepared to face death at any moment. And if they are not, they may easily become so; for God's ear is always open to the cry of His children, and I will take it upon myself to say that no earnest, heartfelt prayer is ever allowed to go unanswered. So, if you have any misgivings about to-night's work, go to God and ask for His mercy and protection and help; and then, *whatever* happens, you will be all right."

So saying, the good old fellow halted just abreast the hatchway, which we had reached at this point in our perambulation fore and aft the deck, and, gently urging me toward it suggestively, released my arm and turned away. I took the hint thus given me and, without a word—for indeed at that moment I was too deeply moved for speech—made my way below to the midshipmen's berth, which I found opportunely empty, and there cast myself upon my knees and prayed earnestly for some minutes. When I arose from this act of devotion I was once more calm and unperturbed; and from that moment I date a habit of prayer that has been an inexpressible comfort and support to me ever since.

Upon returning to the deck the first object that caught my eyes was our gig, with the first luff and little Pierrepoint—our junior mid but one—in the stern-sheets, pulling toward the very handsome Spanish brig — already spoken of as lying at anchor a short distance inside of us—upon a visit of inspection. That the inspection to which she was subjected was pretty thorough was sufficiently attested by the fact that the gig remained alongside her a full hour, the British brig and the Dutch barque being in their turn afterwards subjected to a similarly severe examination; but, as Bates had predicted, nothing came of it, all their papers being perfectly in order, while a rigorous search failed to discover anything of an incriminating character on board either of them.

"Of course not," commented the master, when he learned the substance of the first luff's report to the skipper; "of course not. Bless ye, the people that trade to this river aren't born fools, not they! Just consider the matter for a moment. Let's suppose, for argument's sake, that the Spaniard yonder is a slaver. Would she ship her cargo here in the very spot that would be first visited by every man-o'-war that enters the river? Of course she wouldn't; she'd go away up the river into one of the many creeks that branch into it on either side for the first twenty miles or so, and ship her blacks there, watching for the chance of a dark night to slip out and get well off the land before daylight. If she came in here at all, it would be to fill up her water and lay in a stock of meal upon which to feed her niggers when she'd got 'em; and you may depend on it that when a slaver comes in here upon any such errand as that, a very bright look-out is kept for cruisers, and that, upon the first sight of a suspicious-looking sail in the offing, her irons, her meal, and everything else that would incriminate her are bundled ashore and hidden away safely among the bushes, while her water would be started and pumped out of her long enough before a man-o'-war could get alongside of her. What is that Spanish brig taking in?"

he continued, turning to little Pierre-point, who, with the first lieutenant, had visited her.

"Nothing," answered the lad. "She only arrived yesterday ; and her hold is half full of casks in which she is going to stow her palm-oil."

"Of course," remarked the master sarcastically, turning to me. "What did I say to you this morning? Whenever a ship is found in an African river with a lot of casks aboard, that ship is after palm-oil—at least, so her skipper will tell ye. And that's where they get to wind'ard of us ; for unless they've something more incriminating—something pointing more directly to an intention to traffic in slaves—than mere casks, we daren't touch 'em. But, you mark me, that brig's here to take off a cargo of blacks ; and unless I'm greatly mistaken she'll have vanished when we turn up here again to-morrow."

It was just six bells in the afternoon watch when two boats—one containing fresh water in casks, and the other loaded to her gunwale with fresh meat —mostly goat-mutton strongly impregnated with the powerful musky odour of the animal—appeared paddling leisurely off to the *Barracouta* under the guidance of four powerful but phenomenally lazy Krumen, who would probably have consumed the best part of half-an-hour in the short passage from the wharf to the brig had not our impatient first luff dispatched a boat to tow them alongside. The water was pumped into the tanks, the provisions were passed up the side and stowed away below in the coolest part of the ship ; and no sooner were the boats clear of the ship's side than the boatswain's whistle shrilled along the deck, followed by the gruff bellow of "All hands unmoor ship !" the messenger was passed, the anchor roused up to the bows, and in a few minutes the *Barracouta*, under her two topsails, and wafted by a light westerly zephyr, was moving slowly down the narrow channel toward the estuary of the river.

So light was the draught of air that now impelled us, that, although every cloth was quickly spread to woo it, the ship was a full hour and a half reaching as far as Boolambemba Point, where we met the full strength of the river current ; and when we bore away on our course up the river, our patience was severely taxed by the discovery that, even with studding-sails set on both sides from the royals down, we

could scarcely do more than hold our own against the strong rush of the tide and current together.. Slowly, however, and by imperceptible degrees, by hugging the northern shore as closely as we dared, with the lead constantly going, we managed to creep insidiously past the mangrove and densely bush-clad river bank until, just as the sun was dipping into the horizon astern in a brief but indescribably magnificent blaze of purple and scarlet and gold, we reached the place of our rendezvous with Señor Lobo. And soon afterwards we had the satisfaction of discovering that gentleman making his way toward us out of the narrow creek, his conveyance being a small native canoe about fifteen feet long, roughly hewn and hollowed out of a single log, and propelled by two natives, who apparently regarded clothes as an entirely unnecessary superfluity, for they were absolutely naked. They were fine, powerful specimens of negro manhood, however, and smart fellows withal, for they propelled their ungainly little craft along at a truly wonderful pace with scarcely any apparent effort, sheering her alongside the brig in quite respectable style without obliging us to start tack or sheet in order to pick them up, and shinning up the side with the agility of a couple of monkeys as soon as they had securely made fast the rope's-end that was hove to them.

Our impatience at the slow progress that we had thus far made was somewhat relieved by Lobo's assurance that we might confidently rely upon a brisk breeze speedily springing up that would carry us to our destination as soon as was at all desirable ; his opinion being that our best chance of success lay in the postponement of our attack until about two o'clock in the morning, by which time the moon would have set, and the slaver's crew would probably be wrapped in their deepest slumber. So far as his prognostication relative to the wind was concerned, it was soon confirmed, a strong breeze from the southward springing up, under the impulsion of which, and with considerably reduced canvas, we reached our destination, so far as the brig was concerned, about five bells in the first watch.

This spot was situated on the northern bank of the river, at a distance, up-stream, of about thirteen miles from Boolambemba Point. It was at the mouth of a creek, named Chango

Creek, and in a small bay or roadstead about a mile long by perhaps half that width formed by six islands, the largest of which was nearly two miles long by half-a-mile wide, while the smallest and most easterly of all was a very diminutive affair, of perhaps not more than an acre in area, densely overgrown, like the rest of them, with thick, impenetrable bush. In the very centre of this small roadstead, to which we had been piloted by the Portuguese trader, we anchored the brig in two and a half fathoms of water; when, the canvas having been furled, and all our preparations for the attack having been fully made before dark, a strong anchor-watch was set, and everybody else turned in to get an hour or two's sleep, strict injunctions being laid upon the master, who had charge of the watch, to keep a bright look-out, and to have all hands called at two bells precisely in the middle watch. As for Lobo, he took leave of us directly that our anchor was down, and, rousing out his sable crew, who were fast asleep and snoring melodiously underneath the long-boat, took to his canoe once more and almost immediately vanished among the deep black shadows of the islets that hemmed us in.

I know not what were the feelings of others on board the brig on that eventful night, or how those two short hours of inaction were spent in other parts of the ship, but I am convinced that when we all went below to turn in, a very general conviction had spread among us that the enterprise upon which we were shortly to engage was one that would prove to be more than ordinarily difficult and dangerous, and while not one of us probably had a moment's doubt as to its ultimate result, I believe the feeling was pretty general that the struggle would be fierce and obstinate, and that our loss would probably be unusually heavy. I gathered this from the demeanour of the ship's crew generally, officers as well as men; the former revealing the feeling by the extreme care with which they scrutinized and personally superintended the several preparations for the expedition, and the latter by the grim and silent earnestness with which they performed their share of the work. True, there was some faint attempt at jocularity among a few of the occupants of the midshipmen's berth as we sought our hammocks, but it was manifestly braggadocio, utterly lacking

the true ring of heartiness that usually characterized such attempts, and it was speedily nipped in the bud by Gowland, the master's mate, who gruffly recommended the offenders to "say their prayers and then go to sleep, instead of talking nonsense." Though I was not one of the offenders I took his advice, earnestly commending myself to the mercy and protection of the Almighty, both in the coming conflict and throughout the rest of my life, should it please Him to spare it, after which I sank quickly into a deep, untroubled sleep.

CHAPTER III

THE NIGHT ATTACK

FROM this sleep I was aroused—in a few minutes, it seemed to me, although really it was nearly two hours later—by a boisterous banging upon the mess-table, followed by the voice of the marine who executed the functions of steward to the mess, exclaiming—:

"'All hands,' gentlemen, please! The captain and the first liftenant is already on deck."

This was followed by the rasping scrape of a lucifer match, by the feeble light of which the man's face was seen bending over the lantern which he was endeavouring to light.

"Ay, ay, Jerry, look alive with the lantern, man!" responded the master's mate. "What is the night like?" he continued, as he swung himself out of his hammock and hastily proceeded to thrust his long legs into his breeches.

"Dark as pitch, sir; blowing more than half a gale of wind, and threatening rain," was the cheering answer.

"A pleasant prospect, truly," muttered Good, my especial chum, as we jostled each other in the confined space wherein we were struggling into our clothing.

"It might be worse, however," responded Gowland, as he knotted a black silk handkerchief tightly about his loins. "The darkness and the roar of the wind among the trees will help capitally to mask our approach, while I dare say that the craft which we are going to attack will be in such a snug berth that nobody will think it worth while to keep a look-out, blow high or blow low. I say, Pierrepoint, are you told off for the boats?"

Pierrepoint intimated that he was.

"Then put that rubbishy toasting-fork away and get a cutlass, boy, as

Dugdale has. Of what use do you suppose a dirk would be in a hand-to-hand fight with a great burly Spaniard? Why, none at all. I can't understand, for my part, why such useless tools are supplied for active service! Get a good honest cutlass, boy; something that you can trust your life to. And look sharp about it! Hurry up there, you loafers! Come, Burdett, my boy, stir your stumps if you don't want a wigging from the first luff! Hillo, Jerry! what's that, hot coffee? Well done, my man, I'll owe you a glass of grog for that! Pour it out quickly, and rouse out the bread barge."

Jerry was a smart fellow and looked after us well, I will say that for him. In less than a minute a cup or pannikin of steaming coffee stood ready for each of us, with the bread barge, well supplied, in the centre of the table.

"There's no time for eating now, but take my advice and slip a biscuit into your pocket, each of you, to eat as soon as the boats shove off," advised Gowland. "There is nothing worse for a man, in this climate—or *any* climate, for the matter of that—than to turn out and go into the open air in the middle of the night upon an empty stomach." And, suiting the action to the word, he thrust a biscuit into each of his side-pockets, placed a morsel in his mouth, and, with the exclamation, "Well, I'm off!" darted up the ladder and disappeared.

I followed, and, upon reaching the deck, found that all hands were mustered and waiting for inspection previous to being told off to the boats. The skipper was in his cabin, but a few minutes later—by which time all the laggards had put in an appearance —he emerged from the companion-way and the inspection at once began, great attention being given, I noticed, to those who were to go in the boats, to insure that their weapons were in serviceable order, their pistols loaded, and that each man had his due supply of cartridges. The inspection was conducted by the first lieutenant, accompanied by the captain and a sergeant of marines, the latter carrying a lantern, by the rather dim and uncertain light of which the inspection was made. The moment that this was over the men who were to participate in the expedition were told off, each to his proper boat, the boats were lowered and brought to the gangway, and in less than a quarter of an hour from the moment of our being called we were off.

The expedition consisted of four boats; namely, the gig, the pinnace, and the first and second cutters. The gig was a very fine, handsome boat, beautifully modelled, and exceedingly fast; she was commanded by the captain himself, who led the expedition —a sure indication of the important character, in his opinion, of the impending encounter. She pulled six oars, and in addition to the skipper, my chum, Good, and her crew of seamen, carried half-a-dozen marines, four in the stern-sheets, and two forward. The pinnace was a big, roomy, and rather heavy boat, pulling ten oars, double banked, and mounting a nine-pounder gun in her bows. She was commanded by Mr. Michael Ryan, the second lieutenant, a rollicking, high-spirited Irishman, whose only fault was that he lacked discretion and was utterly reckless; albeit this fault was to a great extent condoned by the effect of his influence upon the men, who would follow him anywhere. His crew, in addition to the ten oarsmen and a coxswain, consisted of little Pierrepoint and ten marines, six aft and four forward. The first and second cutters were sister boats, precisely alike in every respect, each pulling eight oars, double banked. They were rather smarter boats than the pinnace, being nearly as long but with less beam and freeboard, and finer lines. The first cutter was commanded by Gowland, the master's mate, and carried, in addition to her crew of ten men and a coxswain, eight marines. The second cutter was entrusted to me, and carried the same complement as her consort, the first cutter. It will thus be seen that the expedition numbered seventy-seven souls in all—nearly the half of our ship's company, in fact— the brig being left in charge of the first luff, with the master, the purser, the surgeon, young Burdett of the midshipmen's mess, the cook and his mate, captain's, gun-room, and wardroom stewards, and seventy-eight seamen.

The weather, although favourable enough for such an expedition as that upon which we were engaged—and which, if our anticipations should prove correct, would depend largely for its success upon our ability to take the enemy completely by surprise— was decidedly disagreeable; for, as

Jerry had reported, it was dark as pitch, the wind was sweeping athwart the river in savage gusts that roared among the trees with a volume of sound that rendered it necessary to raise the voice to a loud shout in order to make an order heard from one end of the boat to the other, and we had scarcely left the ship when it came on to rain with a fury that rendered the preservation of our ammunition from damage a serious difficulty and a source of keen anxiety. Fortunately for us, we reached the mouth of the creek a few minutes before the rain began to fall, but for which circumstance we should have met with the utmost difficulty in discovering the entrance, and might possibly have lost a considerable amount of valuable time in the search for it. Even as it was, so intense was the darkness that, although the creek was only some two hundred yards wide, we found it impossible to keep the boats in the centre of the channel, and for a little while were constantly running foul of each other or the banks. Luckily for us, we were no sooner in the creek than its eastern bank afforded us a shelter from the direct violence of the wind, the bush and trees growing so thickly right down to the water's edge that close inshore we were completely becalmed; and, thus sheltered, our sense of hearing helped us somewhat despite the deep roar of the gale overhead, while we quickly caught the knack of steering along the outer edge of the narrow belt of calm, in this way avoiding to a great extent the difficulties and petty mishaps that had at first so seriously hampered our movements.

In this way, and exposed all the while to the pelting of the heavy tropical downpour, which quickly drenched us to the skin in spite of the protection of our oilskins, we slowly groped our way along the creek with muffled oars for rather more than an hour, when we unexpectedly found ourselves at the entrance of a fairly spacious lagoon, in the centre of which we speedily made out not one, but *four* craft moored right athwart the channel, completely barring our further passage. From their disposition it looked very much as though they had been moored with springs upon their cables—for their broadsides were presented fair at us—and, if so, it argued at least a suspicion on their part of a possible visit from an enemy, with doubtless a corresponding amount of precaution against the chance of being surprised.

Scarcely had we made this discovery when the gig, which was leading, found her further progress unexpectedly interrupted by a boom composed of tree-trunks, secured together with chains, stretching right across the water-way. As she struck it a loud cry was heard proceeding from the river bank on our starboard hand, immediately followed by a musket shot. The next moment a spark of light appeared in the same quarter, quickly increasing in size and intensity until in less than a minute a large fire, evidently caused by the ignition of a very considerable quantity of highly combustible material, was blazing fiercely in the shelter of a thick clump of overhanging bush, that seemed to almost completely shield it from the rain, which, however, had considerably moderated by this time. The dense mass of bush behind and on either side of the blazing mass acted in some sort as a reflector, concentrating the light of the fire upon the boom and our four boats clustered closely together about it, and defining them with very unpleasant distinctness against the background of impenetrable darkness.

That this was so, and that our projected surprise had proved a lamentable failure, was made clear by the sounds of commotion and the sharp cries of command that at once arose on board the slavers, almost instantly followed by a smart and well-directed musketry fire, the bullets from which came dropping about us in very unpleasant proximity, although, fortunately, nobody was actually hit.

"Separate at once!" cried the skipper, rising in the stern-sheets of the gig as he realized that the time for silence and secrecy was past; "separate at once; spread yourselves along the boom, and let each boat's crew do its best to make a passage through it. Try the effect of a shot from your gun upon it, Mr. Ryan. Marines, return the fire of those craft, aiming at the flashes from their pieces. The first boat to force the boom will report the fact to me before passing through."

We spread well along the boom, maintaining open order, so that we might afford as small a target as possible, and devoted our energies to breaking through the obstruction at points where the trunks were united by chains ; but we found this by no means an easy matter, staples being driven home through the links into the tenacious wood so closely together that it was impossible to find a space wide enough to take the loom of an oar— the only lever at hand, as we had not anticipated or provided for such a contingency. Meanwhile, our adversaries proved themselves fully alive to the advantage which our situation afforded them, and fully prepared to make the most of it, for they kept up a brisk though irregular fire of musketry upon us from which we soon began to suffer rather severely, two of my men being hit within the space of as many minutes, while sharp cries of pain to our right and left told us that the occupants of the other boats were receiving their full share of the slavers' attentions. This was only the beginning of the conflict, however, for before our marines had had time to fire more than thrice in reply to the slavers' musketry fire, five fierce flashes of flame burst simultaneously from the side of the largest of the four craft, accompanied by the sharp, ringing roar of brass nine-pounder guns, and instantly a perfect storm of grape tore and whistled about our ears, splintering the planking of the boats and bowling over our people right and left. Three more of my men went down before that discharge, and the cries of anguish from the other boats told that they too had suffered nearly or quite as severely. The gig fared worst of all, however, for an entire charge, apparently, plumped right into her bows, where the men were clustered pretty thickly, helping two of their comrades who were kneeling upon the boom endeavouring to tear asunder its fastenings, and no less than six of her crew fell before that withering discharge, including the two men upon the boom, who both fell into the water, and were never seen again.

"By Jove ! this will never do," cried the captain. "Out oars, men, and pull alongside the pinnace ! "

This was done ; and as the two boats touched, our gallant leader sprang on board the larger of the two, crying to the second lieutenant—

"Here, Mr. Ryan, I will change places with you. Take the gig, if you please, and see if you can cast the boom adrift at its shore end ; I will look after matters here meanwhile. Mr. Gowland, go you to the other end of the boom, and see what you

can do there. Now then, lads, what is the best news there with that gun ? "

"Just ready, sir," came the answer. "Poor Jim Baker was struck, and fell athwart the breech, wettin' the primin' with his blood just as we was about to fire, so we've had to renew it ; but we're ready now, sir."

"Very well," cried the skipper. "Bear the boat off from the boom, and fire at the chain-coupling ; that ought to do the business for us."

The order was promptly obeyed, and a few seconds later the gun spoke out, the shot hitting fair and square, and dividing the two parts of the chain that formed the coupling between two contiguous tree-trunks. A loud hurrah proclaimed this result, yet when the pinnace pulled up to the boom again, and tried to force her way through, it was found that the logs could not be forced apart ; evidently they were still united under water.

"Load the gun again, lads, as smartly as you can," exclaimed the skipper ; "and then we must try to roll the logs over, and get the chains above water. Well, what news, Mr. Gowland ? " as the first cutter was seen approaching us.

"It's no good, sir," answered Gowland. "We can't get within twenty yards of dry ground for the mud, which is too stiff to permit of our forcing the boat through it, but not stiff enough to support a man. I made the attempt, and went in up to my arm-pits before they could get hold of me to pull me out."

Meanwhile, a hot fire of grape and musketry—the latter from all four of the craft—was being maintained upon us ; our men were falling fast ; and the matter to my mind began to look very serious. Still, those who were not hurt, or whose hurts were not very severe, worked away manfully in an endeavour to break the boom ; but it was clear— to me at least—that our only hope lay in the pinnace's gun. If that failed, it seemed probable that every man of us would be placed *hors de combat* before we could force a passage through.

Our nine-pounder was soon ready again ; and then—Gowland and I having meanwhile stationed our respective boats one on each side of the pinnace, and by the united efforts of our crews succeeded in rolling the logs so far over as to bring the remaining pair of coupling chains out of the water —a second effort was made to divide the boom. The shot was a successful one, both chains being completely cut through. Another ringing cheer proclaimed the good news just as the gig rejoined us with a similar piece of intelligence to that already brought by Gowland, as to the impossibility of landing and getting at the shore-fasts of the boom. That obstacle was now, however, happily severed, and drawing his head as he shouted—

"Out oars, men, and give way for your lives ! Follow me, the rest of the boats. We will tackle the big fellow first, and bring the other three to their senses afterwards with the aid of her guns."

The words were scarcely out of his mouth when another broadside of grape hurtled in among us, now once more huddled closely together about the breach in that deadly boom, and from the dreadful outcry that immediately arose, the tossing of arms aloft, and the dropping of oars, it was evident that fearful havoc had been wrought by it among our already seriously diminished company. And, to make matters worse, it was instantly followed by a louder, deeper report, and a crash on board the pinnace as an eighteen-pound shot struck her gun fair upon its starboard trunnion, dismounting the piece and sending it overboard, while a shower of splinters of wood and metal flew from the slide, wounding and maiming at least four more men. And then, as though that were not enough, the shot glanced and swept the boat fore and aft, crushing in the side of one poor fellow's head like an egg-shell, smashing in the ribs of another, and whipping the captain's sword out of his hand, with all four of his fingers, as it flew over his head into the darkness beyond.

In the teeth of this new disaster the pinnace forced her way through the now divided boom, closely followed by Ryan in the gig, then myself, with Gowland bringing up the rear. "Give way for your lives !" was now the word ; and at racing pace—or as near it as we could get with our sadly diminished crews—we headed for the biggest craft of the four, which we now made out to be a large brig, very heavily rigged and with immensely square yards. We opened out a little to port and starboard as we went, in order that we might show as small a mark as possible for our antagonists to fire at, and,

having already passed the heavy pinnace, I was fast creeping up into the leading position, when Ryan, who saw what I was after, sheered alongside and in sharp, terse language ordered me to change places with him. Of course I could but obey, and the fiery Irishman, finding himself in the best-manned boat of the lot, speedily passed ahead, despite the utmost efforts of the rest of us to keep pace with him. One more broadside of grape greeted us as we pushed somewhat heavily across the lagoon, and that put the poor unfortunate gig practically out of the combat, for it reduced her oarsmen to two, while she had already been so badly knocked about that it needed the utmost efforts of the least severely wounded of her crew to keep her afloat by baling. We kept on, however, in the wake of the other boats, and had at least a good view of the short, sharp fight that followed. The brig was lying with her starboard broadside presented to us, and as the boats advanced toward her they gradually passed out of the broad line of light cast by the still fiercely blazing fire that had been kindled on the shore. No sooner did this happen, however, than half-a-dozen men provided with port-fires sprang, three into her main and three into her fore port rigging, illumining the brig herself brilliantly, it is true, but at the same time revealing the whereabouts of our boats distinctly enough to enable her people to keep up a most galling pistol and musketry fire upon us, besides giving them the advantage that the light was at their backs, while it shone in the faces of our marines with such dazzling effect that they were able to reply but ineffectively to the fire with their own muskets.

The second lieutenant was first alongside, closely followed by Gowland, the pinnace making a bad third and ranging up under the bows of the brig, while the other boats attempted to board her in the waist. But the brig —and the three schooners as well for that matter—was well protected by boarding nettings triced up fore and aft, and as our men made a dash at her they were met by pikes thrust at them out through the ports, by the snapping of pistols in their faces, and the fierce lunge of cutlasses through the meshes of the netting. Nevertheless they persevered gallantly, hacking away at the netting with their cutlasses,

B

and occasionally delivering a thrust through it at any one who happened to come within arm's-length of them. But it was clearly a losing game ; our losses had been so heavy during our attack upon the boom that we were already far out-numbered by the crew of the brig alone, and they possessed a further important advantage over us in that they fought upon a spacious level deck, while our lads were obliged to cling to the bulwarks as best they could with one hand while they wielded their weapons with the other ; moreover, the slavers were able to make a tolerably effective use of their pikes and still keep beyond the reach of our cutlasses. "If it were not for that diabolical netting," thought I, "there would be some chance for us still." And as we ranged laboriously up alongside, my eye travelled up the face of the obstruction to its upper edge, and I saw that it was suspended at four points only, two on the port and two on the starboard side, in the wake of the main and foremasts.

"A sharp knife," thought I, "ought to divide each of those tricing lines at a single stroke, when down would go the net upon the defenders' heads and hamper their movements long enough to give our people a chance." And then I remembered that only a day or two before I had sharpened my own stout clasp-knife—at that moment hung about my neck on a lanyard—to almost a razor edge, and that consequently I had in my possession just the weapon for the purpose.

As my meditations reached this point the gig touched the brig's side, and whipping out my knife and opening it, I made one spring from the boat's gunwale into the netting, up which I at once swarmed with all the agility I could muster—and I was fairly active in those days, let me tell you—a musket-shot knocking my cap off as my head rose above the level of the bulwarks, while a moment later a fellow made a lunge at me with his pike as I skipped up the meshes, and drove its head half through the calf of my left leg. I felt the wound, of course, but was at the moment much too excited and intent upon the task which I had set myself to give it a second thought, and in another instant, so it seemed to me, I had reached the tricing line, which I grasped tightly with one hand while I hacked away vigorously with the other. The rope

parted at the third stroke of the knife, and down dropped the net, sagging so much in the wake of the main rigging that our lads were easily able to surmount the obstacle, and I saw Ryan, with a wild, exultant " Hurroo ! " half fall, half leap down to the brig's deck, where he laid about him so ferociously with fist and cutlass that he at once cleared a space around himself for his followers.

As for me, I was left dangling by one hand at the bare end of the severed tricing line, but within easy reach of the starboard main-topsail sheet, which I promptly grasped and began to lower myself hand over hand down to the deck. Even as I glided down the sheet, I saw that one of our lads had followed my example, and, cutting the fore tricing line, had let the whole of the starboard netting down on deck, while his comrades were pouring in over the bulwarks like an avalanche. The brig's crew still offered a gallant resistance, but the British blood was by this time fairly at boiling point, and, grimly silent, the blue-jackets laid about them in such terrible earnest with fist and cutlass, belaying-pin, clubbed musket, sponge, rammer, or any other effective weapon that they could lay hands upon, that their rush became irresistible, and their antagonists gave way before them in terror.

At this juncture, and while I was still some twelve or fourteen feet above the deck, I noticed a man, whose dress and appearance suggested to me the idea that he might possibly be the leader of this band of outlaws, quietly separate himself from the combatants, and with a certain sly, secretive manner, as though he were desirous of avoiding observation, slink along the deck to the companion, down which he suddenly vanished. There was an indescribable something about the air and movements of this fellow that powerfully aroused my curiosity and excited an irresistible impulse within me to follow him ; and accordingly, swinging myself to the deck abaft the mainmast, which was deserted, the fight still being confined to the waist and forecastle of the brig, I made a dart for the companion, kicked off my shoes before entering, animated by some instinct or idea which I did not stop to analyze at the moment, and drawing my cutlass from its sheath, crept cautiously and noiselessly down the companion-ladder.

The moment that I entered the companion-way I was saluted by a whiff of moist, hot air loaded with a powerful, fœtid, musky odour, of which I had already become vaguely conscious, accompanied by a deep, murmuring sound that seemed to proceed from the vessel's hold; and although this was my first experience with slavers, I knew in an instant that the brig had her human cargo on board, and that the sound and the odour proceeded from it.

The companion-way was in complete darkness, but at the foot of the ladder, and to starboard of it, there was a thin, horizontal line of dim light marking the presence of a door that I had heard slam-to as I kicked off my shoes previous to descending. Making for this, I groped for the door-handle, found it, and, grasping it firmly, suddenly turned it and flung the door open. As I did so I found myself standing at the entrance to a fine, roomy cabin, which seemed to be handsomely, nay, luxuriously furnished. It was but dimly illuminated, however, the only light proceeding from an ordinary horn lantern, which, kneeling upon the deck, the man I had followed was holding open with one hand, while with the other he was applying the end of a slender black cord to the flame of the enclosed candle. The other end of the cord referred to led down an open hatchway close to the fore bulk-head of the cabin; and as I took in the whole scene in a single comprehensive glance—the open hatchway, the black cord, and the dimly-burning lantern—I realized with lightning intuitiveness that every soul on board the brig was tottering upon the very brink of eternity; the reckless villain before me was in the very act of exploding the powder magazine, and blowing the ship and all she contained into the air.

This surmise was confirmed as, turning his head at the sound of the opening door, the fellow withdrew from the lantern the end of the black cord—which was of course a length of fuse composed of spun-yarn well coated with damp powder, now fizzing and spluttering and smoking as the fire swiftly travelled along it. So rapidly did the fire travel indeed, that during the second or so that the desperado paused in surprise at my unexpected appearance, it reached his fingers, causing him to drop it to the deck

with a muttered curse. I knew that in twenty or thirty seconds at most that hissing train of fire would run along the guiding line of the fuse down the hatchway to the powder in which the other end of it was certain to be buried; and bounding forward I placed one foot upon the blazing fuse as I dealt a heavy downward stroke with the hilt of my cutlass upon the upturned temple of the man who, crouching before me, was clearly on the point of springing to his feet. Then, dashing down my cutlass as the fellow sank back with a groan upon the deck, I wrenched my still open knife from my neck, and, while the struggling flame scorched and seared the sole of my naked foot, slashed the blade quickly through the fuse, and with the same movement whirled the severed and unlighted part as far away from me as possible. This done, I knew that the danger was past; and, drawing the short burning fragment of fuse from beneath my foot, I carefully deposited it in the lantern, where it instantly flamed itself harmlessly away. My next act was to secure the remainder of the fuse and cautiously withdraw it from the dark hatchway down which it led; and, this safely accomplished, I closed the aperture by drawing over the hatch, and then sat down to nurse my seared and blistered foot and to await the progress of events; my companion or adversary, or whatever he should be rightly called, still lying motionless where he had fallen, with a large blue lump on his white temple from which a thin stream of blood slowly oozed.

During the few brief seconds that had elapsed between my entrance into the cabin and the flinging of myself upon one of its sofas, I had lost all cognizance of what was happening elsewhere; but as I took my scorched foot upon my knee and ruefully contemplated its injuries, I once more became aware of the sounds of conflict on deck; the fierce, confused stamping of many feet; the cries and ejaculations of encouragement or dismay; the quick jar and clash of blade upon blade; the occasional explosion of a pistol; the dull, crushing sound of unwarded blows; the sharp scream of agony as some poor wretch felt the stroke of the merciless steel; the cries and groans of those who had been smitten down, and, still conscious, were being trampled underfoot by the combatants; the deep muttered curse; the sharp word of command; and the occasional cheer that broke from the lips of our own gallant lads. Suddenly there was a louder hurrah, a quick scurrying rush, a loud shout of command in Spanish for every man to save himself, an outcry of terrified ejaculations in the same tongue, a quick succession of splashes in the water alongside, and a sudden silence, broken the next instant by a gasping but triumphant shout from Ryan of—

"Hurroo, bhoys! By the blessed—Saint—Pathrick — but — that's nately done! Ugh!—pouff!—we've—drove them — clane overboard! Murther! but it's meltin' I am—and as dhry—as a limekiln!"

CHAPTER IV

CHANGO CREEK

THEN I heard the skipper hailing, apparently from the forecastle—

"Is that Mr. Ryan's voice that I hear, aft there?"

"Ay, ay, sorr," answered the second luff; "it's myself, bedad, all that's left ov me!"

A sound of footsteps followed, suggesting that he had walked away forward to join his superior; but as the man at my feet just then stirred uneasily, as though his senses were returning to him, I made a quick grab at my cutlass, and drawing from my belt a loaded pistol, the existence of which I had until then forgotten, I pulled myself together and made ready for the next emergency.

Presently, my prisoner, for such he now was, stirred again, sighed deeply, and opened his eyes, his glance immediately falling upon me. For a few seconds he seemed not to know where he was, or what had happened; then, as we gazed into each other's eyes, I saw that his memory had returned to him, and as he made a motion to rise to his feet, I sprang to mine, and pointing my pistol straight at his head, said in the best Spanish that I could muster—

"Stay where you are! If you make the slightest attempt to move I will blow your brains out, you villain!"

He continued to gaze steadfastly at me for some moments; and then seeing, I suppose, that I fully meant what I said, he smiled bitterly and muttered—

"So it has come to this, has it, that I must lie here in my own cabin, help-

less, at the mercy of a mere boy? Car-r-am-ba!"

He still kept his regards steadfastly fixed upon me; and as I seemed to read in the expression of his eyes a dawning determination to make at least one more effort for freedom, I was not sorry to hear footsteps coming along the deck, and the voices of the skipper and Ryan in earnest conversation.

"We must get a light from somewhere at once, and look to the wounded without a moment's delay," said the former. "I fear that our loss has been very serious in this affair. Ah! there is a faint glimmer of light from the skylight yonder; I will go below and see what it is. Meanwhile, Mr. Ryan, muster your men, and load the guns, if you can lay your hand upon any ammunition. Those schooners will try to slip away if they can, now that we have got the brig; but I shall not be satisfied unless I can secure the whole of them; we *must* have something more than we have got already to account satisfactorily for our loss!"

"Niver fear, sorr," answered the second luff; "they'll not get away from— By all the powers though, there goes one of thim now!"

And away he dashed forward again, shouting out certain orders to the men, while the skipper, after hesitating for a few seconds, entered the companion and began to descend.

My attention had been somewhat distracted from my prisoner by this brief conversation, a fact which had evidently not passed unnoticed by him, for before I fully realized what was happening, he had in some inexplicable manner sprung to his feet with a single, lightning-like movement, and his hand was already upon my left wrist, when with a quick twist of the arm I managed to get my pistol-barrel pointed at him as I pressed the trigger. There was a bright flash, lighting up the whole cabin as though by a gleam of lightning, and glancing vividly from the rolling eyeballs of my antagonist, a sharp explosion, and the Spaniard went reeling backward with a crash upon one of the sofas as the captain entered the cabin at a bound.

"Hillo!" he exclaimed, as he peered at me in the faint light of the lantern, "who are you, and what is the matter here? Why—bless me!—it is Mr. Dugdale, isn't it? And pray who is that man on the sofa?"

In a few brief words I narrated my

adventure, to which he listened quietly, holding his wounded hand, bound up in a handkerchief, in the other meanwhile ; and when I had finished, he glanced at the prostrate figure on the sofa and said, noticing the ghastly paleness of the upturned face, and the lifelessness of the outstretched limbs—

"Well, he looks as though there was not much mischief left in him now, at all events. But it will not do to take any risks ; he is evidently a desperate character, or was before you pinked him, so slip up on deck and get a length of line—a bit off one of the topgallant-braces will do if you can't find anything better—to make him fast with. And call a couple of hands to come below and carry him on deck ; it is scarcely safe to leave such a fellow alone in the cabin, even when securely bound."

I hobbled on deck as well as my burnt foot—which by this time was excruciatingly painful—would permit, and finding a suitable bit of line, and securing the assistance of two of our lads, the slave-captain, as he eventually proved to be, was speedily bound hand and foot, conveyed on deck, and propped up in a reclining position against the bulwarks, well aft out of the way, in such a position as seemed least likely to encourage the bleeding of his wound.

Meanwhile, Ryan, upon leaving the skipper, had rushed forward and hailed the fugitive schooner, in his richest Dublin accent, to heave-to, or he would sink her. To this command, however, whether understood or not, no attention was paid ; and before our people, groping about in the thick darkness among the dead and wounded, could lay their hands upon a single cartridge, they had the mortification of seeing her vanish round a bend of the creek on her way seaward, the lieutenant consoling himself with the assurance that she would infallibly be snapped up by the *Barracouta*, whose slender crew would be certain to be on the alert all through the night. When the skipper and I arrived on deck, after securing our prisoner, Ryan and a few of our lads were busily employed ramming home a charge in the long eighteen mounted upon the brig's fore-castle, a cartridge and shot for which they had stumbled across in their search. The second luff at once began to relate, with many comical expressions of righteous indignation, the

particulars of the schooner's escape ; but he had scarcely got well into his narrative when the faint *screep* of a block-sheave from to windward warned us that another of our slippery neighbours was about to hazard a like experiment. Without waiting for orders, or thinking of what I was doing, forgetting even my injured foot in the excitement of the moment, I sprang upon the rail and hailed in Spanish—

"Hola there, keep all fast on board those schooners, or we will riddle you with grape ! And light a lantern each of you and hoist it to your mainmast-head. I warn you that we will stand no nonsense, so if you value your lives you will attempt to play no tricks !"

To this no reply whatever was vouch-safed ; and I was about to hail again, when the captain remarked, very quietly—

"May I inquire, Mr. Dugdale, what is the nature of the communication—the *unauthorized* communication — that you have just made to those schooners ?"

"I beg your pardon, sir," answered I, considerably abashed ; "I thought I heard a sound just now as though another of the schooners were on the point of attempting to slip away ; so I hailed them that if they attempted any such trick we would treat them to a dose of grape. I also ordered them to each hoist a lantern to the masthead, so that we may see where they are."

"Very good," remarked the skipper suavely ; "it was quite the proper thing to do. But I do not altogether approve of my young gentlemen taking the initiative in any matter unless they happen to be for the time being in supreme command. When that is not the case I expect them to wait for instructions. And now, be so good as to hail them again, and say that unless those lanterns are displayed within three minutes I will fire into them."

My second hail proved effective, the two lanterns being in position well within the time specified. Our skipper was, however, very uneasy ; and after retiring aft and consulting with Ryan for a few minutes, the second luff and Gowland went away in the first and second cutters with two good strong crews, and boarded the schooners, the slavers—who were evidently on the look-out—shoving off in their own boats and escaping to the shore the moment that they detected what we were after. Both schooners had a cargo of slaves on board, and were of course at once taken possession of, an instant search—prompted by our experience on board the brig—revealing the fact that one of them had been set fire to so effectually that it took the prize crew fully an hour to extinguish it.

Meanwhile, lamps and lanterns were found on board the brig and lighted, when those of us whose hurts were the least serious set to work to attend to our more unfortunate comrades. Closer investigation now revealed the welcome fact that we had suffered less severely than had been at first anticipated, our killed amounting to five only—although two more died before they could receive proper surgical attention—while, of the wounded, seven had received injuries serious enough to completely disable them, the rest, amounting to no less than twenty-three, suffering from hurts ranging from such an insignificant prod as I had received in the leg, up to a cutlass-stroke that had all but scalped one poor fellow.

At length, just as we had completed the task of getting our worst cases below out of the persistent rain, and making them in a measure comfortable, the wind shifted and subsided to a gentle breeze from the north-eastward, the weather cleared, the rain ceased, and about half-an-hour later the day broke gloriously, and we were able to get a view of our surroundings.

We found ourselves in a nearly circular lagoon or basin, about half-a-mile in diameter, across the centre of which lay moored the brig and the two schooners, with a gap in the line to mark the berth that had been occupied by the third schooner—the craft that had succeeded in effecting her escape. We were completely land-locked, the shores of the creek being low, and for the most part closely fringed with mangroves, behind which rose dense and apparently impenetrable masses of bush, now in full leaf, and thickly overgrown with flowering parasites, the bush being interspersed with trees of several kinds, some of which were very lofty and handsome. At a short distance above where we were lying, there appeared to be another creek—a small affair, not more than a hundred feet wide—branching off from the main channel ; and, upon its being pointed out to him, the captain at once hailed the schooner of which the second lieutenant was in possession, directing that the latter should take his boat, with

the crew well armed, and make an exploration of the subsidiary and main creeks for a short distance, for the purpose of ascertaining whether, as was exceedingly probable, there was a slave depôt in the neighbourhood. I should greatly have liked to have made one of the party, and indeed asked permission to join it, but my burnt foot was by this time so inflamed and painful that I could not put it to the deck, and Captain Stopford, while expressing his gratification at the zeal manifested by the request, refused, pointing out that, lame as I was, I should not only be useless but an actual encumbrance and embarrassment to the party in the event of resistance being offered to any attempt on their part to land.

In a few minutes Ryan was ready, and the boat shoved off from the schooner, leaving just enough hands to take care of her during the absence of the others. She made straight for the small subsidiary creek, in the first instance, but reappeared in about a quarter of an hour, when the second luff hailed to say that it was a mere *cul de sac*, only some half-a-mile long, and with very little water in it, the banks being of soft, black, fœtid mud, of a consistency which rendered landing an impossibility. Having communicated this intelligence, the cutter next proceeded up stream and quickly vanished round a bend. She had been out of sight fully half-an-hour, and the captain was just beginning to manifest some anxiety, neither sight nor sound having reached us to indicate her whereabouts, when thin wreaths of light brown smoke appeared rising above the bush and trees about a mile away, the smoke rapidly increasing in density and volume, and darkening in colour, until it became quite apparent that a serious conflagration was raging at no great distance. When the smoke at first appeared, there was some question in the mind of the captain whether it might not be the work of the people who had effected their escape from the craft during the darkness, they having perhaps set fire to the bush in the hope of involving the prizes and ourselves in the ensuing destruction ; but a little reflection revealed the unlikelihood of this, the vegetation not only being saturated with the rain that had fallen during the night, but also being so green and full of sap that it would probably prove impossible to fire it. We had just reached this conclusion when Ryan and his party appeared returning, and in a few minutes the cutter ranged up alongside us to enable the second luff to make his report. He stated that he had proceeded about a mile and a half up the creek, the course of which he had found to be very sinuous, when he reached a spot at which the bank on his port hand was clear of bush and trees, with the soil firm enough to admit of a landing being conveniently effected, and as there were signs indicating that the place had been very freely used quite recently, he shoved alongside the bank and stepped ashore. A single glance about him now sufficed to convince him that he had made an important discovery; the grass was much worn, as with the trampling of many feet, and from this well-trodden spot a broad path led into the bush. Leaving two men in the boat to take care of her, with orders how to proceed in the event of an enemy heaving in sight, Ryan at once led his party along this path, and after traversing it for less than a hundred yards, came upon a large barracoon, very solidly and substantially built, and of dimensions sufficient to accommodate fully a thousand slaves; there were also kitchens for the preparation of the slaves' food, tanks for the collection of fresh water, several large thatched huts that looked as if they were for the accommodation of the traders, a large store building, and, in short, everything necessary to complete an important slave-trading establishment. It was evident that it had been very hurriedly abandoned only a few hours previously; but a strict and prolonged search failed to reveal the whereabouts of any of its late occupants; Ryan had therefore first emptied the water-tanks, and had then set fire to the whole establishment, remaining until the flames had taken a strong hold upon the several buildings, when he had retired without molestation.

Meanwhile, by the captain's orders, the hatches had been removed on board the three prizes, and the condition of the unfortunate prisoners looked to. I shall never forget the moment when the first hatch was taken off on board the brig; a thick cloud of steam slowly rose up through the opening, and the fœtid, musky odour, of which I have already spoken,

at once became so pungent and overpowering that the men who were engaged upon the operation of opening the hatchways were fairly driven away from their work for the moment, and until the strength of the stench had been to some extent ameliorated by the fresh air that immediately poured down into the densely-packed hold. What the relief of that whiff of fresh air must have been to the unhappy blacks can only be faintly imagined; but that it was ineffably grateful to them was evidenced by the deep murmur of delight, and the loud, long-drawn inspiration of the breath that swept from end to end of the hold the moment that the hatch was withdrawn, as well as by the upward glance of gratitude that instantly greeted us from the upturned eyes of those who were placed nearest the hatchway! But what a sight that hold presented when in the course of a few minutes the hatches were all removed, and the blessed light of heaven and the sweet, pure air of the early morning had gained free access to its sweltering occupants, dispersing the poisonous fumes which they had been condemned to breathe from the moment when the approach of our boats had been first notified! I had more than once had the hold of a slaver and the mode of stowing her human cargo described to me, but it was necessary to actually *see* it before the full horror and misery of the thing could be completely realized. The space between the planking of the slave-deck and the underside of the beams was just three feet, or barely sufficient to allow the unfortunate wretches to sit upright; and in this confined space they were stowed as tightly as herrings in a barrel, seated on their hams, with the feet drawn close up to the body, and the knees clasped by the arms close to the chest. Let any one try the fatiguing effect of sitting in this constrained attitude for only a single half-hour, and some idea may then be formed of the horrible suffering and misery that the unhappy slaves had to endure cooped up in this fashion for *weeks at a stretch*, not on a steady, motionless platform, but on the heaving, plunging deck of a ship driven at her utmost speed over a sea that was seldom smooth enough to render the motion imperceptible, and often rough enough to sweep her from stem to stern, and to render the closing of the hatches imperatively necessary to save her from foundering. Add to this the fact that the slaves were packed so tightly together that it was impossible to move, and thus obtain the relief of even a slight change of position ; bear in mind that it was equally impossible to cleanse the slave-deck during the entire period of the passage of the ship from port to port ; think of the indescribable foulness of the place, the dreadful atmosphere generated by the ever-accumulating filth, and the exhalations from the bodies of four or five hundred human beings wedged together in this confined space ; and add to all this the horrors of sea-sickness, and it at once becomes a perfect marvel that a sufficient number remained alive at the end of the passage to render the slave-traffic a remunerative business. It is true that, solely in their own interests, and not in the least from motives of humanity, the slavers exercised a certain amount of care and watchfulness over the health of their captives ; that is to say, they allowed one-half to go on deck during meal-times (twice a day), for the double purpose of affording an opportunity for the inspiration of a little fresh air, and at the same time of providing space for the poor wretches below to feed themselves. This, however, was only when the weather and other circumstances were favourable ; if the weather was bad, the hatches were put on and kept on until a favourable change occurred ; and in the case of a gale of wind the unhappy slaves have been known to have been kept without food or water for forty-eight hours, or even longer, simply because it was impossible to give them either. Of course in such a case the mortality was simply frightful, it being no uncommon occurrence for a slaver to lose more than half her cargo in a single gale ; this loss, be it understood, arising not so much from the want of food as from simple suffocation through long confinement in the dreadful atmosphere of the unventilated hold. And when a slaver happened to be pursued by a man-o'-war, the sufferings of the slaves were almost as bad, for in such a case the crew seldom troubled themselves to attend to the wants of their helpless prisoners, devoting all their thoughts and energies to the task of effecting their own escape. But as I shall have more to say upon this subject further on, I will not enlarge upon it here.

Ryan having rejoined his prize, and there being a nice little easterly breeze blowing, the order was given for all three craft to weigh and proceed down the creek ; the captain being rather anxious lest the slavers should return and take us at a disadvantage now that our force was divided. Nothing untoward occurred, however, and in a short time we were all proceeding down the creek, with the second lieutenant in his schooner as pilot.

And here it may be as well to enumerate the few particulars relative to our prizes that the exigencies of the narrative have hitherto not enabled me to give. To begin with the brig : she was, as Lobo had stated, the *Mercedes* of Havana ; a truly beautiful craft, measuring fully five hundred tons, very flat in the floor, and so exceedingly shallow that even in her sea-going trim, with everything on board as when we took her, she only drew a trifle over eight feet of water aft. But what she lacked in depth she more than made up for in beam, her deck being half as spacious again as that of the *Barracouta*. She was a perfectly lovely model, and sailed like a witch, as we soon discovered. This was not to be wondered at, however, for in addition to the beautiful, easy grace of her flowing lines, her scantling was extraordinarily light—less than half that of the *Barracouta*—and all her chief fastenings were *screws !* With so light a scantling she of course worked like a wicker basket in anything of a breeze and seaway, and leaked like a sieve, the latter being of little or no consequence with plenty of negroes to send to the pumps in relays, while the working of her gave her life, and contributed in no small degree toward the extraordinary speed for which she was distinguished. She was armed with eight nine-pounder broadside guns, and a long eighteen mounted upon a pivot on her forecastle ; and in the course of our investigations we discovered that her crew had numbered no less than seventy men, of whom fourteen were killed in her defence, and twenty-six too severely wounded to effect their escape. At the moment of her capture five hundred and sixty-four slaves, all males, were confined in her hold. She was thus, in herself, a very valuable prize, and quite worth all the trouble that we had taken to secure her. But in addition to her there were the two schooners, the larger of which, named the *Doña Hermosa*, was a vessel of close upon one hundred and twenty tons measurement, with nothing very remarkable about her appearance to distinguish her from a perfectly honest trader. Her cargo consisted of exactly three hundred slaves, rather more than half of whom were women and children. She was unarmed save for the few muskets that were found scattered about her decks when our lads boarded and took possession of her. The second schooner, of which Gowland, the master's mate, had temporary command, was a little beauty. She was named the *Felicidad*, and hailed from Santiago de Cuba. She was of one hundred and eighteen tons measurement, and in model generally very much resembled the *Mercedes*, though neither quite so shallow nor so beamy in proportion, while her proportionate length was considerably greater; her lines were therefore even more easy and beautiful than those of the larger vessel. She sat very low in the water, and might have been sworn to as a slaver as far away as she could be seen, her raking masts being short and stout, and her yards of enormous proportionate length — her foreyard measuring no less than seventy-eight feet — with a truly astonishing spread of beautifully cut canvas. In light winds and smooth water she developed a speed that was absolutely phenomenal, easily running away from her two consorts on the passage down the creek under her flying jib and mainsail only. She was pierced for three guns of a side, and was further fitted with a very ingenious arrangement for mounting a gun on a pivot amidships, and at the same time shifting it a few feet to port or starboard so as to permit of its being fired directly ahead or astern clear of the masts. None of her guns, however, were mounted at the time of her capture, they afterwards being found stowed below at the very bottom of her hold in a space left for them among her water-leaguers, from which they could easily be raised on deck when required. Like her consorts, she had on board a full cargo of slaves—numbering two hundred and forty, of whom about one-fourth were women and children—when captured.

Our passage up the creek having been effected in the intense darkness of an overcast and rainy night, it had of course been quite impossible for us to form any conception of the appearance of our surroundings; but now, in the broad daylight and clear atmosphere of a fresh and brilliant morning, every detail of the scene in the midst of which we found ourselves stood out with the most vivid distinctness, and I was not only astonished but delighted with the singularity and beauty of Nature's handiwork that everywhere met my eye in this region of tropical luxuriance. The three craft were the only evidences of man's intrusion upon the scene with which we were confronted; everything else was the work of Nature herself, untrammelled and uninterfered with; and it appeared as though in the riotous delight of her creative powers she had put forth all her energies in the production of strange and curious shapes and bewildering combinations of the richest and most dazzling colours. True, the water of the creek, which in consequence of the sheltering height of the bordering vegetation was glassy smooth, was so fully charged with mud and soil held in suspension that it resembled chocolate rather than water; but its rich brown colour added to rather than detracted from the beauty of the picture, harmonizing subtly with the brilliant greens, deep olives, and splendid purples of the foliage, and the dazzling white, yellow, scarlet, crimson, and blue of the trailing blossoms that were reflected from its polished surface, as well as the delicate blue of the sky into which it merged at a short distance from the vessels. Mangroves with their multitudinous and curiously twisted and gnarled roots and delicate grey-green foliage lined the margin of the creek on either hand, and behind them rose tall, feathery clumps of bamboo alternating with impenetrable thickets of bush, the foliage of which was of the most variegated colours and curious forms, beyond which again rose the umbrageous masses of lofty trees, several of which were clothed with blossoms of pure scarlet instead of leaves, while over all trailed the serpentine convolutions of gorgeous flowering creepers. Euphorbias, acacias, baobabs, all were in blossom, and the fresh morning air was laden with delicious and almost overpoweringly fragrant perfume. Wherever a slight break in the continuity of the mangrove belt permitted the river bank itself to be seen, the margin of the water was ablaze with tall orchids, whose eccentricities of form were matched only by their unsurpassable beauty of colouring ; and even the tall, luxuriant grasses contributed their quota to the all-pervading loveliness of the scene by the delicate purple tints of their stamens ; while the curious, pendent nests of the weaver-bird, hanging here and there from the longer and coarser grass-stalks curving over the water, added a further element of strangeness and singularity to the picture. Brilliant-plumaged birds flashed hither and thither ; kingfishers of all sizes perched solemnly upon the roots and overhanging branches of the mangroves, intently watching the surface of the muddy water for the tiny ripple that should betray the presence of their prey, or flitted low athwart the placid, shining surface of the creek ; bright-coloured parrots were seen clawing their way about the trunks of the more lofty trees, or winging their flight fussily with loud screams from branch to branch ; the cooing of pigeons was heard in every direction ; and high overhead, a small black spot against the deep, brilliant blue of the sky, marked the presence of a fishing eagle on the look-out for his breakfast.

In less than half-an-hour we had traversed the distance to the mouth of the creek, just before reaching which we were astonished to discover the *Barracouta* hard and fast upon a sandbank that lay just off the entrance, with her topgallant-masts struck, and her remaining boats in the water, apparently engaged in the task of lightening her. The captain looked terribly annoyed, but said nothing until we had rounded the last point and come to an anchor near the spot at which we had left the *Barracouta* on the previous night, when he ordered the gig to be hauled alongside, and, directing me to accompany him, gave the word for us to pull to the stranded craft.

CHAPTER V

THE 'FELICIDAD'

THE first lieutenant, looking exceedingly worried and distressed, was at the gangway to meet us.
"Well, Mr. Young," exclaimed the

captain as he stepped in on deck, "what is the meaning of this ?"
"I wish I could tell you, sir," answered Young. "There has been foul play of some sort ; but who is the guilty party I know no more than you do. As you will remember, it blew very hard last night when you left us ; and for some time after you had gone I remained on the forecastle, watching the ship as she rode to her anchor. She strained a little at her cable when the heavier puffs struck her, but by no means to such an extent as to arouse the slightest anxiety ; and after I had been watching for fully an hour, finding that the holding ground was good, and that even during the heaviest of the puffs the strain upon the cable was only very moderate, I felt perfectly satisfied as to the safety of the ship, and retired to the quarter-deck, leaving two men on the look-out on the forecastle, two in the waist, and one on either quarter ; for although I anticipated no danger, I was fully alive to the responsibility that you had laid upon me in entrusting me with the care of the ship, as well as to the fact that in the event of a chance encounter just hereabout, we were far more likely to meet with an enemy than a friend. The same feeling animated the men too, I am sure, for the look-outs never responded to my hail with more alacrity, or showed themselves more keenly watchful than they did last night ; yet I had barely been off the forecastle half-an-hour when we discovered that we were adrift ; and before I could let go the second anchor we were hard and fast upon this bank, fore and aft, and that, too, just upon the top of high water. I of course at once hoisted out our remaining boats, and ran away the stream-anchor to windward ; but, working as we were in the dark, it took us a long time to do it ; and I then sent down the royal and topgallant-yards and masts. When daylight came I examined the cable, thinking that possibly it might have chafed through on a rock ; but to my surprise I found that it had been clean cut at the water's edge. How it was done, or who did it, is impossible to guess, for although I have very strictly questioned both the forecastle look-outs, they persist in the statement that they saw nothing, and were aware of nothing until the ship was found to be adrift."
"Well, it is a most extraordinary

circumstance," commented the captain. "Are you quite satisfied that the men remained fully on the alert all the time?"

"Perfectly, sir," answered the lieutenant. "I hailed them every ten minutes or so, not knowing at what moment some disagreeable surprise might be sprung upon us. Besides, we did not know how you might be faring, and thought it quite possible that the craft you were after might attempt to give you the slip in the darkness. The men on the forecastle were two of the best we have in the ship—William Robinson and Henry Perkins."

"Yes," assented the captain; "they have always hitherto seemed thoroughly trustworthy and reliable men. Where are they? I should like to ask them a question or two."

The two men were summoned, and at once subjected to a very sharp cross-examination, which led to nothing, however, as they both persistently declared that they had neither seen nor heard anything to arouse the slightest suspicion until the discovery was made that the ship was adrift. The captain then went forward and inspected the severed cable; but that revealed nothing beyond the fact that the strands had been cut almost completely through with some very sharp instrument before the stubborn hemp had given way. In short, the whole affair was enshrouded in the deepest mystery. When, however, the captain had heard the whole story, and thoroughly investigated the matter, he freely absolved the first luff from all blame, frankly acknowledging that he did not see what more could have been done to provide for the safety of the ship, and that the thing would undoubtedly have happened just the same had he himself remained on board instead of going away with the boats.

Meanwhile, the dead and wounded had been conveyed from the prizes to the *Barracouta*, where the doctor immediately took the sufferers in hand, while the slain were stitched up in their hammocks ready for burial. At length it came to my turn to be attended to, and when the doctor saw my foot—now so dreadfully swollen and inflamed that my whole leg was affected, right up to the knee—I was promptly consigned to the sick-bay, with the intimation that I might think myself exceedingly fortunate if in that hot climate mortification did not set in and necessitate the amputation of my leg. I am thankful to say, however, that it did not; and in three weeks I was discharged from the doctor's care, and once more able to hobble about with the aid of a soft felt slipper. The dead were buried that same forenoon on the point projecting into the river at the junction of the creek with the main stream, the graves being dug in a small space of smooth, grassy lawn beneath the shadow of a magnificent group of fine tall palms.

A hasty breakfast was snatched, as soon as it could be got ready; and then every man available was set to work upon the task of lightening the stranded brig, her guns and such other heavy weights as were most easily accessible being transferred to the prizes, after which the second bower was weighed and run away to windward in the long-boat by means of a kedge; and such was the activity displayed, that at high-water that same afternoon—the tides were fortunately making at the time—the *Barracouta* floated and was hove off to her anchor. Meanwhile, the missing anchor had been swept for and found, and the severed end of the cable buoyed; before nightfall, therefore, the cable was spliced, and the bonny brig once more riding to her best bower. The men were kept at work until it was too dark to see further; and by six bells in the forenoon watch next day she was again all ataunto, her guns and everything else once more on board her, and the ship herself all ready for sea, it having been ascertained that she had sustained no damage whatever. It may be mentioned that the schooner which had effected her escape from us in the lagoon managed to slip out of the creek and get clear away without being observed by anybody on board the *Barracouta;* but that of course is easily accounted for by the pitchy darkness of the night, and the fact that she must have passed out of the creek a very short while after the brig had grounded upon the sandbank, and when of course our lads would be fully occupied in looking after their own craft.

Proper prize-crews were now told off to the three prizes—Ryan being placed in charge of the *Mercedes;* Gowland, the master's mate, in charge of the *Doña Hermosa;* and Good, one of the midshipmen, in charge of the *Felicidad* —and the order to weigh and proceed in company was given. There was a slashing breeze from the eastward blowing; and this, combined with a strong downward current, carried us along over the ground so smartly that in less than two hours we were abreast of Shark Point, although the *Doña Hermosa* proved to be such an indifferent sailer that the rest of us had to materially reduce our spread of canvas to avoid running away from her altogether. The *Felicidad*, on the other hand, sailed like a witch, and kept her station without difficulty, under a single-reefed mainsail, foresail, and inner jib, with all her square canvas stowed. The master informed me that as we passed Banana Point he had remembered to subject the anchorage to a very careful scrutiny through his telescope, and, as he had foretold, the handsome Spanish brig had disappeared, the Englishman and the Dutchman being the only craft still lying off the wharf. Having made an offing of about twenty miles, we hauled up some three points to the northward for Cape Palmas, our destination being of course Sierra Leone.

On the third day out, the captain of the *Mercedes*—whom I had shot in self-defence in his own cabin, it will be remembered — died of his wound, solemnly declaring with his last breath that he was absolutely innocent of any complicity in the destruction of the *Sapphire's* two boats with their crews, or in the disappearance of the *Wasp*. He admitted that he had heard of both occurrences, and had been told the name of the individual who was said to be responsible for them, but he stubbornly persisted in his refusal to give any information whatever, and carried the secret to his ocean grave with him.

In due time we reached Sierra Leone without mishap and without adventure, after a moderately quick passage ; and, our prizes having been taken *in flagrante delicto*, they were forthwith condemned. At Captain Stopford's suggestion, however, the *Felicidad* was purchased into the service, and with all speed fitted to serve as a tender to the *Barracouta*, her extraordinary speed peculiarly fitting her for such employment, while her exceedingly light draught promised to render her especially useful in the exploration of the various rivers along the coast, many of which are very shallow. We remained in harbour a trifle over three weeks while the necessary alterations were being effected— during which time, owing to the unremitting vigilance and skill of " Paddy "

Blake, our doctor, we lost only one man through fever—and then, all being ready, the *Felicidad* was commissioned, Ryan, our second lieutenant, being given the command of her, with —to my great delight—myself as his chief officer, Pierrepoint and Gowland being our shipmates. We also shipped as surgeon a young fellow named Armstrong, a Scotchman, whom the captain of the *Ariadne* kindly spared to us with a first-rate recommendation ; and in addition we had Warren, the gunner's mate of the *Barracouta*, as gunner ; Coombs, the carpenter's mate, as carpenter ; and Bartlett, the boatswain's mate, as boatswain. And by way of a crew, the captain gave us forty of his best men, as he very well could without weakening his own ship's company, a ship with supernumeraries having most opportunely arrived from home only a few days previously. It will thus be seen that, so far as strength was concerned, we were fairly well able to take care of ourselves. We were expected to do far more than that, however ; the captain, when giving us our instructions, hinting that he looked to us to fully justify him by our services for all the trouble that he had taken in causing the schooner to be fitted out. I think, however, that having put such a dashing fellow as Ryan in command, he had very few misgivings upon this point.

The *Barracouta* and the *Felicidad* sailed together on the evening of the eighteenth of December, and, the captain having given Ryan a pretty free hand, parted company off the shoals of St. Ann ; the schooner keeping her luff and heading about south-west, while the brig bore away on a south-east-by-south course for Cape Palmas ; the idea being that we should do better apart than together. We were to cruise for six weeks, and at the end of that time, if unsuccessful, to rendezvous on the parallel of six degrees south latitude and the meridian of twelve degrees east longitude ; or, in other words, some eighteen miles off the mouth of the Congo. We were to remain on this spot twenty-four hours ; and if at the end of that time the brig had not appeared, we were to proceed on a further cruise of six weeks, and then return to Sierra Leone to replenish our stores and await further orders.

It was a glorious evening when we sailed ; a moderate breeze was blowing from the westward, pure, refreshing, and cool compared with the furnace-like atmosphere in which we had been stewing for the previous three weeks. The sky was without a cloud; the sea a delicate blue, flecked here and there with miniature foam-caps of purest white; while, broad on our lee quarter, the high land about the settlement of Sierra Leone, just dipping beneath the horizon, glowed rosy red in the light of the sinking sun. It was an evening to make one's heart rejoice; such an evening as can only be met with in the tropics; and, just starting as we were upon what all hands regarded as a holiday cruise, it is but small wonder that we experienced and enjoyed its exhilarating influence to an almost intoxicating extent. Jocularity and laughter pervaded the little craft from end to end; and throughout the second dog-watch dancing, singing, and sky-larking—all, of course, within the limits of proper discipline—were the order of the evening. As the sun disappeared in the west, the full, round orb of the moon floated majestically up over the purple rim of the horizon to leeward; and the swift yet imperceptible change from the golden glory of sunset to the silvery radiance of a clear, moonlit night was a sight of beauty that must be left to the imagination, for no mortal pen could possibly do justice to it.

"Now, Harry, me bhoy," exclaimed Ryan, speaking in the broad brogue that always sprang to his lips when he was excited or exhilarated, and slapping me upon the back as we emerged from the companion after dinner that evening, and stood for a moment contemplating the glory of the night, "from this moment we're slavers, we're pirates, we're cut-throats of the first wather, to be hail-fellow-well-met with every dirty blagguard that sails the says—until we can get them within rache of these pretty little barkers," affectionately tapping the breech of one of our long nines as he spoke; "and thin see if we won't give thim such a surprise as they haven't met with for manny a day!"

And he quite looked the character, too—for he was of very powerful, athletic build, though not very tall, swarthy in complexion, and burnt as dark as a mulatto by the sun; with a thick, bushy black beard, and a most ferocious-looking moustache that he had been assiduously cultivating

ever since he had known that he was to have the command of the schooner—as he stepped out on deck at eight bells on the following morning, attired in white drill jacket and long flowing trousers of the same, girt about the waist with a gaudy silken sash glowing in all the colours of the rainbow, the costume being topped off with a broad-brimmed Panama hat swathed round with a white puggaree. He was indeed the beau-ideal of a dandy pirate skipper, and I was not a very bad imitation of him—barring the whiskers. The only things perhaps that a too captious critic might have objected to were the spotless purity of our clothing, and an utter absence of that ruffianly manner which distinguishes the genuine pirate; but, as Ryan observed, the first of these objections would grow less noticeable with every day that we wore the clothes, while the other was not necessary, or, if it should become so, must be assumed as successfully as our talents in that direction would permit. As for the crew, they had by Ryan's orders discarded their usual clothing for jumpers and trousers of blue dungaree, with soft felt hats, cloth caps, or knitted worsted nightcaps by way of head-covering, so that, viewed through a telescope, we might present as slovenly and un-man-o'-war-like an appearance as possible. This effect was further heightened by Ryan having very wisely insisted that not a spar or rope of the schooner should be altered or interfered with in any way, saving of course where it needed refitting; those therefore who happened to know the *Felicidad* would recognize her at once; and it was our business so to conduct ourselves that they should not suspect her change of ownership until too late to effect an escape. Her capture was of course by this time known to many of the craft frequenting the Congo; but that we could not help; our plans were based mostly upon the hope that there were still many who did not know it, and also, to some extent, upon a belief that, even to those who were aware of it, we might by judicious behaviour convey an impression that her people had cleverly effected their own and her escape, and were once more boldly pursuing their lawless trade.

We did not much expect to fall in with anything worthy of our attention until we were pretty close up with the Line; we therefore carried on all through the first night and the whole of the next day, arriving by sunset upon the northern boundary of what we considered our cruising ground proper. And then, as ill-luck would have it, the wind died away, and left us rolling helplessly upon a long, glassy swell, without steerage-way, the schooner's head boxing the compass. This period of calm lasted all through the night and the whole of the next day, varied only by an occasional cat's-paw of scarcely sufficient strength or duration to enable us to get the schooner's jib-boom pointed in the right direction. But this did not trouble Ryan in the least, for, as he reminded me for my consolation, we were now just where we wanted to be, and the first breeze that sprang up might bring with it one of the gentry that we were so anxiously on the look-out for. Meanwhile, he availed himself of the opportunity to prepare a certain piece of apparatus that he had employed his leisure in devising, and which he thought might possibly prove useful on occasion. " I've been think-ing," said he to me on the morning after the calm had set in, "that it mayn't always be convenient for the schooner to go through the wather at her best speed, so I've devised a thriflin' arrangement that'll modherate her paces widhout annyone out of the craft bein' anny the wiser." And there-with he ordered a good stout hawser to be roused up on deck; and from this he had a length of some fifteen fathoms cut off, all along the middle part of which he caused a dozen pigs of ballast to be securely lashed. This done, he ordered the bight, with the pigs attached, to be passed under the ship's bottom, and the two ends of the hawser to be passed inboard through the port and starboard mid-ship ports and well secured, when we had a drag underneath the schooner that would certainly exercise a very marked effect upon her sailing, without making a sufficient disturbance in the water to reveal the fact that trickery was being resorted to.

Towards the close of the afternoon the aspect of the sky seemed to promise that ere long we might hope for a welcome change of weather; the deep, brilliant blue of the unclouded dome became blurred as though it were gradually being overspread by a thin and semi-transparent curtain of mist, which gradually resolved itself into that streaky, feathery appearance called by seamen "mare's tails"; and a bank of horizontal grey cloud gathered in the western quarter, into which the sun at length plunged in a glare of fiery crimson and smoky purple that had all the appearance of a great atmospheric conflagration. A short, steep swell, too, gathered from the westward, causing the inert schooner to roll and wallow until she was ship-ping water over both gunwales, and her masts were working and grinding so furiously in the partners that we had to lift the coats and drive the wedges home afresh, as well as to get up pre-venter-backstays and rolling tackles.

"There is a breeze, and a strong one too, behind all this," remarked Ryan to me, "and it will give us an opportunity to test the little hooker's mettle. I wish it would come and be done with it, for by the powers I'm gettin' mighty toired of this stoyle of thing," as the schooner's counter squattered down with a thud and a splash into a deep hollow, and then rolled so heavily and so suddenly to starboard that we both gathered way and went with a run into the scuppers just in time to be drenched to the waist by the heavy fall of water that she dished in over her rail. This sort of thing soon gave us a taste of the *Felicidad's* quality, for so lightly was she framed that the heavy rolling strained her tremendously, and she began to make so much water that we were obliged to set the pumps going every two hours, while the creaking and complaining of her timbers and bulkheads raised a din that might have been heard half-a-mile away.

"As soon as the breeze comes," said Ryan, as we descended the companion-ladder to shift into dry clothes, "we will bear up and jog quietly in for Cape Lopez, which will give us a chance of being overhauled by some-thing running in for either the Gaboon or the Ogowé, or of blundherin' up against something coming out from one or the other of those same rivers. If we don't fall in with annything by the time that we make the land, we will just stand on and take a look in here and there, beginning with the Ogowé and working our way north-ward gradually until we've thoroughly overhauled the whole of the Bight."

By the time that we were summoned below to dinner, the sky had become entirely overcast with heavy, black, thunderous-looking clouds that entirely obscured the stars, and only allowed the light of the moon to sift feebly through; yet there was light enough to enable us to see our way about the deck, or to reveal to a sharp eye a sail as far away as seven or eight miles, had anything been within that distance. As we left the deck a quivering gleam of sheet-lightning flashed up along the western horizon, and Ryan gave Pierrepoint—who was taking the deck for me while I got my dinner—instructions to keep a sharp eye upon the weather, as there was no knowing how it might turn out. While we sat at table the lightning became more vivid and frequent; and after a while the dull, deep rumble of distant thunder was heard. Presently we heard Pierrepoint singing out to one of the boys to jump below and fetch up his oil-skins for him; and a minute or two later the sound of a heavy shower advancing over the water became audible, rapidly increasing in volume until it reached us, when in a moment we were almost deafened by the loud pelting of the rain upon the deck overhead as the over-laden clouds discharged their burden with all the fierce vehemence of a truly tropical downpour.

At the first crash of the rain upon the deck Ryan and I both with one accord glanced hastily at the barometer that was hanging suspended in gimbals in the skylight; the mercury had dropped slightly, but not sufficient to arouse any uneasiness, and we therefore went quietly on with our dinner, although Ryan shouted across the table to me—

"When the rain comes before the wind,
    Halliards, sheets, and braces mind."

There was little danger, however, of our being caught unawares, for we had long ago clewed up and hauled down everything, except the boom-foresail and jib, to save the sails from thrashing themselves threadbare with the rolling of the ship; we consequently awaited the development of events with perfect equanimity. The downpour lasted perhaps three minutes, and then ceased with startling abruptness, leaving us in absolute silence save for the rush and splash of the water athwart the flooded decks with the now greatly diminished rolling of the schooner, the gurgle of the spouting scuppers, the kicking of the rudder upon its gudgeons, the groaning and complaining of the tim-

bers, or the voices of the people on deck, and the soft patter of their bare feet upon the wet planks as they moved here and there. The shower had knocked the swell down very considerably, rendering the movements of the schooner much more easy than they had been, and we were able to finish our meal in peace and comfort without the continued necessity to steady the plate with one hand and the tumbler with the other, keeping a wary eye upon the viands meanwhile, in readiness to dodge any of them that might happen to fetch away in our direction, and snatching a mouthful or a sip in the brief intervals when the ship became comparatively steady.

When we again went on deck the sky presented a really magnificent spectacle, the vast masses of heavy, electrically-charged cloud being piled one above the other in a fashion that resembled, to me, nothing so much as a chaos of titanic rocks of every conceivable shape and colour, the forms and hues of the clouds being rendered distinctly visible by the incessant play of the sheet-lightning among their masses. Not only the whole sky, but the entire atmosphere seemed to be a-quiver with the silent electric discharges, and the effect was indescribably beautiful as the quick, tremulous flashes blazed out, now here, now there, strongly illumining one portion of the piled-up masses and the reflection in the glassy water with its transient radiance, while the rest of the scene was by contrast thrown into the deepest, blackest, most opaque shadow. Meanwhile the mutterings of the distant thunder had gradually grown louder and drawn nearer, while sudden, vivid flashes of forked or chain-lightning, golden, violet, or delicate rose-tinted, darted at ever-lessening intervals from the lowering masses of intensely black cloud heaped up along the western horizon.

We had been on deck perhaps half-an-hour, when a delicious coolness and freshness began by almost insensible degrees to pervade the hitherto intolerable closeness of the hot and enervating atmosphere, and, looking away to the westward, we saw, by the quick, flickering illumination of the lightning, a few transient cat's-paws playing here and there upon the surface of the water. Gradually and erratically these evanescent movements in the inert air stole down to the schooner, lightly rippling the water round her for an instant, just stirring the canvas with a faint rustle for a moment, and then dying away again. They were succeeded by others, however, with rapidly increasing frequency, and presently a faint blurr upon the glassy surface of the water to the westward marked the approach of the true breeze.

"Sheet home your topsail, and hoist away!" shouted Ryan. "Up with your helm, my man"—to the man at the tiller—"and let her go off east-south-east. Sheet home your topgallant-sail, and man the halliards. Lay aft here, some of you, to the braces, and lay the yards square. Well there, belay! Main throat and peak-halliards hoist away. Ease off the mainsheet. Rouse up the squaresail, Mr. Dugdale, and set it, if you please. Well there with the throat-halliards ; well with the peak ; belay! Away aloft, one hand, and loose the gaff-topsail! Give her everything but the studding-sails while you are about it, Mr. Dugdale ; it will save the canvas from mildew if it does little else."

The breeze—a light air from about west—had by this time crept up to us, and under its vivifying influence the schooner had gathered way, and was soon creeping along at a speed of barely two and a half knots, which, however, rose to three and finally to five as the wind freshened, the sky meanwhile clearing as the heavy thunder-clouds drove away to leeward before the welcome breeze, until the sky was once more cloudless save for the mare's-tails that thickly overspread the blue, through which the stars blinked dimly, and the moon, with a big halo round her, poured her chastened radiance.

"By the powers," exclaimed Ryan, as we paced the deck together after the operation of making sail had been completed—"By the powers, but that dhrag of mine is a wondherful invention entirely! Do ye notice, Harry, me bhoy, how it's modherated the little huzzy's paces? Bedad, she's goin' along as sober as a Quaker girl to meetin' instead of waltzin' away like a ballet-dancer! But wait until one of those light-heeled picaroons comes along, and then won't we surprise thim above a bit! If it's not blowing too hard when ye come on deck in the middle watch ye may give her the stunsails ; it'll look more shipshape, and as if we were in a hurry to make the coast and get our cargo aboard, if we happen to be overhauled by anybody in the same line of business, and the deuce of a fear have I now of outsailing any of them that may happen to be in the neighbourhood. Keep a sharp look-out, Mr. Pierrepoint, and if anything heaves in sight, either ahead or astern, during your watch, give me a call. I'm going below to turn in now."

I followed suit a minute or two later and, with my cabin-door wide open to freely admit the cool, welcome breeze that poured down through the open skylight, soon fell into a deep, refreshing sleep.

CHAPTER VI

A CAPTURE AND A CHASE

WHEN I went on deck at midnight I found that there was no occasion to set the studding-sails, for the breeze had freshened to more than half a gale, and the little hooker was staggering along before it and a fast-rising sea at a tremendous pace—considering the drag—with her royal clewed up and furled, and the gaff-topsail hauled down. Even thus she was being greatly overdriven ; so, as there was no need for *too much* hurry, and as the sky astern had a hard, windy look, I took in the topgallant-sail, and hauled down and stowed the mainsail, letting her go along easily and comfortably for the remainder of the night. I had half a mind to further relieve her by getting the drag inboard, but did not like to do so without first consulting Ryan— since the thing was of his contrivance —so, as the matter was by no means sufficiently urgent to justify me in disturbing him, I let it remain, and very glad was I afterwards that I had done so ; for when I went on deck again at seven bells, there, away about a point on our weather quarter, gleamed in the bright morning sunshine the white upper sails of a large craft that had been sighted at daybreak and that was now coming up to us fast. Ryan was already on deck, having been called immediately that the stranger was made out, and was in a state of high glee at the success of his stratagem, for he informed me that he had been up on the topsail-yard, and had pretty well satisfied himself, both by the look of the craft and the course she was steering, that she was a slaver running in upon the coast to pick up a cargo.

It now became a nice question with us whether we should reveal our true character as soon as the stranger should have approached within reach of our guns, or whether we should try to follow her in, and, lying in wait for her, seize her as she came out with her cargo on board. We were still at a considerable distance from the coast —some twelve hundred miles—and that fact inclined us strongly to make short work of her by showing our colours and bringing her to as soon as she should come abreast of us ; while, on the other hand, there was the chance that by following her in we might fall in with something more valuable than herself.

We were still weighing the pros and the cons of this important question, when the look-out aloft—for Ryan had only half-an-hour previously determined to have a look-out maintained from the topgallant-yard between the hours of sunrise and sunset—the look-out, I say, reported a sail broad on our starboard bow, standing to the northward on a taut bowline, and under a heavy press of sail. She was as yet invisible from the deck; my superior officer and I therefore with one accord made a dash for our telescopes, and, having secured them, hastened forward and made our way up the fore-rigging to the topsail-yard, on to which we swung ourselves at the same moment. From this elevated view-point the upper half of the stranger's topmasts and all above were just visible clear of the horizon ; and, bringing our glasses to bear upon her, we made her out to be a barque-rigged vessel under single-reefed topsails, courses, jib, fore and main-topmast-staysails, and spanker; her yards, which were pretty nearly square on to us, showed a quite unusual amount of spread for a merchant vessel, and the rapidity with which she altered her bearings and forged athwart our fore-foot was conclusive evidence that she was a remarkably speedy craft. For a moment it occurred to us that she might possibly be a cruiser belonging to one or another of the nations who had undertaken to share with Great Britain the noble task of suppressing the inhuman slave-traffic ; but a very little reflection sufficed to disabuse our minds of this idea, for no cruiser would have been carrying so heavy a press of canvas as she was showing, in the teeth of what had by this time become almost a gale, unless she were in chase of something,

and, had she been, we must have seen it. Besides, although everything looked trim and ship-shape enough so far as her spars, sails, and rigging were concerned, there were evidences even there of a certain lack of discipline and order that would hardly have been tolerated on board a man-o'-war of *any* nation, although most of the foreigners were a great deal more free and easy in that respect than ourselves. The conclusion at which we ultimately arrived, therefore, was that she was a slaver with her cargo on board, and "carrying-on" to make a quick passage.

But, fast as she was travelling, we were going through the water still faster, despite our drag, for we were carrying the wind almost square over our taffrail, and Ryan, in order the more thoroughly to hoodwink the craft astern, had double-reefed and set our big mainsail, as though we had been somewhat suspicious of her character, and anxious to keep her at as great a distance as possible ; we were therefore foaming along at a speed of fully eight knots, and rising the stranger ahead so rapidly, that when she crossed our hawse she was not more than eight miles distant, and we had a clear view of her from our topsail-yard. She now hoisted Spanish colours ; and we, not to be outdone in politeness, did the same, as also did the craft astern of us, each of us, I suppose, accepting the exhibition of bunting on board the others for just what it was worth.

Ryan and I had by this time pretty well made up our minds as to the character of both our neighbours ; and as the stranger astern—a large brig—was now barely half-a-mile distant from us, and drawing rapidly up on our starboard quarter, it was necessary to make up our minds without delay as to the course to be pursued ; the question being whether we should meddle at all with the brig, and thus run the risk of exciting the barque's suspicions, or whether we should devote our whole energies to the pursuit of the latter. I was all for letting the brig go, for we knew, by the course she was steering, that she had no slaves on board, and the chances were even that we should find nothing else on board her sufficiently compromising to secure her condemnation by the Mixed Commission. Ryan, on the other hand, could not make up his mind to let the chance go by of making two prizes instead of one.

"'A bird in hand is worth two in the bush, Harry, me bhoy,'" he remarked to me as we stood together near the binnacle, watching the approach of the brig, which was now foaming along not a quarter of a mile away from us; "and I look upon that brig as being quite as much in our hand as though you and I stood upon her quarter-deck, with all her crew safe under hatches. Steady there!" he continued, to the man at the tiller; "mind your weather-helm, my man, or you'll be having that mainsail jibing over, and I need not tell you what *that* means in a breeze like this. Don't meet her quite so sharply; if she seems inclined to take a sheer to starboard, let her go; I will take care that the brig does not run over us. Just look at her," he went on, turning again to me, "isn't she a beauty? Why, she's almost as handsome, and as big too, as the *Mercedes*! D'ye mean to tell me that such a hull as that would ever be employed in the humdrum trade of carrying palm-oil? Why, it would be nothing short of a waste of skilful modelling! No, *sorr*, she was built for a slaver, and a slaver she is, or I'll eat this hat of mine, puggaree and all, for breakfast!"

"I grant all that you say," admitted I, "but if she has nothing incriminating on board her, what then? We shall only be wasting our time by boarding her, while we shall certainly give the alarm to the barque yonder, and, as likely as not, lose her for our pains."

Ryan took a good long look at the barque, that was now about two points before our larboard beam, and some six miles distant, thrashing along in a style that did one's heart good to see, and plunging into the heavy head-sea against which she was beating until her foresail was dark with wet half-way up the weather-leech, and the spray was flying clean over her, and drifting away like smoke to leeward. Then he turned and looked at the brig on our opposite quarter.

"It's risky," he remarked to me through his set teeth, "but, by the powers, I'll chance it! If we happen to be mistaken, why, I'll make the skipper a handsome apology; if he's a true man, that ought to satisfy him. Mr. Bartlett"—to the boatswain—"cast off that drag and get it inboard over the port-rail with as little fuss as may be, so that if those fellows in the brig are watching us they may not know what we're about; I want to keep that conthrivance a saycret as long as I can. Be as smart as you like about it. Mr. Dugdale, I want twenty men to arm themselves forth-

with, and then creep into the waist under the lee of the starboard bulwarks, taking care that they are not seen; pick me out the best men in the ship, if you please. Ah, here is Gowland, the very man I wanted to see! Mr. Gowland, you see that brig——" and as I turned away to muster the men, and see that they were properly armed, he drew Gowland away to the other side of the deck, and began to communicate something to him in a very rapid, earnest manner.

By the time that the drag had been got inboard and stowed away, I had picked out the required men, and had contrived to get them by twos and threes under the starboard bulwarks without—so far as I knew—being seen by those on board the brig, watching the roll of the schooner and giving the word for the men to pass up through the scuttle and make a crouching run for it as the schooner rolled to port and hid her deck from the brig. That craft had by this time overhauled us, and was far enough ahead to permit of our reading her name—the *Conquistador*, of Havana—upon her stern; while our helmsman, taking Ryan's hint, had steered so wildly, that he had sheered the schooner almost to within biscuit toss of her neighbour. Meanwhile, now that the drag was no longer impeding us, we were gradually lessening the small space of water that separated us from the brig, and we could see that the schooner and her movements were exciting much curiosity and speculation, if not actual suspicion, in the minds of three men who stood right aft on her monkey-poop, intently watching us.

"Go for'ard and hail them," said Ryan to me; "I want to get a little closer if I can without unduly exciting their suspicions. You can affect to be deaf if you like; perhaps that will give us a chance."

I took the speaking-trumpet in my hand and, clambering leisurely into the fore-rigging, hailed in Spanish—

"Ho, the brig ahoy! what brig is that?"

"The *Conquistador*, of Havana," was the reply. "What schooner is that?"

I turned to one of the men who was standing near me and asked, in the most natural manner in the world, "What did he say?"

"The *Conkistee* — something, of Hawaner, it sounded like to me, sir," answered the man.

"What did you say?" I yelled at

the brig, raising the trumpet again to my mouth.

"The *Con-quist-a-dor*, of Havana. What schooner is that?"

I assumed the most utter look of bewilderment I could upon the spur of the moment, and then, waving my arm impatiently at our helmsman to sheer still closer alongside the brig, whose quarter was now fair abreast of our fore-rigging, repeated my question—

"*What* did you say?"

My interlocutor, who was evidently the skipper of the brig, stamped on the deck with vexation as he raised his hands to his mouth, and yelled at the top of his voice—

"The *Con-quist-a-dor*, of Havana! Do not sheer so close to me, if you please, señor. You will be foul of me if you do not look out!"

"That will do, Mr. Dugdale," shouted Ryan in English, to the evident astonishment and consternation of the brig's people, "we can manage now. Stand by to jump aboard with me. I shall want you to act as interpreter, for the deuce a word do I understand of their confounded lingo."

And as he spoke he waved his hand to the helmsman, while at the same moment Gowland, who stood close by, hauled down the Spanish and ran up the British ensign to our peak. There was a shout of dismay from those on board the brig, and a quick trampling of feet as her crew rushed to their stations and hurriedly threw the coiled-up braces, halliards, and sheets off the pins with some confused notion of doing something to evade us even at the last moment. But they were altogether too late; Somers, the quarter-master, who had seen what was afoot, and had gradually worked his way aft, sprang to the tiller, and jamming it over to port, sheered us very cleverly alongside the brig in the wake of her main-rigging, into which Ryan and I instantly leaped, followed by our twenty armed men. The surprise was so sudden and so complete that there was no time for resistance, even had the Spaniards been disposed to offer any, and in another moment we had reached the brig's deck and she was in our possession, the schooner instantly sheering off again to a short distance in order that the two craft might not do any damage to each other.

Having taken so very decisive a step as to board and carry the brig, there was now of course nothing for us but to go through with the affair in the same high-handed fashion. I therefore demanded at once to see the ship's papers; and after many indignant protests they were produced and flung down upon the cabin table for our inspection. These fully established the identity of the brig; and as an examination of her hold revealed that she was fitted with a slave-deck, large coppers for the preparation of food for the unfortunate blacks her captain hoped to secure, a stock of water, and farina ample enough to meet the wants of a large "cargo," and an abundance of slave-irons, we were fully justified in taking possession of her, which we did forthwith. Half-an-hour sufficed for us to secure our capture and put a prize-crew on board under Gowland's command, and we then parted company; the brig to stand on for an hour as she was going—so as not to needlessly alarm the barque—and then to haul up and shape a course for Sierra Leone, while we at once hauled our wind in pursuit of our new quarry, which bore by this time well upon our port quarter —as we had hitherto been going—with her topsails just showing above the horizon.

We had no sooner trimmed sail in chase of the barque than we found, to our unspeakable gratification, that we were still far enough to windward to lay well up for her, she being at the commencement of the chase not more than a point and a half upon our weather bow, while, from the superiority of our rig, we were able to look quite that much higher than she did. The question now was whether, in the strong wind and heavy sea that we had to contend against, we could hold our own with a craft so much more powerful than ourselves.

We had of course taken the precaution to get down a couple of reefs in our topsail, and the same in the foresail, as well as to haul down the square-sail and get the bonnet off the jib before leaving the *Conquistador;* but it was not until we had hauled our wind and put the schooner on a taut bowline, that we were able to realize how hard it was actually blowing. Up to then the wind had seemed no more to us than a brisk, pleasant breeze, while the schooner rode the long, creaming surges lightly as a gull. *Now*, however, we had to doff our straw hats in a hurry to save them from being blown away, and to don close-fitting cloth caps instead, as well as our oil-skins, while it was positively hard work to cross the deck against the wind. As for the schooner, she behaved like a mad thing, careening to her gunwale as she soared to the crest of a wave and cleft its foaming summit in a blinding deluge of spray that swept her decks from the weather cat-head right aft to the companion, and plunging next moment into the trough with a strong roll to windward, and a very bedlam of yells and shrieks aloft as the gale swept between her straining masts and rigging. She shuddered as if terrified at every headlong plunge that she took, while the milk-white spume brimmed to the level of her figure-head, and roared away from her bows in a whole acre of boiling, glistening foam. The creaking and groaning of her timbers and bulkheads raised such a din that a novice would have been quite justified in fearing that the little hooker was rapidly straining herself to pieces, while more than one crash of crockery below, faintly heard through the other multitudinous sounds, told us that the wild antics of the barkie were making a very pretty general average among our domestic utensils. But, with all her creaking and groaning, the schooner now proved herself to be a truly superb sea-boat, scarcely shipping so much as a bucketful of green water, despite the merciless manner in which we were driving her; and the way in which she surmounted sea after sea, turning up her streaming weather-bow to receive its buffet, and gaily " shaking her feathers" after every plunge, was enough to make a sailor's heart leap with pride and exultation that was not to be lessened even by the awe-inspiring spectacle of the mountains of water that in continuous procession soared up from beneath her keel and went roaring away to leeward with foaming crests that towered to the height of the cross-trees.

Our first anxiety, of course, was to ascertain whether we were gaining upon the chase, or whether she was maintaining her distance from us; as soon, therefore, as we had secured our morning altitude of the sun for the determination of the longitude, we measured as accurately as we could the angle subtended by that portion of the barque's mainmast which showed above the horizon. The task was one of very considerable difficulty owing to the violent motion of the two craft, and when we had done our best we were by no means satisfied with the result, but we thought it might

possibly be some help to us; so when we had at length agreed upon the actual value of the angle, we clamped our instruments, and, taking them below, stowed them carefully away in our bunks, where there was not much danger of their coming to harm through the frantic plunging of the schooner, our purpose of course being to compare the angle then obtained with another to be measured an hour or two later. If the second angle should prove to be greater than the first, it would show that we had gained on the chase; if, on the contrary, it should prove to be less, it would show that the chase had increased her distance from us. It was shortly before noon when we again brought our sextants on deck, opinion being meanwhile strongly divided as to whether or not we were gaining; some asserting positively that we were, while others as stoutly maintained that we were not. But even our sextants failed to settle the question, for if there was any difference at all in the angle, it was too minute for detection, and we were left in almost the same state of suspense as before. The only relief afforded us was the assurance that we were practically holding our own with the barque, and that unless the weather grew still worse than it was, we stood a fairly good chance of catching her eventually. One thing was certain; light as our draught of water was, and small as was the schooner's area of lateral resistance compared with that of the barque, we were slowly but certainly eating our way out upon her weather quarter, her main and foremasts having been visible to leeward of her mizenmast when the chase commenced, while now they just showed clear of each other to windward, thus conclusively demonstrating that we were gaining the weather-gauge of her, despite the heavy sea. This was certainly a most comforting reflection, and greatly helped to console us for the otherwise slow progress that we were making in the chase. Ryan seemed to be the most disappointed man among us all; he was very impetuous and hotheaded; he liked to do everything on the instant and with a rush; and upon the discovery that we were not gaining perceptibly, he muttered something about giving the schooner more canvas. Luckily, before giving the order he paused long enough to allow the fact to be borne in upon him that the masts were already whipping and bending like fishing-rods, and the gear taxed to its utmost capacity of resistance; and being, despite the characteristics above-mentioned, a reasonably prudent and careful officer, the sight restrained him, and he forbore to attempt anything so risky as the further over-driving of the already greatly over-driven craft.

Not so with the skipper of the barque. It was, of course, impossible for us to know whether he had observed the capture of the *Conquistador*—we hoped and believed not; but, however that may have been, it was certain that he had been keeping his eyes sufficiently open to promptly become aware of the fact that the schooner had altered her course and was standing after him under a very heavy press of sail, and if our surmises as to his character were any-where near the truth, that circumstance alone would be quite sufficient to fully arouse his easily-awakened apprehensions and to urge him to keep us at arm's length at all risks. Be that as it may, we had just made it noon when the quarter-master called our attention to the fact that the barque's people had loosed their main-topgallant-sail and were sheeting it home over the double-reefed topsail. It was an imprudent thing to do, however, for the sail had scarcely been set ten minutes when the topgallant-mast went over the side, snapped short off by the cap. Her skipper instantly availed himself of the pretext afforded by this accident to bear away three or four points while clearing the wreck, his object doubtless being to determine beyond all question whether we really were after him or not; and if this was his purpose, we did not leave him long in doubt upon the point, our own helm being put up the instant that we saw what he was about. Realizing, by this move on our part, the true state of affairs, he now squared dead away before the wind, shook out all his reefs, and set his fore-topgallant-sail, as well as topmast and lower studding-sails. This was piling on the canvas with a vengeance, but Ryan was not the man to be bluffed by any such move as that; every glass we had was now levelled at the barque, and no sooner were her people seen in the rigging than away went our own, and so much smarter were our people than those belonging to the barque, that our own studding-sails were set and dragging like cart-horses while theirs were still being sent aloft. This experiment was tried for about half-an-hour, by which time it became evident that the schooner was

fully as good off the wind as was the barque, if not a trifle better; she seemed to fairly *fly*, while at times, when the breeze happened to freshen a trifle, it really seemed as though she would be lifted out of the water altogether; and I am quite persuaded that but for the preventers we had rigged for the purpose of relieving the masts when she was rolling so heavily during the preceding calm—and which still remained aloft and were doing splendid service—we must have lost both our sticks and been reduced to a sheer hulk long before the half-hour had expired.

I have said that we were doing quite as well as, if not a trifle better than, the barque; for while we held our own with her, so that she was unable to appreciably alter her bearing from us, we were steadily edging up toward her, our gain in this respect being so great that ere the next manœuvre was attempted we had risen her high enough to get a momentary glimpse of the whole length of her rail when she floated up on the crest of a sea. It was clear, therefore, that the barque had gained nothing by running off the wind; on the contrary, we had neared her fully a mile; her skipper, therefore, having given the unsuccessful experiment a fair trial, suddenly took in all his stud-ding-sails again, reduced his canvas once more to a couple of reefs, and braced sharp up to the wind, as before. But here again we had the advantage of him through the superior smartness of our own crew, for he no sooner began to shorten sail than we did the same, handling our canvas so quickly that we were nearly five minutes before him, the result being that we had gained another half-mile upon him and had placed ourselves a good quarter of a mile upon his weather quarter by the time that he had sweated up his top-sail-halliards. We now felt that, bar-ring accidents, the barque was ours; she could escape us neither to leeward nor to windward. Instead, therefore, of continuing to jam the schooner as close into the wind's eye as she would sail, with the object of weathering out on the barque, we pointed the little vixen's jib-boom fair and square at the chase, checked the sheets and braces a few inches fore and aft, and put her along for all that she was worth.

It is astonishing to note the advan-tageous effect that is produced upon the sailing of a ship when it becomes pos-sible to check the sheets and braces even a few paltry inches; it was distinctly noticeable in the case of the schooner; her movements were perceptibly freer and easier, she no longer drove her keen cut-water into the heart of the seas, receiving their blows upon the rounding of her weather bow with a force sufficient to shake her from stem to stern and almost to stop her way for an appreciable instant of time; she now slid smoothly up the breast of the wave, taking its stroke fairly in the bunt of the fore-rigging, where it had little or no retarding effect upon her, surmounted its crest with a long, easy roll, and then sank with equal smoothness down into the trough, along which she sped lightly and swiftly as a petrel. It added a good half-a-knot to her speed.

It was soon apparent that even this comparatively trifling advantage on our part had not escaped the notice of our wary friend the skipper of the barque; it suggested to him yet one more experiment, and he was not slow to make it, keeping his ship away about a point and a half and checking his braces accordingly. This proved very much more satisfactory so far as he was concerned; for by four bells in the afternoon watch we had lost sight of the barque's hull again, and it was unmistakably evident that she was increasing her distance from us. We held on, however, straight after her, as before; for although it was undeniable that she was now drawing away from us, it was but slowly; it would take her a good many hours to run us out of sight at that rate, and we felt pretty confident that when the weather moderated—which we hoped would be before long, as the glass indicated a slight rising tendency —we should have her at our mercy. Meanwhile, however, we felt that we must not count our chickens before they were hatched; for there would be nearly an hour and a half of darkness between sunset and moonrise, and in that time our crafty friend would be pretty certain to attempt some new trickery if there seemed a ghost of a chance of its proving successful.

CHAPTER VII

THE SLAVER'S RUSE

THE sun set that night in a broad bank of horizontal, mottled grey cloud, through which his beams darted in golden splendour at brief intervals for nearly half-an-hour after we had lost sight of the great luminary himself; and just about the time that the spars and canvas of the distant barque began to grow indistinct in the fast-gathering dusk of evening, there occurred a noticeable decrease in the strength of the wind, with every prospect of a tolerably fine night. Of course our glasses were never off the chase for more than five minutes at a time, but up to the moment when it became impossible to any longer distinguish the movements of those on board, no attempt to increase her spread of canvas had been observed. Whether by this apparent apathy her people hoped to lull us into a condition of equal carelessness, it is of course impossible for me to say; but, if so, they signally failed, for immediately that the barque's outline faded into an indistinct blur in the growing darkness, we went to work and shook out a reef all round, never doubting but that they were at that moment doing precisely the same thing. And our supposition was most probably correct—Ryan, indeed, who had sent for his night-glass and brought it to bear upon her, declared that he could detect an increase in the area of her shadowy canvas—for even after we had made sail we could not perceive that we were in any wise decreasing the distance between the two vessels.

As the swift, tropical night shut down upon us every eye in the ship became strained to its utmost power in the effort to keep sight of the chase, for now that there could no longer be any doubt in the minds of her people that we were after them, we felt convinced that should an opportunity present itself for them to elude us in the darkness they would assuredly embrace it; and, being new to the coast and to the service, as most of us were, we had yet to learn by vexatious experience the fertility of resource which had been developed in the slave-trafficking fraternity by the unflagging pursuit to which they were subjected by the slave squadron, and of which they never missed a chance to avail themselves. We had heard many an amusing story of the extraordinarily clever devices that these gentry had resorted to—very often successfully—in their endeavours to elude pursuit, and while we had laughed heartily at the recital of them, or commented admiringly upon their ingenuity, as the case might be, we had no fancy for further illustrating in our own persons their superiority in the art of mystification. And we were rendered all the more anxious by the fact that with nightfall the sky became overspread with a thin canopy of cloud that, while not sufficiently dense to wholly obscure the stars, so dimmed their lustre that it became difficult to distinguish, even through our night-glasses, the forms of the waves at a greater distance than half-a-mile; while as for the chase, we were at length reluctantly compelled to admit to each other that we had lost sight of her altogether, or at least that we could not be absolutely certain whether we could still see her or not; sometimes we were confident that we could, at other times we utterly failed to make her out.

It was while we were in this painful condition of uncertainty that Ryan—who like myself had remained on deck, diligently working away with his glass, and utterly deaf to the more than once repeated statement of the steward that the dinner was on the cabin table—turned quickly to me and said—

" Do you see that greenish-looking star just glimmering through the clouds right over our jib-boom end? Here, stand exactly where I am, and when she pitches you will see it showing about ten degrees above the horizon. There ! do you see the star I mean ? "

" Yes," said I, catching sight of the pale green glimmer as he placed me in position. " Yes, I see it. What of it ? "

" Just carry your eye from it down to the horizon at an angle of about forty-five degrees in an easterly direction, and tell me if you see anything particular."

I did so, and after two or three attempts thought I caught a faint gleam like the light of a lamp shining through a red curtain.

" Yes," I answered, " I fancy I can just make out a dim something." And I described what I saw.

" Precisely ! " exclaimed Ryan delightedly. " There ! now I have it in my glass—no, it is gone again—this jump of a sea renders it almost impossible to use one's telescope on the deck of such a lively little hooker as this—not that I've a word to say against her, God bless her, she's a beauty, every inch of her, but I wish she'd remain steady for a second or two. There, I have it again ! Yes, it's a light in the barque's after-cabin. They've drawn the curtains, never suspecting that the light would show through. Yes, there's no mistake about it, I can see it quite plainly now ;

upon my word I believe we are overhauling her now that the breeze has dropped a bit. Mr. Pierrepoint, d'ye see that light ? "

" Where away, sir ? "

It was pointed out to the lad, and after some searching and prying—for it was so very dim that it was almost impossible to distinguish it with the naked eye—he caught sight of it.

" Very well, then," remarked Ryan, with a return to his old, humorous manner that showed how great a relief to him was the appearance of the faint ruddy gleam, " keep your eye upon it, my bhoy, until I give ye a shpell. Mr. Dugdale and Oi are now goin' below to dinner, and if ye lose soight of that loight, bedad I'll—I'll keelhaul ye, ye shpalpeen. He's edgin' away off the wind, d'ye see, the blagguard ! I wouldn't be surprised if he was to up helm and shquare away before it in a minute or two, hopin' to run us out of soight before the moon rises, so don't let your oye go off that light for a single inshtant if ye value your shkin. Keep her away a bit "—to the man at the helm—" let her go off a point ! So ! steady as you go ! There, Masther Freddy, the light is right forninst your jib-boom end now. Mind that ye kape it there. We're certainly gaining on her." And, patting the lad affectionately on the shoulder, the warm-hearted Irishman turned and beckoned me to follow him down into the cabin.

We had been below about half-an-hour, and were getting well forward with our dinner, when we heard the voices of Pierrepoint and the quartermaster in earnest conversation over the open skylight, and an occasional word or two that reached us seemed to indicate that they were in doubt about something. We both pricked up our ears a little ; and presently we heard Pierrepoint ejaculate in a tone of impatience and with a stamp of his foot on the deck—

" I'll be shot if I can understand it at all, Somers ; I shall call the captain."

" I really think I would, sir, if I was you. I don't believe that's the barque at all ; it's some circumventing trick that they've been playing us, that's my opinion ! "

At this Ryan started to his feet and, hailing through the skylight, asked—

" What is the matter, Mr. Pierrepoint ; have you lost sight of the light ? "

" No, sir," answered poor Freddy, in a tone of distress ; " the light is still straight ahead of us, and we seem to be nearing it fast, but I can't make out anything like the loom of the sails or hull of the barque, and if she is there I think we ought to see her by this time. The red light shows quite plainly in the glass."

"I will join you on deck and have a look at it," exclaimed Ryan; and, rising from the table, he sprang up the companion-ladder three steps at a time, I following close at his heels.

Yes; there was the light, sure enough, right ahead of us; and a glance aloft as well as the feel of the breeze on our faces told us in an instant that the schooner had been further kept away, and was now running well off the wind, although the change had been so gradual that we had not noticed it while sitting in the cabin. Ryan took the glass from Pierrepoint and brought it to bear on the light.

"Yes," he remarked, with the telescope still at his eye, "that is the light, beyond a doubt; but, as you say, Mr. Pierrepoint, I can see no sign of the barque herself. Yet she *must* be there, for that light is obviously moving, and I observe that you have, very properly, kept away to follow it. Surely," he continued, with an accent of impatience and perplexity, "we have not been following some other craft that has hove above the horizon since the darkness set in? And, even so, I can see nothing of the craft herself. Obviously, however, we are nearing the light—whatever it is—fast, for I can see it quite distinctly in the glass, I even fancy that I can see it rising and falling. Take the glass, Dugdale, and tell me what you can make of it."

I took the glass, and, after a long and patient scrutiny of the mysterious light, pronounced my opinion.

"To me, sir," said I, "it has the appearance of an ordinary ship's lantern wrapped in a strip of red bunting and hung from a pole, or something of that sort. For, if you will look at it closely, you will notice that it *sways* with the wash of the sea, and now and then seems to swing for an instant behind a slender object like a light spar. But I could almost take my oath that there is no barque or any other kind of craft there."

Once again Ryan took the telescope, and after a further prolonged scrutiny, he exclaimed—

"By the powers, but I believe you are right, and if so we have been done! It certainly *has* very much the appearance that you describe. But what in the world can it be? It is a moving object, beyond all doubt, for see how we have been obliged to run off the wind in chase of it! However, we are close to it now, for I can make out the swinging of the lantern—and a lantern it *is*—with the naked eye. It is some confounded contrivance for leading us astray, that is what it is! But since we are so close to it, we may as well ascertain its character, if only to be awake to the trick if it ever happens to be played upon us a second time. Hands by the braces here, and stand by to back the topsail. And get two or three lanterns ready to swing over the side, so that we may see just exactly what the thing is."

We had by this time approached the mysterious object so nearly that another three or four minutes sufficed to bring it within a couple of hundred feet of the schooner's weather bow, when the topsail was laid to the mast, and our way checked sufficiently to permit of a careful examination of the thing, whatever it was. By the time that we had forged ahead far enough to bring it on our weather beam it was close aboard of us, and then the light of our lanterns disclosed the nature of the contrivance by which we had been so cleverly tricked. It was in fact nothing more than a raft composed of five nine-inch planks laid parallel to each other with a space of about a foot between each, and firmly secured together by a couple of stout cross-pieces nailed athwart the whole concern. The fore-ends of the planks had been sawn away to the shape of a sharp wedge to facilitate the movement of the raft through the water, and on the foremost cross-piece had been rigged an oar for a mast, upon which was set a hastily-contrived squaresail, made out of a piece of old tarpaulin. To the head of the mast was securely lashed an old lantern with a short length of candle, still burning, in it; the lantern being cunningly draped in red bunting to represent the appearance of a lamp shining through a curtain. And the whole contrivance was rendered self-steering by the attachment of a few fathoms of line to the after-end of the middle plank, at the other extremity of which a drogue, consisting of a short length of plank, was attached. This drogue had the effect of keeping the raft running dead before the wind, and it travelled at a very respectable pace, too—quite five knots an hour, we estimated its speed at—for the sail was quite a big one for so small an affair ; and since we had been steering for it for just about an hour, it meant that we had been decoyed some five miles to leeward of our proper course.

The question now was : Where was the barque ? It did not take us very long to make up our minds upon this point. It was pretty evident that since her skipper had been at so much pains to entice us away down to leeward, he would have held his wind all this time ; and to windward therefore must we look for him. Whether, however, he had tacked and stood away to the westward immediately after launching his raft, or whether he had held on upon the port tack to the northward, we could not possibly tell, for a diligent and prolonged use of our night-glasses failed to reveal the slightest indication of his whereabouts. Ryan, however, was not long in arriving upon a con- clusion in the matter. He argued that if he had tacked we ought also to tack forthwith, because, if we stood on as we were going until the moon rose, we might run out of sight of him ; whereas, if he had *not* tacked, he would be at that moment somewhere about broad on our weather bow. If therefore he *had* tacked, we should be doing the right thing to tack also, since we should then be standing directly after him ; while if he had not tacked, we should still be doing right to heave about, since even in that case we should probably see something of him from our masthead when the moon rose, as she would in less than half-an-hour. We therefore at once put the helm down and hove round on the starboard tack, keeping the schooner as close to the wind as she would lie, while still allowing her to go along through the water.

A faint brightening in the sky by and by announced the welcome approach of the moon upon the scene ; and shortly afterwards the beautiful planet herself, considerably shrunken from her full-orbed splendour, rose slowly into view above the horizon, her cur- tailed disc showing of a deep, ruddy orange-colour through the dense, humid vapours of the lower atmosphere. Two hands were at once sent up to the top- gallant-yard to take a look round ; but even after they had been there an hour —by which time the moon had risen high enough to give us plenty of light —they failed to discover any sign of

the barque or anything else ; and we were at length reluctantly compelled to admit that we had been very cleverly tricked, and that our cunning neighbour had fairly given us the slip.

"But I'll not give him up, even now !" exclaimed Ryan, when this con- viction had fairly forced itself upon us. "Come down below, Dugdale, and let us reason this thing out."

We accordingly descended to our snug little cabin and seated ourselves at the table, Ryan producing a sheet of paper, a scale, and a pencil where- with to graphically illustrate our line of reasoning.

"Now, here," said he, drawing an arrow near one margin of the paper, "is the wind, coming out at west as nearly as may be ; and here," laying the scale upon the paper, measuring off a distance, and making two pencil dots, "are the positions of the barque and the schooner when the former was last seen. Now, I estimate that the barque was going about eight and a half knots, and we were reeling off nine by the log at that time ; and this state of affairs continued at least until the light was seen, which was about half- an-hour after we lost sight of our friend. Consequently, when the light was first seen, the schooner was here "—making another dot—"and the barque there," making a fourth.

"Now, what would the blagguard be most likely to do when he had safely launched his raft ? He knew that it would go skimming away to leeward, taking us with it ; and I therefore think it most probable that he would tack at once, going off in this direc- tion," laying down a line upon the paper. "Meanwhile, the raft went scudding away to leeward until we met it there," making another dot. "Then we tacked, and, laying a point higher than he can, stood along this line," ruling one carefully in as he spoke. "Now, we have been travelling along this line, say an hour and a quarter, which brings us here. But where is the barque ? If she had tacked, and *continued to stand on* until now, she would be *there*, eleven or twelve miles away, and we should see her. Sup- posing, however, that she continued to stand on as she was going when we last saw her, she would now be *there*, twenty-eight miles away ! Phew ! I was a long way out of my reckoning when I thought that we should still have her in sight, even if we tacked.

We've lost her, Harry, my bhoy, and that's a fact. However, we know where she's bound to, and that's the island of Cuba, or I'm a Dutchman. Very well. Having given us the slip she will make the best of her way there without further delay; and it is my opinion that *if* she is still standing to the northward she will not continue to do so for very much longer, because, d'ye see, my bhoy, she'll be afraid of falling in with some of our cruisers if she stands in too close to the coast. Therefore, as we can hug the wind closer than she can, we'll just stand on as we are going for a day or two longer, or until the wind changes—in fact, we will shape a course for Cuba—and if we don't fall in with her again within the next seventy-two hours I shall give her up. Meanwhile the wind is dropping fast, so we will get some more muslin upon the little hooker."

As Ryan had said, the wind was dropping fast, so rapidly, indeed, that when eight bells was struck at midnight the schooner was under all the canvas that we could set, and even then was only creeping along at a speed of some two and a half knots per hour. Oh, how fervently we wished then that we could see even as much as the mere mastheads of the barque! for we felt certain that in such a light air the schooner would make short work of overtaking her. But nothing hove in sight; and when the next morning dawned we were still alone upon the face of the vast ocean.

With the rising of the sun the small draught of air that still remained to us fell dead; and we had it calm the whole day and well on into the succeeding night. Then the weather became unsettled and thundery, with light baffling airs interspersed with fierce squalls from all quarters of the compass, during which we made scarcely sixty miles in the twenty-four hours.

It was about midnight of the third day after we had lost sight of the barque, and the seventy-two hours that Ryan had allowed himself in which to find her again were fully spent, without affording us another glimpse of her. All hands, from Ryan himself down to the smallest boy in the ship, were dreadfully disgusted and crestfallen at our want of success; and we were only waiting for a breeze to spring up from somewhere to enable us to shape a course back to our cruising ground.

The weather, however, was still very overcast and lowering, with signs not wanting that another heavy thunderstorm was brewing, which would probably bring us the desired breeze. There was not much swell running, but sufficient, nevertheless, to tumble the schooner about a good deal; and I had accordingly taken it upon myself to clew up, haul down, and furl every stitch of canvas, in order to save the sails from battering themselves to rags. The thunder had been gradually working up ever since sunset, and in fact even before that, and when eight bells struck at midnight, and my watch below came round, the weather had such a curious and portentous look, and the atmosphere was moreover so close and heavy, that I determined to stretch myself out "all standing" on the stern grating instead of going below, so that I might be all ready in case my presence should be required.

It was shortly after two bells when Pierrepoint came and roused me out with the remark—

"I am sorry to disturb you, Dugdale, but I think it is going to rain very shortly, and if you remain there you stand a very good chance of getting soaked to the skin. And what do you think of the weather? Is it merely a thunder-squall that has been brewing all this time, or what is it? Just look at those clouds overhead, their edges look quite red, as though there was a fire somewhere behind them. Do you think I should call the captain?"

It was as he had said. The sky was banked up from horizon to zenith, all round, with enormous cloud-piles, black as ink in the body of them, but their fringes or edges, which had a curiously tattered appearance, were of a distinct fiery red hue. All this time there was not a breath of wind save what was created by the schooner as she rolled heavily on the gathering swell; not a sound save those which arose within her as the bulkheads and timbers creaked and groaned dismally, the cabin doors rattled, the rudder kicked as the water swirled and gurgled about it and under her counter with the heave of her, and the jerk of the spars aloft, or the slatting of the braces as she swayed, pendulum-like, from side to side.

"What does the glass say?" inquired I, in response to Pierrepoint's last question. I walked to the open skylight and peered down through it at the barometer, the tube of which was just sufficiently illuminated by the turned-down cabin lamp to permit of its condition being noted. It had fallen an inch since I last looked at it, during my watch on deck!

"Phew!" ejaculated I, "there must surely be something the matter with the thing; it can never have fallen that much in scarcely two hours!"

I hurried below and, turning up the lamp, subjected the instrument to a careful examination; but, as far as I could make out, there seemed to be nothing wrong with it; the fall had all the appearance of being perfectly genuine. But, whether or not, it was certain that the captain ought at once to be made acquainted with the state of affairs; I therefore went forthwith to his cabin and aroused him.

"Ay, ay," he answered sleepily, to my call. "What is it, Mr. Dugdale? Has the barque hove in sight?"

"No such luck, sir, I am sorry to say," replied I. "But I think you ought to know that the weather has a very peculiar and threatening appearance; and the glass has dropped a full inch within the last two hours."

"An inch?" ejaculated Ryan, starting up in his bunk. "An inch? Surely, Dugdale, you must be mistaken!"

"Indeed, sir, I am not," said I. "I examined the barometer very carefully, and satisfied myself that I had made no mistake before calling you."

"By Jove, then, it is high time that I was on deck!" exclaimed he, leaping out of his bunk. "Just put a match to my lamp, Harry, my lad, will ye; you will find a box there on the shelf. Is there any wind?"

"Not a breath, sir; but I shall not be surprised if we have a great deal more than we want before long," I answered.

"Um!" said he. "Well, almost anything short of a hurricane would be better than these exasperating calms. The swell seems to have risen a bit since I turned in, hasn't it?"

"Quite perceptibly," said I, "and it seems to be coming more out from the northward than at first."

"Well," said he, thrusting his bare feet into his slippers, "let us go on deck and take a look round."

And, he leading the way, we forthwith trundled up the companion-ladder and stepped out on deck.

It seemed to have grown blacker and more threatening than ever during the short time that I had been below, although that may have been due to the contrast between the light of the cabin and the darkness on deck; the ruddy tinge on the cloud edges, however, was even more pronounced than before, the colour having slightly changed and grown more like the hue of red-hot copper. Ryan was evidently much astonished — and, I thought, somewhat dismayed—by what he saw.

"By the powers!" he ejaculated, "you did right to call me, Dugdale. If we were in the Indian Ocean, now, I would say that a cyclone was brewing; and, now I come to think of it, there is no Act of Parliament against one brewing here. How is the glass *now*? has it dropped anything since you last looked at it?"

I went to the skylight and once more peered at the mercury.

"Yes, indeed, sir, it has," answered I, "it has gone down nearly one-tenth!"

"Then, by the piper, we're in for something out of the common, and the sooner we set about preparing for it, the better!" exclaimed Ryan. "Ah! I see you have already furled everything; well, that leaves us so much the less to be still done. Call all hands, however, for we may have it upon us at any moment, by the look of things up there," pointing to the frowning, ruddy sky. "Rig in the jib-boom, and send down all but the lower-yard on deck, and both topmasts as well. Set some of the men to secure the canvas with double gaskets; and close-reef the boom-foresail and set it. Let the carpenter look to the hatches and see that they are securely battened down, and he had better examine the pumps also; our lives may depend upon them before all is over. Where is the boatswain? Oh, is that you, Bartlett? Give an eye to the boats' gripes, will you, and see that they are all right. I have known a boat to be blown clean from the davits before now. Hurrah, men! look alive with those yards, and let us have them down here on deck as quickly as possible."

The schooner was by this time as busy as a beehive in swarming-time, the men working with a will, since they knew, from the sharp, incisive tones in which Ryan issued his orders, as well as by the menacing aspect of the sky, that the occasion was pressing. Fortunately, in so small and lightly-rigged a craft as the *Felicidad*, the task of preparing her for the forthcoming battle with the elements was not a heavy one, and, being well manned for our size, we were soon ready.

None too soon, however. For hardly had the finishing touches been given to our preparations, and the guns and boats made thoroughly secure, than we were momentarily dazzled and blinded by a terrific flash of blue lightning that seemed to dart from the clouds immediately overhead, and to strike the water close to us, filling the dead and heavy air with a strong odour of brimstone, while simultaneously we were deafened and stunned by a most awful, ear-splitting *crack* of thunder that made the schooner quiver from stem to stern as though she had been struck by a heavy shot.

Ryan, Pierrepoint, and I were all standing close together near the companion at the moment when the lightning flashed out, illumining the whole scene for an instant with a light as brilliant as that of the noonday sun, and while I was still in process of recovering from the shock produced by the terrifying crash of the thunder, I heard my fellow-mid exclaim to the captain—

" There ! did you see that, sir ? There is a craft of some sort away out there," pointing in a north-easterly direction. " I saw her as distinctly as possible. She is about six miles away, and is stripped to her close-reefed topsails——"

" Did you see that ship out there on our port quarter, sir ? " hailed one of the men from the forecastle, interrupting Master Freddy in his tale.

" No," answered Ryan sharply. " I wasn't looking that way. What did she look like ? "

" She is a square-rigged craft of about three or four hundred tons, under close-reefed topsails, lying end-on to us, sir," answered the man.

" Surely it can't be our old friend the barque that has drifted within view of us again during the darkness ? " exclaimed Ryan excitedly. " Keep a good look-out for her, lads, when the next flash comes," he added in an eager tone of voice, that showed conclusively how secondary a matter the impending outburst of the elements had already become to him in view of this new discovery.

No second flash came, however, but instead of it, and almost as the last words left Ryan's lips, the clouds above us burst, and there descended from them the heaviest downpour of rain that I had ever up to that time witnessed. Those who have never beheld a tropical thunder-shower can form no conception of what it is like. Imagine yourself to be standing immediately under a large tank of warm water, and then further imagine that the contents of this tank are suddenly capsized right on top of you ; multiply the quantity of falling water a million times, and suppose the descent of the water to be continued for from three to six or seven minutes, and you will then have an imperfect conception of the sort of drenching that we received on the occasion of which I am now speaking. The decks were flooded in an instant, and before I could wriggle into my oil-skins I was soaked to the skin, and the warm water was washing above my ankles with the roll of the schooner. The scuppers were wholly inadequate to the occasion, and we were obliged to open the ports to get rid of the water and prevent it from getting below. The downpour lasted some four minutes or so, ceasing as abruptly and with as little warning as it had commenced ; but in that time it had beaten down the swell so effectually that our motion was scarcely more perceptible than it would have been in a well-sheltered roadstead ; and the effect of the sudden cessation of the noises that had been so recently sounding in our ears, and of the crash of the downpour, was very weird and curious, the dead silence now being broken only by an occasional faint creak or jar of bulkhead or boom, and the loud gush and gurgle of the water pouring from the scuppers.

The silence was of no long duration, however, for we had scarcely found time to become sensible of it when a faint moaning sound arose in the air, coming from no one knew where ; and, presently, with a still louder moan, a sudden, furious scuffle of wind swept past us, causing our reefed foresail to flap loudly, and was gone. The moanings grew louder and more weird, sounding now on the port quarter, now on the starboard bow, then broad abeam, and anon high over our mastheads ; it was clear that small, partial currents of air were in violent motion all round us, and that the crisis was at hand.

CHAPTER VIII

CAUGHT IN A CYCLONE

THE watch below had been dismissed upon the completion of our work of preparation, but not a man had left the deck, their anxiety to see and know the worst of what was to befall having completely overcome their usual propensity to make the utmost of every moment allotted to them for necessary rest, and they were now all huddled and clustered together upon the forecastle, discussing the situation in low, murmured tones, and holding themselves in readiness, like hounds in the leash, to spring into activity at the first word of command.

The moaning and wailing sounds were now floating all round us, and presently, making itself rapidly audible above them, we became conscious of a deep, fierce, bellowing roar that seemed to be approaching us on our starboard beam, the schooner's head being then about north-west.

"Here it comes!" exclaimed Ryan, in a hoarse tone of suppressed excitement. "Get hold of a belaying-pin each, you two, or you will stand a very good chance of being blown overboard. Starboard your helm; hard over with it, my man. Get under the lee of the starboard bulwarks, men. Carpenter, are your axes ready in case we should be obliged to cut anything away?"

"All ready, sir," came the reply, scarcely audible above the roar of the tempest that was now close upon us; and as the man spoke a fierce gust of wind laden with salt mist swooped down upon us and careened the schooner almost to her covering-board as it filled the foresail with a jar and a report like that of a nine-pounder. This blast was only momentary, however, it was upon us and gone again in an instant, but it was quickly succeeded by others; and then, away in the gloom, right abeam of us, appeared a white, spectral glimmer swooping down upon the schooner with the speed of a race-horse, and spreading momentarily wider athwart the blackness as it came. It was a line of white foam churned up on the surface of the sea by the advancing hurricane, and all behind it the ocean was white as milk. The air was now in violent motion all about us, fierce eddies swooping hither and thither, but generally in the same direction as that from which the gale was approaching. Another heavy salt-laden gust struck us, lasting just long enough to give the schooner way and render her obedient to her helm, and then the deep bass roar rose into a deafening, yelling medley of indescribable sounds as the gale struck us, and the poor little schooner bowed beneath the blow until the water poured in over her lee gunwale and I thought that she was going to "turn the turtle" with us. The foresail stood the strain for just an instant, and then it split to ribbons, and was torn from the bolt-ropes as cleanly as though the work had been done with a knife. But the good sail had already done its work before the hurricane proper had struck us, in that it had imparted some life, even though ever so little, to the schooner; she was already paying slowly off when the first stroke of the hurricane beat her down, and she continued to do so until, as she got dead before it, she rose suddenly to an even keel and went scudding away to leeward like a frightened sea-bird. The awful volume of sound given out by the fierce, head-long swoop of the wind as it bore down upon us quite prepared me to see both masts blown clean out of the schooner; but all her gear fortunately happened to be sound and good, and the loss of the foresail was the full extent of the damage sustained by us.

Having satisfied myself upon that point, I ventured to raise my head a little above the bulwarks to see how the strange sail was faring. Pierre-point had reported her as being visible in the north-eastern quarter, and if this were so she ought now to be somewhere astern of us, since we were running off about south-west; and, sure enough, there she was, about a point and a half on our starboard quarter, just visible in the midst of the ghostly glare of the phosphorescent foam. She was, like ourselves, running dead before the gale, and I thought I could make out that her topsails had withstood the tremendous strain of the outburst and were still doing their duty. If this were so, since we were scudding under bare poles, she would soon overtake and pass us quite as closely as would be at all consistent with the safety of the two craft, and we should be afforded an opportunity to learn something of her character, and to judge whether she was the barque that we had been so industriously seeking. I made my way over to Ryan, who was standing

—as well as he could against the violence of the wind that threatened to sweep him off his feet—close to the helmsman, pointed toward the stranger, and, clinging to the companion, we stood and watched her for a minute or two, half suffocated with the difficulty of breathing in so furious a tempest. She was now about four miles from us, and it soon became apparent that she was overhauling us fast, although by no means so fast as I expected; and she was so nearly end-on to us that I suggested to Ryan the advisability of our showing a light, as it looked very much as though she had not yet seen us and might approach us so closely as to put both craft in imminent peril.

"All in good time," shouted the captain in my ear, in response to this suggestion. "I do not believe that she *has* seen us yet; but that is not of much consequence, since both of us are steering as steadily as pleasure-boats on a river, and I will take care to make her acquainted with our whereabouts if there appears to be the slightest danger of her running over us. But I want her to pass as near us as possible, so that we may have a good view of her. For there seems to me to be a something familiar-looking about her, as though I had seen her before; and, between you and me, Harry, I believe her to be our old friend the barque again. And, if so, we must keep up with her at all costs until the weather moderates sufficiently to bring her to; so just step for'ard, will you, my lad, and get the fore-trysail on deck and bent ready for setting in case we need it. And let one hand bring aft a lantern, *not* lighted, mind ye; he can take it below, light it *there*, and leave it at the foot of the companion-ladder all ready to show a light if yonder stranger seems likely to sheer too close to us in passing."

I went forward, as requested, and found that the watch below had already returned to their hammocks, the crisis having passed, and the schooner scudding as comfortably as could be before the gale. The trysail was got up from below, bent, halliards and sheets hooked on, and, in short, made all ready for setting, and I returned aft to Ryan's side, having to claw my way to him along the rail in preference to creeping along the deck upon all fours, which seemed to be the only alternative method of making headway against

the wind. The sea was by this time getting up, and the air was full of spume and scud-water, caught up from the surface of the sea and the crests of the waves and swept along in a blinding, drenching shower by the gale. My superior officer was still clinging to the companion, with his eyes intently fixed upon the strange sail astern, which, now that the dense masses of cloud overhead were torn into shreds of flying scud by the fury of the wind, was pretty distinctly visible, at a distance of about a mile and a half, by the dim, misty moonlight that filtered through.

"I've been trying to get a peep at her through my night-glass," exclaimed Ryan, with a wave of his hand toward the dark blotch in the midst of the white foam, "but there is no holding it in such a breeze as this; you have to keep a tight grip on the thing or the wind will take it away from you altogether. But I'm pretty certain that it is the barque; and if so I'll stick to her as long as this schooner will hang together."

"Do you think that she has seen us yet?" I asked.

"Yes, I fancy so," answered Ryan. "She appears to me to be edging away a trifle, so as to pass us to starboard, giving us as wide a berth as possible. But even although she may have seen us, I do not believe that we are recognized, as yet; indeed, how should we be? At this distance, and end-on as we are, with no canvas set and our topmasts struck, we must look like little more than a dot on the water."

. This was quite true, and I fully believed, with Ryan, that we had *not* been recognized, for although our companion had indeed manifested signs of an inclination to edge away from us, the tendency was only to a sufficient extent to insure her passing us in safety. Had she suspected us of being an enemy, it would not have been positively dangerous for her to have altered her course fully a point, although, blowing as it then did, it would have been exceedingly imprudent to have attempted more than that.

In about half-an-hour after I had joined Ryan the strange craft overtook us; but while she was yet some half-a-mile astern of us we had made her out to be a barque of just about the same size as the one that we had been hunting for; and when she came up abreast of us at a distance of not more than a quarter of a mile, we saw that her main-topmast had gone just at the cap, and her people were still busy with the wreck of it; a pretty tough job they seemed to be having with it, too. That she was much more strongly manned than is usually the case with a merchantman of her size was also evident, for we could see that while one gang was at work clearing away the wreck, another was busy securing the fore-topmast by getting up preventer-backstays, and so on. How they managed to work aloft at all in such terrific weather passed my comprehension; but there they were, at least *trying* to do something. And, as Ryan remarked, it showed conclusively what a resolute set of fellows they were on board her, and afforded us a clue as to the sort of resistance we were likely to meet with should it ever come to a game of fisti-cuffs between them and ourselves.

Having once overtaken us she seemed to very quickly pass ahead, and when she was once more about two miles distant, Ryan gave the order to set the storm fore-trysail, a step that we might then very well take without exciting any very strong suspicion on board the barque as to our ulterior intentions. since the sea was by this time getting up to an extent which made the exhibition of a small amount of canvas on board the schooner not only justifiable but absolutely necessary. The sail was accordingly set, and all risk of being pooped was, for the time at least, done away with, and what was almost of equal importance in our eyes, we now appeared to be holding our own with the sail ahead.

The watch had just been called when we noticed that the wind was backing further round from the northward—a pretty conclusive indication that it was a cyclone, or revolving storm, that we had encountered—and Ryan began to be exceedingly anxious upon the subject of heaving-to, since, as he explained to me, every mile that we now travelled carried us nearer to the terrible vortex or "eye" of the storm. Still he could not bring himself to do so while the barque held on, thus allowing her to effect her escape from us a second time —assuming, of course, that she really was, as we very strongly suspected, our former acquaintance; it was therefore with a feeling of considerable satisfaction that we shortly afterwards saw her start her fore-topsail sheets with the evident intention of clewing up the sail, if possible, preparatory to heaving-to.

"Ah!" exclaimed Ryan, admiringly, "that fellow is no fool; he scents danger ahead; he has been in a cyclone before to-day, I'll warrant, and seems to know exactly what he is about. There goes his topsail, clean out of the bolt-ropes, as I expected it would; but I do not suppose he ever seriously hoped to save the sail. And now over goes his helm, and there he rounds-to —ah-h! look at *that!* on her beam-ends, by all that's—no—no—she is righting again—good! very prettily done, *v-e-r-y* prettily done indeed! *Now* she luffs!—excellent! capital! You are all safe now, my man. We will run down to him, Harry, my bhoy, and heave-to about a mile to leeward of him; then perhaps he will not suspect us; he will gradually settle down towards us, as we shall lie closer than he will; and when the wind drops we shall have him to do as we like with."

It was a very anxious moment with us when, having run down to the spot selected by Ryan, we eased the helm over to bring the schooner to *on the starboard tack*—that being the correct tack upon which to heave-to in a cyclone in the northern hemisphere — and I shall never forget the feeling of absolute helplessness that seized me when, as our little craft gradually presented her broadside to the gale, I felt her going over — over — over — until the water poured in a raging cataract over her lee rail, and she laid down beneath the strength of the howling blast—that now seemed to have suddenly increased to twice its former fury—until the lee side of her deck was buried almost to the combings of the hatchways. But as her bows came round and presented themselves more obliquely to the gale she righted somewhat, and although she still careened until her lee rail was all but awash, she rode the furious seas as gallantly and buoyantly as a gull. Ryan had displayed a very considerable amount of judgment in conducting the schooner down to the berth he had chosen for her, and had placed her there in so natural a manner that we scarcely believed it possible that our presence so near the barque would be likely to arouse any suspicions of our intentions in the minds of her crew; and as we had never been very near her during the time of our former pursuit of her, we were in hopes that we should not now be recognized. We had taken up a position exactly to leeward of our neighbour; and, as Ryan had anticipated, we soon found that the schooner was looking up a full point higher than the bigger craft ; but this was very evenly balanced by the greater amount of lee drift that we made, in consequence of our much lighter draught ; we therefore contrived to maintain our position with almost perfect exactitude, except that the schooner manifested the greater tendency to forge ahead, thus placing herself gradually further upon the barque's lee bow.

The wind continued to blow with unabated fury, and when day broke and we were able to look about us, the scene was grand and awful beyond all power of description. The sky was of an uniform deep, slaty, purple-grey hue, across the face of which careered a constant succession of lighter grey, smoky-looking clouds, all shredded and torn to tatters by the headlong sweep of the gale. The colour of the sea was a dirty green, deepening in tint to purple-black in the hollows, and capped by long ridges of dirty yellowish foam, that was continuously snatched up by the wind and hurled through the air in drenching sheets that cut and stung the skin like the lash of a whip. The sea, although not so high as might have been expected from the force of the wind, was still formidable enough to be almost terrifying in its aspect as it swept down upon the schooner in long, steep, mountain-like ridges, that soared to nearly half the height of our main cross-trees, with a hollow of fully one hundred and eighty feet in width between them, each wave crowned with a roaring, foaming crest that reared itself above our low hull as though eager to hurl itself upon and destroy us.

As the day wore on we received a temporary addition to our company, in the shape of a brig. She hove in sight in the eastern quarter, about six bells in the forenoon watch ; and the first sight that we got of her revealed that her jib-boom and both her topmasts were gone. She was showing a storm-staysail ; and at first sight we supposed her to be hove-to ; but she drove down towards us so fast that we soon came to the conclusion that there must be something wrong with her steering-gear, and as she drew nearer it became evident that she was unmanageable, falling off occasionally until she was almost dead before the wind ; and we could see that whenever this happened the sea made a clean breach over her. When within about a mile of us she showed the Russian ensign, upside down, in her main-rigging, to which we responded by hoisting Spanish colours —to lull any doubts that might possibly be lurking in the minds of our friends on board the barque, who did not condescend to favour us with a sight of their bunting. As for the brig, she drove straight down towards us, occasioning us a considerable amount of anxiety, for so erratic were her movements that when she had arrived within a couple of cables' lengths of us it became impossible to say whether she would pass ahead or astern of us. The only thing that we could do to avoid her was to fill upon the schooner and forge ahead out of her way, and this we would have done but for the possibility that after our having done so the brig might take a sheer in the wrong direction and fall foul of us, when the destruction of the schooner, if not of both vessels, must inevitably have happened. At length it became evident that something must be done, for she was settling bodily down upon us, and another two minutes would bring the two craft into collision.

Ryan therefore ordered the helm to be shifted, and we were just forging clear, as we thought, and leaving her room to pass under our stern, when a terrific sea swept down upon her, throwing her quarter round, sweeping her from stem to stern, and driving her crew into the rigging, and in an instant there she was, driving along stem-on right for us—or, rather, for the spot that we should occupy when she reached it. There was now only one way of avoiding a disastrous collision, and that was by putting our helm hard up, and, at all risks, jibing round upon the other tack ; and this we accordingly did, missing the brig by a hair's-breadth, but springing our foremast-head so badly as the trysail jibed over, that we had to get in the sail at once, and set a close-reefed main-staysail instead. As for the brig, she was little better than a wreck, for as she drove past us we saw that her rudder was gone, her bulwarks carried away on both sides, from cat-head to taffrail, and her decks swept of everything that was movable. It was of course utterly impossible for us to help them in any way in the wind and sea that then raged ; nor could we follow them in their helpless progress to leeward, and stand by them, the damage to our foremast being so serious as to utterly preclude the possibility of getting any head sail upon the schooner until it had been at least temporarily repaired, while the little hooker, having again been brought-to on the starboard tack, absolutely refused to pay off under her staysail only, which was perhaps just as well, so far as we were concerned, since any attempt on our part to run to leeward would almost certainly have resulted in the swamping of the schooner. What became of the brig, and whether she outlived the gale or not, we never knew, for she continued her erratic course to leeward, and we lost sight of her in about an hour and a half from the time when she so nearly fell on board us, and we saw her no more. But she was driving in a direction that would carry her right into the track of the vortex of the storm, to encounter which, in her wrecked and helpless condition, would infallibly mean her destruction.

As the day wore on, the wind gradually shifted round further from the eastward, and by nightfall it was blowing from about east-south-east, and showing some signs of moderating, although it still blew very heavily; much too heavily indeed to justify us in sending any hands aloft to fish our sprung masthead. Nevertheless, every preparation was made for the commencement of the operation at the earliest possible moment, as we had detected signs on board the barque indicative of an intention to send a new main-topmast up without delay; which might or might not mean that a suspicion as to our true character had begun to dawn upon them. By midnight the gale had moderated to a strong breeze, and the sky had cleared sufficiently to permit of a little moonlight percolating through between the denser clouds, and we were then able to make out—to our inexpressible chagrin—that the barque's people had already got their new topmast aloft and fidded, and were getting their ma'ntopsail-yard across, having been hard at work, doubtless, ever since darkness set in, though how they had managed to perform their task was a puzzle to us. It was, however, another evidence of the resolute character of their skipper; another hint to us that we should have all our work cut out to bag him; and the carpenter was therefore at once sent for, and set forthwith to the task of fishing our mast-head with all possible expedition. The task was not half executed, however, when we had

the mortification to see our neighbour sheet home his double-reefed topsails and make sail to the westward. This sight put our men upon their mettle; they could vividly picture to themselves the laugh that the slavers would be enjoying at our expense, should they have suspected our intentions toward them, and before the barque was absolutely out of sight from aloft, Chips had managed to make such a job of his work as enabled us to make sail also.

Daylight brought with it a clear sky, dappled with high, fleecy, white, fine-weather clouds, and a moderate breeze from the south-east, with a very heavy, confused sea still running, however; and as the barque's royals were still in sight above the horizon, we cracked on after her, although the carpenter had warned Ryan that the work done during the night was scarcely as satisfactory as might be, and that the mast-head was hardly to be trusted. But the fellow was a thoroughly good man, and eager to avoid all possibility of it being said that we had lost the chance of a prize through him. As soon therefore as it was light enough to see, he was aloft again; and by eight bells he had finished his work, and reported that we might now pack sail upon the schooner to our hearts' content, which we forthwith did, giving her everything that would draw, from the royal down, the wind being very nearly aft, that is to say, about two points on the larboard quarter. By noon it became apparent that we were gaining, although but slowly, on the barque, her royals and half her topgallant-sails being by this time above the horizon; and now all was anxiety on board the schooner as to the character of the coming night; for we had no doubt that, seeing, as they now must, that we were following them, the ever-vigilant suspicions of the barque's people would prompt them to avoid us should the night prove dark enough to permit of such a manœuvre. The indications were all for fine weather, however; the glass was rising steadily, the sky was becoming of a deeper clearer blue; the white clouds were melting away, promising a clear, star-lit night between the hours of sunset and moonrise, and, what was equally as much in our favour, both wind and sea were going down steadily.

Toward eight bells in the afternoon watch we sighted another sail — a schooner this time; she was beating up to the eastward, and crossed the

D

hawse of the barque at no great distance, exchanging signals with her, although what was their nature we could not see, and even had we been near enough to have made out the flags, it is exceedingly improbable that we should have understood them. We had a suspicion, however, that they in some way referred to us; for shortly afterwards the schooner tacked and stood towards us, crossing our bows at a distance of about a mile, and exhibiting the French ensign. We replied by showing Spanish colours, as before; upon which the stranger threw out some signal that we could not understand, and after displaying it for some few minutes hauled it down and hoisted another. We thought it would never do to display a total ignorance of the signals; Ryan therefore ordered the signal-bag to be produced, and we strung some flags together haphazard, and hoisted them. This signal the schooner acknowledged, tacking at the same time and standing toward us once more; but we were far too busy to wait for her, for although she had all the looks of a slaver, we knew, from the course she was steering, that she could have no slaves on board, and was therefore altogether unworthy of our attention with so promising a craft as the barque in plain view. She made no attempt to follow us, and in an hour was out of sight to the northward.

By sunset that night the weather was everything that we could wish, and we had risen the chase to her topsails; everybody on board the *Felicidad* was therefore in the highest spirits, and hope ran high that by daybreak on the morrow we should have our neighbour under our guns, and be able to give her an overhaul. The stars came out brilliantly, and although the moon would not rise until after midnight—and would not give us much light even then, since she had entered her fourth quarter—we soon found that we should have light enough to prevent the barque from giving us the slip, provided that we kept both eyes open. Nevertheless, darkness had no sooner set in, than she made an effort to do so by edging off to the northward, a couple of points, which move, however, we soon detected and frustrated by steering directly after her.

During the night the wind breezed up again somewhat, and this gave the chase so great an advantage that at daybreak she was still about eight miles ahead. Shortly after sunrise, however, it dwindled away again, and gradually dropped to a gentle air that barely fanned us along at a speed of five knots.

By noon we had brought the chase to within five miles of us, and Ryan deemed that the time had now arrived for us to declare ourselves; we accordingly hoisted British colours, and fired a gun as a signal to the barque to heave-to; the only notice taken of which was the exhibition of Spanish colours by the chase, and the firing of a shotted gun of defiance; so now at last we knew each other.

Meanwhile the wind was very gradually dropping, and the schooner as gradually gaining upon the craft ahead, until at length, late in the afternoon, we had reached within a mile and a half of her. And then began one of those barbarous practices that I had heard of, but had hitherto been scarcely able to credit as sober truth, namely, the throwing of slaves overboard in order to retard pursuit by causing the pursuer to stop and pick up the poor wretches, as British men-o'-war invariably did whenever it was at all practicable.

The mode of procedure was generally to launch the unhappy black overboard, securely lashed to a plank or piece of timber large enough to float him, and as he was dropped exactly in the track of the pursuing man-o'-war, he was certain to be seen by some one on board, and an effort made to pick him up. In waters infested by sharks, however, this had been found to be of very doubtful utility, since it happened as often as not that long before the unfortunate wretch had served the purpose for which he was sacrificed, the sharks had found him and torn him to pieces. In order, therefore, that certain hundreds of good dollars—or their value—might not be wasted, and not from any motives of humanity to the slave, or any desire to give him a better chance for his life, but merely that he might last long enough to delay the man-o'-war to the extent of picking him up, an improved plan had been devised for use on occasions where the presence of sharks might be expected; this plan consisting simply in *heading the black up in a cask!* This was the plan now adopted by the people on board the barque.

CHAPTER IX

THE GOVERNOR'S COMMUNICATION

AT the distance which now separated us from the barque all the movements of her crew were distinctly visible to us with the aid of our glasses—which of course were scarcely off her for a moment—and we accordingly witnessed the launching of the first slave overboard. The unhappy creature was placed in a cask, and, as I have said before, headed up therein, an aperture being cut in the two halves of the head just sufficient to admit his neck; and the cask was then slung by a whip from the main-yardarm, and secured by a toggle, the withdrawal of which at the right moment, by means of a lanyard, enabled the cask to be dropped gently, right end up, in the water, where it floated, with its inmate a helpless prisoner, to be picked up or not as the case might be. To render this ruse of real service, a smart breeze should be blowing, because under these conditions the pursuer has not only to lower a boat to pick up the floating black, but she has also to heave-to and wait for her boat; and however smartly the operations of lowering, picking up, and hooking on again may be performed, they still absorb quite an appreciable amount of time, during which the fugitive craft increases her lead more or less according to her speed. In the present case, however, the conditions were by no means favourable to the pursued craft; for, since we were only moving through the water at a speed of about three knots, it was an easy matter for us to drop a boat into the water and send her on ahead to pick up the man, and pull alongside again without detaining the schooner for an instant. The slaver tried the trick four times in succession, and then, finding that it did not answer, gave it up.

The sun was just dipping beneath the horizon in a magnificent array of light cirrus clouds, painted by his last rays in tinctures of the most brilliant purple and rose and gold, and the wind had died away to the merest zephyr when we arrived within gun-shot of the chase; and Ryan at once ordered the long eighteen between the masts to be cleared away and a shot fired as close to the barque as possible without hitting her, just by way of a gentle hint that we were disposed to stand no more nonsense, and that the time had now arrived for her to surrender without giving us any further trouble. But evidently the last thought in the mind of her skipper was to yield, for instead of hauling down his colours like a good sensible man, he blazed away at us in return with a couple of twelve-pounders that he had run out through his stern-ports. The shots were well aimed, but did not quite reach us, striking the water twice fair in line with us, and then making their final scurry, and sinking within about thirty yards of our bows.

"By the piper, I believe the fellow intends to fight us!" exclaimed Ryan. "As a rule these gentlemen are particularly careful of their skins, and have no fancy for hard knocks, giving in when they find that their only choice lies between a fight and surrendering, but there are occasional exceptions to this rule, and I fancy that this fellow will prove to be one of them. Now, Harry, me bhoy, we must be careful what we are after when it comes to boarding and carrying yonder gintleman; for if he happen to be one of the reckless desperado kind he may play us a scurvy trick. I have heard of men who blew their ship and everybody in her into the air rather than allow her to be captured; and, for aught that we can tell to the contrary, the fellow who commands the barque may be one of that stamp. Now, if he is, we may rest assured that he will do nothing desperate until the capture of the ship is certain; until then he will be the foremost man in the fray; so we must both keep a sharp look-out for him and put him *hors de combat* before he has the chance to do any harm. I hope this breeze will hold long enough to enable us to get alongside; should we be becalmed and have to attack him with the boats, it will give him an important advantage, and perhaps result in the loss of some of our men."

This hope of Ryan's was destined to disappointment; for the wind continued to dwindle after sunset until it finally died away altogether, and left both craft without steerage way. By this time, however, we had drifted within range of the barque's guns, and she had opened a rather desultory but well-directed fire upon us whenever any of her guns could be brought to bear, the result of which was that one of our men had already been hurt by a splinter, while the schooner's rigging was beginning to be a good deal cut up. Meanwhile we were precluded from returning the barque's fire lest we should injure or kill any of the unhappy wretches pent up in her hold. At length a round shot entered the schooner's bows, traversed the decks, and passed out over the taffrail, glancing hither and thither as it went, and, although it did no material damage, affording several of the men a very narrow escape.

"Why, this will never do!" exclaimed Ryan, as the shot made its exit after passing between the legs of the man who was standing at the now idle tiller. "A few of those fellows, as well aimed as that one was, would make a very pretty general average among us. We shall have to get out the boats —or, stop!—yes, I think that will be better; we will arm the men and make all ready for boarding; load the guns with a double charge of grape; and then man the sweeps, and sweep the schooner alongside, firing our guns as we heave the grappling-irons, and boarding in the smoke. We shall thus have all hands available when we get alongside, and our bulwarks will meanwhile afford the men a certain amount of protection."

The necessary orders were accordingly given, and a few minutes later the men, stripped to the waist, had rigged out the heavy sweeps and were toiling away at them. And now the advantages of the schooner's light scantling, light draught, and fine lines made themselves fully apparent, for, having once overcome the inertia of the hull and put it in motion, the men found the little craft very easy on her sweeps, and capable of being moved at quite a respectable pace through the water.

The barque was of course much too large and unwieldy a craft to be moved by the same means, and nothing of the kind was even attempted; her crew, however, maintained a smart fire upon us as we approached; but as we were careful to keep her end-on so that only her two stern chasers could be brought to bear upon us, and as we kept up a hot musketry fire upon that particular part of her, we did not suffer very severely; and without any further casualties we at length arrived near enough, with good way on, to permit of the sweeps being laid in, preparatory to our ranging up alongside. Ryan now divided the boarders into two parties, one to be led by himself from aft, while I was instructed to head the other party from our forecastle, the idea being to pin the

slaver's crew between the two parties, thus attacking them simultaneously in front and rear as it might be.

Ryan himself conned the schooner alongside; and when we were within some ten yards of the barque, our guns having previously been trained well forward, the whole of our small broadside was poured in upon her deck, with terribly destructive effect it would seem from the outburst of shrieks and groans and curses that immediately arose on board her. Our fire was instantly returned, but in such a partial irregular way as only tended to confirm the impression that the slaver's crew had suffered severely, yet it gave us a tolerably clear idea of what would have been the result to us had we withheld our fire for just a second or two longer. Then, while both craft were still enveloped in the motionless smoke-wreaths, we felt the schooner's sides rasping against those of the barque; and, with a shout to my little party to follow, I sprang upon our own bulwarks, from thence to those of the barque, and so down on the slaver's deck—for a slaver she was, as our olfactory nerves now assured us beyond dispute.

It was by this time quite dark, or at least as dark as it was likely to be at all that night; but the sky was cloudless, the atmosphere was clear, and the stars were shining with a lustre quite unknown in our more temperate clime; we therefore had but little difficulty in seeing what we were about, or in distinguishing friend from foe; still, I must confess that I felt a little awkward, and, having commenced by discharging both my pistols into the thickest of the crowd that I found opposed to me, confined myself pretty much to a random system of slashing right and left with my cutlass, my principle—if I had one—being to strike the blows, leaving to others the task of warding them if they could. The fight that now ensued was brief, but sharp; the slavers disputing every inch of their deck with us; but our fellows were not to be resisted; there was a brief space of time during which the air seemed full of the sound of clashing steel, popping pistols, shouts, shrieks, groans, and execrations, and the barque was ours, her crew throwing away their weapons and crying loudly for quarter, which of course was granted to them.

The fight being over I at once made my way aft, and was greatly shocked to find that during the brief struggle poor Ryan had been badly wounded in a hand-to-hand fight with the skipper of the barque, whom he had at once singled out and engaged. It afterwards appeared that as soon as matters seemed to be going badly for the barque's people her skipper had attempted to slip out of the fight and slink below; but Ryan, suspecting some sinister object in this projected movement, had stuck to the man so closely, getting between him and the companion, that his object, if he had one, was frustrated; and in his desperation he had struck a blow at Ryan that clove the unfortunate Irishman's skull open, only to be impaled himself upon our dashing captain's sword at the same moment.

Ryan had thus fulfilled his purpose of putting the slaver's skipper *hors de combat*, but at serious cost to himself; the poor fellow was so desperately hurt that he could do nothing but murmur his gratification at finding that I had emerged from the fray unhurt, and an injunction to me to take the command, when he fainted, and I at once had him carefully conveyed to his own cabin on board the schooner, where Armstrong the surgeon immediately took him in hand.

Our capture was named the *San Sebastian*, and hailed from Havana; she had four hundred and twenty-one slaves on board, out of a total of four hundred and seventy-six that she had brought out of the Gaboon river only ten days before; she was a very fine handsome vessel of three hundred and forty-five tons measurement; and our recent experiences with her had proved that she sailed like a witch. We secured our prisoners; conveyed our own wounded—amounting to nine in all—on board the schooner; and then, having put Pierrepoint and a prize crew on board the barque, both vessels made sail in company for Sierra Leone, where we arrived safely, after a passage of exactly a week, and where we were rejoined by Gowland and the prize crew of the *Conquistador*, which vessel had arrived six days before us.

Here, as the repairing of our damages and the provision of a new foremast for the schooner threatened us with a considerable amount of delay, Ryan went ashore to the hospital, where he made pretty fair progress toward recovery, although the improvement was not so marked or rapid as it had been on board the schooner at sea; the intense heat, he complained, was against him,

and his first inquiry every morning when I went to see him was, "When did I think the schooner would be ready for sea again?" It was therefore with a feeling of intense satisfaction that I was at length able to inform him that another day would see us out of the hands of the shipwrights and riggers, and that we might sail on the day following if he so pleased. This news acted like a cordial upon his spirits; he brightened up wonderfully, and improved more rapidly within the ensuing twenty-four hours than he had done during the whole time of his sojourn in hospital, and but for the firmness of the doctor, would at once have taken his discharge, and actually busied himself about the final preparations for our departure. He, however, insisted upon joining me in the acceptance of an invitation to dine with the Governor that evening; and at the appointed hour I called for him, and we sauntered slowly to Government House together. The party was not a very large one, nor did we sit very late; but as the other guests were taking their leave, his Excellency intimated that he desired to have a word or two with us in private, and we accordingly deferred our departure.

When at length we were alone, our host invited us to light up another cigar, and, himself setting us the example, proceeded to a cabinet that stood in the corner of the room, opening which he produced a folded document from a drawer, and unfolding it, laid it before us.

"This, gentlemen," said he, "is a rough sketch-chart of the embouchure of the Congo. It does not profess to be drawn to scale; but I am told that it shows with approximate accuracy the relative positions of the various creeks and indentations that discharge into the main river, up to the Narrows. Now, the individual from whom I obtained this chart informs me that at a distance of about two and a half miles up a certain creek on the south bank—this one, the mouth of which is indicated by a star—there is a rather considerable native settlement, ruled by a savage, known to the few Europeans who possess the doubtful honour of his acquaintance as King Plenty. And, if my informant is to be depended upon, this potentate, whose chief characteristics are avarice and brutal ferocity, has discovered a very simple method of combining business with pleasure by making ruthless war upon his neighbours, and, after his lust for slaughter is satisfied, disposing of his prisoners to certain slave-dealers, who have established themselves on the southern bank of the creek, where they have erected barracoons, factories, and every convenience for carrying on their nefarious trade. I am told that within the last six months this spot, known only to a select few, has been frequently visited, and large numbers of slaves have been carried away from it; its natural characteristics rendering it especially suitable for the traffic. For instance, it would appear that this creek, like most of the others that discharge into the Congo, and like the African rivers generally, has its own little bar at its mouth, upon which there is only one and three-quarter fathoms of water, and is therefore unapproachable by any of the men-o'-war on the station—excepting perhaps the *Barracouta*, and she is away cruising just now—while the character of the banks is such as to afford every facility for a galling and continuous fire upon a flotilla of boats advancing up the creek. I have therefore thought that the breaking up and destruction of this slave-trading station would be a piece of work admirably suited to the *Felicidad* and her gallant crew"—Ryan and I simultaneously bowed our appreciation of the compliment—"because it is especially a case wherein valour and discretion must go hand-in-hand, the service being of an especially hazardous nature; and I feel that in no one are the two qualities that I have mentioned more admirably combined than in the person of Captain Ryan."

Ryan bowed again, and remarked— "I am obliged for your Excellency's good opinion of me; and still more so for the information that you have been good enough to give us to-night. I have been very fortunate, so far, in the schooner, and I suppose I may reckon upon my promotion as certain; but I am eager to have further opportunities of distinguishing myself, and if we can only be lucky enough to find two or three slavers up that creek, and to capture them, it would afford me just the opportunity that I require. I shall sail to-morrow, and shall hope to be back here again in a month or six weeks, with two or three prizes in company, and the assurance that the establishment in question is completely destroyed."

We sat a few minutes longer, drank a final glass of wine, and then took our leave and walked down to the schooner together, Ryan having determined to sleep on board her that night.

We sailed from Sierra Leone on the following day, as Ryan had resolved we should; but, as usually happens when matters are hurried, we met with an endless succession of petty delays at the last moment that detained us at anchor until nearly nightfall, and occasioned us a vast amount of trotting about in the broiling sun to put some life into the dilatory people who were keeping us waiting; the consequence of which was that when at last we lifted the anchor and stood out of the bay with the very last of the sea breeze, to run into a calm when we had attained an offing of some two miles, I felt altogether too tired and knocked up to eat or drink; while, as for Ryan, he was in a state of high fever once more.

We got the land breeze about eight o'clock that night, and stood away to the southward and westward until midnight, in order that we might obtain a good offing, when we hauled up on a south-east course for the Congo. I remained on deck until midnight— at which hour I was relieved by Pierrepoint—and then was obliged to send for the doctor, who, after feeling my pulse, ordered me to my bunk at once, and when I was there administered to me a tremendous dose of some frightfully bitter concoction, telling me at the same time, for my comfort, that he would not be in the least surprised if, when he next visited me, he should find me suffering from a severe attack of coast fever. Happily, his anticipations, so far as I was concerned, were unfounded; but by daybreak poor Ryan was in a state of raving delirium, with three men in his cabin told off to keep him in his bunk and prevent him from inflicting upon himself some injury. As for me, the medicine that I had taken threw me first into a profuse perspiration, and afterwards into a deep sleep, from which I awoke next morning cool, free from pain, and with a quiet, steady pulse, but very weak; and I did not fully recover my strength until a day or two before we made the land about the Congo mouth, which we did after a long passage that was uneventful in everything save the persistency with which we were beset by calms and light, baffling airs. By this time Ryan, too, had recovered to a certain extent; that is to say, he was able to leave his bunk and to stagger up on deck for an hour or so at a time, but he was still frightfully weak; and it often appeared to me, from the rather wild talk in which he sometimes indulged, that he had not thus far fully recovered his mental balance.

We made the land about six bells in the forenoon watch, and stood straight in for Shark Point, which we hugged pretty closely, in order to cheat the current, which, as usual at that time of the year, was running out pretty strongly. The sea breeze was blowing half a gale, however, and despite the current the little *Felicidad* slid over the ground bravely, arriving abreast the mouth of the creek to which we were bound about four bells in the afternoon watch. We here cleared the schooner for action, sent the men to their quarters, and, with a leadsman in the fore-chains, both on the port and on the starboard sides, and with Ryan, sketch-chart in hand, conning the vessel, steered boldly into the creek. The soundings which we obtained at the entrance proved the chart to be so far correct, and with our confidence thus strengthened we glided gently forward over the glassy waters of the creek, every eye being directed anxiously ahead, for we knew not at what moment we might encounter our enemy, nor in what force he might be. To me it appeared that we were acting in rather a foolhardy manner in thus rushing blindfold as it were upon the unknown, and earlier in the day—in fact, just after we had entered the river—I had suggested to Ryan the advisability of taking the schooner somewhat higher up the stream and anchoring her in a snug and well-sheltered spot that we had noticed when last in the river in the *Barracouta,* and sending the boats away at night to reconnoitre. But this happened to be one of the captain's bad days—by which I mean that it was one of the days when the fever from which he had been suffering seemed to partially regain its hold upon him, making him impatient, irritable, and unwilling to receive anything in the shape of a suggestion from anybody; and my proposal was therefore scouted as savouring of something approaching to timidity. I had long ago got over any such feeling, however; and even now, when we momentarily

expected to come face to face with the enemy, I found myself sufficiently calm and collected to note and admire the many beauties of the scene as the creek opened up before us.

For the scene *was* beautiful exceedingly with a wild, tropical lavishness of strange and, in some cases, grotesque forms and rich magnificence of colour that no words can adequately describe, and even the artist's palette would be taxed to its utmost capacity to merely suggest. The creek was, as usual in the Congo, lined with an almost unbroken, impassable belt of mangroves, their multitudinous roots, gnarled and twisted, springing from the thick, mud-stained water, and presenting a confused, inextricable tangle to the eye, from the deep shadows of which flitted kingfishers of many species and brilliant plumage; while above swayed and rustled in the gentle breeze the delicate grey-green foliage of the trees themselves, now in full and luxuriant leaf, affording a delicious contrast of cool green shadow, with the glints of dazzling sunshine that streamed here and there through the verdant masses. Great clusters of magnificent orange-tinted orchids gleamed like galaxies of golden stars between the mangrove trunks at frequent intervals; clumps of feathery bamboo swayed gently in the soft warm breeze; the dense background of bush displayed every conceivable tint of foliage, from brilliant gold to deepest purple bronze; and magnificent forest trees towered in stately majesty over all, rearing their superb heads a hundred and fifty feet into the intense blue of the cloudless sky; while everywhere, over bush and tree and withered stump, blazed in thousands the trailing blossoms of brilliant-hued climbing plants that loaded the air to intoxication with the sweetness of their mingled perfumes. Parrots and other gaily-plumaged birds flitted busily hither and thither with loud and—it must be admitted — more or less discordant cries; inquisitive monkeys swung from branch to branch, and either peered curiously at us as we passed, or dashed precipitately, with loud cries of alarm, into the concealment of the deepest shadows at our approach; and at one point, where the belt of mangroves was interrupted, and a small, open, grassy space reached down to the water's edge, a stately antelope stepped daintily down into the water, as though to slake his thirst, but catching sight of the approaching schooner, bounded off again into the contiguous bush, where he was instantly lost sight of in the sombre green gloom.

At a distance of about two miles from the mouth of the creek we reached a spot where it forked, one arm—the wider of the two—running in a due east-by-south direction, while the other trended away to the west-south-west, communicating—as we afterwards discovered—with another creek which, although too shoal for navigation by sea-going craft, would have afforded us excellent facilities for a reconnaissance with the boats. At this point the southern shore of the creek exhibited signs of cultivation, small patches of bush having been cleared here and there and planted with maize, or sugar-cane, or yams, a small reed-hut thatched with palm-leaves usually standing in one corner of the plot, with a tethered goat close by, a few fowls, or other traces of its being inhabited. Of the human inhabitants themselves, however, strangely enough, nothing was to be seen. But it was clear that we were nearing our goal ; and word was passed along the deck for the men to hold themselves prepared for instant action.

There were several memoranda jotted down upon the chart for our guidance, and among these was an intimation to look out for a clump of exceptionally tall trees on the southern bank of the creek, under the broad shadow of which the slave barracoons were stated to be built. A few minutes after passing the branch creek already referred to we arrived at a bend, and as the schooner glided round it, and entered a new reach, these trees swept into view ; there could be no mistaking them, for they lifted their majestic heads—there were five of them—fully fifty feet clear above those of their brethren. Moreover, they stood quite close to the margin of the creek, thus confirming the statement made upon the sketch-chart. But had there been any lurking doubt in our minds about the matter they would have been quickly dispelled, for as we glided forward, a small sandy beach —also referred to in the chart—was made out projecting from the southern bank, at which some twenty or thirty large canoes lay with their bows hauled sufficiently out of the water to prevent their going adrift. That a vigilant watch was being kept upon the waters of the creek became quickly apparent,

for we had scarcely made out the canoes when we saw several negroes rush down to one of them, launch it, and paddle swiftly away up the creek and round another bend, while, as we advanced, a crowd of naked blacks, armed with spears, shields, and muskets, gathered upon the beach, and, from their actions, seemed fully prepared to forcibly resist any attempt on our part to effect a landing.

Still advancing up the creek, we gradually opened the vista of the reach beyond—that in which the canoe had a few minutes previously vanished— and at length, when only a short half-mile intervened between us and the beach—which projected boldly nearly half-way across the channel—the mainmast of a schooner crept into view beyond the concealment of the hitherto intervening bush and trees ; and bringing our glasses to bear upon her, we detected signs of great bustle and confusion on board her, and made out that her crew were busily engaged in tricing up boarding nettings, and otherwise making preparations for her defence.

Ryan now ordered our ensign and pennant to be hoisted, thus boldly announcing at once our nationality and the fact of our being an enemy—an announcement which I should have deemed it perfectly justifiable to defer until the last possible moment—and the schooner at once replied by hoisting French colours and firing a gun of defiance. This greatly amused our people, to whom the act seemed a piece of ridiculous braggadocio—for the stranger was no bigger than ourselves—but the laugh left their faces and was succeeded by a look of grim resolution when presently we opened out another and a larger schooner and a heavy, handsome brigantine, the first flying Spanish colours and the brigantine *a black flag !* But this was not all, for before we arrived abreast the beach we had opened out still another schooner with the Spanish flag floating from her mast-head ; and by what we saw going on board the four craft it became evident that we had by no means caught these bold rovers napping, and that we might confidently reckon upon meeting with a very warm reception. Moreover, it was clear that, snug as was their place of concealment, and unlikely as it was to be discovered save, as in our case, by betrayal, they had left nothing to chance, but had taken every possible precaution to insure their safety, the four craft being moored in pairs, with springs on their cables, stern to stern right across the stream, so that, the fair-way being very narrow, they would have to be fought and taken in succession, a necessity which I at once recognized, and which, to my limited experience, seemed to militate very strongly against our chances of success. It was, however, altogether too late now to hesitate or alter our plans ; we had plunged headlong and, as it were, blindfold into a hornet's nest from which nothing but the coolest courage and determination could extricate us, and, while I had long ago completely conquered the feeling of trepidation and anxiety that almost everybody experiences more or less when going into action for the first time, I could not altogether suppress a doubt as to whether Ryan, in his then very indifferent state of health, possessed quite all the coolness and clear-headedness as well as the nerve that I anticipated would be necessary to see us safely out of our present entanglement.

CHAPTER X

A DISASTROUS EXPEDITION

UPON arriving abreast the beach, which we were obliged to hug pretty closely in consequence of the contracted width of the channel and the fact that the deepest water lay close to it, we found it occupied by fully five hundred naked blacks, all of whom appeared to be profoundly excited, for they yelled continuously at the top of their voices and fiercely brandished their weapons. They appeared to be acting under the leadership of a very tall and immensely powerful man who wore a leopard-skin cloak upon his shoulders, and a head-dress of brilliantly-coloured feathers. He was armed with *two* muskets, and had a ship's cutlass girt about his waist. A white man—or a half-caste, it was difficult to tell which at that distance, so deeply bronzed was he—accompanied him ; a man attired in a suit of white drill topped off with a broad-brimmed Panama hat wrapped round with a white puggaree ; and it appeared that all the excitement and animosity manifested by the blacks at our approach was instigated by him, for we saw him speaking earnestly to the apparent leader of the blacks, gesticulating violently in our direction as he did so, while the savage now and then turned to his followers and addressed a few sentences to them which seemed to arouse them to a higher pitch of frenzy than ever.

Beyond the sand beach a wide open space extended that had evidently at one time been carpeted with grass, for small tufts and patches of it still remained here and there, but for the most part the rich, deep chocolate-coloured earth was worn bare by the trampling of many feet. This open space was occupied by a native village of considerable dimensions, the houses —or huts, rather—being for the most part square or quadrangular structures, although there were a few circular ones among them, built of upright logs with panels of mud and leaves between them, roofed in with palm-leaf thatch, the eaves projecting sufficiently at each end to form a verandah some six or eight feet deep. At a little distance from the village, a hundred yards or so, towered the clump of lofty trees under which the slave barracoons were said to be erected ; but whether this was so or not we could not tell, as a belt of bush interposed between us and the trees, affording an effectual screen to any buildings that might stand beneath their shadow.

As the schooner glided up abreast of the beach, with the hands at the sheets, halliards, and downhauls, clewing up and hauling down preparatory to running alongside the schooner nearest us, a great shout was raised by the negroes, immediately followed by a confused discharge of their muskets and the hurling of a few spears, but where the bullets went we never knew, for certainly none of them came near us, and as for the spears, they fell short and dropped harmlessly into the water. To this salute we of course made no reply, as our business was not to make war upon the natives unless absolutely compelled to do so, and three minutes later, having taken as much room as the width of the creek would permit, our helm was eased over and the *Felicidad* swept round toward the object of her first attack, which was the schooner flying French colours. A death-like and ominous silence now prevailed on board the four craft that we were so audaciously attacking, and not a man was to be seen on board either of them. This state of things continued until we were within forty fathoms of the nearest craft, when a shouted command arose from on board the *brigantine*—which was the third craft away from us—and instantly the ports of the two nearest schooners were thrown open, and a rattling broadside of nine guns loaded with round and grape was poured into us with terrible effect, for we were almost bows-on at the moment, and the shot swept our deck fore and aft. No less than eleven of our people went down before that murderous discharge, and as five of them lay motionless, I greatly feared that the poor fellows would never rise again. We reserved our fire until the sides of our own schooner and the Frenchman were almost touching, and then gave him our broadside and the contents of Long Tom as well; then, as the *Felicidad* struck her opponent pretty violently, Ryan waved his sword above his head, snatched a pistol from his belt with his left hand, and shouted—

" Heave the grapnels ! Come along, lads, follow me, and hurroo for ould Oireland ! "

The two schooners being fast together, every man Jack of us sprang after our leader, only to be confronted by the boarding nettings triced up on board our antagonist, however ; and as we sprang on the bulwarks and commenced hacking away at the obstruction they opened a hot and most destructive fire upon us with their muskets and pistols. I saw our men dropping to right and left of me, and then one of the tricing-lines of the netting gave way—one of our lads had shinned aloft and cut it—and we half tumbled, half scrambled down upon her deck all in a heap, and were instantly engaged in a desperate hand-to-hand struggle with her crew, who greatly outnumbered ourselves, weakened as we were by the casualties that had already seriously reduced our force. Moreover, we soon discovered that our antagonists were by no means the despicable poltroons that we are perhaps too prone at all times to believe them to be ; on the contrary, they fought manfully, and held their own with a sturdy determination worthy of a better cause. The casualties were rapidly multiplying on both sides, yet we were slowly driving the Frenchmen forward, when they were unexpectedly reinforced by a crowd of at least sixty people who had come alongside in boats from the other craft, boarding

on the larboard side of the schooner, on which side, as it had been impossible for us to reach it with the *Felicidad*, the nettings had not been triced up, and in an instant we found ourselves confronted by overwhelming odds. Above the tumult of shouts and oaths and groans, of pistol-shots and clashing steel, I heard Ryan give a ringing cheer and an encouraging shout of " Hurroo, bhoys, the more the merrier ! Lay on with a will, now, and make short work of it ; " and I saw him at the head of a small division of our men laying about him manfully and driving himself and his little band wedge-like through the thickest of the crowd, and I turned and struck out right and left to get to his assistance, for it seemed to me that he must be speedily overpowered. Before I could reach him, however, he suddenly threw up his hands, and striking one of them to his temples sank in an inert heap to the deck, and at the same instant a sickening blow fell upon my head, the whole scene whirled confusedly before my eyes for the fraction of an instant, and for a time I knew no more.

* * * * * .

When at length I recovered my senses I found that I was undressed and comfortably stowed away in a bunk in a small but light and airy state-room that certainly was not my own, nor had I ever seen it before. The snuggery was very tastefully fitted up, the bunk itself being of polished mahogany, enclosed with handsome lace curtains, that I presumed were intended as a protection against the mosquitoes, the sharp, ringing buzz of multitudes of which pertinacious tormentors I heard distinctly as I lay, weak, sick, and with a most distracting headache, safe within the shelter of the curtains. These curtains were suspended from a polished brass rod that traversed the underside of the deck above close to the ship's side, so that they sloped over the bunk tent-fashion, an ingenious arrangement of frilling along the upper edge imparting a sufficient stiffness to the flimsy material to cause it to stand up close to the planking, thus leaving no opening by which the persevering little insects could obtain access to the interior. The bulkhead was panelled with pilasters of satin-wood supporting a handsomely-carved cornice, and the panels, like the underside of the deck, were painted a delicate cream colour, the former being decorated with a thin gilt moulding which formed the framework of a series of beautifully-painted pictures of tropical flowers, butterflies, and birds. There was a polished mahogany washstand in one corner of the room, and a small mahogany swing-table against the bulkhead between the bunk and the closed door of the berth ; a horsehair sofa ran along the ship's side, opposite the doorway ; a small lamp, apparently of silver, hung in gimbals from the ship's side, near the head of the bunk, and the apartment was amply lighted by a large round open port or scuttle, through which the gentle sigh of the evening breeze came pleasantly, and the rich, orange beams of the setting sun poured with so brilliant an effulgence that I could scarcely endure the dazzling light, and was obliged to close my eyes again.

Where was I? Certainly not on board the *Felicidad;* for she had no such luxurious sleeping-accommodation as this on board her. Then, if not on board her, I must most probably be on board the French schooner ; a surmise that was to some extent confirmed by the powerful effluvium that pervaded the ship, and proclaimed her character beyond all question. Then there were sounds on deck—the voices of men laughing and jesting together, and addressing occasional brutal remarks to, presumably, the wearers of certain chains, the clanking of which, together with the sounds of boats or canoes coming alongside, and an occasional order issued by some one nearly overhead, powerfully suggested the idea that the craft, whatever she was, was now taking in her human cargo. I soon recognized, however, that the orders and conversation generally were in Spanish, not French ; still, this proved nothing, for slavers were as a rule by no means particular as to the colour of the flag that they fought or sailed under, often hoisting the first ensign that happened to come to hand.

But Spanish or French, the vessel on board which I now found myself could scarcely be other than one of those that we had engaged earlier in the afternoon ; and if so, I was in the hands of the enemy—an enemy, be it said, that, if report spoke truly, showed but scant mercy to such of its legalized opponents as happened to fall into his hands. Yet this scarcely tallied with the evident care that had been taken of me, and the exceedingly comfortable—not to say luxurious—quarters wherein I now found myself.

I was parched with thirst, and looked round the state-room for some liquid wherewith I might quench it. There was none; but I now observed a small mahogany shelf, close to the head of the bunk, which had hitherto escaped my notice, and upon it stood a small silver hand-bell, quaint of shape, and elegantly adorned with *repoussé* work. With considerable pain and giddiness I contrived to turn my body far enough round to seize the bell and ring it ; in instant response to which the state-room door opened—revealing a glimpse of a small but elegantly - furnished cabin—and a young mustee lad, clad only in a white shirt thrown open at the neck, and white drill trousers girt to his slender figure by a crimson sash, entered, and demanded in Spanish—

"Can I do anything for you, señor?"

"What is your name, my lad?" said I, answering his question with another.

"I am called Pedro, señor."

"Well then, Pedro," said I, "you can do two things for me, if you will. In the first place you can get me something to drink, if you will be so kind ; and, in the next, you can tell me the name of this ship and her captain."

"I will willingly do both, señor, with pleasure. The drink first," answered the lad, with a bright smile that disclosed an array of small and beautifully regular, ivory-white teeth. And, turning on his bare heel, he retired as noiselessly as he had entered, only to reappear, a moment later, with a tumbler in one hand, and a large glass jug full to within an inch of the brim with lemonade, upon the surface of which floated two or three slices of the fruit and a curl of the rich golden green rind. He filled and handed me a bumper, which I instantly drained and begged for another. The lad laughed, and handed me a second tumblerful, which I also drained. The liquid was deliciously cool, and of that peculiar acid and slightly bitter flavour that seems so ineffably refreshing when one is parched with fever.

"Another yet, señor?" asked Pedro, with a laugh, as I handed the glass back to him.

"Well—n-o—not just now, I think, thank you," answered I. "And now, Pedro, my boy, tell me about this ship and her captain, and how I came to be here."

"That is easily done, señor," answered the lad. "In the first place, the brigantine is named the *Francesca*, after my mother; she hails from Havana; and is commanded by my father, Don Fernando de Mendouca; and you were brought here by him, when he found you lying apparently dead upon the deck of the *Requin* after your people had been driven off and compelled to beat a retreat."

"*What?*" I exclaimed. "Driven off? Compelled to retreat?"

"Certainly, señor," the lad answered proudly. "You surely did not seriously expect to capture all four of us with that paltry schooner of yours, and so small a force as you brought against us, did you?"

"Well," I admitted, "I must confess that when I saw what we had to contend with, I had my doubts as to the issue. But then, you see, I was not the captain."

"Your captain must have been *mad* to have attacked us in broad daylight, as he did. And, indeed, he *seemed* to be mad by the desperation with which he fought. I never saw anything like it in my life."

"*You?*" I exclaimed again. "Do you mean to say that you took part in the fight?"

"Certainly, señor; why not?" demanded Pedro haughtily. "True, I am very young; but I am strong. And I am bigger than the little officer who was fighting near you when the French sailor struck you down with the handspike."

"Yes; that is very true," I agreed, knowing, from the lad's description, that he was referring to Freddy Pierrepoint. "So you were in the fight, and saw our captain, eh, Pedro? Can you tell me what became of him?"

"He was shot—by one of our men, I believe; and I think he was killed, but am not quite sure. He was carried back into his own schooner by two of his men; and after the fight had lasted about two minutes longer a very handsome, light-haired officer appeared to take the command, and seemed to order a retreat; for your men steadily retired to their own vessel, and, fighting to the very last, cast her adrift, set the sails, and retired, hotly pursued by the *Requin*."

"Phew!" exclaimed I; "we seem to have made rather a mess of it this time. Poor Ryan! I am sorry for him; very sorry indeed. You are right,

Pedro, our captain *was* mad; the poor fellow was badly wounded in the head not long ago, and he had by no means recovered from his injuries. And now he is wounded again, if not killed outright. I am *very* sorry for him. And now, Pedro, can you tell me how your father proposes to dispose of *me?*"

"No, señor, I cannot. Nor can he at present, I think," answered the lad. "It was at my entreaty that he brought you on board here; otherwise you would have been thrown overboard to the crocodiles that swarm in the creek just here. He said that prisoners were only a useless encumbrance and an embarrassment; but somehow I liked your looks as you lay, white and still, upon the French schooner's deck, and I begged him so hard to save you that he could not deny me. And I am sure that we shall be friends—you and I—shall we not? There is no one on board here that I can be intimate with —except my father, of course—and he is so much older than I, that I can scarcely look upon him as a companion. Besides——"

The lad stopped, embarrassed.

"Besides what?" demanded I.

"Well—I—perhaps I ought not to say. You see we are strangers yet, and father has often said that it is a great mistake to be confidential with strangers. Some other day perhaps I may feel that I can speak more freely. And that reminds me that I have let you talk far too much already; you need rest and perfect quiet at present, if you are to escape a bad attack of fever, so I shall leave you for a little while to sleep if you can. But first let me bathe your wound for you, and bandage it afresh."

"You are very kind, Pedro," remarked I, as the lad with singular deftness proceeded to remove the stiff and bloodstained bandage from my head. "And I must not allow you to leave me until I have thanked you— as I now do, very heartily—for having saved my life. Perhaps I may have an opportunity some day to show my gratitude in some more convincing form than that of mere words, and if so, you may depend upon me to do so. Meanwhile, I see no reason whatever why we should not be friends, and good friends too, if your father is willing that it should be so. At the same time— but there, we can talk about that too, when we know a little more of each other, and understand each other better. Thanks, Pedro; that is very soothing and comfortable indeed. Now, another drink of lemonade, if you please—by the way, you may as well leave the jug and glass within my reach—and then, if you insist upon running away, why, good-bye for the present."

The lad left me, and I fell into a rather gloomy reverie upon the fate of poor Ryan and that of the gallant fellows who had fallen in our ill-planned attack upon the occupants of this unlucky creek, as well as upon my own future, the uncertainty of which stood out the more clearly the longer I looked at it. I think I must have become slightly light-headed eventually, for twice or thrice I caught myself muttering aloud in a rather excited fashion, now imagining myself to be in the thick of the fight once more, and anon fancying myself to be one of the slaves that were imprisoned in the brigantine's noisome hold; until finally my ideas became so hopelessly jumbled together that I could make nothing of them, and then followed a period of oblivion from which I awoke to find the state-room faintly illumined by the turned-down lamp screwed to the ship's side near the head of my bunk, and by the more brilliant rays of a lamp in the main cabin, the light of which streamed through the lattices in the upper panel of the state-room door. The ship was heeling slightly, and I knew by the gurgle and wash of water along her side that she was under weigh, but still in perfectly smooth water, for I was unable to detect the slightest heave, or rising and falling motion in her. There was an intermittent faint murmur of voices overhead, an occasional footfall on the deck, and now and then the creak and clank of the wheel-chains following a call from the forecastle, all of which led me to the conclusion that the brigantine was effecting the passage of the creek on her way seaward. This state of things continued for perhaps a quarter of an hour, when I felt the vessel lift as if to a small swell, the wash and splash of the water along her side became more pronounced, then came a light plunge, with a corresponding roar of the bow wave; her heel perceptibly increased, and the pipe of the wind took a more sonorous sound; an expression or two in tones that seemed to indicate a feeling of relief and satisfaction passed between the persons overhead, and

then a string of orders pealed forth from one of them, followed by the clatter of ropes thrown down on the deck, and the cries of the crew as they made sail upon the vessel. The movements of the craft now rapidly grew more lively; she heeled still more steeply under the pressure of the wind; the splash and rush of water alongside grew momentarily more confused; bulkheads began to creak, and cabin-doors to jar and rattle upon their hooks; the two people overhead began to pace the deck to and fro; the wind whistled and blustered with increasing loudness through the rigging; and as the craft plunged more sharply I caught the sound of an occasional clatter of spray upon the deck forward. This went on for some considerable time, and then I became aware of the sound of surf booming distantly, but rapidly increasing in strength and volume, until after a period of perhaps ten minutes its thunder seemed to suddenly fill the air, as the brigantine brought it square abeam; then it rapidly died away again until it was lost altogether in the tumult of wind and sea that now stormed about the vessel, and I knew that we had passed close to either Shark or French Point, and were fairly at sea. This conviction was confirmed a few minutes later by the descent of some one—presumably the captain—into the cabin, where, as I could tell by the clink of bottle and glass and the gurgle of fluids, he mixed and tossed off a glass of grog, after which he retired to a state-room on the opposite side of the cabin and closed the door. Then, lulled by the motion of the ship and the sound of the wind and sea, I gradually sank into a feverish sleep, from which I did not fairly awake until the sun was streaming strongly in through the glazed scuttle of my state-room next morning.

Shortly afterwards Pedro entered and bade me good-morning with a cheery smile.

"You are looking better, señor," he remarked; "your eyes are brighter, and there is more colour in your face. I hope you were not greatly disturbed last night by the noise of getting the ship under weigh?"

"Not at all," I answered; "on the contrary, I did not awake until you were clear of your moorings and passing down the creek. I remained awake until the ship seemed to be fairly at sea, and then I went to sleep again. I suppose we are out of sight of land by this time?"

"Yes, thanks be to the blessed Virgin! And I hope we shall see no more until we make Anegada," was the reply.

"Anegada?" I queried. "Where is that?"

"What!" exclaimed Pedro, "do you not know Anegada? Then you have never been to the West Indies?"

"That is very true," I admitted. "I have never been to the other side of the Atlantic."

"I was certain of it, or you would know Anegada," answered Pedro. "Anegada is the most easterly of the Virgin Islands; and my father always endeavours to pick it up on his westerly runs. It makes a good landfall, and enables us to continue the rest of our run with confidence, and to dodge those pestilent cruisers of yours. Anegada once sighted, my father knows every inch of the rest of the way, and could take his ship from thence to Havana blindfold, I believe. But while we are talking this water is cooling, and I want to bathe your wound and bind it up afresh. So; am I hurting you?"

"Not at all," I answered. "Your touch is as light as a woman's. By the way, where are my clothes, Pedro? I shall turn out as soon as you have done with me, if you will kindly send somebody with some water. That ewer seems to be empty."

"It can soon be filled, however," remarked the lad. "As to your clothes, they are forward, drying. They were so stained and stiff with blood that you could not possibly have put them on again, so I had them washed. You see my clothes would not be big enough for you, while my father's would be too big; so you will be obliged to make shift with what you have until we reach Havana. I am glad that you feel well enough to dress, for I am anxious that you should meet my father as soon as possible. I fervently hope that you will succeed in impressing him favourably."

"Why?" I demanded, laughingly. "Is he so very formidable a personage, then?"

"Formidable enough, for one in your situation, if he should happen to take a dislike to you," the lad answered gravely. "Not that I have very much fear of that, however," he continued; "and in any case, my father is all right except when anything has occurred to vex him."

"Well, I suppose that holds good of most people," I remarked. "However, we must hope for the best. And now, since you have coopered me up so nicely, if you will let me have some water and my clothes, I will make my toilet as far as I can."

Upon leaving my bunk I found that I was still very shaky, with a tendency to giddiness, added to which my head was aching most distressingly; but I thought it possible that these disagreeable symptoms would perhaps pass off as soon as I found myself in the open air; I therefore dressed as quickly as possible, and made my way on deck.

The morning was brilliantly fine, with a slashing breeze from about east, a trifle northerly, and the brigantine was bowling along before it, with all studding-sails set on the starboard side, in a manner that fairly made me stare with astonishment, although I had been accustomed to fast vessels. The *Francesca* was an exceedingly fine and handsome vessel, of enormous beam, and sitting very low upon the water, but the pace at which she was travelling conclusively demonstrated that, beamy as she was, her lines must be the very perfection of draughting; indeed this was proved by the ease with which she appeared to glide along the surface of, rather than *through*, the water, her progress being marked by singularly little disturbance of the element, considering her very high rate of speed. Her sails were magnificently cut, setting to a nicety, and drawing to perfection, and they were white enough to have graced the spars of a yacht. I noticed, too, that the inside of the bulwarks, her deck-fittings, brass-work, and guns, were all scrupulously clean and bright, while every rope was carefully coiled upon its proper pin, the principal halliards and sheets being Flemish-coiled on the deck. In fact, the whole appearance of the vessel was far more suggestive of the British man-o'-war than of the slaver. The watch on deck consisted of about a dozen men—one or two of whom looked remarkably like Englishmen—and it did not escape me that, one and all, they had the look of resolute, reckless fellows, who would be quite ready to fight to the last gasp, if need be. And I was impressed, at the very first glance, with the fact that they were all quietly and steadily going about their work, talking quietly together, and behaving without a single trace of that lawlessness that I had expected to prevail among a slaver's crew.

CHAPTER XI

DON FERNANDO DE MENDOUCA

THE most striking figure in the ship, however, was, beyond all question, a tall, well-built man, with a firmly-knit, powerful frame, every movement of which was eloquent of health and strength and inexhaustible endurance, while it was characterized by that light and easy *floating* grace that is only to be acquired by the habitual treading of such an unstable platform as a ship's deck. He was very dark, his hair, moustache, and beard being coal-black and wavy, while his skin—or at least the exposed parts that met my eye —was tanned to so deep a bronze as to give him quite the complexion of a mulatto. But there was not a drop of black blood in him; his nose alone— thin, shapely, and slightly aquiline— was evidence enough of that. He was clad in the inevitable suit of white drill, girt about the waist with a crimson cummerbund; his head-covering was the equally inevitable Panama broad-brimmed hat, and his otherwise naked feet were thrust into a pair of Turkish slippers of red morocco, embroidered with gold thread. And, early as was the hour, he held a half-smoked cigar between his large, even, white teeth. As I emerged from the companion he was standing to windward, near the helmsman, critically eyeing the set of the brigantine's beautifully cut canvas; and upon seeing me he — without moving from his position or offering me his hand — bowed with all the stately grace of a Spanish hidalgo, and exclaimed in Spanish, in a firm, strong, and decidedly musical voice—

"Good-morning, señor! I congratulate you upon being sufficiently recovered to leave your cabin. I suppose I ought, by every rule of good manners, to bid you welcome to my ship; but I have discarded conventional forms of speech—among other things—and now make a practice of speaking only the strict truth; and—as Pedro has probably told you—I had little to do with your being here beyond the mere issue of the order for your transfer from the deck of the French schooner. But, if I cannot at this moment truthfully bid you welcome, I can at least say that I sincerely hope we shall be good friends; and should that come about, you shall be welcome not only to my ship, but, as we Spaniards say, to my house and all that is in it."

"Thank you, Don Fernando," I answered. "I can easily understand that you find it exceedingly difficult to regard me as a welcome guest, and believe me, I am not going to be so foolish as to feel hurt at your frankly telling me so. And I heartily unite with you in the hope that as long as we may be compelled into intimate association with each other, we shall be able to forget that our professions are antagonistic, and that personally it may be quite possible for us to be good friends. And now, señor, permit me to seize this, the first opportunity that has presented itself, to express to you my most grateful thanks for having saved my life yesterday——"

"Stop, señor, if you please," he interrupted, holding up his hand. "I have already explained to you that I had absolutely nothing to do with that beyond the mere issuing of an order. To be perfectly frank with you, I was in no mood to show mercy to any one just then, for you and your pestilent, meddlesome crew fought like fiends, and cost me several good men that I could ill spare. Your gratitude, therefore," and I thought I detected an echo of something very like scorn in his voice, "is due solely to my boy Pedro, whose whim of saving you I did not even then care to thwart. But enough of this; you are my guest, and may, if you will, become my friend. I hope your accommodation is to your liking?"

"Excellent, indeed," answered I, glad enough to get away from a topic that seemed to be somewhat distasteful to my host. "Excellent, indeed, and far more luxurious than anything to which I have been accustomed on board my own ship."

"Yes," he smiled; "the English are clearly anxious that their officers shall not become enervated through over-much luxury. I have been on board several of your ships, and saw but little to admire in the accommodation provided for and the arrangements made for the comfort of their officers. How long have you been on the West African station, señor?"

I told him, and the conversation gradually took a more agreeable turn, my host proving himself not only a thorough man of the world, but also surprisingly well educated and well read for a Spaniard. He was well acquainted with several of our best English writers, and professed an admiration for our literature as great and thorough as was his evident hatred of ourselves and our institutions as a nation. He had very considerably thawed out of his original coldness of manner, and was discussing with much animation and in well-chosen language the British drama, and especially Shakspeare, when we were summoned to breakfast and found Pedro waiting for us in the cabin. The lad was very demonstrative in his delight at finding me so much better, and I could see that he was also greatly pleased—and I thought relieved—at the prospect of amicable if not cordial relations becoming established between his father and myself.

I have said that the morning was brilliantly fine, and so it was; but I had noticed even when I first went on deck, that there was a certain pallor and haziness in the blue of the sky, the appearance of which I did not altogether like; and when after breakfast we went on deck—Mendouca with his sextant in his hand, for the purpose of finding the ship's longitude—our first glance aloft showed us that a large halo had gathered round the sun, and certain clouds that had risen above the horizon were carrying windgalls in their skirts. I drew Mendouca's attention to these portents, and he agreed with me that we were probably about to have bad weather. And sure enough we had, for that afternoon it came on to blow heavily from the eastward, and after running before it as long as we dared —indeed a good deal longer than in my opinion was at all prudent—we were compelled to heave-to; and we thus remained for sixty-two consecutive hours, during which Mendouca fumed and raved like a madman; for the sea was making clean breaches over the brigantine during the whole of that time, so that a considerable portion of our bulwarks and everything that was not securely lashed was washed away, and, worst of all, it was imperatively necessary to keep the hatches battened down during the entire continuance of the gale, thus depriving the unhappy slaves pent up below of all air save such as could penetrate through a small opening in

the fore-bulkhead, communicating with the forecastle, and used for the purpose of gaining access to the hold in bad weather, in order to supply the slaves with food and water. As, however, the sea was breaking more heavily over the fore-deck than anywhere else, the utmost care had to be exercised in opening the fore-scuttle, a favourable opportunity having to be watched for, and the hatch whipped off and on again in a moment. Very little air, therefore, was obtainable from that source, and none whatever from elsewhere; the blacks, therefore, were dying below like rotten sheep, of suffocation, as was reported by those who came up from time to time after attending to the most pressing wants of the miserable creatures. And to make what was already bad enough still worse, it was impossible to remove the dead from among the living so long as the bad weather continued.

When at length the gale moderated and the sea went down sufficiently to permit of sail being once more made, the hatches were lifted; and never to my dying day shall I forget the awful, poisonous stench that arose from the brigantine's hold. The fumes could be actually *seen* rising through the hatchway in the form of a dense steam that continued to pour up for several minutes, and when the men were ordered below to pass up the dead bodies, even the toughest and most hardened of them recoiled from the task, and staggered away forward literally as sick as dogs. At length, however, after the lapse of about a quarter of an hour, a gang ventured down into the now comparatively pure atmosphere, and the work of passing up the dead bodies began. I stood to windward, as near the hatchway as I could get without being sickened by the still pestilential effluvium that even now arose from the hold, and watched the operation, not from any feeling of morbid curiosity, but in order that I might become aware, by the evidence of my own eyesight, of some of the blacker horrors of this most foul and accursed trade, and the sights that I then witnessed literally beggar description. The unhappy wretches had been packed so tightly together that they had been unable to move more than an inch or so, while the slave-deck was so low that a sitting posture with the head bowed to the knees and the hands clasped in front of them had been absolutely necessary; and the miserable creatures had died and stiffened in this cramped and painful posture; it was gruesome enough, therefore, to see the bodies passed up and thrown overboard in so woful an attitude; but the worst sight of all was in those cases where, in the dying agony, some unfortunate wretch had writhed his head back until it looked as though the neck had become dislocated, thus revealing the distorted features, with the eyeballs rolled back until only the whites were visible, and the mouth wide open as though gasping for air. The brigantine had left the Congo with four hundred and fifty-five slaves on board, about three-fifths of whom were men, the remainder being young women and children; and of these every woman and child, and one hundred and twenty-seven men had succumbed, leaving, out of the grand total, the miserable moiety of only one hundred and forty-six survivors! It was horrible beyond the power of words to express, and to crown all, as the work went on, the water in the ship's wake became alive with sharks, who fought and struggled with each other for their prey, literally tearing the bodies limb from limb in their frantic struggles to secure a morsel. It was a sight that, one might have thought, would have excited pity in the breast of the arch-fiend himself, but with Mendouca it only had the effect of goading him into a state of mad, ungovernable fury. "See," he exclaimed at last, stalking up to me and grasping me savagely by the arm—"see the result of the thrice accursed meddlesome policy of your wretched, contemptible little England and the countries who have united with her in the hopeless task of suppressing the slave-trade! But for that, these negroes might have been comfortably stowed in three or four ships, instead of being packed like herrings in a barrel in the hold of one only, and then all this loss of life and money might have been avoided. By this infernal mishap I am a loser to the extent of over thirty thousand dollars, and all for what? Why, simply because you British, with your sickly sentimentality, choose to regard the blacks as human beings like yourselves. You are all virtuous indignation because forsooth we slave-traders have bethought ourselves of the plan of removing them from their own country, where their lives would have been passed in a condition of the lowest and most degrading

barbarism, and transporting them to another where they can be rendered useful and valuable; where, in return for their labour, they are fed, clothed, tended in sickness, and provided with comfortable homes; where their lives may be passed in peace and comfort and perfect freedom from all care; and where, if indeed they *are* human, like ourselves, which I very much doubt, they may be converted to Christianity. You violently object to this amelioration of the lot of the negro savage; but you shut your eyes to the fact that thousands of your own countrymen and women are actually slaves of the most abject type, made so by your own insatiable and contemptible craving for *cheap* clothing, *cheap* food, cheap everything, to satisfy which, and to, at the same time, gratify his own perfectly legitimate desire to make a living, the employer of labour has to grind his employés down in the matter of wage until their lives are a living lingering death to them, in comparison with which the future of those blacks down below will be a paradise. Bah! such hypocrisy sickens me. And yet, in support of this disgusting Pharisaism, you, and hundreds more like you, claiming to be intelligent beings, willingly endure hardships and face the perils of sickness, shipwreck, shot and steel with a persistent heroism that almost compels one's admiration, despite the mistaken enthusiasm which is its animating cause. Nay, do not speak, señor; I know exactly what you would say; I have heard, until I have become sick of it, the canting jargon of those meddlesome busy-bodies who, knowing nothing of the actual facts of slavery, or for their own purposes, hunt out exceptional cases of tyranny which they hold up to public execration as typical of the system—I have heard it all so often that I have long passed the point where it was possible to listen to it with even the faintest semblance of patience; so do not attempt the utterly useless and impossible task of trying to convert me, I pray you, lest in my anger I should say words that would offend you."

Good heavens! did the man suppose that he had not offended me already? I saw, however, that I might as well attempt to quell the hurricane as argue with him in his present mood; moreover I am but a poor hand at argument; I therefore bowed in silence, turned away and went below, fully determined

E

to have the matter out with the fiery Spaniard the first time that I caught him in a more amenable temper. Pedro would have followed me, and indeed attempted to do so, but as I entered the companion, I heard his father call him back and bid him remain on deck.

With the moderating of the gale the wind had come out dead ahead, and the brigantine was consequently on a taut bowline on the starboard tack when the hatches were opened and the bodies of the suffocated negroes were passed up on deck and thrown overboard. She remained so for the rest of that day; but when I awoke next morning, I at once became aware, from the steady, long, pendulum-like roll of the ship, that she was once more before the wind, and I naturally concluded that the wind had again become fair. To my great surprise, however, when I emerged from my state-room and caught a glimpse of the tell-tale compass hanging in gimbals in the skylight opening of the main cabin, I saw that the ship was heading to the *eastward!* Wondering what might be the meaning of this, I went on deck, but neither Mendouca nor Pedro was visible, and I did not choose to question the mate—a surly, hang-dog, cut-throat-looking scoundrel, who had chosen to manifest an implacable hostility to myself from the moment that our eyes had first met. However, I had not been on deck long when Mendouca made his appearance, and in response to his salutation I said—

"Good-morning, captain; I see you have shifted your helm during the night."

I saw, when it was too late, that my remark was an unfortunate one, for Mendouca scowled as he replied—

"Yes; it was not worth while to make the trip across the Atlantic and back for the mere purpose of landing one hundred and forty odd negroes—even could we have got them over without further loss, which I greatly doubt—so I am going back to the coast for more—unless I can pick them up without going so far," he added, after a momentary pause, and with a peculiar look which I could not at the moment fathom. "And all this loss of life, and money, and time, and all this extra risk are forced upon me by the meddlesome policy of Great Britain. *Great!* Faugh! Could she but see herself as others see her she would, for very shame, strike out that vaunting prefix, and take that obscure place

among the nations which properly befits her. Señor Dugdale, do you value your life?"

"Well, yes, to a certain extent I do," I replied. "It is the only one I have, you see; and were I to lose it the loss would occasion a considerable amount of distress to my friends. For that reason, therefore, if for no other, I attach a certain amount of value to it, and feel bound to take care of it so far as I may, with honour."

"Very well, then," remarked Mendouca, with a sneer, "so far as you can *with honour*, refrain, I pray you, from thrusting your nationality into my face; for I may as well tell you that I have the utmost hatred and contempt for the English; I would sweep every one of them off the face of the earth if I could; and some day, when this feeling is particularly strong upon me, I may blow your brains out if I happen to remember that you are an Englishman."

"I hope it will not come to that, Don Fernando, for many reasons," I remarked, with a rather forced laugh, "and among them I may just mention the base cowardice of murdering an unarmed man. I rather regret that you should be so completely as you appear to be under the dominion of this feeling of hatred for my nation; it must be as unpleasant for you as it is for me that we are thus forcibly thrown together; but it need not last long; you can put me out of the ship at the first land that we touch, and I must take my chance of making my way to a place of safety. It will be unpleasant for me, of course, but it will remove from you a constant source of temptation to commit murder."

Mendouca laughed—it was rather a harsh and jarring laugh, certainly—and said—

"Upon my honour as a Spanish gentleman, you appear to be mightily concerned to preserve me from the crime of bloodshed, young gentleman. But do you suppose it would not be murder to put you ashore, as you suggest, at the first land that we reach? Why, boy, were I to do so, within six hours you would be in the hands of the natives, and lashed to the torture-stake! And would not your death then be just as much my act as though I were to shoot you through the head this moment?"

And to my astonishment—and somewhat to my consternation, I must admit—he whipped a pistol out of his belt and levelled it full at my head, cocking it with his thumb as he did so.

"I presume it would," I answered steadily; "and on the whole I believe that to shoot me would be the more merciful act of the two. So fire by all means, señor, if you *must* take my life."

"By the living God, but you carry the thing off bravely, young cockerel!" he exclaimed. "Do you *dare* me to fire?"

"Yes," I exclaimed stoutly. "I dare you to fire, if you can bring yourself to perpetrate so rank an act of cowardice!"

"Well," he returned, laughing, as he lowered the pistol, uncocked it, and replaced it in his belt; "you are right. I cannot; at least not in cold blood. I dare say I am pretty bad, according to your opinion, but my worst enemy cannot accuse me of cowardice. And, as to putting you ashore, I shall do nothing of the kind; on the contrary, widely as our opinions at present diverge upon the subject of my calling, I hope yet to induce you to join me. You can be useful to me," he added, in pure English, to my intense astonishment; "I want just such a cool, daring young fellow as yourself for my right hand, to be a pair of extra eyes and ears and hands to me, and to take command in my absence. I can make it well worth your while, so think it over; I do not want an answer now."

"But I *must* answer now," I returned, also in English; "I cannot allow a single minute to elapse without assuring you, Don Fernando, that you altogether mistake my character if you suppose me capable of any participation whatever in a traffic that I abhor and detest beyond all power of expression; a traffic that inflicts untold anguish upon thousands, and, not infrequently, I should imagine, entails such a fearful waste of human life as I witnessed yesterday. Moreover, it has just occurred to me that when we attacked you and your friends in the creek this brigantine was flying a *black* flag. If that means anything it means, I presume, that you are a pirate as well as a slaver?"

"Precisely," he assented. "I am both. Some day, when we know each other better, I will tell you my story, and, unlikely as you may now think it, I undertake to say that when you have heard it you will acknowledge that I have ample justification for being both."

"Do not believe it, Don Fernando," I answered. "Your story is doubtless that of some real or fancied wrong that you have suffered at the hands of society; but *no* wrong can justify a man to become an enemy to his race. I will hear your story, of course, if it will afford you any satisfaction to tell it me; but I warn you that neither it nor anything that you can possibly say will have the effect of converting me to your views."

"You think so now, of course," he answered, with a laugh; "but we shall see, we shall see. Meanwhile, there is my steward poking his ugly visage up through the companion to tell us that breakfast is ready, so come below, my friend, and take the keen edge off your appetite."

It was on the day but one after this, that, about four bells in the forenoon watch, one of the hands, having occasion to go aloft to perform some small job of work on the rigging, reported a strange sail ahead. The brigantine was still running before a fair wind, but the breeze had fallen light, and it looked rather as though we were in for a calm spell, with thunder, perhaps, later on. We were going about four or maybe four and a half knots at the time, and the report of the strange sail created as much excitement on board us as though we had been a man-o'-war. For some time there seemed to be a considerable amount of doubt as to the course that the stranger was steering; for, as seen from aloft, she appeared to be heading all round the compass; but it was eventually concluded that, in general direction, her course was the same as our own.

As the morning wore on the wind continued to drop, while a heavy bank of thunder-cloud gathered about the horizon ahead, piling itself steadily but imperceptibly higher, until by noon it was as much as Mendouca could do to get the sun for his latitude. By this time we had risen the stranger until we had brought her hull-up on the extreme verge of the horizon; and the nearer that we drew to her the more eccentric did her manœuvres appear to be; she was heading all round the compass, and but for the fact that we could see from time to time that her yards were being swung, and some of her canvas hauled down and hoisted again in the most extraordinary manner, we should have set her down as a derelict. I ought, by the way, to have said that she was a small brig of, apparently, about one hundred and forty tons. Mendouca was thoroughly perplexed at her extraordinary antics; his glass was scarcely ever off her, and when he removed it from his eye it was only to hand it to me and impatiently demand whether I could not make out something to elucidate the mystery. At length, after witnessing through the telescope some more than usually extraordinary performance with the canvas, I remarked—

"I think there is one thing pretty clear about that brig, and that is that she is in the possession of people who have not the remotest notion how to handle her."

"Eh? what is that you say?" demanded Mendouca. "Don't know how to handle her? Well, it certainly appears that they do not," as the foretopsail-halliard was started and the yard slid slowly down the mast, leaving the topgallant-sail and royal fully set above it. "By Jove, I have it!" he suddenly continued, slapping his thigh energetically. "Yonder brig is in possession of a cargo of slaves who have somehow been allowed to rise and overpower her crew! Yes, by heaven, that must be the explanation of it! At all events we will run down and see. Blow, good breeze, blow!" and he whistled energetically after the manner of seamen in want of a wind.

The breeze, however, utterly refused to blow; on the contrary, it was growing more languid every minute, while our speed had dwindled down to a bare two knots; and the thunder-clouds were piling up overhead blacker and more menacing every minute. At length, when we were a bare three miles from the brig, the helmsman reported that we no longer had steerage way, and as the *Francesca* slowly swung round upon her heel, bringing the brig broad on her starboard quarter, Mendouca stamped irritably on the deck, and cursed the weather, the brig, the brigantine; in fact he cursed "everything above an inch high," as we say in the navy when we wish to describe a thorough, comprehensive outburst of profanity. At length, having given free vent to his impatience, he stood for a moment intently studying the lowering heavens, strode across the deck and glanced through the open skylight at the barometer, then turned to me and said, in English—

"What think you, Dugdale; would it be safe, in your opinion, to send away a couple of boats to take possession of that brig? The glass has dropped nothing to speak of since it was set this morning, and that stuff up there promises nothing worse than a sharp thunderstorm and a pelting downpour of rain. The boats could reach her in forty minutes, when their crews would take possession, shorten sail, and wait for us to join. I'll be bound there is sufficient 'black ivory' aboard there to spare me the necessity to return to the coast and to make good all my losses."

In my turn I too looked at the sky intently.

"I hardly know what to make of it," I answered at length. "It may be, as you say, that there is nothing worse than thunder brewing up there; yet there is something in the look of those clouds that I do not altogether like; their colour, for instance, is too livid a purple for thunder alone, according to my idea, and I do not like the way in which they are working; why, they are as busy as a barrel of yeast; depend on it, señor, there is wind, and plenty of it, up there. As to how long it may be before the outburst comes, you have had more experience than I of this part of the world, and ought to know the weather better than I do."

"Well, I dare say I do," he assented, with apparent relief, and again raised his eyes and anxiously scrutinized the clouds. "I'll risk it," he at length exclaimed, decisively, and forthwith turned and issued the necessary orders to his chief mate, who trundled away forward, bawling to the men as he went; and in a few minutes all was bustle and activity about our decks, the arm-chests being brought on deck, and the selected boats' crews coming aft and receiving their weapons from Mendouca himself, while the gunner served out the ammunition. The rascals were a smart, active lot—I will give them credit for so much—and in less than ten minutes from the announcement of Mendouca's decision, the boats, two of them, with ten men in each, were in the glassy water, and their crews stretching out lustily for the brig.

It was perfectly evident to me that Mendouca was possessed by a feeling that his eagerness to acquire the brig's cargo of negroes had warped his judgment and egged him on to an unduly risky course of action in sending his boats and so many of his people away in the face of that threatening sky; the boats had no sooner shoved off than he became consumed by anxiety, and, oblivious of the suffocating heat and closeness of the atmosphere, proceeded to pace the deck to and fro with hasty, impatient strides, halting abruptly at frequent intervals to scrutinize the aspect of the sky, and, anon, to watch the progress of the boats. The crews of the latter were evidently quite aware that the expedition upon which they were engaged was by no means free from peril, for until they had reached a distance too great to enable us to distinguish their actions, I could see first one and then another glancing aloft and over his shoulder at the sky, the action being invariably followed by the exhibition of increased energy at the oar. They were clearly doing their utmost, one and all; in fact the boats were making a downright race of it for the brig; the men bending their backs and throwing their whole strength into every stroke, churning the oily-looking surface of the water into foam with their oar-blades, and leaving a long, wedge-like wake behind them, while the two mates in charge, and who had hold of the yoke-lines, were bowing forward at every stroke in true racing style. Yet, rapid as their progress was, it did not satisfy Mendouca, who, every time that he paused to watch their progress, stamped upon the deck with impatience, and cursed the oarsmen for a set of lazy, good-for-nothing lubbers.

And there was ample justification for his anxiety; for scarcely had the boats reached a quarter of a mile from the *Francesca* than there was a sudden and very perceptible darkening of the heavens, followed by a vivid flash of lightning low down toward the eastern horizon, the low, muffled boom of the thunder coming reverberating across the glassy water with the sound of a cannon-shot rolled slowly along a timber floor.

CHAPTER XII

AN AWFUL CATASTROPHE

PRESENTLY, after one of his frequent halts, Mendouca turned and gave orders to shorten sail. "Clew up and haul down fore and aft; stow everything except the main-staysail; and see that you make a snug furl of it, men!" he cried; adding, as he turned to me—

"We might as well be snugging down as doing nothing; and perhaps the sight will put some life into the movements of those lazy rascals yonder," pointing with his cigar as he spoke towards the boats.

"Possibly," I agreed. "And in any case it appears to me that the time has fully arrived for the commencement of such preparations as you may think fit to make for the coming blow, which, in my humble opinion, is going to be rather sharp while it lasts."

"Yes; no doubt," Mendouca assented. "Curse those lazy hounds! Have they no eyes in their heads to see what is brewing? If they don't wake up, they will have the squall upon them before they reach the brig."

"In which case," said I, "you may say good-bye to the brig and to the slaves in her; and may think yourself lucky if you are able to recover your boats."

I do not know whether he heard me or not. I think it probable that he did; but he made no reply, turning his back upon me, and keeping his glances alternately roving between the boats and the sky, which latter had by this time assumed a most sinister and threatening aspect, so much so, indeed, that had I been in Mendouca's place I should have recalled the boats without another moment's delay. But I could see that he had set his heart upon securing possession of the brig, and was willing to run a considerable amount of risk in the effort to do so.

At length, when the boats were, according to my estimation, a little better than half-way to the brig, another flash of lightning, vivid and blinding, blazed forth, this time from almost overhead, only the very smallest perceptible interval of time elapsing between it and the accompanying thunder-crash, which was so appallingly loud and startling that for a moment I felt fairly deaf and stunned with it, and before I had fairly recovered my dazed senses the rain came pelting down in drops as large as crown-pieces. The rain lasted for only three or four seconds, however, and then ceased again abruptly, while almost at the same instant a brief scurry of wind swept past us, just lifting the staysail—which was by this time the only sail remaining set on board us—and causing it to flap feebly for a moment, when it was once more calm again ; but we could trace the puff a long distance to the westward by its track along the oily surface of the water.

Mendouca turned to me with an oath. " When it comes, it will come to us dead on end from the brig ! " he exclaimed. " It is just like my cursed luck ! Do you think it is too late to recall the boats ? "

"Yes," I answered decidedly. "They are now nearer the brig than they are to us, and their best chance certainly is to keep on as they are going."

Mendouca turned and bestowed upon the boats yet another long scrutinizing glance ; and then said, with his eyes still fixed upon them—

" I do not agree with you. I think they are quite as near to us as they are to the brig ; and if they keep on and the squall bursts before they reach the brig, they will have to pull against it, and may perhaps not fetch her after all, whereas if I recall them, and they are overtaken before they reach us, they will have the wind all in their favour instead of dead against them."

" That is very true," I assented. "It appears to me, however, that the whole question hinges upon the point whether they are nearer to us or to the brig ; and in my opinion they are much nearer to the latter."

For fully another minute Mendouca continued to watch the boats ; then he suddenly exclaimed—

" I shall recall them. Clear away the bow gun there, and fire it with a blank cartridge ; and, Pedro, get out the recall signal, and stand by to run it up to the main truck at the flash of the gun."

The signal was made, the boom of the gun seeming to echo with a hollow, long-drawn-out reverberation between sea and sky ; and within a minute the boats, with seeming reluctance, had turned and were pulling back to the brigantine.

Meanwhile the heavens had continued to darken, until, by the time that the boats had turned, the whole scene had become involved in a murky twilight, through the gloom of which the brig, still with every stitch of canvas set, could with difficulty be made out. Still, although it seemed to me that the brooding squall might burst upon us at any moment, the atmosphere maintained its ominous condition of

stagnation until the boats had reached within some four cables' lengths—or somewhat less than half-a-mile—of us ; when, as I was intently watching their progress, I saw the sky suddenly break along the horizon just above them, the clouds appearing as though rent violently apart for a length of some ten or twelve degrees of arc, while the rent was filled with a strong yet misty glare of coppery-yellow light, in the very centre of which the brig stood out sharply defined, and as black as a shape cut out of silhouette paper.

" Here it comes, at last ! " I exclaimed ; and as the words passed my lips I felt a spot of rain upon my face, and in another instant down it came, a regular deluge, but only for about half a minute, when it ceased abruptly, and, looking toward the brig, I saw a long line of white foam sweeping down towards her.

" God help those poor, unhappy blacks ! " I cried. " If that craft's spars and rigging happen to be good she will turn the turtle with them, and probably not one of them will escape ! "

" It is a just punishment upon them for rising against the crew," exclaimed Mendouca savagely ; " but if I had only succeeded in laying hands upon them I would have inflicted a worse punishment upon them than drowning. I would have—ah ! look at that ! Now the squall strikes her, and over she goes. Taken flat aback, by heaven ! "

It was as Mendouca had said ; the brig when struck by the squall happened to be lying head on to it, and her topmasts bent like reeds ere they yielded to the pressure, and snapped short off by the caps. Then, gathering stern-way, she paid off until she was nearly broadside on to us, and we could see that her stern was becoming more and more depressed as it was forced against the comparatively stubborn and unyielding water, while her bow was raised proportionally high in the air. Foot by foot, and second by second, her stern sank deeper and deeper into the water until the latter was flush with her taffrail, and then, with the aid of a telescope, I saw it go foaming and boiling in upon her deck, driving the dense crowd of negroes forward foot by foot. By this time her forefoot was raised clear out of the water, and, enveloped in mist and spray though she was, I could see the bright, glassy glare of the sky beyond and below it. For a second she remained thus ; then her bow rose still higher in the air, and, with a long sliding plunge, she disappeared stern foremost.

"Gone to the bottom, every mother's son of them—as they richly deserved!" exclaimed Mendouca, with a savage curse. "And if those loafing vagabonds of mine don't bestir themselves they will follow in double-quick time! What do you think, Dugdale? Shall we be able to save them?"

I shook my head. "I would not give very much for their chance," I replied. "It is a pity that you recalled them, I think. They would have had time to reach the brig, and could at least have got her before the wind, even had they no time to do more."

"Yes," he assented; "as it happened, they could. But how was a man to know that the squall was going to hold off so long, and then burst at the most unfortunate moment possible?"

All this, it must be understood, had happened in a very much shorter time than it has taken to tell of it, and the squall had not reached as far as the boats when the brig disappeared; while, as for us, we were lying motionless in a still stagnant atmosphere, with our starboard broadside presented fair to the approaching squall. But as the last words left Mendouca's lips the squall swooped down upon the boats, and in an instant they were lost sight of in a smother of mist and spray, while the roar of the approaching squall, that had come to us at first as a faint low murmur, grew deeper and hoarser, and more deadly menacing in its overpowering volume of tone. Then the air suddenly grew damp, with a distinct taste of salt in it; the roar increased to a deafening bellow, and with a fierce, yelling shriek the squall burst upon us, and the brigantine bowed beneath the stroke until her lee rail was buried, and the water foamed in on deck from the cat-head to the main-rigging. I thought for a moment that she, too, was going to turn turtle with us, and I believe she would, had the staysail stood; but luckily at the very moment when it seemed all up with us, the sheet parted with a report that sounded even above the yell of the gale; there was a concussion as though the ship had struck something solid, and with a single flap the sail split in ribbons and blew clean out of the bolt-ropes. Meanwhile Mendouca had sprung to the wheel and lent his

strength to the efforts of the helmsman to put it hard up, and, after hanging irresolute for a moment, as though *undecided whether to capsize* or not, the *Francesca* gathered way, and in obedience to the helm gradually paid off until she was dead before it, when she suddenly righted and began to scud like a terrified thing. The boats were of course left far behind; and I made up my mind that we should never see them again.

The squall was as sharp a thing of its kind as I had ever beheld, and it was fully three-quarters of an hour before it became possible to bring the ship to the wind again, which Mendouca did the moment that he could with safety. The wind continued quite fresh for another half-hour after the squall had blown itself out, and then it dwindled away to a very paltry breeze again, the clouds cleared away, the sun reappeared and shone with a heat that was almost overpowering, and the weather became brilliantly fine again; much too fine, indeed, for Mendouca's purpose, he being anxious to get back again as quickly as possible to the spot where he had been obliged to abandon his boats, a lingering hope possessing him that perchance they might have outlived the squall, and that he might recover his men. I may perhaps be doing the man an injustice in saying so much, but I firmly believe that this desire on his part was prompted, not by any feeling of humanity or regard for the men, but simply because the loss of so many out of his ship's company would leave him very short-handed, and seriously embarrass him until he could obtain others to fill their places; and I formed this opinion from the fact that his many expressions of regret at being blown away from his boats were every one of them coupled with a petulant repetition of the remark that his hands would be completely tied should he fail to recover their crews. So persistently did he hang upon this phase of the mishap, that at length I ventured to ask him whether there were none of them that he would be sorry to lose for their own sakes, apart from any question of inconvenience; in reply to which he stated, with a brutal laugh, that they were, one and all, a lazy set of worthless rascals, of whom he should have rid himself in any case on his arrival in Havana.

However, be his motive what it

might, he cracked on every stitch of canvas that the brigantine would bear, as soon as the strength of the squall had sufficiently abated to permit of his bringing her to the wind, making sail from time to time as the wind further dwindled, until he had her under everything that would draw, from the trucks down. To add to his anxiety, it was about two bells in the first dog-watch before he could bring the ship to the wind, and he feared, not without reason, that it would be dark before he could work back near enough to the spot at which we had left the boats, to see them again—always supposing, of course, that they still floated. However, he did everything that a seaman could do, sending a hand aloft to the royal-yard to keep a look-out as soon as the ship had been got upon a wind, and making short boards to windward—the first one of a quarter of an hour's duration, and the others of half-an-hour each, so as to thoroughly cover the ground previously passed over—as long as the daylight lasted. But when, all too soon, the sun went down in a blaze of golden and crimson and purple splendour, no sign of the boats had been seen; Mendouca, therefore, worked out a calculation of the distance run by the brigantine from the spot where the squall first struck her, subtracted from it the distance that the boats would probably traverse in the same time, and having worked up to this spot as nearly as he could calculate, he hove-to for the night, with a bright lantern at his main-truck, firing signal rockets at intervals of a quarter of an hour, and wearing the ship round on the other tack every two hours. The night was brilliantly star-lit, but without a moon, still there was light enough upon the water to have revealed the boats at a distance of half-a-mile, while the weather was so fine that a shout raised at twice that distance to windward of the ship might have been heard on board her above the soft sigh of the night wind, and the gentle lap of the water along the bends; moreover, apart from the rockets fired, she might have been plainly seen against the sky at a distance of fully three miles from the boats, while her progress through the water was so slow that they could have pulled alongside her without difficulty; when, therefore, midnight arrived without any news of them, I

gave them up for lost, and turned in. Not so Mendouca, he would not give them up; moreover, he refused to leave the deck—declaring that now he had lost his two mates he had nobody on board that he could trust in charge—preferring to have a mattress laid for him upon the skylight bench, where he snatched catnaps between the intervals of wearing the ship round.

However, the matter was cleared up shortly after sunrise next morning, when Mendouca again sent a hand aloft to look round, for the fellow had only got as far as the foretop when he reported two objects that looked like the boats, about five miles to leeward; adding, that if they *were* the boats, they were capsized. The topsail was accordingly filled, and the ship kept away, when, after about an hour's run, first one boat and then the other was found, the first being capsized, while the second was full of water and floating with the gunwale awash. One drowned seaman was found under the capsized boat, but the rest were nowhere to be seen. Both boats were easily secured, and found to be undamaged; and several of the oars and loose bottom-boards were also recovered, being found floating at no great distance from the boats. The drowned seaman, I may as well mention, was not brought on board, but instead of this a boat was sent away with a canvas bag containing three nine-pound shot, which they secured to the poor wretch's ankles, and so sunk him.

Mendouca now, in no very amiable mood, resumed his course toward the coast; and that same afternoon—having meanwhile been engaged apparently in a tolerably successful effort to recover his temper—approached me with a proposal that he should tell me the story of his life, to which I of course cheerfully assented.

I will not inflict upon the reader the tale that he told me, because it has no direct bearing upon this present history; suffice it to say, that I now learned with some astonishment that he was a born Englishman, and that, moreover, he had begun his career in the British navy, from which—if his story were strictly true, as I afterwards had the opportunity of learning was the case—he had been ousted by a quite unusual piece of tyranny, and a most singular and deplorable miscarriage of justice. It was the latter,

I gathered, even more than the former, that had soured him, and warped everything that was good out of his character; for it appeared that he had a keen sense of justice, and a very exalted idea of it; he had undoubtedly been most cruelly ill-used—he had in fact been adjudged guilty of a crime that he had never committed—and this appeared to have utterly ruined the character of a man who might otherwise have been an ornament to the service, distorted all his views of right and wrong, and filled him to the brim with a wild, unreasoning, insatiable desire for vengeance.

This much for the man's story, which, however, I soon found had been told me with a purpose; that purpose being nothing less than the inducing of me to join him and take the place of his lost chief mate, whereby —according to his showing—I might speedily become a rich man. Had the proposal come before I had heard his story I should have resented it as an insult, but the recital to which he had treated me, and the sentiments expressed during its narration, convinced me that his sense of honour had been so completely warped that he could see no disgrace in the abandonment of a service and a country capable of treating any other man—myself, for instance, as he carefully pointed out— as he had been treated; I therefore contented myself with a simple refusal, coupled with an assurance that such a step would be wholly discordant with my sense of right and wrong, utterly irreconcilable to my conscience, and not at all in accord with my views. I had expected him to be furiously angry at my refusal, but to my great surprise he was not; on the contrary, he frankly admitted that he had been fully prepared for a refusal—at first— but that he still believed my views might alter upon more mature reflection.

"Meanwhile," said he, "you see how I am situated; I have lost both my officers, and have no one on board but yourself in the least capable of taking their places. I saved your life—or spared it, which comes to the same thing—and I now ask you to make me the only return in your power by assisting me in my difficulty."

"Before I give you any answer to that," said I, "I must ask you to explicitly define and accurately set forth the nature of the assistance that you desire me to render."

"Certainly," said Mendouca. "All that I ask of you at present is to relieve me by taking charge of a watch, and assisting me to navigate the ship. With regard to the latter, I consider myself capable of taking the ship anywhere, and have as much confidence in myself as a man ought to have; but 'to err is human,' and it increases one's confidence, and confers a feeling of security, to have some one to check one's calculations. And as to the watch, unless you will consent to keep one for me, I shall be compelled to keep the deck night and day. Now, it is no great thing that I am asking of you *in return for your life*; will you do it?"

"Give me half-an-hour to consider the matter, and you shall then have my reply," said I.

"So be it," he answered. And then the matter ended, for the moment.

It was a question that I found it by no means easy to decide. Here was I, an officer in the service of a country pledged to do its utmost to suppress the abominable slave traffic, actually invited to assist in the navigation of a ship avowedly engaged not only in that traffic but—according to the acknowledgment of her captain—also in, at least, occasional acts of piracy! What was I to do? On the one hand, I was fully determined to do nothing that could be construed into even the semblance of tacit acquiescence in Mendouca's lawless vocation; while, on the other, I undoubtedly owed my life to the man, and therefore shrank from the idea of behaving in a manner that might appear churlish. Moreover, it appeared to me that by rendering the trifling service demanded of me, I should find myself in a position to very greatly ameliorate in many ways the condition of the unhappy blacks down in the dark, noisome hold. The end of it all was, therefore, that at the expiration of the half-hour I had determined—perhaps weakly and foolishly —to accede to Mendouca's request. I accordingly went to him and said—

"Señor Mendouca, I have considered your request, and have decided to accede to it upon certain conditions."

"Name them," answered Mendouca.

"They are these," said I. "First, that my services shall be strictly confined to the keeping of a watch and the checking of your astronomical observations. Secondly, that you undertake to perpetrate no act of piracy while I am on board. And, thirdly, that you will allow me to leave your ship upon the first occasion that we happen to encounter a sail of a nationality friendly to Great Britain."

"Is that *all?*" demanded Mendouca. "By my faith, but you appear to attach a somewhat high value to your services, señor midshipman! I spared your life; yet that does not appear to be a sufficient reason why you should afford me the small amount of help I require without hedging your consent about with ridiculous and impossible restrictions! I am surprised that, while you were about it, you did not also stipulate that I should abandon the slave-trade while the ship is honoured by your presence! I am obliged to you, Señor Dugdale, for your condescension in giving your distinguished consideration at all to my request, but your terms are too high; I can do better without your help than with it, if it is to be bought at the price of such restraint as you demand."

And he turned his back upon me and walked over to the other side of the deck.

Presently he turned and re-crossed the deck to my side, and remarked, in English—

"Look here, Dugdale, don't be a fool! In coupling your consent to help me with those restrictions, you doubtless suspected me of an intention to involve you in some of those acts that you deem unlawful, and then to renew my proposal that you should join me. Well, if you did you were not so very far from the truth; I confess that I *do* wish you to join me. I have somehow taken a fancy to you, despite those old-fashioned and absurd notions of yours about conscience, and duty, and the like. Why, if you would only put them away from you it would be the making of you, and you would be just the sort of fellow that I want; you are pluck all through, and, once free from the trammels of the thing that you call conscience, you would stick at nothing, and with you as my right hand I should feel myself free to undertake deeds that I have only dared to *dream* of thus far, while, with our views brought into accord, we should be as brothers to each other. I am ambitious, Dugdale, and I tell you that if you will join me we *can* and *will* revive the glories of the old buccaneering days and make ourselves feared and reverenced all over the globe; we will be sea-kings, you and I. What need is there for hesitation in the matter? Nay"—and he held up his hand as he saw that I was about to speak—"do not inflict upon me those musty platitudes about *conscience* and *duty* that I have heard so often in the old days, and that have been made the excuse for so many acts of gross tyranny and injustice that my gorge rises in loathing whenever I hear them mentioned. What *is* conscience? The inward monitor that points out your duty to God and restrains—or tries to restrain—you from doing wrong, you will perhaps say. Well, let us accept that as an answer. I will then ask you another question. Do you really believe in the existence of the Being you call God? No, I am sure you do not; you cannot, my dear fellow, and remain consistent. For what is our conception of God? or, rather, what is the picture of Him that our ghostly advisers and teachers have drawn of Him? Are we not assured that He is the personification and quintessence of Justice, and Love, and Mercy? Very well. Then, if such a Being really exists, would the tyranny, the injustice, the cruelty, and the suffering that have afflicted poor humanity, from Adam down to ourselves, have been permitted? Certainly not! Therefore I unhesitatingly say that He cannot exist, and that the belief in Him is a mere idle, foolish superstition, unworthy of entertainment by intelligent, reasonable, and reasoning beings. And if there is no God, whence do we derive our conception of duty? I tell you, Dugdale, there is no such thing as duty save to one's self; the duty of protecting, and providing for, and avenging one's self, as I am doing, and as you may do if you choose to join me."

"Have you finished?" I asked, as he paused and looked eagerly into my face. "Very well, then; I will answer in a few words. If facts were as you so confidently state them to be, I might possibly be induced to cast in my lot with yours; but, fortunately for humanity, they are not so, and I must therefore most emphatically decline."

"Then I presume," said he, with a sneer, "you still believe in the existence of God, and His power to work His will here on earth?"

"Certainly," I answered, without hesitation.

"Do you believe that He is more potent than I am?"

"I really must decline to answer so absurd a question," said I, and turned away to leave him.

"Stop!" he thundered, his eyes suddenly blazing with demoniac fury. "Answer me, yes or no, *if you are not afraid!* If your faith in Him is as perfect as you would have me believe, answer me!"

I hesitated for a moment—I confess it with shame—for I felt convinced that in the man's present mood a reply in the affirmative would assuredly provoke him to some dreadful act in proof of the contrary; the hesitation was but momentary, however, and, that moment past, I replied—

"Yes; I believe Him to be omnipotent, both on earth and in heaven."

It was as I had expected—my reply had provoked him to murder; for as the words left my lips he, for the second time, drew his pistol from his belt, cocked it, and deliberately pressed the muzzle of the barrel to my temple, exclaiming, as he did so—

"Very well. Then let us see whether He has the power to save you from my bullet!"

And, glaring like a madman straight into my eyes, he held it there while one might perhaps have slowly counted ten, and then pulled the trigger. There was a sharp click and a little shower of sparks as the flint-lock fell, and—that was all.

"Missed fire, by all the furies!" he exclaimed, dashing the weapon violently to the deck, *where it instantly exploded.* "Well, you have proved your faith, at all events, and have escaped with your life by the mere accident of my pistol having missed fire, and there is an end of it for the present. Here, take my hand; you are a plucky young dog and no mistake, but you did wrong to provoke me; take my advice and don't do it again, lest worse befall you."

"No," said I, "I will *not* take your hand. You saved—or rather, spared—my life once, it is true, but you have threatened it twice, and it is no thanks to you that I am alive at this moment. We are now quits, for this last act of yours has wiped out whatever obligation I may have owed you for your former clemency. I will not take your hand; and I warn you that I will leave your ship on the first opportunity that presents itself."

And I turned away and left him.

Shortly afterwards Mendouca went below; and a few minutes after his disappearance the steward came up to me and informed me that "supper"—as the evening meal is called at sea—was ready.

"I shall not go below, steward," I said. "If Captain Mendouca will allow you to do so, I should like you to bring me a cup of coffee and a biscuit up here."

"Very well, señor," the man answered. "I will bring them."

He disappeared, but returned, after an interval of a minute or two, and handed me a note scrawled on a small slip of paper. It was written in English, and read as follows—

"You are the last fellow I should ever have suspected of so contemptible a weakness as sulking. Come below, like a sensible lad; I have that to say to you which I do not choose to say on deck in the presence of the men.
                    "MENDOUCA."

"Oh!" thought I, "so he has returned to his right mind, has he? Very well, I will go below and hear what he has to say; for it would certainly be unpleasant to be in a ship for any length of time with the captain of which one is not on speaking terms."

Accordingly I descended the companion, and as I entered the cabin Mendouca rose from a sofa-locker upon which he had flung himself, and again stretched forth his hand.

"I want you to forgive me, Dugdale," said he, with great earnestness. "Nay, but you must; I will take no denial. I am not prone to feel ashamed of anything that I do, but I frankly confess that I *am* ashamed of my behaviour to you this afternoon, and I ask your pardon for it. To tell you the whole truth, I believe that there is a taint of madness in my blood, for there have been occasions when I have felt myself irresistibly impelled to actions for which I have afterwards been sorry, and that of this afternoon was one of them."

I believed him; I really believed that, as he had said, there was a touch of madness in his composition, and that he was not always fully accountable for his actions. I therefore somewhat reluctantly accepted his proffered hand and the reconciliation that went

with it, and with a suggestion that perhaps it would be as well henceforth to
avoid theological arguments, took my
accustomed seat at the cabin table.

Later in the evening, while Mendouca was reading in his cabin, my
friend Pedro joined me on deck, and,
with many expressions of poignant distress at his father's behaviour to me,
endeavoured to excuse it upon the plea
of irresponsibility already urged by
Mendouca himself; the poor lad assuring me that even he was not always
safe from the consequences of his
father's .violence.   And during the
half-hour's chat that ensued I learnt
enough to convince me that Mendouca
was in very truth afflicted with
paroxysmal attacks of genuine, un-
doubted madness; and that, in my
future dealings with him, I should
have to bear that exceedingly alarming and disconcerting fact in mind.

CHAPTER XIII

HOW MENDOUCA REPLENISHED HIS "CARGO"

I COULD see that Mendouca was pretty
thoroughly ashamed of himself, for
despite his utmost efforts, there was a
perceptible shrinking and embarrassment of manner apparent in him during
the progress of the meal.   Nevertheless, he exerted himself manfully to
obliterate the exceedingly disagreeable impression that he knew had been
made upon me by his late conduct;
and it was evident that he was sincerely
desirous of re-establishing friendly
relations between us, whether from
any selfish motive or not I cannot of
course say, but I think not—I believe
his pride was hurt at his late lamentable exhibition of weakness, and he
was chiefly anxious to recover his own
self-respect. Whatever his motive may
have been, his demeanour was a perfect blending of politeness and cordi-
ality that won upon me in spite of
myself; and before the meal was over
I had determined to render him the
small amount of assistance that he had
asked of me, reserving to myself the
right to withdraw it at any moment
that I might deem fit. He seemed
sincerely grateful for my offer, and
accepted it frankly and cordially with
the reservation that I had attached to
it; and having accompanied me on
deck and turned the hands up, he informed them that I had offered to

temporarily perform the duties of chief
mate, and that they were to obey my
orders as implicitly as they would
those from his own lips; after which,
as I had offered to take charge until
midnight, he said that he was tired
and would try to get a little sleep, and
so retired below to his own cabin.

The breeze continued easterly, and
very moderate, frequently dropping
almost calm, on which occasion we
were almost invariably treated to
deluges of rain, with occasional thunder
and lightning.   Our progress to the
eastward was therefore slow, and for
three whole days and nights nothing
occurred to break the monotony of
the voyage. On the morning of the
fourth day, however, when I went on
deck just before eight bells—it having
been my eight hours in, that night—I
found the brigantine once more before
the wind, with a slashing breeze blowing after her, and she with every rag
of canvas packed upon her that could
be induced to draw. But, to my ex-
ceeding surprise, we were heading to
the *westward*, and, hull-down about
ten miles distant, was another craft
dead ahead of us, also carrying a press
of canvas.

I turned to Mendouca for an explanation; and in answer to my look of
inquiry he said—

"Yes, I want to overtake that brig,
if I can. I am ashamed to say that
among us we let her slip past in the
darkness of the early part of the last
watch, and so I missed the opportunity
of speaking her. But I believe I know
her; and if my surmise as to her
identity proves correct, I think I shall
have no difficulty in persuading her
skipper to transfer his cargo to me,
and so save me the trouble and risk
of returning to the coast for one—a
risk which was every day growing
greater as we drew nearer to the ground
haunted by your lynx-eyed cruisers, to
fall in with one of which just now, with
those niggers down in the hold, would
mean our inevitable condemnation, as
I need scarcely tell you."

"Quite so," I assented. "But should
you fail to overtake yonder craft, you
will lose a good deal of ground, will
you not?"

"Oh, we shall overhaul her, if she
be the brig I believe her to be, and I
have very little doubt upon that point,"
answered Mendouca. "She is a smart
craft, I admit, but the *Francesca* can
beat her upon any point of sailing, and

in any breeze that blows; and, that being the case, the distance that we may have to run to leeward before getting alongside her is a matter of indifference to me, since it will be so much of our voyage accomplished."

"Have you gained anything on her since you bore up in chase?" I asked.

"About a couple of miles, I should think. But then the wind has been light with us until within the last hour. If this breeze holds I expect to be alongside her about four bells in the afternoon watch."

"By which time we shall have run close upon seventy miles to leeward," I remarked.

"Nearer eighty," observed Mendouca. "We are going close upon thirteen now. But, as I said before, that does not trouble me in the least, since we shall be that much nearer Cuba."

This was serious news to me, for Cuba was about the last place that I desired to visit, at least on board the *Francesca*, for I foresaw that if once we got over there the difficulty of effecting my escape from the accursed craft would be very greatly increased; indeed, I had quite reckoned upon her being fallen in with and captured by one of our cruisers, either while standing in for a fresh cargo of slaves, or when coming out again with them on board, to which chance alone could I look with any reason for the prospect of deliverance from my present embarrassing and disagreeable situation. True, there was just a possibility of our being picked up by one of the West Indian squadron; but I had not much hope of that, our vessels on that station being mostly slow, deep-draught craft, altogether unsuited for the pursuit and capture of the swift, light-draught slavers, who, unless caught at advantage in open water, could laugh us to scorn by the simple expedient of taking short cuts across shoals, or seeking refuge among the shallow lagoons that abound among the islands, and are especially plentiful and spacious along the northern coast of Cuba. However, there was no use in worrying over a state of things that I had no power to mend; I therefore assumed charge of the deck, and allowed matters to take their course—since I needs must.

The breeze continued to freshen as the sun increased his distance above the horizon, and we went bowling along at a most exhilarating pace, overhauling the brig ahead, slowly but surely; and when at one o'clock the steward summoned me to the cabin to dinner, a space of barely two miles separated the two craft. She had just hoisted Portuguese colours, of which, however, Mendouca took no notice, somewhat to my surprise, since he reiterated the statement that she was the craft he had believed her to be, and that the captain of her and he were old friends. It was my afternoon watch below; so when I rose from the dinner-table I said—

"Captain Mendouca, I have no wish to identify myself in any way with the transaction you are about to negotiate; you must excuse me therefore if, it being my watch below, I retire to my cabin."

"Very well, Dugdale," he answered, quite good-humouredly, "I can manage the business perfectly well without you; if therefore *your conscience*"—with just the faintest suggestion of a sneer— "will not permit you to take an active part in it, you are quite welcome to stay below until the affair is at an end, when I will call you."

I even thought that he spoke with an air of relief, as though my withdrawal had smoothed away a difficulty.

About an hour later I was awakened from a nap by the sound of hailing in a language which I did not understand, but which, from its decided resemblance to Spanish, I concluded to be Portuguese. I could not hear what passed, nor did I attempt to do so, being of opinion that the less prominently I was mixed up with the affair, and the less I knew about it, the better. The hailing soon ceased, and then the brigantine was hove-to, as I could tell by the difference in her movements. I had the curiosity to rise from my bunk and take a peep through the scuttle at the sea, but it was bare as far as my eye could reach; so, as my state-room was to windward as the *Francesca* then lay, I came to the conclusion that the brig was hove-to to leeward of us. The moment that our topsail was backed I heard the creaking of davit blocks, and the other sounds of a boat being lowered; and a few minutes later I heard the roll of the oars in the rowlocks as she was pulled away from the ship. Then the hatches were taken off fore and aft, and in about half-an-hour from the time of our having hove-to I became aware that the first boat-load of slaves had arrived alongside and were being driven down into the hold. The boats now began to arrive in rapid succession, and there was a good deal of bustle and confusion on deck, which lasted until close upon sunset, and in the midst of it I laid down and went to sleep again, for want of something better to do. When I awoke the dusk was thick upon the glass of my scuttle, the steward was lighting the lamp in the main cabin, and I could feel that we were once more under way again ; concluding, therefore, that the exchange had been completed, I rolled out of my bunk and, slipping my feet into my shoes, left my state-room and went on deck, where I found Mendouca in jubilant spirits, but rather disconcerted, I thought, at my appearance. •

" Hillo ! " he exclaimed in English, " where the deuce did you come from, and how long have you been on deck ? "

" I came from my state-room, and have but this moment emerged from the companion. Why do you ask ? " said I.

" Because," he answered, " to tell you the truth you startled me, making your appearance in that quiet manner. I thought you were going to stay below until I called you ? "

" It was *you* who said that, not I," answered I. " And, to tell you the truth, I felt tired of being below, and so—finding that you were under way again—came on deck."

The brig was about five miles astern, and, as far as I could see in the fast-gathering darkness, still hove-to, which struck me as being so peculiar that I made some remark to that effect.

" Oh no ; nothing strange about it at all," answered Mendouca carelessly. " Her people are getting their supper, probably, and are too lazy to start tack or sheet until they have finished their meal. Bless you, you have no idea what lazy rascals the Portuguese are ; their laziness is absolutely phenomenal; they are positively too lazy to live long, and so most of them die early. Moreover, I expect her skipper is still below poring over his charts and trying to make up what he is pleased to call his mind what spot to steer for in order to get another cargo."

" Very possibly," I assented, with a laugh. " By the way, it is curious, but I could almost fancy her deeper in the water than she was ; does it not strike you so ? "

" Deeper in the water ? " he exclaimed sharply. " No, I cannot say that it does ; and even were such a thing possible, it would need an uncommonly sharp eye to discern it in such a light as this. She may be, however, for that rascal José wrung enough good Spanish dollars out of me, for his rubbish, to sink her to her waterways. But come, here is the steward, so I suppose supper is ready, and if so we may as well go below and get it, for I must plead guilty to being most ravenously hungry."

Notwithstanding which statement I could not avoid noticing that he toyed a great deal with his food and ate very little ; which was not to be wondered at under the circumstances, for I afterwards learned that while I was below in my berth, suspecting nothing worse than the purchase and transfer of a cargo of slaves from one ship to another, a most atrocious and cold-blooded act of piracy had been committed, and that, too, under the shadow and disguise of the British flag ; Mendouca having coolly hoisted British colours the moment that I left the deck, and, in the guise of a British cruiser, compelled the Portuguese brig to heave-to and disgorge her cargo ; after which he had confined the crew below, bound hand and foot, and had scuttled their ship, leaving them to perish in her when she went down ! But of this I had not the faintest suspicion until the tale was told me some time afterwards by one of the *Francesca's* own crew.

With the setting of the sun the wind evinced a very decided tendency to drop, growing steadily lighter all through the first watch, until when Mendouca relieved me at midnight the ship was moving at a rate of barely five knots, although she was carrying studding-sails on both sides ; and when I went on deck again at four o'clock next morning it was a flat calm, and the ship was lying motionless upon the water, with her head swung round to the south-east ; the swell, too, had gone down, and there was every appearance of the calm lasting for several hours at least. The appearance of the sun, as he rose, also confirmed this impression, the sky being—for a wonder in that latitude—perfectly cloudless, and of a clear, pure, soft, crystalline blue, into which the great luminary leapt in dazzling splendour, palpitating with breathless heat that promised to soon become almost unendurable. It was my custom to indulge in a salt-water bath every morning in the ship's head, one of the men playing the hose upon me for a quarter of an hour or so, and never did that bath seem a greater luxury to me than on this particular morning, for the heat came with the sun, and I envied the fish their ability to escape it by sinking deep into the cool, blue, crystalline depths; indeed I should most probably have been tempted to imitate them as far as possible by plunging overboard and swimming twice or thrice round the ship, had I not happened to have noticed a large shark under her counter, when, to test the clearness of the water, I happened to lean over the taffrail to look at the rudder and stern-post. Even the men dawdled over the job of washing decks that morning, using a much greater quantity of water than usual, and placing themselves where there was a chance to get the hose played upon their bare feet and legs. And if it was hot on deck, what must it have been down in the crowded hold? It was Mendouca's habit to have the gratings put on the hatchways and secured every night—when the weather would permit of the use of them instead of the solid hatches—in order to prevent anything in the shape of a rising on the part of the negroes; and all night long a thin, pungent vapour had been rising through them, telling an eloquent tale of the frightful closeness and heat of the atmosphere down there, while at frequent intervals could be heard the sound of a restless stirring on the part of the living cargo, accompanied by a long-drawn, gasping sigh, as if for breath. There was usually a good deal of carelessness and remissness manifested by the men in the removal of the gratings in the morning. I have frequently gone on deck at seven bells—when it was my eight hours in—and found them still on, although it was well understood that they were to be taken off at four bells. I was always very particular, when it was my morning watch on deck, to have the gratings removed prompt to time; on this particular morning, however, I did not wait until four bells, but took it upon myself to have the hatches thrown open as soon as there was daylight enough to enable us to see clearly, and I am sure that the poor wretches below were grateful for even so small a measure of relief.

As the day advanced the heat grew

intolerable, and the consequent suffering of the blacks more intense. It is the custom on board slavers, I believe —at least it was so on board the *Francesca*—to feed the slaves twice a day, the food consisting of a fairly liberal quantity of boiled rice, farina, or calavance beans—these latter being used on account of their great fattening powers, whereby the slaves are maintained in a tolerably good condition of body—with a pint of water at each meal. Mendouca made it a rule to vary the diet of the slaves as much as possible on these three articles, one or the other of which was given every third day, he having found that the poor wretches thus thrived better, and took their food with more enjoyment than when fed during the entire voyage upon one kind of food only; and whenever the weather was sufficiently moderate to permit of it, he always had one-half of the slaves on deck for an airing during the time that the other half were being fed below, thus allowing room for the men who dispensed the food and water to move about, and also for the slaves to use their hands in the process of feeding; and on the particular morning of which I am now writing it was unspeakably moving and pathetic to note, as I did, the feverish eagerness and longing with which the unhappy creatures waited and watched for the arrival of the moment when they might come on deck and breathe for a few brief minutes the pure and—to them—cool and refreshing outer atmosphere. My heart ached with pity for them, and I determined that I would utilize my presence on board this accursed ship by doing everything in my power to ameliorate as far as possible the condition of the unfortunates that were imprisoned within her. And I made up my mind to begin on that very morning, if, when Mendouca made his appearance, he seemed to be in a temper amenable to persuasion.

When he came on deck, however, the conditions appeared anything but promising, for he was in a frightfully bad humour at the calm, cursing the weather, his own ill-luck, and everything else that he could think of to execrate. I allowed him to give unrestrained vent to his ill-humour for some minutes, and when at length he had calmed down somewhat I said—

"And yet it appears to me that this calm, about which you are complaining so bitterly, may be made excellent use of, if you will, to benefit and increase the value of your property."

"Indeed ? in what way, pray ? " he demanded.

"Well," said I, "there is no sail trimming to be done in this weather, and it would be downright cruelty to send the men aloft to work about the rigging in this blazing heat ; why not therefore spread an awning aft, here, and set the entire watch to work, beneath its shade, to patch up such of your canvas as needs repairing ? And while they are engaged upon that job I will see—if you approve of the plan—whether I cannot get the negroes to take a bath in batches in a studding-sail rigged on the fore-deck, and thus rid themselves of some of the filth that is fast accumulating on their bodies ; it will do them more good and tend more to keep them in health than a double allowance of food for the remainder of the voyage. And when they have done that they can be divided into two gangs, one on deck to draw and pass water, and the other below, with all the scrubbing brushes and swabs that can be mustered, to give the slave-deck a thorough cleansing. That is what I should do, were they my property."

"Well,' he said musingly, "I dare say it would do the rascals a lot of good, and would certainly make the ship sweeter—I'll be bound that she could be scented a mile away in her present condition. But who is to undertake the supervision of such work ? Not *I*, I tell you, frankly ; and I believe the hands would refuse, to a man, were I to attempt to set them to such work."

"If they will rig me a studding-sail, or an old fore course for'ard, I will do the rest—or *try* to do it," said I.

"Will you ?" exclaimed Mendouca, in surprise. "Then I am sure you may, and I heartily wish you joy of the job."

"Very well, then, I will set about it the first thing after breakfast," said I.

And I did. I got the poor wretches forward in batches of thirty, induced them to stand in the basin-like hollow of the sail, and then set half-a-dozen of their number pumping and drawing water, and playing upon their fellows with the hose, or sluicing buckets of water over them, and the exquisite enjoyment, the unspeakable luxury of that bath, as the cool, sparkling liquid dashed upon the filth and sweat-begrimed bodies, was a sight to see ! Enjoyed it ? Why they revelled in it, so

that it was with difficulty that I could get them out ; the stony look of hopeless, utter despair faded temporarily out of their eyes, and some of them actually *laughed !* It was by no means a pleasant or a savoury job that I had undertaken, but witnessing the keen enjoyment that I had thus bestowed made it the most delightful that I had ever been engaged in. It occupied me the whole morning to pass the entire cargo through the bath and secure the thorough cleansing of their persons, and the whole of the afternoon to get the slave-deck properly cleansed and purified ; but when the sun set that evening the ship was once more sweet and wholesome, while the slaves had—taking one with another—been on deck and actively exercised for about half a day instead of about twenty minutes morning and evening. As I had said, it did them more good than double rations for the entire voyage. Even Mendouca was fain to acknowledge that the day, instead of being wasted, had been well spent.

We had been hoping all day that with sunset a breeze would spring up from *somewhere*—I think nobody was very particular as to the quarter from which it should come, so long as it came at all—but our hopes were doomed to disappointment ; the sun went down in a perfectly clear sky, and there was no sign whatever of wind from any quarter. The same weather conditions prevailed all through the night ; and when the sun rose next morning there was still not the slightest sign of wind, while the glass exhibited a slight tendency to rise. Under these circumstances I thought I would endeavour to secure a repetition of the proceedings of the previous day, and so well pleased was Mendouca with the improved appearance of the blacks when, as usual, half of them came on deck at breakfast-time, that he readily gave his consent ; and accordingly the poor creatures were again treated to the luxury of the bath, while the slave-deck received another thorough scrubbing to cleanse it from the filth accumulated during the night. And thus the negroes were enabled to pass a second day in pure air, to the great improvement of their health and spirits ; indeed, the ecstatic delight with which they lingered over their bath, and the cheerfulness with which they afterwards worked at their task of drawing water and scrubbing, chattering almost gaily together all the time, were, to me, most eloquent testimony as to the miseries that they had previously endured, cooped up, tightly wedged together, *day and night*, in the close and noisome hold.

I must not omit to mention a very curious phenomenon of which I had often heard, but had never before beheld until this day. It is known among sailors as the phenomenon of "the ripples." I was on the forecastle superintending the bathing operations when it first made its appearance, the sky being at the time clear and cloudless, with the sun blazing in its midst like a huge ball of living flame, while the water was so oil-smooth and glassy that it was quite impossible to distinguish the horizon, or to determine where the sea ended and the sky began. It was hotter than I had ever felt it before; dressed only in a thin shirt and the thinnest of white trousers, the perspiration was gushing so freely from every pore of my body that my light and airy garments were saturated with it, while the atmosphere was so stagnant that it seemed impossible to inhale a sufficiency of air for breathing purposes. Under these trying conditions we were, of course, all anxiously watching for a breeze; and it was with a feeling of exquisite delight that, happening to look abroad toward the north, I saw the horizon strongly marked with a line of delicate blue, indicating, as I believed, the approach of a thrice-welcome breeze. In the exuberance of my delight I shouted to Mendouca, who was reclining in a hammock aft slung from the main-boom, and, of course, under the shelter of the awning—

"Hurrah! here comes a breeze at last, although I do not know where it has sprung from, for there is not a cloud to be seen."

Mendouca sprang up in his hammock at this news, and looked in the direction to which I was pointing; then sank back again, disgustedly.

"Pshaw, that is no breeze—worse luck!" he cried. "That is only 'the ripples.'"

"The ripples?" I ejaculated. "Surely not. It has every appearance of a genuine breeze!"

Mendouca, however, was too intensely disgusted to reply. Meanwhile, the streak of blue, stretching right athwart the horizon, was advancing rapidly, bearing straight down upon the brigantine, and soon it became possible to see the tiny wavelets sparkling in the dazzling sunlight, and to detect a soft, musical, liquid-tinkling sound, such as one may hear when the tide is rising on a flat, sandy beach on a calm summer's day. But by this time I had made the disappointing discovery that the blue line was merely a belt of rippling water about a quarter of a mile wide, with a perfectly calm, glassy surface beyond it, and, as there was no advance-guard of cat's-paws, such as may usually be seen playing on the surface of the water as forerunners of an approaching breeze, I was reluctantly compelled to acknowledge to myself that Mendouca was right. And so it proved; for although the line—or rather belt—of rippling water not only advanced right up to the ship, giving forth a most pleasant and refreshing liquid sound as it came, and lapping musically against the brigantine's sides for a few minutes when it reached her, but also passed on and traversed the entire visible surface of the ocean, finally disappearing beyond the southern horizon, the whole phenomenon was absolutely unaccompanied by the slightest perceptible movement of the air. This curious disturbance of the ocean's surface was twice repeated on that same day.

The long, hot, breathless, and wearisome day at length drew to an end, and still there was no sign of wind; the night passed; another day dawned; and still we lay, like the craft in Coleridge's *Ancient Mariner*, "as idle as a painted ship upon a painted ocean." That day too waxed and waned without the sign of so much as a cat's-paw to revive our drooping hopes; and although during the succeeding night we were visited by a terrific thunderstorm, accompanied by a perfect deluge of rain, during which a few evanescent puffs intermittently filled our sails, and moved us perhaps a mile nearer Cuba, when day again dawned there was a further recurrence of the same staring, cloudless sky of dazzling blue, the same blazing sun, the same breathless atmosphere, and the same oil-smooth sea. And as these days of calm and stagnation succeeded each other with relentless persistency, I kept up the custom of bathing the negroes and thoroughly cleansing the slave-deck, until at length the poor creatures actually grew fat and merry, so that Mendouca, despite his fast-growing impatience and irritability at the continued calm, was obliged to admit that he had never seen a cargo of "black ivory" in such promising condition before. This, however, was not all; for while superintending these bathing and scrubbing operations I talked cheerfully and pleasantly to the fellows, giving them such names as Tom, Bob, Joe, Snowball, and so on, to which they readily answered, instead of abusing them and ordering them about with brutal oaths and obscenity, as was the habit of the crew; and although the poor wretches understood not a word of what was spoken to them either by the crew or by myself, yet they readily enough distinguished the difference of manner, and not only so, but they seemed to possess the faculty of interpreting one's meaning from the tones of one's voice, so that they quickly grew to understand what I wanted them to do, and did it cheerfully and with alacrity. In this manner, with persistent calm recurring day after day, we passed no less than the almost incredible time of over three weeks without moving as many miles from the spot where the wind had deserted us, Mendouca's temper growing steadily worse every day, until at length he became absolutely unbearable, and I spoke to him as little as possible. And the climax was reached when one day the steward, who had been sent down into the hold to overhaul the stores, came on deck with a face as long as the main-bowline, and reported that there was only food and water enough in the ship to last ten days longer.

CHAPTER XIV

"ONLY ten days longer?" roared Mendouca, his face livid with fury and consternation. "Nonsense, Juan! you must have made some stupid mistake; there surely is—there *must* be—more than that!"

"I have not made any mistake at all, señor," answered the man sulkily; "it is just as I have said; there are only provisions and water enough to last us, on a full allowance, ten days longer."

"Then, if that is the case, all hands must be put on short allowance—half rations—at once!" exclaimed Mendouca, with an oath. "But, stop a little; there *must* be some mistake. Light your lantern again, and I will go down below with you, and satisfy myself on the point."

Accordingly Mendouca and the steward went down into the hold together, and gave the stores an exhaustive overhaul, with the result that the original report of the latter was fully confirmed!

Mendouca came up from the hold, raging like a maniac, cursing the weather, the provisions, and everything else that he could think of, including myself, whom he denounced as a Jonah, his ill-luck having commenced, according to his assertion, with the sparing of my life and my reception on board the *Francesca*. As for the calm, he declared that it should detain him no longer; and, having searched the sky and examined the barometer in vain for any signs of a change, he gave orders for all canvas to be furled, and for the negroes to be set to work forthwith upon the sweeps, his intention being, as he stated, to keep them at it in relays or gangs until the region of apparently eternal calm had been left, and a breeze of some sort found. There were ten of these sweeps, or long, heavy oars, working through the ports, in beckets firmly lashed to ringbolts in the stanchions, that were evidently placed there expressly for that particular purpose. The loom of the sweep was long enough to admit of four men working at it, and accordingly the boatswain, having received his orders from Mendouca, selected forty of the strongest-looking of the negroes, and set them to this exhausting labour, the rest of the unfortunate creatures being driven below out of the way. The vessel, lying there inert as a log on the water, proved very heavy to start, especially as the blacks knew not how to handle the sweeps, having evidently never touched one before; but, once fairly started, the craft was kept moving with comparative ease at a speed of about three and a half knots per hour. But it was cruel work for the unhappy blacks, who, naked as when they were born, were remorselessly kept at it by the boatswain and his mate, both of whom paced the deck, fore and aft, armed with a heavy "colt," which they plied unmercifully upon the shoulders of any man whom they chose to believe was not fully exerting himself, although the perspiration poured from the dark naked hides like rain. "Short spells and hard work" was, however, the order of the day, and after half-an-hour of almost superhuman exertion a relief was called, a fresh gang was set to work, and the exhausted toilers were hustled below to rest and recover themselves as best they could. I remonstrated hotly with Mendouca upon the needless cruelty practised by the boatswain and his mate, but I was roughly told that I did not know what I was talking about; that negroes would never work unless kept continually in wholesome dread of the lash; and that it was absolutely necessary to get every ounce of work out of them if we were not one and all to perish miserably of hunger and thirst. So, as I could do no better, I got a piece of the oldest and softest canvas I could find, and a bucket of water, with which I descended to the slave-deck and carefully bathed the poor lacerated shoulders of those unfortunates who had suffered most severely at the hands of the boatswain and his mate, a little piece of attention that I saw was most gratefully received.

We made fully twenty miles of westing that day, from the time when the negroes were first set to work up to sunset, to Mendouca's great gratification. Indeed, so delighted was he with his own brilliant idea, that he did that night what I had never known him to do before, he indulged rather too freely in the contents of the rum-bottle. And, as a consequence, he grew garrulous and good-humouredly sarcastic over the efforts made for the suppression of the slave-trade, which he emphatically asserted would never be put down.

"One very serious disadvantage which you labour under," he remarked, referring particularly to the operations of the British slave-squadron, " is that you are altogether too confiding and credulous; you accept every man as honest and straightforward until you have learned, to your cost, that he is the reverse. Take the case, for example, of your attack upon Chango Creek. You were led to undertake it upon the representations made and the information given by Lobo, the Portuguese trader of Banana Point, weren't you? Oh, I know all about it, I have heard the whole story," he interrupted himself to say, in reply to my ejaculation of surprise. "You were all very much obliged to Lobo, of course; and your captain paid him handsomely for his information and assistance. I suppose there was not one of you, from the captain downward, who ever had the ghost of a suspicion that the fellow was playing you false, and that the affair was a bold yet carefully arranged plot to exterminate the whole of you, and destroy your ship, eh? No; of course you hadn't; yet I give you my word that it *was*. Ay; and the only wonder to me was that it did not succeed. I suppose it was that you had a good deal more fight in you than any of them gave you credit for; and that is where so many excellently arranged traps have failed; the plotters have never made sufficient allowance for the fighting powers of the British, as I have told them over and over again. It was just that important oversight that caused what ought to have been a splendid success to result in a serious disaster; the intention was good, but, as is much too often the case, they had reckoned without their host."

"But I do not understand," I cut in, as Mendouca paused. "What was the plot? and how was Lobo concerned in it? It appears to me that the man acted in perfect good faith; he gave us certain information which proved to be substantially correct—except that he was mistaken as to the force that we should have to encounter—and he safely piloted us to the spot from which our boat attack was to be made; I can see nothing like a plot or treachery in that."

"No; of course you cannot, you sweet innocent," retorted Mendouca, with fine sarcasm, "for the simple reason, as I say, that the British are altogether too trustful and confiding to see treachery or double-dealing until it is thrust openly in their faces. You are altogether too simple and unsuspicious, you navy men, to deal with the tricks and ruses of the slave-dealing fraternity; and before your eyes are opened you either die of fever, or are killed in some brush with us, or are invalided home."

"It may be so," I agreed; "but so general a statement as that does not in the least help me to see what was the character of Lobo's plot, or even that there was a plot at all."

"Well, I will tell you," said Mendouca thickly, helping himself to another caulker of rum—he had already swallowed two tumblers of stiff grog since the subject had been broached, in addition to what he had previously taken—"I will tell you, because, having made up my mind that you shall never rejoin your own people, the information is not likely to do Lobo any harm. When you arrived at Banana

Point on that particular morning, your presence seriously threatened to entirely upset a very important transaction which Señor Lobo had in hand, namely, the disposal and shipment of a prime lot of nearly a thousand able-bodied, full-grown, male blacks that he had got snugly stowed away in two big barracoons a short distance up the creek from his factory. Had your captain taken it into his head to land a party and make a search of the peninsula, the barracoons would have been discovered, and friend Lobo would have been a ruined man. So, as soon as your brig was identified as a man-o'-war—and that was as soon as she could be distinctly made out—another mistake that you man-o'-war's men make, friend Dugdale ; you can scarcely ever bring yourselves to disguise your ships ; they declare their character as far as it is possible to see them.—Let me see, what was I saying? I have run clean off my course, and don't know where I am."

"You were going to tell me what happened when the *Barracouta* was identified from Banana Point as a man-o'-war," said I.

"Ah, yes, exactly," answered Mendouca. "Well, as soon as it was discovered that your brig was a British man-o'-war, every available hand was set to work to clear everything of an incriminating character out of the two brigs that were going to ship the slaves ; so that, should you overhaul them—as I was told you did—nothing might be found on board to justify their seizure. This job was successfully completed only a few minutes before you entered the creek. But that would have availed Lobo nothing had your captain happened to have thought of landing upon the peninsula ; the next thing, therefore, was to furnish him with a totally different subject to think about ; and this Lobo found in the opportune presence of the four craft in Chango Creek. The captains of three out of the four vessels happened to be down at Banana when you arrived ; and Lobo—who is gifted with quite an unusual measure of persuasiveness—had very little difficulty in convincing them that you would be absolutely certain to discover their hiding-place sooner or later, and that consequently it would be a good plan to inveigle you into making an immediate attack upon them ; when, by concerting proper measures of

defence, they might succeed in practically annihilating you, and so sweeping a formidable enemy out of their path. The three skippers fell in readily with his plan, when he had propounded it, and also undertook to secure the cooperation of the fourth ; and· as the creek offered exceptional facilities for a successful defence, it was accepted that you were all as good as done for, especially as Lobo had undertaken to cut the brig adrift at the right moment, so that she might be driven ashore and rendered useless for the time being, if not altogether. This matter arranged, the slave-captains left Banana forthwith to carry out their plans for the defence of the creek, taking a short cut by way of the back of the creek, and taking with them also every available man that Lobo could spare ; the idea being to allow you to advance unmolested as far as the boom—which they never dreamed that you would succeed in forcing—and then destroy you by a musketry fire from the banks, when, weakened by your unavailing attack upon the boom, you should at length be compelled to retire. Your astounding pluck and perseverance in forcing the boom completely upset all their plans, and converted what would have been for them an easy and bloodless victory into a disastrous defeat, while it saved the lives of the survivors of the attacking party. But though it turned out disastrously for Aravares, of the *Mercedes*, and his friends, the plot served Lobo's purpose perfectly ; the shipping of the slaves on board the two brigs which were waiting for them proceeding immediately that you were clear of the creek, and both vessels getting away to sea that same night. So that, you see, it is by no means as difficult a matter to deceive and hoodwink you man-o'-war people as you choose to suppose."

"No," answered I ; "so it would seem. Yet, by your own showing, we were not the only deceived parties ; and, after all, the attack was successful, so far as we were concerned."

"That is very true, and only confirms what I have always insisted upon ; namely, that, in making their plans, foreigners do not allow sufficiently for British pluck and obstinacy. Now *I* do ; I never leave anything to chance, but always lay my plans so carefully that the destruction or capture of my enemies is an absolute certainty. But for such careful forethought on my part, the *Sapphire's* two boats would never have fallen into my power."

"The *Sapphire's* boats?" I exclaimed. "Surely you do not mean to tell me that *you* are responsible for the massacre of those two boats' crews?"

"No, not the massacre of them, certainly, but their capture," answered Mendouca, with a smile of gratified pride.

"And are the people still alive, then?" I asked.

"They were when I last heard of them," answered Mendouca. "But it is quite possible that by this time they —or at least a part of them—have been tortured to death by Matadi— the chief to whom I sold them—as a sacrifice to his fetish."

"Gracious powers, how horrible!" I exclaimed. "And to think that you, an Englishman, could consign your fellow-countrymen to such a fate as that!"

"Why not?" demanded Mendouca fiercely; "why should I be more gentle to my countrymen than they have been to me? Do you think that, because I carry my fate lightly and gaily, I do not feel keenly the depth to which I have fallen? I might have been a post-captain by this time, honoured and distinguished for great services worthily rendered; but I am instead a slaver and a pirate masquerading under the disguise of a Spanish name. Do you think I am insensible of the immeasurable gulf that separates me from what I might have been? And it is my own countrymen who have opened that gulf—who have robbed me of the opportunity of reaching that proud eminence that was at one time all but within my reach, and have hurled me into the abyss of crime and infamy in which you find me. And you are surprised, forsooth, that I should avenge myself whenever the opportunity comes!"

I knew now from experience that it was quite useless to argue with Mendouca when he got upon the subject of his grievances; I therefore gave the conversation a turn by asking—

"Where, then, are these wretched people now, if indeed they are still alive?"

"I presume," answered he, "that, if still alive, as you say, they are where I last heard of them; namely, at Matadi's village; a place on the south bank of the Congo, about one hundred miles, or rather more, from its mouth. But why do you take such a profound interest in them?" he asked. "Possibly you are contemplating the formation of an expedition for their rescue, as soon as you have effected your escape from me?" and he laughed satirically.

My reply and his laugh were alike cut short by the sound of heavy footsteps on the companion-ladder outside the cabin, and the next moment the boatswain made his appearance in the doorway with the intimation that a craft of some sort had just been made out, at a distance of about three miles broad on the starboard bow; and he wished to know whether the course of the brigantine was to be altered or not.

Mendouca sprang to his feet and hurried on deck, I following him.

On our first emergence from the brilliantly-lighted cabin the night appeared to be dark; but as our eyes accommodated themselves to the change of conditions, it became apparent that the cloudless sky was thickly gemmed and powdered with stars of all magnitudes, from those of the first order down to the star-dust constituting the broad belt of the Milky Way, all gleaming with that soft, resplendent lustre that is only to be witnessed within the zone of the tropics. Moreover, there was a young moon, a delicate, crescent-shaped paring, about two days old, hanging low in the western sky, yet capable, in that pure, translucent atmosphere, of yielding quite an appreciable amount of light. The water was still smooth as polished glass, even the swell having gone down so completely that its undulations were not to be detected by even the delicate test of watching the star reflections in the polished depths, while the brigantine was as steady as though still on the stocks where she took form and substance. The negroes were still toiling at the sweeps, and the watch, armed to the teeth, were clustered fore and aft, on the alert to guard against any attempt at an outbreak among them. The canvas was all closely furled, so that we had an uninterrupted view of the sky from horizon to zenith, all around, toward the latter of which the delicate, tapering, naked spars pointed as steadily as the spires of a church. The boatswain, however, was eagerly directing Mendouca's attention toward a small, dark object, broad on our starboard bow ; and turning my gaze toward it, I made out a brig under her two topsails, jib, and trysail, with her courses in the brails. Mendouca had already seized the night-glass, and with its aid was subjecting her to a prolonged and searching scrutiny, upon the completion of which he handed the instrument to me, with the remark, in English—

"Take a good look at her, Dugdale, and tell me what you think of her ?"

I took the glass, and, having brought the stranger into its field, soon managed, by an adjustment of the focus, to get a clear, sharply-defined image of her, as she floated motionless, a black silhouette, against the deep, velvety, purple-black, star-spankled sky. And as I did so a certain sense of familiarity with the delicate, diminutive . black picture upon which I was gazing thrilled through me. Surely I knew that low, long, shapely hull ; those lofty, slightly-raking masts ; those spacious topsails? Even the very steeve of the bowsprit seemed familiar to me, and I felt certain that the superbly cut jib and handsome trysail could belong only to the *Barracouta!* And, if so, how was I to act ? It was plainly my duty to do anything and everything that might be in my power to promote the capture of the daring slaver and unscrupulous pirate, whose guest—or prisoner —I was ; but had I the power to do *anything?* With that now thoroughly alert and even suspicious individual at my side, and the watch on deck all about me, it was clearly evident that nothing in the shape of signalling could even be attempted with the slightest hope or chance of success ; and the only other mode of action that remained to me appeared to be to carefully conceal my knowledge—or, rather, very strong suspicion—as to the identity of the brig. I had barely arrived at this conclusion when Mendouca, with an accent of impatience, interrupted my reverie with the exclamation—

"Well, surely you have seen all that it is possible to see by this time ? Or cannot you quite make up your mind as to her character ?"

"I have an impression that I have seen her before, and it seems to me that she bears a very striking resemblance to the Spanish brig that was lying off Lobo's factory on the day of our first arrival in the Congo," said I ; the happy idea suggesting itself to me, as I began to speak, that I might safely make this statement without any breach of the truth, all of us on board the *Barracouta* having observed and remarked upon the striking resemblance between the two craft.

"Um l it *may* be so," muttered Mendouca, with a strong accent of doubt in his voice, however. "Let me have another look at her."

I handed over the glass with alacrity, for it was about my last wish just then to be questioned too closely as to the character of the stranger ; and Mendouca subjected her to a further long and exhaustive scrutiny. At its termination he turned to me, and, with an accent of unmistakable suspicion, inquired—

"It hasn't suggested itself to yoμ, I suppose, that yonder craft may be a British man-o'-war ? You have seen nothing so like her in your own squadron as to lead to the suspicion that she may be a dangerous enemy whom I ought to be promptly warned to avoid ? "

Now, had I not known that he had never seen the *Barracouta*, I should have scarcely known what reply to give to this home question ; as it was, however, I answered at hazard—

"Well, at this distance yonder vessel offers to my eye very little resemblance to the usual type of British gun-brig ; she is longer, and much lower in the water, and her masts are certainly further apart than is the case with our brigs generally, you must see that for yourself ; and it would be unreasonable to expect me to give a more decided opinion at this distance and in so vague a light."

"Will you swear to me that you are honestly of opinion that yon brig is *not* a man-o'-war ? "

"Certainly not," answered I, with pretended annoyance at his pertinacity. "She may be, or she may not be ; it is quite impossible to express a more decided opinion, under the circumstances, and I therefore must decline to do so."

And I turned and walked away from him with an air of petulance.

Mendouca laid down the telescope, walked to the binnacle, and peered intently for a moment at the compass.

"Keep her way two points more to the southward," he ordered the helmsman.

This alteration in our course brought the brig about one point before our beam, distant about two and a half miles, and if persisted in, would soon have the effect of increasing the distance between the two craft; and, unless we were already seen, rendered it quite possible that we might slip past unobserved, our spars standing naked to the dark sky, and our hull lying low upon the equally dark water. There was, however, the hope that, even at the distance separating the two vessels, the roll and grinding of the heavy sweeps would be heard in the perfect stillness of air and water; and I felt confident that, if yonder brig were indeed the *Barracouta*, and the sounds referred to extended so far as to reach the sharp ears on board her, they would be identified, and their significance at once understood. But even as the thought passed through my mind it seemed to have also occurred to Mendouca; for he strode toward the waist and exclaimed in a low, clear voice that was distinctly audible fore and aft, but which would probably not have been audible half a cable's length away—

"Let those niggers knock off sweeping for the present, and send them below. And as soon as they are there and you have clapped the hatches on—noiselessly, mind—let all hands set to work to muffle the sweeps with mats, old canvas, pads of oakum, or anything else that you can lay your hands upon. It is unfortunate that this was not thought of before; but it may not yet be too late."

The negroes, grateful for this unexpected respite from their exhausting toil, and of course quite ignorant as to its cause, gladly tumbled below, and the gratings were carefully secured over them. Meanwhile the boatswain, with one hand, dived below, and in a short time the two men reappeared with a load of miscellaneous stuff and some balls of spun yarn; and all hands went diligently to work under Mendouca's personal supervision, to muffle the sweeps, which was so effectually done that when, half-an-hour later, they were again manned, they worked with scarcely a sound beyond the rather heavy splash of their blades in the water. Meanwhile, during the progress of the muffling process—in which I had not offered to participate—I kept a keen watch upon the distant brig, taking an occasional squint at her through the night-glass when I thought it possible to do so without attracting Mendouca's attention. I do not quite know what I expected to see, for of course I knew perfectly well that every eye in the brig might be steadfastly watching us, without our being able to detect any sign of such scrutiny; and I was moreover fully aware that should we have been discovered, and our character suspected, no visible indication of such discovery or suspicion would be permitted to reveal itself to our eyes; and the same studied concealment would equally apply to the preparations for any investigation that they might be moved to undertake. Still, I thought it just barely possible that by maintaining a strict watch I might chance to detect some sign of alertness on board the brig, if she were indeed the *Barracouta*, as I strongly suspected. Nor was I disappointed, for I did at length detect such an indication, not on board the brig herself, but at some considerable distance from her, and immediately under the slender crescent of the setting moon, where, while sweeping the surface of the water, moved by some vague instinct, I caught two faint momentary flashes of dim orange radiance that to me had very much the appearance of reflected moonlight glancing off the wet blades of oars. And if this were so it meant that we had been seen, our character very shrewdly suspected—most probably from the steady plying of the sweeps for no more apparently urgent reason than that we were becalmed—and that a surprise attack was about to be attempted from the very quarter where, under the circumstances, it was least likely to be looked for, namely, straight ahead. Of course what I had seen might merely have been a ray of moonlight glancing off the wet body of a porpoise, a whale, or some other sea creature risen to the surface to breathe; but it had so much the appearance of the momentary flash of oars that I was loath to believe it anything else. Assuming it to be what I hoped, my cue was now of course to distract attention as much as possible from that part of the ocean that lay immediately ahead of us; and this could not be better done than by concentrating it upon the brig, which now lay practically abeam of us, a short three miles away. I therefore—no longer surreptitiously but ostentatiously—again brought the night-glass to bear upon her, and allowed myself to be found thus when Mendouca came aft, after having personally superintended the muffling of the sweeps and the putting of them in motion again.

"Well," he said, as he rejoined me, "have you not yet been able to satisfy yourself as to the character of that brig?"

"No," said I; "but, whatever she is, they all seem to be asleep on board her. If she is a slaver, her skipper has more care and consideration for his property than you have, for he at least allows his slaves to rest at night."

"That is quite patent to us all," answered Mendouca drily. "But then, you know, he may not be running short of food and water, as we are. Or—he may not be a slaver."

"Of course," I assented, with the best accent of indifference that I could assume. "But, slaver or no slaver, I have not been able to detect a sign of life on board that brig for the last half-hour, or indeed from the moment when I first began to watch her. I can make out the faint light of her binnacle lamps, and that is all. But the fact of their being allowed to continue shining would seem to argue, to my mind at least, that, be they what they may, they have no reason for attempting to conceal their presence from us. If you feel differently toward them I think you would do well to extinguish your binnacle lights for awhile; the helmsman can steer equally well by a star, of which there are plenty to choose from."

"Yes, of course; you are right," he assented hastily; "there can be no harm in doing that."

And going to the binnacle, he glanced into it, saw that the ship was heading on the course he had last set for her, directed the helmsman to choose a star to steer by, and then himself carefully withdrew the lamps and extinguished them.

CHAPTER XV

THE AFFAIR OF THE 'FRANCESCA' AND THE 'BARRACOUTA'S' BOATS

I CONTINUED to industriously scrutinize the brig through the night-glass, and, by so doing, contrived to keep Mendouca's attention also pretty closely centred upon her; but I could see that he was fully on the alert. He appeared to instinctively scent danger in the air, for he frequently assumed an anxious, listening attitude, with a growing irritability that manifested itself in repeated execration of the slaves for the quite unavoidable splashing sounds that they made in working the sweeps. He was also intently watching the thin crescent of the setting moon that was by this time hanging on the very verge of the western horizon; and I suspected that he was awaiting her disappearance to put in practice some stratagem—such as, perhaps, a further alteration of the ship's course—as an additional safeguard. But, whatever may have been his intentions, they were all altered by an unlucky discovery made by one of the men on the forecastle, who, at the very moment when the moon was in the act of sinking behind the horizon, caught sight for a moment of a large boat full of men strongly outlined against the golden crescent, and immediately reported the fact, coming aft that he might do so without raising his voice.

"A boat!" exclaimed Mendouca anxiously, when the man had told what he had seen. "Are you *quite* sure?"

"As sure as I am that I am now standing here speaking to you, señor," answered the man, in a tone of conviction. "José saw it also. We were both watching the disappearing moon, and when she was about half-way below the horizon we suddenly saw a large boat, pulling, I should say, at least twelve oars, glide swiftly across her face, as though steering to the southward on a line that would cross our course."

"Phew!" ejaculated Mendouca; "that looks serious. For it undoubtedly means that the brig's people are by no means as fast asleep as you have imagined them to be, Dugdale. How far off did you judge the boat to be when you saw her?" he demanded, turning again to the seaman.

"A matter of a mile and a half, or perhaps a trifle more," was the answer.

"Very well, then, that will do," answered Mendouca. "'Forewarned is forearmed,' as the English say. As you go forward pass the word along for the sweeps to be laid in and stowed away, and for the negroes to be sent below, and the hatch gratings put on and secured. And, do you hear, everything must be done as noiselessly as possible."

"Bueno, señor," answered the man, as he turned away to do Mendouca's bidding; and in a few minutes the sweeps were laid in and stowed away, and the brigantine's head gently turned more to the southward, in order that she might drift in that direction as long as she retained her way. Then, the slaves having been driven below and secured, the decks were rapidly but noiselessly cleared for action, the guns were cast loose and loaded, a liberal supply of grape and canister was passed on deck, arms were served out to the men, and the boarding nettings were triced up all round the ship. The whole of the work was executed so rapidly and silently as to clearly demonstrate that the crew was a thoroughly seasoned one, inured to fighting, and by no means averse to it when the chances were in their favour, as they certainly were in the present instance; and I was filled with chagrin and disgust at the thought of how simple an accident had sufficed to mar and defeat what might otherwise have proved a perfect surprise to Mendouca and his crew. Still, although I could not conceal from myself the fact that this apparently trivial accident had placed the attacking party at a woful disadvantage, by warning their antagonists of the intended attack, and thus putting them on the alert, I had seen enough of British pluck to hope that even yet, despite all, it might still prove successful; and I awaited the event with no small anxiety, quite determined that if the slightest chance offered of affording any aid to the assailants, I would avail myself of it, let the consequences to myself be what they would. But Mendouca soon proved that he was not the man to overlook any such peril as this; for presently, when by personal inspection he had satisfied himself that everything was in readiness, he came up to me and said, with just the suspicion of a sneer in the tones of his voice—

"Now, Dugdale, I will not pay you so poor a compliment as to suppose you capable of treacherously making use of your present position on board my ship, to raise your hand against the man who gave you your life, at the moment when his whole attention will be needed to protect himself against outside enemies. Still, your conscience appears to be a very curious and inscrutable thing, and there is no knowing what it may prompt you to do under the influence of excitement and misguided enthusiasm. In order therefore that you may be placed beyond the danger of temptation to do something that you would probably afterwards have cause to bitterly regret, I will ask you to go below to your cabin, where, for your own safety's sake, I will take the liberty of locking you in, with a companion whose duty it will be to see that you remain there and do not commit yourself by any rash act."

"Oh, certainly!" I answered, rather bitterly. "Needs must when the devil drives; so lead on, most courteous señor."

"Look here, Dugdale," said he, apparently rather hurt by my tone, "you must not feel yourself aggrieved at my action in this matter. What I propose to do is for your own good and safety, quite as much as by way of a safeguard of my own. My men are fairly amenable to discipline in their calmer moments, as you have doubtless discovered by this time; but I should be sorry to answer for them in the excitement of a fiercely-contested fight, such as this is likely to be; and since you have persistently refused to join us out and out, I honestly think it will be safer for you to be below out of sight until we have driven those meddlesome boats off."

"Very well," said I; "it must of course be as you please. Only, for mercy's sake, spare me the humiliation of mounting a guard over me!"

He looked me intently in the eyes for a moment, and then said—

"All right, I will; you shall be locked up by yourself. Only, for your own sake, be careful to behave exactly as you would in the presence of a guard; for I promise you that, if I have the slightest reason to suspect any treachery on your part, you will be sorry that I ever spared your life. Now, come along, for there is no time to spare."

I accordingly followed him below and entered my cabin, closing the door behind me, and I immediately heard him turn the key and withdraw it from the lock, after which he went on deck again; and for a time the most perfect stillness and silence reigned throughout the ship.

The silence was not of long duration, however; for I had scarcely been in my cabin ten minutes when I heard a low murmur of voices overhead, and the next instant Mendouca's voice pealed out, loud and clear, in English—

"Ho, the boats ahoy! Who are you, and what do you want?"

There was some reply that I could not catch, the voice evidently coming from a point at some distance from the ship, on the opposite side to that occupied by my cabin. It was probably an inquiry as to name and destination of the brigantine, for Mendouca shouted—

"The *Nubian Queen*, of and for Liverpool, from the Brass river, with oil and ivory. Keep off, or I will fire into you! I warn you that we are armed, and are quite prepared to defend ourselves."

A long hail from the boats now followed, to which Mendouca replied—

"If you do it will be at your peril; I have been cleared out once before just about this same spot, and I do not intend to be robbed a second time. Keep off, I tell you! If you advance another stroke I will fire!"

And instantly afterwards I heard him say to his own men in Spanish—

"Now, lads, you have them all in a cluster, let them have it. Fire!"

The sharp, ringing report of the brigantine's nine-pounders immediately pealed out, and even through the shock and concussion of the discharge I thought that, as I stood with my ear at the open port, I caught the sound of a crash. Whether this was so or not, there could be no mistake about the screams and groans of agony that came floating over the water in response to our broadside, mingled with cries of command, the roll and dash of oars in the water, a rattling volley of musketry, and the deeper notes of two boat-guns fired almost together, the shot of one at least of which I heard and felt strike the hull of the brigantine.

All was now in an instant noise and confusion on deck; the silence that had held the tongues of the crew was now no longer necessary, and the jabber, the oaths, the shouting, the loud, defiant laughs, the rumbling of the gun-carriages, the creaking of tackle-blocks, the thud of rammers and sponges, the calls for cartridges, all combined to create a hubbub that would not have shamed the builders of Babel; and through all and above all rose Mendouca's voice in short, sharp sentences of appeal, encouragement, and direction to his men. I could hear, by the furious grinding of handspikes, the breathless ejaculations

of the men, and the crash of the gun-carriages as the guns were run out, that the *Francesca's* crew were working like demons; and almost before I could have believed it possible, they had again loaded their guns and a second broadside rang out over the still water, to be again followed by a still more gruesome chorus of cries and groans, and the sudden cessation of the sound of the oars, loud above which rose the exultant cheers of the ruffians on deck.

"Hurrah, lads!" I heard Mendouca exclaim joyously; "load again smartly, but with grape and canister only this time. We have checked them for a moment, but they have not yet had enough, I fear; they will come at us again as soon as they have picked up their shipmates, so now is your time; load and let them have it while they are stationary!"

And while he was speaking I could also hear a voice—that, unless I was greatly mistaken, belonged to Young, the first luff of the *Barracouta*—exclaiming at no great distance—

"Pull starboard, back port; now back, hard, all, and let us pick up those poor fellows before the sharks get the scent of them! Easy all; steady, lads, steady; hold water! Now then, my hearties, lay hold of the oars and let us get you inboard sharp; we can't afford to lie here to be peppered. Help the wounded, those of you who are unhurt. That's your sort, Styles, bring him along here; is he still alive, do you think? All right, I have him! Now then, coxswain, heave with a will, but don't hurt the poor fellow more than you can help. Gently, man, gently; now lift handsomely, so——"

Crash! the relentless broadside of the *Francesca* again pealed forth, and again uprose that dismal wail of shrieks in testimony of its too terribly truthful aim. Frantic cheers and shouts of exultation burst from the lips of the slaver's crew, in the midst of which Mendouca's voice rang out—

"Now, stand by, men! here they come; but there is only one boat-load of them, and half their number must be killed or wounded. Stand by with your pikes, pistols, and cutlasses, and let not one of them show his head above the rail. Give them a volley from your pistols as they range alongside, and then trust to cold steel for the rest. *Now* is your time! Fire!"

And at the word there followed a tremendous popping of pistols, mingled with the yells of the men on deck, a British cheer that sent the blood tingling through my veins and made me anathematize my helpless condition, the sharp, ringing clash of steel upon steel, and a furious trampling of bare feet upon the planks overhead.

The scuffle continued for fully three minutes, and must have been very hot while it lasted, for all through the hubbub the cries and groans of the freshly-wounded were continuous. I could hear the dull crunching sound of the sharp cutlasses shearing through bone and muscle, the shrill scream of agony, the heavy thud of bodies falling to the deck, oaths and execrations both in Spanish and in English, shouts of mutual encouragement, yells of deadly hatred, the ceaseless trampling of feet, and all the indescribable medley of sounds that accompany a sharp and stubbornly - contested hand - to - hand conflict; and in my feverish anxiety to share in the struggle I forgot all about Mendouca's warning, and dashed myself frantically against the stout cabin door in an effort to burst my way out. Before, however, I could succeed the hurly-burly suddenly ceased, to be almost instantly followed by a yell of exultation from the crowd overhead as the hasty rattle and splash of oars proclaimed that the attacking party had been driven off.

"Now, men, to your guns again, quick! Load smartly and give them another broadside before they get out of range!" shouted Mendouca. "Sweep them off the face of the water, if you can; let not one of them escape to tell the tale!"

A loud shout of exulting assent to this brutal exhortation pealed forth; and I heard the rumbling of the wheels on the deck as the guns were run in. This was more than I could endure; and again hurling myself furiously against the cabin door, I at length succeeded in bursting it off its hinges. To emerge from the cabin and rush on deck was the work of a moment, and I reached the scene of action just as the loaded guns were being run out.

"Stop!" I shouted. "What are you about to do, men? You have utterly mistaken your captain's orders if you suppose he meant you to fire upon that boat! Order them to secure the guns," I continued, turning to Mendouca; "it surely *cannot* be that you are going to allow the excitement of battle to betray you into the committal of a cold-blooded murder? You have beaten off your enemies, and they are in full retreat; let that satisfy you. Hitherto you have been *fighting*, and, as you are aware, the present state of the law is such that you are held justifiable in your act of self-defence; but should you fire upon that boat now it will be *murder*, and I swear to you that if you do I will testify against you for the deed, if I live so long. Man, have you no regard for *yourself*? Do you suppose that the captain of yonder brig will be content to take the beating off of his boats as a final settlement of this night's doings? I tell you he will follow you and hunt you to the world's end, ay, and *take* you, sooner or later! And what do you suppose will be your fate if you murder that retreating boat's crew? Why, you will swing for the deed, as certainly as that you now stand there glaring at me!"

"Have you finished?" he demanded, in a voice almost inarticulate with fury, his hand resting meanwhile upon the butt of a pistol that was stuck in his sash.

"Yes," said I, "I have. That is to say, I have finished if I have succeeded in preventing the perpetration of an act of miserable cowardice that in your cooler moments would cause you to hate and despise yourself for the remainder of your life; not otherwise."

Slowly he removed his hand from the butt of his pistol and, with a bitter laugh, drew a cigar from his pocket and lighted it.

"Secure the guns!" he shouted to his men. Then walking up to me and clutching me by the shoulder, he said—

"You have triumphed again. But I warn you that some day you will go too far, and pay for your temerity with your life. Do you know that while you were speaking you were actually tottering upon the very brink of the grave? Why I did not blow your brains out, I do not know. Boy, if you have any wish to live out your days, never taunt me with cowardice again! There, go below, and do not let me see you again until I have recovered my self-command, or even yet I shall do you a mischief."

"No," I said, "I will *not* go below; it is my watch on deck, and I mean to keep it. I have no fear of your temper getting the better of you now, so I shall remain where I am—that is, if you will trust me with the charge of the deck. I am fresh, while you are fagged with exertion and excitement, so it is for *you* to go below and get some rest, not I."

Mendouca laughed again, this time quite genially, and said—

"Very well, let it be as you say; I *will* go below and rest. And if it is any comfort to you to know it, I do not mind acknowledging *now* that I am glad you intervened to prevent me from firing on that boat. Keep her as she is going and let the niggers man the sweeps again; you are right about that brig, she will follow us to the world's end—if she can, so we must put all the distance possible between ourselves and her while this calm lasts."

And, repeating to the boatswain his orders respecting the manning of the sweeps, this singular man nodded shortly to me and dived out of sight down the companion-way.

In a few minutes a gang of slaves was again brought on deck and put to the sweeps; and steering a course of about south-south-west, we were soon once more moving through the water at a speed of about three knots. This course was followed all through the night and up to eight o'clock the next morning, at which hour—one of the men having been sent aloft as far as the royal-yard to see whether any sign of the brig could be discovered, and having returned to the deck again with an intimation that the horizon was clear all round — the brigantine's position was pricked off upon the chart and her head once more pointed straight for Cuba.

We had by this time traversed a distance of fully sixty miles under the impulsion of the sweeps alone, and everybody was anxiously watching for some sign of a coming breeze; yet, despite the already long continuance of the calm, the heavens were still as brass to us, clear, cloudless, blue as the fathomless depths beneath our feet, not the merest vestige of cloud to be seen, the mercury still persistently steady at an abnormal height, the sea as smooth and motionless as a sheet of glass, and not the smallest sign to justify us in hoping for any change. The heat was something absolutely phenomenal; the deck planking was so hot that we all had to wear shoes to protect our feet from being scorched; a gang of negroes was kept constantly at work drawing water with which to

flood the deck; yet, despite this precaution, and despite, too, the awnings which were now spread fore and aft, the pitch in the seams of the planking became so soft that if I stood still for only a few seconds I found myself stuck fast. I pitied the unfortunate blacks from the bottom of my heart, for they were relentlessly kept toiling at those horrible sweeps without intermission all through the day, and that, too, upon a short allowance of water; but it was useless to interfere, for even I had begun to understand by this time that, unless the brigantine could be taken out of that awful region of apparently eternal calm, every one of us, black and white together, must inevitably perish miserably of thirst.

This terrible weather lasted all through that and the following day, during which, with torment indescribable from thirst and the lash of the boatswains' colts, the miserable slaves propelled the ship no less a distance than one hundred and fifty miles. Oh, how fervently I begged and entreated Mendouca to have mercy upon the unhappy creatures, and to at least give orders that they must be no more flogged, even if inexorable necessity demanded that they must be kept toiling at the sweeps. But the wretch was as adamant, he laughed and jeered at my sympathy with the poor creatures, and—as much, I believe, to annoy me as for any other reason—persistently refused to give the order, declaring that, since they would receive many a sound flogging when they got ashore—if indeed they ever lived to reach it—it was just as well that they should learn to endure the lash at once. At which brutal statement I went temporarily mad, I think—at all events I did what looked like a thoroughly mad thing; I went on deck and, walking up to the boatswain, informed him that if he or his mate dared to strike a negro again I would knock them both down. Mendouca, highly amused at my heat and excitement on behalf of the negroes, had followed me on deck, probably to see what I would do next; and upon hearing this threat he called out, jeeringly—

"Look out, José, my man! Señor Dugdale has warned you, and you may be sure that if you strike one of those niggers again he will carry out his threat!"

The boatswain saw at once how the land lay, and that Mendouca was only amusing himself at my expense; feeling confident therefore of his captain's countenance and protection, I suppose, he, for answer, raised his colt and smote the nearest negro a savage blow over the shoulders with it.

Of course, after my possibly foolhardy threat there was but one thing to do, and I did it forthwith, hitting out with my whole strength, catching the boatswain fair between the eyes, and rolling him over like a ninepin.

"Ha, ha! well hit!" exclaimed Mendouca, laughing heartily at the sight of the boatswain as he reeled and fell under the feet of the negroes. "I warned you, José, my lad; and now you see the evil results of neglecting my warning! No, no," he hastily continued, starting to his feet; "put up your knife, man; that will never do! I cannot afford to spare Señor Dugdale—at least not just yet—ah! would you? Look out, Dugdale! bravo! well hit again! Serves you right, José; you should never draw your knife upon an unarmed man."

For the fellow had hastily scrambled to his feet, and, with his drawn knife in his hand, made a rush at me, his eyes blazing with fury. And, as the only way of defending myself at the moment, I had seized his uplifted right hand with my left, giving it a wrench that sent the knife spinning over the bulwarks into the sea, while with my right I again knocked him down.

"Now, José," exclaimed Mendouca, "that ends the matter; do you hear? I cannot spare Señor Dugdale, so if he is found with a knife between his ribs I shall hold you responsible for it, and I give you my solemn promise that I will run you up to the yardarm and leave you there until it will not matter to you what becomes of your miserable carcase. And I hope that the thrashing you have received will make you use a little more discrimination in the use of your colt. If a nigger *won't* work, *make* him, by all means; but so long as they are willing to work without thrashing, leave them alone, I say. As for you, Dugdale," he continued, in English, "had I suspected that you really meant to carry out your threat, I would have taken steps to prevent it. I will not have my men interfered with in the execution of their duty. If they do not perform their duty to my satisfaction, *I* will take such steps as may seem necessary for their correction, so you need not trouble yourself further in that direction. Why, man, if I were to give you a free hand, we should have a mutiny in less than a week. Moreover, you have made one deadly enemy by knocking José down, and you may consider yourself exceedingly fortunate if my authority proves sufficient to protect you from his knife. Take care you make no other enemies among the men, or I will not be answerable for your safety."

This occurred shortly before sunset, and all through the hot and breathless night the unhappy negroes were kept toiling at the sweeps in gangs or relays, the result being that when morning dawned the poor wretches seemed, one and all, to be utterly worn out. Yet still there was no respite for them; and when I again attempted to remonstrate with Mendouca, that individual simply pointed to the serene, cloudless sky, with the blazing, merciless sun in the midst, and savagely asked whether I wanted all hands to perish of hunger and thirst. This occurred while we were at breakfast; and when we went on deck at the conclusion of the meal, my enemy the boatswain drew Mendouca's attention to the upper spars and sails of a ship just rising slowly above the horizon on our starboard bow. I never saw so sudden a change in a man's demeanour as took place in that of Mendouca when his eye rested upon that distant object; hitherto he had been growing every day more savage and morose, but now his good-humour suddenly returned to him, and, ordering the brigantine's head to be pointed straight for the stranger, he shouted, in the gladness of his heart—

"Hurrah, lads, there is relief for us at last! We shall find what we want —food and water—on board yon stranger, and also a way of persuading them to let us have it, or I am greatly mistaken!"

The significance of the last part of this remark was, to my mind, unmistakable. If he could not get by fair means what he wanted, Mendouca had already made up his mind to take it by force; in other words, to commit an act of piracy.

I was sorry for the crew of the unlucky craft, for I felt convinced that Mendouca would have but scant consideration for their future wants while satisfying his own ; yet the sight of the stranger filled me with almost delirious delight, for here was a chance —if I could but contrive to avail myself of it—to make my escape from my present surroundings. True, if I were permitted, or could contrive, to throw in my lot with those people yonder, I should probably have to face terrible suffering in the shape of hunger and thirst, but, after all, that would be less unendurable than my present situation ; and I determined that, whatever might happen, I would certainly make an attempt to join them, always provided, of course, that the craft was honest, and not of a similar character to the *Francesca*.

As we neared the stranger she proved to be a handsome, full-rigged ship of about a thousand tons measurement, or thereabouts, and I thought that she had somewhat of the look of one of the new British clipper India-men that were just at this time beginning to supersede the old-fashioned, slow, lumbering tubs that had been considered the correct kind of thing by John Company ; if she were, she would probably have a crew strong enough not only to successfully resist the demands of Mendouca, but also to protect me, should I be able by any pretext to get on board her. The difficulty, of course, would be to do this ; but if, as I rather expected, Mendouca should elect to lay the *Francesca* alongside the ship and endeavour to carry the latter by a *coup de main*, I would board with the rest, taking my chance of being run through or shot down in the attempt, and immediately place myself under the protection of the stranger's crew. It was of course easy enough to arrange this scheme in my own mind, but even a very slight deviation on Mendouca's part from the programme which I expected him to adopt might suffice to nullify it ; nevertheless, it appeared probable that my surmise as to Mendouca's intentions would prove correct, for if he did not mean to lay the stranger aboard and carry her with a rush, I could scarcely understand the boldness with which he was approaching her in broad daylight, with his strongly-manned sweeps proclaiming to the most unsuspicious eye the dubious character of the brigantine.

CHAPTER XVI

THE CAPTURE AND PLUNDERING OF THE 'BANGALORE,' INDIAMAN

IT was just six bells in the afternoon watch when we at length arrived within a distance of about half-a-mile of the stranger, which had by this time been unmistakably made out to be a British passenger ship of one of the crack lines ; first by her having hoisted British colours some time before, and secondly by the crowd of well-dressed ladies and gentlemen that, with the aid of the telescope, we could see congregated on her poop. Mendouca also had hoisted the British ensign, and, to my supreme indignation, a man-o'-war's pennant, his object in doing so being, of course, to disarm suspicion as long as possible, and thus leave the ship only a very brief length of time to prepare for defence when our intention to attack her became no longer possible of concealment. I remonstrated with him upon this desecration of the colours that he had once fought and hoped to win fame under ; but of course my remonstrance was quite useless, the rascal only laughed at me.

Having arrived within the above-named distance of the ship, Mendouca ordered the sweeps to be laid in, and the slaves to be driven below and secured. This done, to my disgust his next order was to hoist out the boats —of which the *Francesca*, unlike most slavers, carried three ; and as soon as they were in the water, the entire crew were armed, and the whole of them, except my especial enemy, José, and an Englishman—a very quiet, inoffensive fellow, whom I was surprised to find among a crew of such ruffians— were ordered down over the side. This completely upset my plans, for, of course, the only way now of reaching the stranger was by means of the boats, or by swimming ; and while I would gladly have gone in one of the boats, and taken my chance of reaching the stranger's deck alive, I was not quite prepared to throw away my life in an unsuccessful effort to swim to the ship —for that is what it would have meant, the water being alive with sharks that had followed us, day after day, with alarming persistency, ever since we had taken to the use of the sweeps. Besides which, I should of course not have been permitted to make the attempt. Of course, had I chosen to tell a deliberate falsehood, and declared my readiness to throw in my lot with Mendouca and his crew, it is possible that I might have been given the command of one of the boats ; but not even for the purpose of effecting my escape did I consider that such a course would be justifiable. So I had perforce to remain where I was, under the jealously watchful eye of José, if not of the Englishman also ; Mendouca asking me ironically, as he went down the side last of all, whether I had no letters for home or elsewhere that I would like to forward by means of the stranger.

Now that the sweeps were laid in, and their everlasting grind and roll and splash were no longer heard, the silence of nature seemed so profound as to be almost awe-inspiring ; there was literally not a sound to be heard save such as were caused by human agency, such as the movements and voices of the men in the boats, or the gasping sighs of the unhappy negroes cooped up below in the stifling hold. Occasionally a slight murmur of sound reached us from the distant ship ; the call of an officer uttering a command, the "Yo-heave-oh" of the crew, or a gang of them, engaged upon some heavy job, and an occasional rumbling that to my ear sounded very much like that of carronade slides in process of being trained to bear upon some object. But if the ship was armed there was no sign of it, her sides being decorated with *painted* ports only, so far as I could see. When, however, the boats had traversed about half the distance between the brigantine and the ship, a man appeared in the mizen rigging of the latter, and, hailing them in English in a voice which rendered his words perfectly audible to us on board the *Francesca*, demanded to know what they wanted. I saw Mendouca rise in the stern-sheets of his boat, and heard him make some reply, but I could not distinguish what it was, perhaps because he had intentionally made it unintelligible. Whatever the words may have been, they were clearly unsatisfactory ; for the figure in the rigging waved its hand warningly, and shouted—

"Keep off, whoever you are ; you are far too strong a party to be allowed to come alongside us ; and I warn you that if you attempt to do so we shall fire upon you ! If you have any legitimate business with us let *one* boat,

with a crew of not more than five, come alongside, and welcome ; but we will not have the whole of you if we can help it, and I think we can ! "

The boats had, up to this time, been paddling quietly and composedly along, the men evidently husbanding their strength for a final effort ; but now, in response to a shout from Mendouca, they bent to their work, and sent the boats foaming along in a style for which I certainly should never have given them credit ; they could scarcely have done better had they been the British man-o'-war's men that they had pretended to be ; the oars bent, the water was churned into foam, and a miniature surge gathered under each boat's bow as the little craft was suddenly urged to racing speed. Then the figure in the ship's mizen rigging waved an arm, and stepped quietly down on to the poop, which by this time was occupied only by a band of men — evidently passengers — who, under the leadership of a military-looking man, were handling their muskets and making ready to open fire. At the signal given by the individual who had just stepped out of the ship's rigging—and who was no doubt her captain—eight hitherto closed ports in the stranger's bulwarks were suddenly thrown open, as many dark, threatening, iron muzzles appeared, and, at a second command, the whole eight blazed forth, and their contents, consisting of round-shot with a charge of grape on top of each, went hurtling through the air in the direction of the boats. The aim was excellent, the shot flashing up the water all round the boats ; but, so far as I could see, not a man among either of their crews was touched. I heard Mendouca cheer his men on, urging them to stretch out, and get so close to the ship, that by the time that the guns were again loaded, it would be impossible to depress the muzzles sufficiently to hit the boats ; and the men responded with the nearest approach to a cheer that, I suppose, a Spaniard can give, pulling manfully the while. The ship's crew were, however, too quick for them, and managed to give them another broadside just before the boats got within the critical limit where it would have been impossible to touch them ; and this time the discharge was very much more effective, a round-shot striking Mendouca's own boat square on the stem just at the water-line, destroying her bows and tearing several feet of her keel away, while the accompanying charge of grape bowled over three of her men and shattered Mendouca's left arm at the elbow. The crews of the other two boats suffered nearly as badly, one of them losing three men, while the other lost one man killed and five more or less severely wounded, besides having to stop and pick up Mendouca and his crew, his boat sinking almost immediately.

I thought that this severe punishment would have sufficed the Spaniards, and that they would have abandoned the attack, and so, I imagine, thought the skipper of the ship, for while they were in this perilous predicament, he magnanimously withheld his fire, giving them an opportunity to retire without further loss. And so they would, in all probability, had Mendouca been a born Spaniard. But, renegade as he was, the British blood in his veins still told, and, despite the anguish of his terrible wound, he no sooner found himself in the boat that picked him up than his voice again rang out almost as loudly and clearly as before, still urging his men to press forward, and reminding them that they were fighting for their lives, or—what was the same thing—food and water. It was probably this reminder that turned the scale among the waverers, for at the mention of the word "water" they again seized their oars, and with a yell gave way for the ship. Evidently exasperated at this quite unexpected exhibition of determination on the part of the pirates, the little band on the poop now opened a smart and very galling fire with their muskets upon the boats, and I saw three or four pairs of arms tossed skyward as the discharge rattled forth. But before the weapons of this little party of volunteers could be reloaded the boats were alongside the ship, the pirates dropped their oars, and made a simultaneous dash for the fore and main channels, and there instantly ensued a desperate *mêlée*, in which the popping of pistols was for the first half-minute or so a very prominent feature. I fully expected to see Mendouca and his crew driven back into their boats with a very heavy loss; but, to my astonishment and sorrow, I soon saw that they were more than holding their own, and in less than three minutes they had actually forced their way inboard, and the fight was transferred to the

ship's decks. It was evident that the British crew were now making a most determined and desperate resistance, for the fight was protracted to fully a quarter of an hour, the clink and clash of steel, the shouts of the combatants, and the cries of the wounded being distinctly audible to us on the deck of the *Francesca*. Then the hubbub suddenly lulled, and I heard cries for quarter, cries which, to my bitter grief, I knew to be the sure indication of defeat on the part of the British crew. Then utter silence fell upon the unfortunate ship for a few minutes, to be broken by the muffled sound of women's shrieks, men's voices uplifted in fierce, impotent anger and denunciation, two or three pistol-shots that sounded as though they had been fired in the ship's cabin, and then silence again; an ominous, dreadful silence that to my foreboding mind might mean the perpetration of horrors to which those already enacted on the blood-stained decks were as nothing.

This silence prevailed for fully an hour, during which no sign of life was visible on board the ship; then arose the sound of hilarious shouts and drunken laughter; there was a sudden stir and commotion about the decks; a crowd of men gathered on the poop, many of them with their hands bound behind them—as I could see with the aid of a telescope—while others had their heads swathed in blood-stained bandages; a long plank was rigged out over the taffrail; and then Mendouca appeared to be making some sort of a speech. If such was the case the speech was a very brief one; and when it terminated a short pause ensued, and I saw that a few of the prisoners—perhaps three or four, as nearly as I could make out—were being released from their bonds. Then occurred another short pause, at the expiration of which a man was led forward, blindfolded, and guided to the inner extremity of the plank, along which I could see that they were urging him to walk. He advanced a few paces, paused, as though he had been addressed, and I distinctly saw him shake his head. As though this movement of the head were a prearranged signal, the inner end of the plank suddenly tilted up, and the unfortunate man, with a staggering movement as though to save himself, fell with a resounding splash into the sea, where for a few seconds he seemed to struggle desperately. Not for long, however; the sharks that had been haunting us for so many days heard the splash, and after a few restless movements, as though unwilling to leave us, darted off toward the ship. I saw the horrid triangular fins cleaving the surface of the glassy water, each leaving its own delicate wedge-shaped wake spreading astern as it went, until the small ripples of the different wakes met and crossed each other; then, as the distance between them and their prey lessened, there was a sudden increase of speed which soon became a rush, the black fins merged toward each other, the water swirled round the drowning man, there was a single ear-piercing shriek of agony, and the poor wretch had disappeared.

This dreadful spectacle appeared to have had its desired effect, for I saw that several more of the prisoners were now being released from their bonds, the released men, one and all, slinking down off the poop and away forward toward the forecastle. There were others, however—fifteen in all, for I counted them—whose courage was not to be shaken even by this awful ordeal, and one after the other they boldly trod the fatal plank, and went to meet their dreadful doom! All honour to them, say I, for the lofty courage that enabled them to choose death rather than an ignoble and crime-stained life!

Then there was another long pause, during which, as I afterwards learned, the *Francesca's* crew were rummaging the ship—a homeward-bound Indiaman, named the *Bangalore*—and loading her decks with booty of every imaginable description, preparatory to its transfer to the brigantine. Mendouca, I must mention, had already compelled the *Bangalore's* surgeon to dress his wound for him; and now, having given his orders to one of the men whom he considered the most reliable and trustworthy of his crew, he returned to the *Francesca*, and, with the aid of his son Pedro, was got into his bunk, where I could hear him from time to time grinding his teeth in agony, although, such was the spirit of the man, not a groan would he permit to escape him.

The sun had set, and the velvet dusk of the tropics was closing down upon the scene, when at length the *Bangalore's* boats were hoisted out,

and the work of transhipping the booty began. Mendouca must have felt himself a second Kidd, for the ship was almost as rich a prize as one of the old Acapulco galleons; there were bales of rich silks and shawls, spices, caskets of gems, ingots of gold, exquisite embroidered muslins, and I know not what beside—goods of a value sufficient, it seemed to me, to make every rascal on the books of the *Francesca* rich for the remainder of his life, although they were of course unable to take more than a comparatively small quantity of the *Bangalore's* entire cargo. Nevertheless, they contrived to find room for a goodly proportion of the most costly and valuable contents of the vessel's hold, the transfer of which, and of as much food and water as they deemed necessary to their requirements, occupied the crew until midnight; for in Mendouca's absence, as may be supposed, they did not trouble to exert themselves overmuch. Moreover, a large proportion of them were in such a state of intoxication they scarcely knew what they were doing—my especial *bête-noir* the boatswain among the number, he having seized an early opportunity to board the ship after Mendouca had been safely bestowed in his own cabin. I did not know this until told so by Simpson, the Englishman whom I have already mentioned as having been left on board the *Francesca* that afternoon with the boatswain and myself, who added to his information—

"Better keep your weather-eye liftin', Mr. Dugdale, sir; that José 's full of spite as an egg's full of meat; he has never forgiven you for knockin' him down, and have swore over and over again to put his knife into you. And now that he's full of drink, and the skipper's on his beam-ends, he's just as likely as not to try it."

"Yes, I suppose he is. Thank you for the warning, Simpson," said I. The man put his finger to his forehead in acknowledgment of my thanks, but continued to linger near me; and presently it dawned upon me that he had something further to say. So I turned to him and inquired—

"Is there anything particular that you wish to say to me, Simpson?"

"Well, yes, sir, there is, if I only knowed how to say it," answered the man, in a low, cautious tone of voice and with a somewhat hesitating manner. He paused for a second or two, as though in consideration, and then, looking me full in the face, said—

"I hopes you'll excuse me askin' of you the question, Mr. Dugdale, but might you be a-thinkin' of gettin' away out o' this here brigantine, supposin' that you sees a good chance for to do so? I ain't askin' out of any impertinence or curiosity, sir, I beg you to believe; but my meanin' is this here, if so be as it happens that you *was* thinkin' of any such thing, I was wonderin' whether we mightn't be able to go together, and be of sarvice to one another in a manner of speakin'."

"Oh," said I, "that is your idea, is it? Are you not satisfied with your present berth then, Simpson?"

"No, sir, I'm not, to tell the truth of it," answered the man. "I know that it's rather a risky thing to say aboard of this here wessel; but the truth is that I *ain't* satisfied at all, and haven't been for a long while; not since Mr. Arrowsmith—or Señor Mendouca, as he now calls hisself—took up to the piratin' business. So long as it was just a matter of runnin' a cargo of slaves across the Atlantic, I didn't mind so much, for there was plenty of dollars goin', and I didn't see that there was much harm in it, for I don't suppose the poor beggars is any worse off on the sugar and 'baccy plantations than they are in their own country. But when it comes to work like what's been done to-day, I wants to be out of it; and I don't mind sayin' so to you straight out, Mr. Dugdale, because you're a naval hofficer, you are, sir, and of course as such you're bound to be dead against such things as has happened since you've been aboard here. Besides, I've been a-watchin' of you, sir—askin' your pardon for the same, Mr. Dugdale—and I've seen that this ship and her doin's ain't no more to your taste than they are to mine."

"You are right, Simpson, they are not," said I; "and since you have been so frank with me, I will be equally so with you. You have rightly guessed that I would gladly make my escape from this accursed brigantine, if I could; and I had quite made up my mind that if, as I fully expected, Captain Mendouca had run alongside that ship this afternoon, I would board with the rest, and then join the British crew in their defence of their own ship."

"It's perhaps just as well then for you, sir, and for me too, that matters was arranged different," answered Simpson; "because, if the thing had come off as you planned it, I don't suppose that your joinin' of the other side would have made that much difference that they'd have beat off the skipper and his lot; and if they hadn't, and you'd fallen alive into the hands of the skipper, he'd have—well, I don't know what he wouldn't have done to you; but I'm mortal sure that you wouldn't have been alive now. But perhaps, sir, you've been thinkin', as I have, that even now it mayn't be too late to do somethin'."

"Yes," said I, "I have. While you have been talking to me a multitude of ideas have thronged through my mind, disconnected and vague, certainly, but still capable perhaps of being worked into shape. And I do not mind admitting to you, Simpson, that your proposal to join me in any attempt that I may be disposed to make simplifies matters a great deal. The most important factor in the problem before us is: How will yonder ship be dealt with when the *Francesca's* people have done with her? Will she be destroyed, or will she be left, with those unfortunate passengers—most probably with no knowledge whatever of nautical matters—to drift about at the mercy of wind and sea, to take her chance of being fallen in with, or to founder in the first gale of wind that happens to come her way?"

"No, sir, no," answered Simpson. "You may take your oath that Captain Mendouca won't run the risk of leavin' her afloat to be picked up and took into port, where her passengers could tell what tales they liked about him and his doin's. She'll be scuttled, sir, and left to go down with all them passengers in her, the same as that unfortunit' Portugee brig was that we took the slaves out of. But I've been thinkin', sir, that, even so, two sailormen, like you and me, might do a good deal, with the help of the gentlemen passengers, to put together some sort of a raft that would hold all hands of us and keep us above water until somethin' comes along and picks us up. Of course I knows quite well that it'll be a mighty poor look-out for the strongest of us, and a dreadful bad time for the poor women-folk, to be obliged to take to a raft; but I expect they'd rather do that and take their chance of bein' picked up than go down with the ship ; and if you're willin' to face the job, *I* am too, sir, and there's my hand on it."

I took the fellow's proffered hand and grasped it warmly.

"You are a good fellow, Simpson, and a true British seaman, whatever your past may have been," said I, "and I accept your proposal, which I can see is made in perfect good faith. Now, it seems to me that all that we have to do, in the first place, is to get on board yonder ship. The question is : How is it to be done without the knowledge of any of the *Francesca's* people ? "

"Well, sir," said Simpson, "I don't think as there'll be any great difficulty about that, so far as I'm concerned ; and I don't think there need be much with you neither, if you wouldn't mind changing your rig and shiftin' into some togs of mine, so as these chaps of the *Francesca* won't recognize you. Then, when the next boat comes from the ship, we'll tumble down into her and offer to give two of the others a spell ; they'll be only too glad of the chance to get a little relief from the job of pullin' backwards and for'ards and the handlin' of a lot of stuff, and, once aboard the ship, we can stow ourselves out of sight until they leave her for good and all."

"Very well," said I, "that seems as good a plan as any, and we will try it. Let me have some of your old clothes, Simpson—a flannel shirt and a pair of canvas trousers will do—and I will shift into them at once. And there is another thing that occurs to me. If we could manage to secure a little further help it would be so much the better. Now, if I am not mistaken, a good many of the crew of yonder ship joined the *Francesca* this afternoon as the only means of saving their lives. We must get hold of a few of them, if we can, and, by means of a few judicious questions, find out whether they would be willing to throw in their lot with us and take their chance of ultimate escape, rather than become slavers and pirates. With only half-a-dozen stout, willing seamen a great deal might be done to better the state of affairs generally."

"You are right, sir, it would make a lot of difference, and I'll see what can be done," answered Simpson. "And now, sir, shall I go and get you the togs? I s'pose that whatever we do might as well be done at once ?"

"Certainly," said I, "the sooner the better. I can see no object in delaying our movements, now that we have determined upon a definite plan."

"All right, sir, then here goes," answered Simpson. "I'll be back with the duds in a jiffey."

Simpson's "jiffey" proved to be a pretty long one, for it was fully twenty minutes before he returned with the clothes—a thin flannel shirt that had seen its best days, and was so faded from its original colour and so thoroughly stained with tar and grease that it was difficult to say what that original colour had been, but was therefore so much the better suited to the purpose of a disguise—a pair of equally faded dungaree trousers, and a knitted worsted cap. But his delay had not been profitless, for happening to find in the forecastle two of the crew of the *Bangalore*, who had been compelled to join the *Francesca*, and who, from their dejected appearance, he conjectured were not altogether pleased or satisfied with the arrangement, he entered into conversation with them, and soon contrived to elicit from them that his conjecture was well founded. Thereupon, as there was no time to lose, he took the bold course of asking them outright whether, in the event of there being a scheme afoot on the part of others to escape from the brigantine to the ship, they would be disposed to join in it, to which they replied that they would gladly, and that indeed they had been discussing the possibilities of such an attempt when he interrupted them by his descent into the forecastle. This was enough for Simpson, who at once brought them aft to me, and I, finding them fully in earnest in their expressed desire to have nothing to do with the pirates, forthwith unfolded my plans to them, carefully directing their attention to the somewhat desperate aspect of the adventure, but at the same time pointing out to them that every additional seaman whose help we could secure added very materially to the chances of a successful issue. What I said seemed only to render them the more determined to sever their brief connection with the pirates at any cost, and they unhesitatingly declared their readiness to join me, and to implicitly obey my orders. More than this, they informed me that there were others of the *Bangalore's* crew who, they were sure, would be equally ready with themselves, if permitted, to take part in the adventure, and they consented to hunt up as many of these men as possible at once, and to have them ready to meet me on the forecastle to discuss the matter in a quarter of an hour.

My scheme, which, prior to my conversation with Simpson, had been of the most vague and nebulous character, had now taken shape and wore so promising an appearance that I felt sanguine of its ultimate success; so without further ado I retired right aft to the wheel grating—that part of the brigantine being now quite deserted, and wrapped in total darkness save for the dim and diffused light that issued from the cabin skylight—and there, unseen, shifted into the clothes that Simpson had brought me. They were not particularly comfortable nor quite so well-savoured as I could have wished; but it was no time for ultra-squeamishness, and I was soon transformed into a very colourable imitation of a fo'c's'le hand. This done, I went forward, past the open hatchway down which the plunder from the *Bangalore* was being struck, noticing with bitter distress and anger the forlorn, dejected, worn-out, and despairing attitudes of the unfortunate blacks closely huddled together on the slave-deck, their forms faintly indicated in the yellow, smoky light of the lanterns which the men were working by, and noticing too, with keen satisfaction, that most of the crew had reached that stage of intoxication wherein the victim's whole attention is required for the conduct of his own affairs, with none to spare for those of others. Many had gone considerably beyond this stage, and were staggering about, pulling and hauling aimlessly at the first object that they could lay their hands upon, and proving far more of a hindrance than a help to their less intoxicated comrades; while there were some who had reached the final stage of bestiality, and were lying about the decks in a helpless condition of drunken stupor. Nothing more favourable for our scheme than this condition of general intoxication could possibly have happened, unless it were that Pedro was below, fully occupied in attending to his father, and was therefore the less likely to discover my absence from the brigantine until it should be too late to take any steps toward the investigation of the phenomenon; I therefore hurried

to the rendezvous with a sudden feeling of elation and joyousness and confidence in the conviction that the time of release from my exceedingly uncongenial and disagreeable, if not absolutely hopeless, situation had at length arrived.

Upon reaching the forecastle-head —the appointed spot of our rendezvous—I found it tenantless; but presently a man came lounging up to me from the group of workers about the hatchway, and, after peering into my face, inquired—

"Got any 'baccy about you, mate? Mine's down below in my chest, and I haven't unlashed it yet. If you've got any, just give me a chaw, will ye, and maybe I'll do as much for you another time."

"I am sorry to say that I have not any," I answered. "I do not use it except in the form of a cigar now and then. But I expect my mate Simpson on deck every moment, and I have no doubt that he will be able to accommodate you. You are one of the new hands, shipped from the *Bangalore*, are you not? I don't seem to remember having seen your face before."

"No, perhaps not, and it's precious little you can see now, I should think, unless you've got cat's eyes, and can see in the dark," was the somewhat surly response. "Yes," he continued, "I'm Joe Maxwell, late carpenter of the *Bangalore*, and—well, yes, 'shipped' is the word, I suppose. And pray who may *you* be, my buck, with your dandified talk—which, to my mind, is about as like any fo'c's'le lingo that I ever heard as chalk is like cheese? Are all hands aboard this dashin' rover of the same kidney as yourself?"

"Scarcely that, I think, as you seem to have already had an opportunity of judging," I answered, laughingly, as I glanced in the direction of the hatchway. "No," I continued, determined to sound him forthwith, as his speech and manner seemed to indicate that he was by no means satisfied with his changed lot, "I am a naval officer, and a prisoner, I suppose I must call myself, although, as you see, I have the liberty of the ship. And now, having told you thus much, I should like you to tell me candidly, Maxwell, did you join this afternoon of your own free will, or under compulsion?"

The man looked at me searchingly for a moment, and then said—

"Well, I suppose when a man is

asked a straightfor'ard question the best plan is to give a straightfor'ard answer. So, mister, I don't mind tellin' you that I j'ined because I was obliged to; 'twas either that or a walk along a short plank."

"In fact, you joined merely to save your life," I suggested.

"Ay; pretty much as you, yourself, may have done," was the answer.

"I?" I exclaimed. "Surely, my good fellow, you do not mean to say that you imagine me—a naval officer —to have joined this crew of thieves and murderers?"

"Blest if I know, or care," the fellow answered roughly. "Only, if you're a naval officer, as you say, and haven't joined the 'thieves and murderers,' as you call 'em, I should like to know how you come to be rigged like a fo'c's'le Jack?"

I saw that the man was suspicious of me—perhaps thought I was endeavouring, for purposes of espionage, to fathom his real feelings with regard to the service into which he had been pressed; I saw, moreover, that my conjecture was correct, and that, despite his cautious replies, he was by no means satisfied with the arrangement, and so determined to be frank with him at once, tell him what I contemplated, and invite him to join me. As carpenter of the *Bangalore* he would be an especially valuable acquisition to our party. I accordingly did so; and before I had finished I had the satisfaction of seeing that his suspicions had completely disappeared, and that he was listening to me intently and respectfully. When I had brought my disclosure and proposition to an end, he at once said—

"I'm with you, sir, heart and soul! *Anything*—even a raft—will be better than this thievin' and murderin' hooker and her cut-throat crew! Yes, sir, I'm with you, for life or death. But, please God, it shall be life and not death for all hands of us. Let us get away aboard at once, sir; I'm just longin' to tread the beauty's planks again; and as to scuttlin' her—why, I'll make it my first business, when I get aboard, to shape out a few plugs and take 'em down into the run with me—that's the only place where they'll be able to get at her under-water plankin'—and as soon as they've gone I'll plug up them holes so that she'll be as tight as a bottle, and never a penny the worse for what little they're likely

to do to her. But it would please me a precious sight better to knock out the brains of whoever dares to go down below to do the scuttlin' business."

"No, no," said I, "that would never do; the man would be missed, a search would be instituted, and heaven only knows what the consequences would be. No, the scuttling must be allowed to proceed, and the pirates must finally leave the ship with the conviction that she is slowly but surely sinking. If all goes well this craft will be out of sight before morning, and then, once clear of them, we shall have leisure to make our plans and carry them out."

"Right you are, sir, and right it is," answered Maxwell. "You'll have to be our skipper now, sir, for poor Capt'n Mason and all three of the mates is gone—one on 'em—Mr. King—killed in the scrimmage, and t'others made to walk the plank—so you'll be the only navigator that we can muster among the lot of us, as well as the 'riginator of this here scheme for gettin' the better of these here Spaniards, so you're the fittest and properest person to take charge. All that you've got to do, sir, is to give your orders, and I'll answer for it as they'll be obeyed."

CHAPTER XVII

I ESCAPE FROM THE BRIGANTINE

AT this moment Simpson rejoined me, bringing with him three more of the *Bangalore's* crew; and while I was talking to them the other two men— those whom Simpson had previously discovered—came forward from the hatchway, where they had been lending a hand to strike the booty down into the hold, and informed me that they had found and spoken to eight of their shipmates, at work at the gangway and hatchway, all of whom were quite ready and more than willing to join me at any moment when the signal should be given. A little further inquiry elicited the information that our party now comprised all the survivors of the *Bangalore's* crew who had, so to speak, made a virtue of necessity and shipped under Mendouca in order to save their lives; there being four others who had shipped *willingly*, and whom it had, therefore, been deemed inexpedient to approach with a proposal to join us, lest, in their zeal for their new chief, they should refuse and betray us all. Our party, therefore, was now complete, and all that remained to be done was to carry out our plans with as little delay as possible, and with twelve men at my back I felt tolerably confident of success ; indeed, when I first learned our 'full strength, the wild idea flashed through my mind of attempting not only to save the *Bangalore*, but also to capture the *Francesca*. A moment's reflection, however, convinced me of the impracticability of this scheme, for although, with the assistance of the ten male passengers who, I learned, were at that moment prisoners in their own cabins on board the Indiaman, it might be possible to capture the *Francesca*, in the then disorganized condition of her crew, it would certainly involve some loss of life on our side, which we could not spare, and we should be able to do nothing with her when we had her, our whole available strength being hardly sufficient to handle and take care of the ship, should it come on to blow, much less to look after a prize as well. I therefore abandoned the idea, the more readily that I knew my story need only be told to the proper authorities to cause the brigantine to be hunted off the ocean, and her atrocities put an end to at once and for all.

Our arrangements, therefore, were soon made ; and this done, we sauntered away to the hatchway, singly and by twos at a time, and began to lend a hand in getting the plunder out of the boats and sending it below. Presently the *Bangalore's* long-boat came alongside, loaded down to the gunwale with booty, and manned by half-a-dozen Spaniards who were so drunk that they could scarcely stand. One of them, indeed, would have lost his life but for Simpson and Maxwell ; for the boat was steered alongside stem on, and the shock of her collision with the brigantine completely upset the balance of the man who was standing in the bows to fend her off, so that he fell overboard between the boat and the brigantine's side. The fellow was partially sobered by his sudden immersion, and finding himself overboard, began at once to sing out lustily for help, fully aware that there were probably several sharks still hanging about the two vessels, and momentarily expecting to feel their teeth ; whereupon Simpson and Maxwell, both of whom happened to be

at the gangway at the moment of the accident, sprang down into the boat and succeeded in dragging the fellow safely out of the water, though not a moment too soon, the water being all aswirl with the rush of the sea-monsters as the man was dragged inboard. The fright that he had received completely sobered him, but at the same time so thoroughly shook his nerves that he at once scrambled on board the brigantine, declaring with many oaths that he had had enough of boating for one night. His mates were but little better, and were glad enough to leave the boat at my suggestion and allow me and my party to take their places.

We quickly roused the boat's cargo out of her, and then shoved off for the ship again, making a great fuss and splash with the oars as we did so. When a few fathoms away from the brigantine, however, where in the darkness our movements were not likely to attract a too curious attention, first one oar and then another was laid in until all had been laid in but one ; and this one we shifted aft, sculling the boat with it not to the *Bangalore's* larboard gangway, at which the other boats were working, but under the ship's stern and to her starboard mizen channels, where we made her fast, and cautiously scrambled up on to the poop, one by one.

Here we separated, the carpenter boldly making his way forward past the noisy, jabbering, drunken crowd who were grouped about the main hatchway, engaged in hoisting on deck the goods that the boatswain, down in the hold, was selecting from the ship's heterogeneous cargo, while the rest—excepting Simpson and myself—quietly stole up the mizen rigging, three of them concealing themselves in the top, while the rest, continuing on up the topmast rigging, made for the main and foretops by way of the stays ; the lanterns which were being used to light the pirates at their work about the main hatchway so effactually dazzling the drunken ruffians' eyes, that there was not the slightest fear of any of the silent, sober figures stealthily moving about aloft being seen by them ; indeed so deep was the gloom created between the masts by the towering expanses of the Indiaman's canvas that even I, far away as I was from the dazzling light of the lanterns, was unable to follow with my eye the dusky, indistinctly-seen figures any further than the rim of the mizen-top. As for Simpson, it was quite possible for him to move freely about the ship and go wherever he pleased without exciting any suspicion, he being one of the *Francesca's* regular crew ; I therefore instructed him to go down into the saloon and ascertain whether any of his quondam shipmates were there, and to return to me with his information as speedily as possible.

While he was gone I had time to look about me a little, and note such of the most prominent characteristics of the ship as were to be seen by the dim light of the stars. She was a noble craft, as big as the generality of our first-class frigates, though not quite so · beamy, perhaps, in proportion to her length, not quite so high out of the water, and of course not so heavily rigged. She carried a magnificent full poop that reached as far forward as to within about twenty-five feet of the main-mast, with companion, skylight, deck fittings generally, and poop ladders of polished teak, handsomely and elaborately carved. The fore-part of the poop extended some six feet beyond the cabin front, and underneath it her steering-wheel was placed, with a door on each side of it giving access to the grand saloon. A long row of hencoops ran along each side of the poop ; and the deck was further littered with a large number of deck-chairs that had been hurriedly bundled out of the way behind the companion, probably when it was seen that the brigantine undoubtedly meant to attack. The main-deck exhibited all the confusion incidental to a sea-fight, the guns—sixteen twelve-pound carronades—still unsecured, with their rammers and sponges flung down on the deck beside them, shot lying in the scuppers, overturned wadding-tubs, cutlasses, pistols, boarding-pikes, strewed all over the deck, and — horrible sight—several dark, silent figures lying stark and still in pools of blood, just as they had fallen in the fight. The ship's davits were empty, both her gigs having been lowered to facilitate the transfer of the plunder to the brigantine ; her long-boat also was in the water, as already stated, but there were two fine cutters lying bottom up over the quarter-deck, their sterns resting on the break of the poop and their bows on the gallows. It was a strange sight to look abroad into the dusky starlit night and observe the boundless Atlantic stretching silent and still on every hand, and then to turn one's eyes inboard and note the noisy, drunken, ruffianly rabble grouped about the hatchway, naked to the waist, and toiling in the dim lantern light at the tackles by which they were hoisting the bales of costly merchandise out of the hold.

But I had not much time to devote to moralizing upon the incongruous sight, for after an absence of some three minutes Simpson reappeared from the saloon with the information that the place was clear, and that, judging from the sounds he had heard, the passengers had all locked themselves, or been locked, into their cabins.

This being the case, I determined to go below and make a brief investigation of the condition of the unfortunate passengers, as well as to afford them such comfort as was to be derived from a communication to them of my intentions. I accordingly descended the companion-way leading down from the poop, and found myself in a small vestibule, the arrangement of which I could not very well see, as it was unlighted, save for the lamplight that issued from the open door of the saloon; I caught a glimpse, however, of polished panels of rare, ornamental woods, with gleams of gilded mouldings and polished metal handrails, and found my feet sinking into the pile of a soft, thick carpet, which gave me a hint as to the luxurious appointments of the ship. From this vestibule I passed into the saloon itself by a partially open door on the port side, and at once found myself in an exceedingly handsome and luxuriously furnished apartment. It was long and rather narrow in its proportions, having state-rooms on each side, as I could tell at a glance by the doors with Venetian slatted upper panels that occurred at regular intervals in the longitudinal bulkheads on each side of the cabin. These bulkheads were divided into panels by fluted pilasters with richly-carved and gilded capitals, supporting a heavily-carved cornice picked out with gold. The panels and pilasters were enamelled in a delicate tint of cream, with mouldings picked out in French grey, the former being decorated with very handsome paintings illustrative of Oriental views and scenery. Richly-upholstered divans occupied the spaces along the bulkheads between the several state-room doors; a long table of polished mahogany, having sofa seats with reversible backs on each side of it, stretched down the centre of the saloon, with another and shorter table flanking it athwartships at the after-end; a buffet loaded with richly-cut decanters and glass, backed up by a large gilt-framed mirror, occupied the whole space against the fore-bulk-head between the two entrance doors; and a very handsome piano, open, and with some music on it, occupied a similar position at the after-end of the saloon, two doors in the after-bulk-head proclaiming the existence of at least two more state-rooms. The apartment was lighted during the day by a large skylight filled in with painted glass—in which were fixed opposite each other a barometer and a tell-tale compass—and at night by two very fine silver-plated chandeliers each carrying six lamps, only four of which, however, were now lighted; and the deck was covered with a rich, thick carpet, apparently of Oriental manufacture, into which one's feet sank with noiseless tread. The state-rooms were all in total darkness apparently, for I could catch no gleam of light issuing from the pierced upper panels of any of them; but the sound of an occasional sob or moan told me that some at least of them were occupied.

I located one of the cabins from which these sounds came, and tapped gently at the door; there was no response, but the sounds instantly ceased. I tapped again, and said—

"Will you open the door, please? I am a friend, and have some intelligence to communicate that may be interesting to you."

Still no response; but from the next cabin there now issued a man's voice, inquiring—

"Do I hear some one out there proclaiming himself *a friend?*"

"Yes," answered I. "I *am* a friend; and my present object is to communicate to you some intelligence that I hope may prove agreeable and comforting. I am quite alone and unarmed, and you may therefore open your cabin door without fear."

"Sir," replied the voice, "I know not who you are, or how you come to be on board this most ill-starred ship.

Your voice, however, has a reassuring tone in it, and I would risk opening my door to you if I could; but I cannot, for—like all the rest of the passengers, I believe—I am bound and absolutely helpless, and I think that, if you will take the trouble to try, you will find that we are all locked in. Pray, who are you, sir? and how did you find your way on board the *Bangalore?* Are the pirates gone yet?"

"No," said I, as I tried the door and found that it was indeed locked. "I regret to say that they are not, and therefore I am for the present obliged to leave you in your uncomfortable situation. But take comfort, and believe me that it shall not be for one moment longer than I can help; the pirates are unlikely to very much prolong their stay now, and as soon as they are at a safe distance I will come again and release you all—provided, of course, that my plans do go amiss. My name is Dugdale, and I am a naval officer—a midshipman—who has been unfortunate enough to fall into the hands of the pirates in an unsuccessful attack upon them more than a month ago, and this is the first opportunity that I have had to attempt my escape. I must go again now, as my discovery on board here by the pirates would mean utter ruin to us all; but I will return as soon as I can with prudence. Meanwhile," slightly raising my voice so that all might hear, "take comfort, and hope for the best."

"Good-bye! Heaven bless and prosper you!" fervently ejaculated the unknown, as I moved away from the door; and I thought I heard faint murmurs of a similar import from some of the other cabins, but could not be certain, as one of the outer doors giving direct access to the main-deck suddenly opened, and I had to make a dash of it for the dark vestibule in order to reach the concealment of the still darker companion-way to avoid detection. My alarm was groundless, however; for the new-comer proved to be Joe Maxwell, the carpenter, whom I saw enter the saloon, after a careful reconnaissance of its interior, with several plugs under one arm, and a maul in his hand. Seeing who it was, I followed him, and unexpectedly ran against him as he was again coming out.

"Who the—oh, it's you, sir! beg

your pardon, I'm sure, but I thought it was one of them sneakin' pirate chaps a-prowlin' round," he exclaimed. "I thought I heard a sound o' some sort as I comed in from the deck, and thinks I, 'That's one o' them cowardly villains that has sneaked aft for some purpose of his own that ain't no good, I dare swear. I'll just see what the scoundrel's up to, and if he's after anything *very* houtragis, I'll maybe take the liberty of smashin' his skull with this here maul, and droppin' him over the starn to the sharks, where many a better man than he went this a'ternoon.' Lucky for him that it's you, sir, as the Irishman says. I'm just a-goin' to make my way down into the run, so as to be all handy for pluggin' up the holes again that these here murderin' thieves intends to bore through the dear old gal's skin. I *think* they'll be pretty sure to come aft to do it; it'll either be there or down in the fore-peak, where they'd have to shovel away a lot of coal to get at her below the water-line, so I expect they'll make for the run. Now, sir, it's a very good job as I met you just here, because I can show you the lazarette hatch —here it is, under our feet." And he turned back a large mat upon which we were standing, disclosing a small, square hatch flush with the deck.

"Now, sir," he continued, "I'll be off below at once; because, from what I saw as I comed aft, I fancy them Spanish thieves is thinkin' about toppin' their booms, and if so, we've no time to spare. There," as he raised the hatch and dropped through the opening, "I'm all right now, sir; I can make my way well enough without a light, though I've got a candle and matches in my pocket that'll give light enough to work by as soon as them villains have cleared out. Now, sir, please put on the hatch again, will ye, and don't forget to spread the mat over it. And when them blackguards have gone you can send somebody to let me out."

"All right, Maxwell, never fear; I'll see to that," I answered, as the man disappeared in the gloom. "Good luck to you. And whatever those fellows may do, be sure that you keep silent and do not attempt to interfere with them; let them do their work and go away, and as soon as you hear the hatch close after them, go ahead and plug the holes as quickly as you like,

and be sure that you make a thorough job of it."

"Ay, ay, sir," came his reply, already muffled by distance and the intervening casks and cases among which he was making his way, "you may trust me for that."

I carefully replaced the hatch, adjusted the mat over it, and made my way cautiously up on the poop. It was evident, from what I now saw, that Maxwell was only just in time; for the pirates had knocked off work and were coming up out of the hold, refreshing themselves as they emerged by copious draughts from a tub of strong grog that stood on the deck conveniently near the hatchway. They were all pretty far gone in a state of intoxication, and were singing a jumble of at least a dozen forecastle ditties in tones of maudlin sentiment, or laughing and jeering at nothing in particular as they reeled and staggered about the deck. Disgusting as was the sight, I was glad to see it, for I felt that men in their condition would never notice the absence of Simpson or myself from the brigantine, still less that of the unaccustomed faces of those of the *Bangalore's* crew who had joined me and were now snugly concealed aloft. Nor were they capable of doing very much more mischief, unless perchance they should accidentally set the ship on fire, which was what I most greatly dreaded; if, happily, we escaped this danger all might yet be well, for I felt convinced that, once on board the brigantine again, and the unhappy negroes once more set to the sweeps, nearly every man in the accursed craft's forecastle would betake himself to his hammock and stay there until morning. There was of course the risk that Mendouca might send for me and ask me to look after his vessel for him through the night, knowing or guessing as he would the condition of his crew; but I did not believe that he would, at least not so soon after the perpetration of such fearful atrocities as he had openly committed that afternoon.

The men having helped themselves freely from the grog-tub, until it seemed that they could take no more, tumbled rather than scrambled down into the boat alongside, and I was just beginning to cherish the hope that after all they would go away forgetting to scuttle the ship, when I saw José, the boatswain—who appeared to have assumed the command of the party—seize and detain the only man except himself who still remained on the ship's deck. He said something to this man, and then they both staggered away forward and I lost sight of them in the deep shadows that enshrouded the fore-part of the ship. They were gone about ten minutes; and then they re-appeared, the boatswain armed with a large auger. As they passed the main hatchway, on their way aft, José seized one of the still lighted lanterns that were standing on the deck, and seemed to direct his companion to take another. This the man did, and continuing their way aft, the pair entered the saloon from the main-deck; and presently, peering cautiously down through the open skylight, I saw that the two ruffians were groping about under the cabin table, no doubt searching for the lazarette hatch. Their search was of course in vain; and at length I overheard the boatswain assert with an oath that it was useless to search for it any longer, they must get the steward out of his pantry, and make him show them where it was. They then left the saloon, and there was silence for a few minutes; then, going to the head of the companion-ladder, I heard José demanding in broken English, with a profusion of expletives, where was the opening of the lazarette. A strange voice replied in trembling tones; and then I heard the mat flung back and the hatch wrenched off with a clatter. A few more oaths followed, there was a scrambling sound, and I concluded that the two miscreants had descended to the performance of their dastardly task.

Then ensued what seemed like a very long—although it was actually a comparatively short—period of anxious suspense, for completely successful as we had been thus far, our absence from the brigantine might easily be discovered at any moment; and in that case there was no alternative for us between fighting to the death and ignominious surrender. I was more anxious on my own behalf than on that of the others, for their absence was scarcely likely to be noted by their drunken comrades until the next morning, while, as for me, should Mendouca take it into his head to require my presence, it would no sooner be reported to him that I

was not to be found than he would have a very shrewd suspicion of what had happened; and I felt convinced that, with my knowledge of the enormities that he had perpetrated on that dreadful day, he would never willingly suffer me to escape from him alive. Then there was Pedro, too. The lad had, for some inscrutable reason, taken a violent fancy for me, and, although I have not very frequently referred to him in the telling of this story, had attached himself to me with almost the fidelity of a dog, sharing in my watch, and seizing every opportunity to be in my company. Should he find himself at liberty to seek me I should be lost, for he would not be content until he had found me. There were just two chances in my favour against many adverse possibilities: the first being that Mendouca's condition would confine the lad to his side all through the night; the second lying in the fact that I had taken the precaution to lock my cabin door and remove the key before leaving the brigantine, so that should it chance that I was sought for, it might be thought that I had locked myself into my cabin in anger at the piratical deed that had been perpetrated. But I grew increasingly uneasy as the minutes dragged their slow length along, expecting every moment to hear a hail from the brigantine inquiring as to my whereabouts. It was therefore with a feeling of keen delight that, at the expiration of about twenty-five minutes, when my state of suspense had become almost unendurable, as I stood listening at the head of the companion-way I heard José's voice again, and the sounds of his own and his companion's emergence from the lazarette.

"There," I heard him exclaim in Spanish, in a drunken voice and with a jeering laugh, "that job is done, and pretty effectually, too; I don't suppose she will float longer than three hours more, or four at the most, and then who is to know what has become of her? It will be supposed that she foundered in a gale; and that will be the end of the matter. It is a pity, Miguel, that we should be obliged to destroy so fine a ship, but she could never be of any use to us, and necessity has no law, you know. Now—let me consider—there is one thing more to be done before we leave; what is it? It was in my mind a moment ago! Ah, yes, of course, that is it; we have to put this miserable poltroon of a steward back into his pantry, lock the door upon him, and—yes, that is all, I think. Come along, *amigo*!"

I heard the steward begging piteously not to be locked up again; for although the fellow had probably not understood a single word of what José had said, he had sense enough to know that the two ruffians before him had scuttled the ship, and that if locked up in his pantry again he would probably drown there, like a rat in a trap. His entreaties, however, were of course unavailing with two men who knew not the meaning of mercy; there was a Spanish oath or two, the sound of a scuffle, mingled with further cries of distress from the steward, the slamming of a door, the sharp click of a lock; and a moment later José and his companion emerged upon the deck, staggered to the gangway, scrambled down the side, and the boat was shoved off.

I waited until the boat was fairly away from the ship's side, and then, slipping down the dark companionway, groped about until I had found the pantry, which I unlocked, to find the unhappy steward, bound hand and foot, prostrate on the deck, weeping bitterly. In reply to my question he told me where I could lay my hand upon a knife, finding which I cut him adrift, and directed him to go forward to the forecastle to ascertain whether any of the crew were imprisoned down there. Then, making my way to the still open lazarette, I swung myself down into it, and called Maxwell's name as loudly as I dared. He heard and answered me at once.

"The rascals have left the ship," I cried, "so you may ram those plugs home as tightly as you can, and perhaps even venture to give them a gentle tap or two, but we must leave the final driving until the brigantine has moved off; everything has gone right thus far, and it will never do to spoil it all now by being impatient. Has she taken in much water?"

"Not more than we can pump out of her in ten minutes," was the reply, as I sighted him creeping toward me along the narrow space underneath the beams. "They only bored five holes through her, and I've already plugged 'em tight enough to stop the water from comin' in—though of course

they'll want a few good taps on the head to make 'em all secure. But that job can wait until the brigantine is a mile or two further away."

"Had you any difficulty in plugging the holes?" I asked, as honest Joe emerged into the more open spaces about the hatchway.

"Not a bit, sir," he answered. "You see the way of it was this: As soon as I got to understand that they was likely to scuttle the ship, the first thing I says to myself was: 'I wonder,' I says, 'what size auger them murderin' scoundrels is likely to use? Because if I only knowed that, I could make my plugs to fit the holes.' Then the next thing I thought was that prob'ly they wouldn't remember to bring a tool aboard with 'em, and that they'd hunt for some'at of the sort aboard here. So I goes to my cabin, gets out a inch and a half auger, a chisel, a hammer and some nails, and places 'em on the tarpaulin of the fore-hatch, where anybody going for'ard couldn't help seein' of 'em; and 'There,' I says to myself, 'if those fellers haven't brought no auger aboard with 'em, that's the tool they'll use.' So I chanced it, and made my plugs to fit a inch and a half hole; and, as it turned out, I was right; they used my auger what I had left for 'em, and as soon as their backs was turned I slipped down and screwed the plugs into the holes."

"Excellent!" said I. "And now, Maxwell, the next job is to break open the state-rooms and release the poor ladies and gentlemen who are confined there. Do you think you can do it without making much noise?"

"Lord bless you, yes, sir," was the cheerful reply. "I'll just go for'ard and get a bit of wire, and I'll pick the locks of them cabin doors in next to no time, and make no noise about it either."

"Then come along and let us get it done at once. That must be our first job," said I.

CHAPTER XVIII

RE-APPEARANCE OF THE 'FRANCESCA'

WHILE Maxwell stole forward to get his wire, I crept up on the poop again, and carefully avoiding the skylight, so that my figure might not be revealed by the coloured rays that streamed from it, found that the boat with José and his companions, and the last of the plunder, was just going alongside the brigantine. The first to scramble out of her was José ; and there was light enough about the brigantine's decks to enable me to see that he went straight aft to the companion, which he descended. He was absent from the deck but a very few minutes, however ; and when he re-appeared I supposed that he had been below to make his report to Mendouca and to receive that individual's orders, for as he passed along the deck I heard him shout to the crew—

"Now, then, look alive there with those bales, and get the deck clear as quickly as possible, so that we can get the niggers on deck and the sweeps at work once more. We've got all that we can take from the Englishman, and now the sooner we are off the better, for she won't float above two or three hours longer ; and if a breeze was to spring up, and bring a cruiser along with it, it would be bad for us if we were found in this neighbourhood. So bundle those bales down the hatch-way anyhow, men, and clear the decks at once. We must stow the goods properly afterwards."

This was excellent—very much better than I had expected ; for a dreadful idea had suggested itself to me, that Mendouca might take it into his head to remain by the ship until she should show unmistakable signs of sinking, in which case there would be nothing for us but another fight, which, short-handed as we were, would not suit our book at all.

The men on board the *Francesca* woke up a little at José's order, and soon had the last boat unloaded and the decks clear ; the slaves were then ordered on deck, the *Bangalore's* boats cast adrift, the sweeps rigged out, and, with I think the most fervent emotion of gratitude and delight that I had ever experienced, I at length had the satisfaction of seeing the brigantine stir sluggishly against the background of the star-spangled heavens, turn her bows slightly away from us, and finally glide off, with a quiet, gentle, scarcely-perceptible motion, in a westerly direction.

While I was still watching her I caught sight of Maxwell creeping along the deck from forward, under the shelter of the bulwarks, so that the light from the still burning lanterns

that the pirates had left behind them might not disclose his moving figure to any of the eyes on board the *Francesca* that might be turned upon the ship ; and making my way down the companion, I joined him in the vestibule, and we entered the cabin together.

I led him straight to the door of the state-room with the occupant of which I had previously held a short conversation, and directed Maxwell to open it, at the same time knocking upon the panel and saying—

"Sir, I am happy to inform you that the pirates have at length left us, and we are about to make an attempt to release you."

"Thank God for that !" fervently ejaculated a voice that I had not heard before. "Be as quick as you can, pray, for I fear that my poor husband here is dead or dying ; and he should be attended to without a moment's delay."

"That's Mrs. Maynard's voice !" exclaimed the carpenter, as he worked away with his wire ; "I know it well. Somebody told me that the colonel was hurt—stabbed, I think they said, in protectin' his daughters from the ill-usage of some of them Spanish ruffians."

"Say you so, man ?" I exclaimed. "Then never mind fiddling with that wire any longer. Let us put our shoulders to the door and burst it open !"

"Half a second, sir ; I've got the thing now, and—there, that's all right ! Now try the door, sir !"

As the man spoke I heard the click of the lock as it went back, and, turning the handle, the door opened, and I entered.

The cabin was a fine, roomy one, and of good height, as cabins went in those days ; it contained two standing bunks, one above the other, fitted with brass rods and damask curtains, a sofa against the side of the ship, a wash-stand in a recess between the bunks and the bulkhead adjoining the saloon, a framed mirror above it, a folding mahogany table against the transverse bulkhead, brass pins upon which to hang clothing, a curtain to draw across the doorway, a handsome lamp with a ground-glass globe hung in gimbals in the centre of the transverse bulkhead, two large travelling trunks and three or four smaller cases, broken open and the contents strewn upon the carpeted deck, and prone among them, bound hand and foot and lashed together, were the figures of a man and woman, both evidently elderly, although their precise ages could hardly be guessed by the imperfect light that streamed in from the saloon through the open door.

As I entered the apartment, noting these details in a single comprehensive glance, the woman moaned—

"Oh, sir, for the love of God pray release us from these cruel bonds as quickly as possible; they are bound so tightly that the circulation of the blood is stopped, and we have been suffering the most excruciating agony for hours."

"I will cut you adrift at once, madam," said I, unsheathing the long knife which was attached to the belt that Simpson had lent me with the clothes. "Had I known that you were in this cruel plight, I would have risked everything in the endeavour to release you when I first entered the cabin."

I cut the unfortunate couple adrift, and, having first taken the precaution to draw the curtain of the side-light, lighted the lamp, and, with Maxwell's assistance, raised the lady into a sitting position; after which we lifted her husband and placed him on the bed in the lower berth. He was a very fine, handsome man of about fifty years of age, with that indescribable and unmistakable look of the soldier about him that seems to set its mark upon every military man. His wife was perhaps seven or eight years his junior, still exceedingly good-looking, and must, at her best, have been a singularly lovely woman.

The colonel, it appeared, had, in common with the other passengers who had any womankind on board, locked his wife and daughters into their cabins when it was foreseen that an attack upon the ship was inevitable; and it was after the fight was over that he was severely stabbed in resisting an attempt on the part of one of the *Francesca's* crew to force open his daughters' cabin. Probably the poor man would have been murdered outright but for the opportune appearance of Mendouca, who sternly ordered every one of his men out of the cabin, except two, whom he personally supervised as they executed his order to bind all the survivors hand and foot and confine them in the cabins. Luckily for the unfortunate passengers, the first thought of the men had been drink, and the second, plunder; and by the time that these two appetites had been satisfied, all thought of further violence had passed out of their heads.

The first thing now to be done was to find the ship's surgeon—if he were still alive; so, leaving Maxwell in the cuddy to continue his lock-picking operations, I sallied out on deck and, first softly calling to the men aloft that they might now venture to come down, hunted up the steward, and inquired of him whether he knew where the surgeon was to be found. He answered that the surgeon, purser, and three mates were all berthed in the after-house, between the main-mast and the main-hatch, and that probably the man I wanted would be found there, adding that, as he believed the pirates had flung all the keys overboard, he would take the liberty of going into poor Captain Mason's cabin, and bringing me a bunch of spare keys that he knew were always kept there. This he did, and, finding the key of the after-house, we entered it together, to find the unhappy surgeon and purser bound hand and foot, and lashed together in such a manner that neither of them could move, upon the floor of the cabin. To release the pair was but the work of a moment; after which, having directed the doctor to hasten to the cuddy and attend to the colonel's injuries, I made a survey of the deck, with the result that fourteen more of the *Bangalore's* crew were found, of whom six were dead, and eight more or less seriously wounded; the latter were removed to their bunks in the forecastle forthwith and attended to by Mr. Grant, the surgeon, as soon as he had dressed the wounds of Colonel Maynard and two other passengers. I may as well say here, to save time, that, thanks to Grant's skill and unremitting attention, all the wounded were reported to be doing well and, with the exception of Colonel Maynard, out of danger.

The keys of all the cabins having been found, and the doors unlocked by the steward, Maxwell's services were no longer required in the cuddy; as therefore the brigantine had by this time reached the tolerably safe distance of a mile from us, I sent him down into the run again to drive the plugs well home and make them perfectly secure, and set to work with the steward to release the remaining passengers from their exceedingly uncomfortable condition. This was not a long task, and when it was completed I found that we mustered nine gentlemen, of whom three were wounded, eleven ladies, three children—two boys and a girl—seven maids, and an Indian ayah or nurse. One family, consisting of a lady and her daughter, were in a dreadful state of distress, the husband and father—a Mr. Richard Temple, resident magistrate of one of the up-country districts —having been shot dead while gallantly fighting in defence of the ship. The rest were in fairly good spirits, now that they found that there was a hope of ultimate escape from the perils that had so unexpectedly beset them ; for I learned that although their personal baggage had been rifled and all money and jewellery taken, they had been spared any further outrage than that of being bound with unnecessary and cruel rigour and confined to their cabins.

The poor souls had been without food or drink since tiffin. I thought therefore that it would not be amiss to set them down to a good meal, and with that object directed the steward to find his mates and also the cook, if possible, it appearing that none of the individuals named had been seen either during or since the attack, which gave rise to the suspicion that they had contrived to conceal themselves somewhere about the ship. This proved to be the case, the cook, with his mates, and the three under-stewards being eventually discovered in a disused pig-sty under the topgallant-forecastle, carefully concealed beneath a lot of lumber that they had dragged over themselves. From this secluded retreat they were speedily routed out, and, being solemnly assured that all danger was now past, were at length prevailed upon to resume their duty and to prepare a long-delayed dinner —or supper, as it might be more appropriately called—for the cuddy occupants.

When at length the meal was served, I took the liberty of occupying the poor murdered captain's seat at the table ; and while we were eating and drinking, I managed to gain a pretty clear idea of the incidents of the attack upon the *Bangalore*, each one having passed through some more or less trying experience which he or she was anxious to relate to the rest ; and when the meal was over Mr. Molyneux, a Calcutta merchant, rose to his feet and, while formally thanking me

on behalf of himself and his fellow-passengers for what I had already done, expressed their perfect concurrence in the wish of the surviving crew that I should take command of the ship, merely suggesting the great desirability of navigating her forthwith to the nearest civilized port. This, of course, was my own fixed intention, and I suggested Sierra Leone as the most suitable spot for which to make, it being as near as any other, with the advantage that the necessary officers to navigate the ship home, and a sufficient number of men to make up the full complement of the crew, might almost certainly be reckoned upon being found there.

The brigantine had left us, and with her departure everybody appeared to consider the danger as past. This, however, was an opinion which I by no means shared; for, knowing Mendouca so well as I did, I felt that it was by no means unlikely that, having reached an offing of some ten or twelve miles, he might order the sweeps to be laid in until daylight, in order that he might remain in our neighbourhood and assure himself by the actual demonstration of his own— or Pedro's—eyesight that the *Bangalore* had foundered, taking with her to the bottom all evidence of the atrocious crime of which he and his crew had been guilty. And, even should no uncomfortable doubts on this point assail him, he *must* learn, ere the lapse of many hours, that I and others were missing; and then, guessing, as he would at once, at the explanation of our absence, nothing would prevent him from returning and taking, or attempting to take, such measures as would insure our eternal silence.

I therefore considered it a singular if not an actually providential occurrence that when I went out on deck after dinner—or supper—the sky should have become overcast, with scarcely a star to be seen, with every appearance of both wind and rain ere long. It had become exceedingly dark, so much so that no sign of the brigantine was to be discovered, but by listening intently the roll and clatter of her sweeps were still to be caught ; and it was with very deep and fervent thankfulness that, after listening intently for several minutes, I felt convinced that she was still receding from us. I had given strict orders that the lanterns should be allowed to remain burning on deck, just as the pirates had left them, that no other lights should be kindled anywhere about the ship except where it was possible to effectually mask their light, and that no one should show anything of himself above the level of the topgallant-rail upon any consideration; but now, the brigantine having been gone from us rather more than two hours, I gave instructions that all the lanterns on deck and all lights of every kind visible from outside the ship might be simultaneously extinguished, so that, should anybody happen to be watching our lights, they might come to the conclusion that the ship had filled and we were gone to the bottom. This done, I mustered my entire crew and, first hoisting in the long-boat, sent them aloft to stow all the lighter sails, so that we might not be wholly unprepared should the change of weather that now seemed impending be ushered in with a squall. This occupied the men a full hour and a half, at the end of which, having brought the ship into tolerably manageable condition, I gave them permission to lie down and snatch a nap if they could, but to hold themselves ready for any emergency that might arise.

It was by this time long past midnight, and so pitchy dark that, all lights having been extinguished, it was impossible to see one end of the poop from the other. The stars had all vanished, and the silence was so profound as to be quite oppressive, not even the sound of the pirate's sweeps now being audible; though whether they had been laid in, or whether the vessel had increased her distance so greatly as to have passed beyond the range of sound, I knew not, but I strongly suspected the former contingency. This profound silence was maintained for nearly an hour, and then my hearing—rendered unusually acute no doubt by the intense darkness that enveloped me—once more became conscious of a regular, measured, rhythmical sound, the sound of sweeps again being plied, and, without doubt, on board the *Francesca*. What did it mean? Had Mendouca, in his feverish and painful condition, grown impatient of delay and ordered the sweeps to be again manned, after having given instructions for them to be laid in? Or, as my forebodings whispered to me, had the absence of myself and others

been already discovered, and was the brigantine returning in search of us? For the first quarter of an hour or so after the sounds had once again broken in upon the silence this was a question very difficult to decide; but when half-an-hour had passed the fact was indisputable that the pirates *were returning*, for the sounds had become distinctly clearer and stronger than they had at first been.

What was now to be done? There was but one course for us ; namely, to take every possible measure for the defence of the ship to our last gasp, for I felt assured that, should Mendouca recover possession of her, his fury at the trick that we had played him would be sated by nothing short of our absolute destruction. Having quickly made up my mind upon this point, I was in the act of groping my way along the poop, with the object of calling the men, when I thought I felt a faint stirring of the air, and, pausing for a moment, I moistened the back of my hand and held it up, turning it this way and that until I felt a distinct sensation of coolness. Yes, there was no doubt about it, I had felt a cat's-paw, and it seemed to be coming over our starboard quarter ; while the sound of the sweeps was away broad on our port bow. I could scarcely restrain a cheer as the hope of a breeze thus came to encourage me at the very moment when a new and terrible danger was threatening us. I paused for an instant and reflected ; and my thoughts took somewhat this shape : " If Mendouca is returning—and he undoubtedly is— it is because through some unfortunate combination of circumstances my absence has already been discovered, and he has at once jumped to the correct conclusion that I have somehow contrived to escape from the brigantine to the ship. And he knows me well enough to feel assured that, once here, I shall not tamely allow the Indiaman to go down under my feet ; or, if that should prove unpreventible, that I shall at least release the prisoners and concoct with them some plan of escape, such as taking to the boats, or constructing a raft. And he also knows that, in either case, should we succeed in preserving our lives until we are fallen in with, or picked up, his atrocious act of piracy and murder will be proclaimed, and every craft in the squadron will b specially ordered to keep a look-r for him and effect his capture at all hazards. Therefore he will spare no effort to find the ship and destroy her. Now—ah, there is another little breath of wind, I felt it distinctly that time ! —should he fail to find us, what course will he pursue? Why, he will certainly expect us to make our way northward—for Sierra Leone, most probably, the port that we have already determined to steer for—and he will do his best to overtake and recapture us. Therefore our best course will obviously be to head to the *southward*, and thus increase the distance between the two craft as rapidly as possible, so that they may be out of sight of each other at daybreak ; and then to proceed upon our proper course under easy sail."

This seemed to me to be a very fair and sound line of reasoning, and I determined to act upon it forthwith. I accordingly made my way forward, routed out the men, told them there was a breeze coming, and ordered them to brace up the yards and trim the sheets aft for a close-hauled stretch on the port tack, at the same time cautioning them to work silently, as I had only too much reason to fear that the pirates were returning to search for the ship. This news, confirmed as it was by the now perfectly audible sound of the sweeps, was enough for them, and they went about the decks so silently, speaking in whispers, and carefully taking each rope off its belaying-pin, and *laying* it down on deck, instead of flinging it down with clatter enough to wake the Seven Sleepers, that I am certain no one in the cabins, even had they been awake, could possibly have been aware of what was happening.

By the time that we had got our canvas trimmed the breeze had become quite perceptible, and the ship had gathered steerage way ; we therefore wore her round, and presently had the ineffable satisfaction of hearing a slight but distinct tinkling and gurgle of water under the bows.

With the springing up of this most welcome little breeze the sound of the sweeps first became by imperceptible degrees less audible and then was lost altogether, but whether this arose from the fact that the wind carried the sound away from us, or whether it was that they had laid in the sweeps, and were making sail upon the brigantine, it was impossible to tell, nor did I greatly care, provided that the breeze freshened

sufficiently to carry us out of sight before daybreak, this now being my great anxiety. Maxwell assured me that the *Bangalore* was a real clipper, easily beating everything that they had fallen in with, both on the passage out and on their homeward voyage. But no ship can sail fast without a fair amount of wind, and so far this breeze that had come to us was a mere breathing, just enough perhaps to waft us along at a speed of about two knots, or two and a half, maybe, whereas what I wanted was at least a seven-knot breeze, that would take us clean out of sight of our starting-point before dawn. For I knew that, if the *Bangalore* was a clipper, so too was the *Francesca;* and if her people once caught sight of so much as the heads of our royals from their own royal-yard, they would chase us as long as there was the slightest hope of overhauling us. And the knowledge of this fact made me wonder whether I had not acted rather imprudently in stowing all the lighter sails, instead of leaving them abroad to give us all the help of which they were capable. I was just inwardly debating this point, and had arrived at the conclusion that we ought to set them again, when the atmosphere seemed suddenly to grow more dense, and in a moment down came the rain in a regular tropical deluge, like the bursting of a waterspout, the sails flapped to the masts, and we were becalmed again. This was horribly vexatious, not to say disheartening ; but, happily for our peace of mind, it was a state of things that did not last long ; it merely meant a shift of wind, for presently, when the shower had ceased as abruptly as it had begun, the breeze sprang up again, this time coming out from the northward, and with gay and thankful hearts we squared away before it, or rather, headed just far enough to the eastward of south to permit everything set to draw properly. Moreover, the breeze gradually but steadily freshened, until in about an hour from the time when the ship first began to move we were going seven knots at the very least.

This was so far satisfactory, especially as the sky remained overcast and the night intensely dark, rendering it utterly impossible to see anything beyond a distance of three or four of the ship's lengths on either hand, and I now had good hopes of running the brigantine out of sight before daylight. That she was still engaged in the search for us, however, soon became evident ; for about three-quarters of an hour after the springing up of the true breeze our attention was suddenly attracted by the outburst of a brilliant glare of bluish-white light on our port quarter, which was nothing less than the brigantine burning port-fires, probably in an attempt to discover our whereabouts by the reflection of the light on our sails, or possibly in the expectation of catching sight, by means of the light, either of our boats, or a raft, or perhaps a hen-coop and grating or two floating about as evidence of our having gone down. However, she was about five miles distant from us at that time, and although the light of the port-fires rendered her perfectly visible to us, I had little or no fear that it would betray our whereabouts to er people. She remained dodging ab ut and occasionally burning port-fires or fully another hour—by which time we had sunk her to her foreyard below the horizon, as viewed from our deck—and then, as she discontinued her pyrotechnic display, we lost sight of her. At daybreak I sent a man right up to the main-royal-yard, where he remained until the light was thoroughly strong, and then came down with the report that the horizon was clear.

This was highly satisfactory, inasmuch as it confirmed my hope that if Mendouca was still prosecuting a search for us—as I felt sure he was, he having of course failed to discover any evidence of the ship having foundered—he was looking for us in a northerly direction, very probably cracking on in the belief that we had gone that way and that there was still a chance of overtaking us.

At eight bells in the morning watch we brought the ship to the wind on the larboard tack, with her head about east-north-east, and I then divided my scanty crew into two watches, with Joe Maxwell, the carpenter, as my chief mate, and a very smart A.B., named Tom Sutcliffe, as second. This done, the watch was set, and put to the job of straightening-up generally and pumping out the ship, this latter job being accomplished and the pumps sucking in just under the ten minutes that Maxwell had allowed for it. It was clear, therefore, that our hull was sound, and that in that respect, at all events, with the best—or rather the

worst—intentions in the world, the pirates had done us little or no harm.

Our most serious difficulty was the want of water, Mendouca having literally cleared the ship of every drop she possessed, save some eight or ten gallons in the scuttle-butt, which they had either overlooked, or perhaps had considered not worth taking. But here again it appeared as though God in His infinite mercy had taken compassion on us ; for about noon the wind died away, and I had only just time to take my meridian observation for the latitude when the heavens clouded over, and toward the close of the afternoon we were visited by a terrific thunderstorm accompanied by a perfect deluge of rain, during which, by loosely spreading all the awnings fore and aft, we were enabled to catch a sufficient quantity of water to carry us without stint as far at least as Sierra Leone.

It remained calm until about midnight, when a little breeze sprang up from the eastward which enabled us to lay our course nicely while it fanned us along at a speed of about five knots. The next morning broke bright and clear ; and with the first of the light the look-out reported a sail broad on our weather bow. Maxwell, fearing that it might be our old enemy, the *Francesca*, showing up again, came down at once and called me, stating his fears, and causing me to rush up on the poop just as I had sprung from my cot, quite regardless of appearances, although I could scarcely believe that Mendouca, if indeed we should be so unfortunate as to fall in with him again, would make his appearance in the eastern board. I must confess, however, that when I first reached the deck and beheld the stranger, I experienced a slight qualm of apprehension, for the craft was undoubtedly square-rigged, forward at least, and she was steering as straight as a hair for us, with studding-sails set on both sides, and coming down very fast. A few minutes' work with the telescope, however, sufficed to remove our apprehensions, so far at least as the *Francesca* was concerned, for as the light grew brighter we were enabled to discern that the stranger was a brig, and as I continued working away with the glass the vessel seemed to assume a familiar aspect, as though I had seen her before. At first I thought that it might possibly prove

H

to be the Spanish brig that had been anchored just ahead of us off Banana Peninsula ; but as she drew nearer I recognized with intense delight that it was none other than the dear old *Barracouta* herself. " And with her appearance," thought I, "all my troubles are ended ; for doubtless Captain Stopford will not only lend me men enough to carry the ship to Sierra Leone, but will also escort me thither."

CHAPTER XIX

TO THE CONGO AGAIN UPON A SPECIAL MISSION

THERE was very great delight manifested fore and aft when I was able to announce that it was a British man-o'-war that was bearing down upon us ; for all hands felt, like myself, that we had only to state our recent experiences to secure her protection at least until our arrival in safer waters. There was one exception to this, however, in the person of Simpson, who no sooner learned the true character of the strange sail, than he came aft and told me his story ; which, in brief, was to the effect that he had originally belonged to our navy, but had deserted, out of affection for Mendouca—who had shown him great kindness—when that individual chose to shake off his allegiance and abjure his country. And now, of course, he dreaded nothing so much as recognition and seizure, for not only was he a deserter, but he had also been guilty of taking an active part in more than one deed of piracy perpetrated by his chief ; he therefore implored me to let him keep below out of sight during the presence of the man-o'-war — which clearly meant to speak us—and also to omit all mention of or reference to him in the narrative of my own personal adventures. This I readily promised to do ; for although I was fully conscious that, in making such a promise, I was screening an individual who had most seriously transgressed the laws of his country, I could not help feeling that he had also contributed in a very important degree toward the saving of the *Bangalore*, and all on board her ; and I considered that this to a very great extent made amends for his past misdeeds, although it was quite probable that if he were arraigned for it, his judges might not take quite as lenient a view of the case. There it was, however ; but for him I might

never have succeeded in effecting my escape from the *Francesca*, and in that case the *Bangalore* and all on board her would have gone to the bottom. I therefore felt fully justified in promising to afford him all the protection that lay in my power.

When the brig was within a mile of us she hoisted British colours, and fired a gun for us to heave-to, which we of course at once did, displaying our ensign at the mizen-peak at the same time. The ladies and gentlemen in the cuddy, learning from the stewards what was happening, at once turned out to do honour to the occasion, so that when, a few minutes later, the *Barracouta*, with all her studding-sails collapsing and coming in together, rounded to within biscuit-toss of our weather quarter, our poop must have presented quite an animated appearance.

As the beautiful craft swept gracefully yet with a rush up into the wind, a figure that I recognized with delight as that of Young, our beloved first luff, sprang on to the hammock-rail with a speaking-trumpet in his hand. The next moment he had raised it to his lips, and was hailing—

" Ho, the ship ahoy ! What ship is that ? "

" The *Bangalore*, eighty-two days out from Calcutta, bound to London ; and plundered two days ago by a pirate. I hope you are none the worse for your boat adventure, Mr. Young, in the attack upon that same pirate last week ? I have news and to spare for you, so shall I lower a boat, or will you ? If you can conveniently do so it will perhaps be better, for I am rather short-handed," I replied.

I saw Young staring at me with all his eyes ; evidently he had not as yet recognized me in the longshore rig with which I had been fitted by the kindness of one of the cuddy passengers.

He raised the trumpet to his lips, and began—

" Who in the name of——? " when I saw little Freddy Pierrepoint scramble up alongside him excitedly and utterly regardless of etiquette, and say something eagerly. Young lowered the trumpet, stared hard at me, raised it again, and roared through it—

" Can it be possible that you are Dugdale—the Harry Dugdale that we have all been mourning as lost ? "

" Ay, ay, Mr. Young, it is myself, sure enough, alive and well, I am thankful to say ; and more glad than I can express to see the dear old *Barracouta* again ! "

As I uttered these words the watch on deck gave a ringing cheer, which thrilled me to the heart, for it told me better than words how sincerely attached to me the honest fellows were, and how delighted to see me again ; and although the outburst was by no means in accordance with strict discipline, Young—thoroughly good fellow that he was — never checked them, but, as their voices died away, simply waved his trumpet, and shouted, " I will come on board you ! " and disappeared behind the brig's high bulwarks.

A short pause now ensued, during which I suspected that the first luff was conferring with Captain Stopford, the *Barracouta's* people gazing curiously at us meanwhile through the brig's open ports ; and then the sound of the boatswain's pipe came floating to us from the brig across the tumbling waters, and we heard his gruff voice bellowing—" Gigs away ! "

The call was followed by a slight, muffled scurrying of feet, and the gig's crew were seen leaping, light as figures of india-rubber, into the elegantly-moulded craft that hung at the brig's davits, the falls were eased away, and in a moment the boat, light as a bubble, was dancing upon the sparkling blue tumble at the brig's lee gangway. Then the first lieutenant and Freddy Pierrepoint appeared at the head of the side ladder, the latter descending first and the lieutenant instantly following, the boat's bow was borne off from the ship's side, the oars dropped with a clean cut into the water, the men bent their backs as they gave way, and the dancing craft came bounding over the long surges towards us.

Meanwhile, on board the *Bangalore* I had caused the side-ladder to be shipped and the ropes rove in readiness for the lieutenant's arrival ; and in a few minutes he and Freddy were standing on the Indiaman's broad deck and greeting me with a handgrip the heartiness of which there was no mistaking.

I told my story as briefly as possible, and at its conclusion Young said—

" Well, we must of course let you have a few men ; but it will be a few only that we shall be able to spare, for I am sorry to say that our loss was terribly heavy in our boat attack upon

your friend Mendouca, no less than eight killed and twenty-three wounded, only four of the latter having as yet been able to return to duty. You must, however, lay your case before Captain Stopford—who, by the way, hopes you will take breakfast with him—and I dare say that when he learns how very short-handed you are, he will strain a point to spare you a dozen men to take the ship to Sierra Leone. And now, suppose you introduce us to your passengers, who, judging from what I have been able to see of them from here, appear to be a very pleasant lot of people."

Upon this hint I led the way to the poop, where by this time nearly the entire cuddy party had assembled, and introduced my companions in due form, and in a few minutes Young and Freddy were each surrounded by a large party, Master Freddy's, I noticed, being mainly composed of the younger members of the gentler sex, who petted and made much of the juvenile warrior, to that young gentleman's entire content.

In due time I proceeded on board my old ship ; and on reaching the deck was fully repaid for all that I had gone through by the heartiness of the greeting that I received from my shipmates, one and all of whom seemed sincerely delighted at finding that I was still in the land of the living. For, as fate would have it, the *Barracouta* had fallen in with the *Felicidad*, with the French schooner *Mouette* in company as a prize—the latter vessel having pursued the *Felicidad* out of the creek, only to find that she had caught a Tartar, which captured her after a short but determined struggle —and from her the *Barracouta's* people had learned all particulars of our somewhat disastrous enterprise, including the news that I was missing, and was believed to have been killed in the unsuccessful attack upon the schooner in the creek.

Captain Stopford was kindness itself in his reception of me, commiserating with me upon all the hardships of my late adventure, and heartily congratulating me upon my escape from the *Francesca*, and the saving of the Indiaman, the latter of which, he assured me, he would take care to report in the proper quarter in such a way as should further my advancement in the service. With regard to supplying me with men, he promised to do the best that he could; and at Young's suggestion—he being one of the rather large party that the captain had invited to meet me at breakfast—it was arranged that I should have a dozen; and as he fully agreed with me that there was just a chance that the *Francesca* might be at no great distance to the northward, still actively pursuing her search for us, it was further arranged that I should crowd sail for Sierra Leone, in the hope of turning the tables upon Mendouca by overtaking him, in which case we were to do our best to detain him until the arrival of the *Barracouta* upon the scene, it being the captain's plan to follow us at a distance of some fifteen or twenty miles. As an incentive to expedition—and no doubt, incidentally, to the promotion of the capture of the *Francesca*—the captain informed me that if we managed to accomplish a quick run to Sierra Leone, I should probably be in time to rejoin the *Felicidad*, which schooner was then at that port, refitting after her engagement with the *Mouette*. I was very grieved to learn that poor Ryan, although not nearly so severely wounded as I had believed, was lying in the hospital at Sierra Leone, prostrate with a bad attack of fever, from which, when the *Barracouta* left, it was greatly feared that he would not recover.

As soon as breakfast was over the crew were mustered, and Young picked out for me twelve good, stout men, who were ordered to pass their bags down into the boat and go on board the *Bangalore* with me; and, this most welcome addition to our crew having been received, I made sail, packing upon the good ship every rag that would draw, the *Barracouta* remaining hove-to until we had placed a sufficient distance between her and ourselves. But although we carried on day and night—the Indiaman proving such a flyer that the *Barracouta's* people had their hands full to keep us in sight—nothing more was seen of the *Francesca*, and we were at length driven to the conclusion that, failing to find us, Mendouca had resumed his voyage at a much earlier period than we had anticipated. We reached Sierra Leone on the afternoon of the third day after falling in with the *Barracouta*; and there I left the Indiaman, which, after a detention of four days, sailed for England with a

full complement, made up of the officers and men of a large barque that had been wrecked upon the coast only a week or two before, supplemented by a few out of the many white seamen who had been left behind in hospital when their ships were ready to sail for home, and who, contrary to the general rule, had recovered from, instead of succumbing to, the deadly malaria of the coast.

As for me, I found that I had arrived most opportunely, so far as the *Felicidad* was concerned, for the repairs to that small hooker were completed, as it happened, on the very day of our arrival; and Captain Stopford very generously offered me the command of her, asserting that my conduct with regard to the Indiaman had conclusively demonstrated my entire fitness for the post, and that if I chose to accept it he should have no anxiety whatever, either on the score of my courage or my discretion. Ryan, poor fellow, was, contrary to expectation, still alive, and hopes were now entertained that he might ultimately recover; but he was still so weak that when I went to the hospital to see him, he was so overcome with emotion at the sight of me—although he had been carefully prepared for the meeting—that he burst into tears and was seized with a fit of hysterical sobbing so violent that I had to retire again at once without exchanging a word with him; and, to my very deep regret, I had not another opportunity to see him. I grieve to say that although, when I paid him that unfortunate visit, he appeared to be making slow but sure progress toward recovery, he suffered a relapse a few days afterwards, from which he never rallied; and his ashes now repose, with those of many another gallant spirit, in the spot that is known throughout the world as "The White Man's Grave."

The repairs to the *Felicidad* being completed, her final preparations for sea were vigorously pushed forward, and on the third day after our arrival, having first visited the *Bangalore* and bade farewell to her passengers—each and every one of whom insisted that he (or she) owed his (or her) life to me, and that henceforward I must regard myself as a dearly cherished friend—I joined the little hooker as her commander, and sailed the same afternoon for the Congo; my especial mission being to test the truth, or otherwise, of Mendouca's statement respecting the fate of the *Sapphire's* boats' crews, and—in the event of its being true—to attempt the rescue of any of the unfortunate people who might perchance be still alive.

We made the high land to the northward of the river mouth about midnight, after a rather long and uneventful passage; and, the wind being light, and the river current strong, even at a considerable distance from the entrance, we then reached in toward the land, and anchored in fourteen fathoms, at about as many miles from the shore, where we remained, rolling and tumbling about on the heavy swell, until the sea-breeze set in, about eight o'clock the next morning. We then hove up our mud-hook, and ran in, anchoring in Banana Creek, opposite Lobo's factory, about six bells in the forenoon. There was only one other vessel in the creek at the time, a Portuguese brig; and her build and general appearance so unmistakably proclaimed her honest, that I never gave her a second thought. Besides, I had a special mission to accomplish —namely, the discovery and deliverance, if possible, of between thirty and forty of my own countrymen, languishing in a bitter captivity, and in daily, if not hourly, peril of death by torture as cruel and protracted as the fiendish malignity of merciless savages can possibly devise.

Now, I was as well equipped for such an expedition as I could possibly wish, save in one particular. I had a smart, light-draught vessel, capable of "going anywhere where a duck can swim," as we say at sea; we were well armed, had plenty of ammunition, mustered a crew of twenty-six prime seamen, the pick of the *Barracouta's* crew—men who would go anywhere, and face anything—we carried an ample supply of blankets, beads, brass wire, old muskets, and tawdry finery of various descriptions, priceless in the eyes of savages, for the purpose of peaceable ransom, if such could be accomplished; but we lacked an interpreter, a man acquainted with the barbaric language of the up-river natives, through whom we should be able to communicate with them and carry on the necessary negotiations. And such a man it was now my first duty and anxiety to secure. I had given this matter a great deal of careful consideration during our pas-

sage, and had at length determined upon the course of action that seemed to promise the most successful results; and it was in accordance with this determination that I anchored in Banana Creek instead of proceeding forthwith up the river to the spot named by Mendouca as the scene of the captivity of the *Sapphire's* boats' crews.

I entered the river without any disguise of any sort, showing British colours and the man-o'-war's pennant; and, as I had expected, our old friend Lobo soon came alongside in his gig, with his usual stereotyped smiles and bows, and offers to supply us with anything and everything that we might happen to want. I took care to be below when he boarded us; and, in accordance with previous arrangements, Gowland, who met the fellow upon his arrival, proposed that he should go down into the cabin and see me personally upon the business of his visit. He at once assented, willingly, Gowland following him down, and when the two had entered, the sentry at the cabin door closed it after them.

"Ah, good-morning, sar," exclaimed Lobo to me, as he entered. "Glad to see you back in the river, sar! I hope dat de capitan and officers of de beautiful *Barracouta* are all well? Ah, gentlemen, dat was a ver' fine bit of vork, dat attack of yours upon Chango Creek; ver' fine and ver' successful. I 'ave alvays been proud of *my* share in dat exploit. But, gentlemen, you mus' please never so much as whisper dat I, Joaquin Miguel Lobo, had anything to do vid it. My vord, if you did, de rascal slavers vould cut my t'roat for me, and de man-o'-war gentlemen vould lose a fait'ful ally."

"No doubt, Señor Lobo," agreed I genially. "But, never fear, you are perfectly safe from betrayal to the slavers, so far as we are concerned; you shall find us as faithful to you as you have been to us. But sit down, man, and let me offer you a glass of wine."

With many bows and wreathed smiles, and deprecating elevations of the shoulders, Lobo took the seat to which I pointed him, and I touched a bell.

"Steward, put the wine and some glasses on the table, will you; and also a box of cigars that you will find on the shelf in my cabin."

The wine and cigars were brought; we helped ourselves; and I began—

"I am very much obliged to you for coming aboard, Señor Lobo, for you are the very man that I most desired to see. I require some assistance of a rather peculiar kind, and I believe that you, above all others, are the one who can best help me to it."

Lobo bowed and smiled, sipped his wine, and assured us that he was in all things our very obedient, humble servant, and that nothing pleased him so much as to be of assistance to the man-o'-war gentlemen, who honoured the river by paying it an occasional visit. At the same time—he pointed out—his friendly relations with those same man-o'-war gentlemen, and the services that he had been so glad to render them from time to time were, if not well known, at least very strongly suspected by the slavers and slave-dealing fraternity generally who used the Congo for their nefarious purposes; and in incurring this suspicion he also incurred a very serious risk, both to property and life, for which he considered that he was justly entitled to be remunerated on a generous scale.

"Most assuredly," I agreed. "And I may tell you at once, Señor Lobo, that I am prepared to reward you very munificently for the efficient and faithful performance of the service that I require of you; I am prepared, in fact, to offer you no less a reward than *your life*. Ah, you turn pale, I see; and well you may when I inform you that your true character is by this time known to probably every British commander on the coast; you are known as a bare-faced traitor to the cause that you have pretended so zealously to serve, and I don't mind mentioning to you, in confidence, that, if this ship had happened to be the *Barracouta* instead of the *Felicidad*, you would now in all probability have been dangling from one of that ship's yard-arms, as a wholesome warning and example to all betrayers— Nay, keep your seat, man; there is a sentry outside the door, and you are a prisoner beyond all possibility of escape. But you have no cause for fear on that account, provided that you can prevail upon yourself to act honestly for once. I require a certain service from you, and I promise you that if you render that service faithfully I will set you free at the termination of the adventure, with full liberty to seek safety by flight elsewhere. But until the adventure of which I speak is brought to a favour-

able conclusion, you are my prisoner; and I give you my word of honour that upon the first attempt to escape which you may be ill-advised enough to make, I will put you in irons and chain you to the deck. If, therefore, you are wise, you will submit to your present predicament with a good grace, rather than tempt a worse one. And now, tell me everything you know with regard to the fate of the crews of the *Sapphire's* boats."

"The *Sapphire's* boats?" ejaculated the now thoroughly terrified wretch. "I swear to Gad, sar, dat I had not'ing to do vid dat! I know not'ing about dem; not'ing whatever! But I can tell you de name of de man who had; ay, and I can put him into your power, if you like; he is a villain, and it would be only doing a good action to betray him to justice. I vill do it, too, if you vill release me at vonce; I vill tell you all about him, vhere he is to be found vhen he visits de river, de name of his cheep, and—and—all dat is necessairey for you to know."

"Yes; no doubt," I answered. "But you will have to purchase your release in some other way, señor; unfortunately for you we know all about Don Fernando de Mendouca, captain of the brigantine *Francesca*, and have every confidence in our ability to get hold of him without your assistance. And I may tell you that, *up to the present*, no charge has been made against you in connection with the disappearance of the *Sapphire's* boats; you have therefore nothing to fear from us just now on that score. *Now*, will you tell us what you know about those unfortunate missing men?"

"Yes; yes, I vill, gentlemen; I vill tell you all dat I know; but it is not much," answered Lobo, with evident relief. "I only know dat de scoundrel Mendouca managed to trap de two boats in some vay—how, I know not—and dat he gave dem de choice of being massacred, dere and den, or of surrendering and having dheir lives spared. And vhen dhey had surrendered he exchanged dhem to Matadi for slaves—t'ree slaves for every white man—so dat Matadi might have plenty of victims—white victims dhey consider *very* good—for de annual—de annual—what you call it, eh? festa."

"Festival, I suppose you mean," said I, with an involuntary shudder. "And, pray, Señor Lobo, do you happen to know the date of this festival?"

"No, I canot say dat I do; but I t'ink about one week from now," was the answer.

"Then, thank God, we are still in time!" I ejaculated. "Now, Señor Lobo, I presume you are acquainted with this chief, Matadi, are you not? You have probably had dealings with him, eh? Do n#t be afraid to give a truthful answer, because by so doing you cannot betray anything about yourself that we do not know already. We are fully aware, for instance, that you are a slave-dealer—among other things—and I have very little doubt that, if I chose to land a party, we should find a choice lot of negroes in that barracoon of yours in the bush, yonder—you look surprised, but, you see, I know all about you; so your best plan will be to answer my questions truthfully and unreservedly. Now, as to this Matadi, who is he, and what is he?"

"Sair," said Lobo, in great perturbation, "I see dat you know all about me, so I will be perfectly open and frank wid you. I *do* know Matadi. He is a very powerful chief, de head of a tribe numbering quite t'ree t'ousand warriors; and his chief town is far up de river—four, five days' journey in a canoe. It lies on de sout' bank of de river 'bout eight miles below de first—what you call?—where de water runs very furious over de rocks, boiling like —like de water in a pot."

"Ah, rapids, you mean, I suppose?" suggested I.

"Yes, yes; rapids; dat is de word," agreed Lobo. "His town is near de first rapids; and he is very powerful, very dangerous, very fierce. What do you want wid him, señor?"

"I want those white men that he holds in captivity; and I mean to have them, by fair means or foul!" said I. "I will buy them of him, if he is willing to part with them in that way; and if not, I intend to take them from him by force, for have them I *must* and *will*. And I require your assistance in this matter, señor, as an interpreter, through whom I can treat with the fellow and carry on the necessary negotiations; and if those negotiations are successful, you will be released on our return here, and allowed thirty days to complete your arrangements for removal elsewhere. But if we fail you will be retained as a prisoner, and taken to Sierra Leone, to be dealt with as your past treacheries

deserve. Now, do you quite understand the position?"

"Yes, señor, I understand," answered Lobo, in great distress. "But, oh, gentlemen, I beg, I pray you, do not take me away from my business; it will all go wrong widout me, and I shall lose hundreds, t'ousands of dollars, *all* my property will be gone before I can get back! I shall be ruin'!"

"I am sorry to hear that," I remarked; "but even supposing that matters go as badly with you as you seem to fear, that will be better than *hanging*, will it not? And, you see, I *must* have somebody with me, as interpreter, whose interest it will be that I shall be successful in my mission; and I know of no one whose interests can be made more completely identical with my own than yourself, señor. Therefore I shall take you with me, regardless of consequences. But if you have any assistants ashore to whom you would like to send a very brief message to the effect that you are taking a little business-trip up the river with me for a few days, and that they must do the best they can for you during your absence, I have no objection to your sending it. Otherwise, I will dismiss your boat; for we must not miss this fine sea-breeze, which ought to take us a good many miles up-stream before it dies away."

"Well, gentlemen, if you are quite determined, I must submit," answered Lobo, with a very disconsolate air. "But I protest against being thus carried off against my will; I protest against it as a—an—a—what do you call him?—yes, an outrage—an outrage, gentlemen; and the Portuguese Government will inquire into the matter."

"All right," said I cheerfully; "there can be no objection to that, so far as *we* are concerned. And now that we have arranged this little matter, shall I dismiss your boat?"

"No, no; not yet, not yet," hastily answered Lobo. "Give me one littl' piece of paper, if you please, and I will write a few words to Diego, my manager, telling him what to do in my absence."

"No," said I determinedly, "I can permit no written messages; a *verbal* one, if you like, but nothing more."

"Ver' well," answered Lobo resignedly. "Then I will go up and speak to my boatmen."

";No need for that," said I. " Tell us which of your men you wish to see, and I will send for him to come here."

Poor Lobo made a gesture of impatience, but saw that I had quite determined to afford him no shadow of an opportunity to make any secret communication whatever ; so he submitted to the inevitable, and sent for one of his men, to whom he delivered such a message as I suggested, adding a request that a small supply of clothing might be sent off to him at once. This ended the matter, so far as the obtaining of an efficient interpreter was concerned ; the clothes were brought off ; and shortly after noon we weighed and, with a brisk breeze, stood out of the creek on our way up the river.

For the first twelve miles or so our course was the same as that which we had followed in our memorable expedition to attack Chango Creek ; the river being, up to that point, about three miles wide, with a fine deep channel averaging perhaps a quarter of that width up as far as abreast the southern extremity of Monpanga island, where this deep channel terminates, and the average depth of the entire stream dwindles to about six fathoms for the next fourteen miles, the channel at the same time narrowing down to a width varying from about two miles to less than half-a-mile in some parts, notably at the spot where it begins to thread its devious way among the islands that cumber the stream for a length of fully thirty miles, at a distance of about twenty-eight miles from Shark Point.

By carrying a press of sail, and hugging the northern bank, keeping as close to the shore as our little draught of water would permit, thus to a great extent cheating the current, we contrived to get as far as the spot where the above-mentioned chain of islands commences ; and there, the wind failing us toward sunset, we came to an anchor close to the southern shore, on a sand-bank, in three fathoms, under the lee of a large island that sheltered us from the rush of the main current ; and there we remained all night, a strict anchor watch of course being kept not only to see that the schooner did not drive from her berth, but also to guard against possible attack on the part of the natives. In this spot, to my inexpressible chagrin, we were compelled to spend the following two days, the

wind blowing down the river, when it blew at all, a little variety being infused into the weather by the outburst of a most terrific thunderstorm which brought with it a perfect hurricane of wind and a deluge of rain ; after which we again got a fair wind and were able to pursue our way for a time, getting ashore occasionally upon unsuspected sand-banks, but always contriving to heave off again, undamaged, thanks to the fact that we were proceeding up-stream against the current instead of down-stream with it. And—not to dwell unduly upon incidents that were exciting enough to us, although the recital of them would prove of but little interest to the reader—in this way we contrived to creep up the river the hundred and twelve miles or so that were necessary to bring us to Matadi's town—having passed, and with some difficulty avoided, two whirlpools on the way, reaching our destination about two bells in the afternoon watch on the fifth day after leaving Banana Creek.

CHAPTER XX

SUCCESS. THE FATE OF THE PIRATE SLAVER

MATADI'S "town" was situate, as Lobo had informed us, on the south bank of the stream, on the sloping side of a hill that rose rather steeply from the water's edge ; the scenery of this part of the river being totally different from that of the mouth ; the change occurring gradually, but becoming quite decided about the point where the chain of islands is left behind on the traveller's upward way. For whereas on the lower reaches of the Congo— that is to say, for the first forty miles or so from its mouth—the banks of the river are low and flat, and to a great extent mangrove-lined, beyond this point their tendency is to become higher and steeper, in some places, indeed, quite precipitous, until where we now were the ground sloped up from the river margin to a height of fully four hundred feet, for the most part densely covered with bush interspersed here and there with masses of noble forest trees.

Matadi's town was situate, as I have said, upon the sloping hillside that constituted the south bank of the river, and consisted of some four or five hundred buildings arranged with tolerable regularity on either side of two broad streets or roads that crossed each other at right angles, their point of intersection being a spacious square, in the centre of which stood a circular structure with a high-peaked, pointed roof of thatch, that Lobo informed me was the fetish-house. I was greatly surprised at the neatness and skill displayed in the construction of the buildings in this important town ; for while they were insignificant in size, as compared with the dwellings of a civilized race, being about the size of a small two-roomed cottage, such as may be found in almost any rural district in England, they were very considerably larger and more carefully and substantially-built than the huts that we had noticed in King Plenty's town, when we made our disastrous attack upon Mendouca and his consorts. There was even a certain attempt at ornamentation discernible in the larger structures, many of which had what I believe is called in England a bargeboard, elaborately carved, under the projecting eaves of the roof that formed the verandah, the wooden posts that supported those same projecting eaves being also boldly sculptured. These particulars I noted through my telescope on rounding the bend of the river just beyond the town ; and I could not help feeling that a community of savages intellectual enough to find pleasure in the adornment of their houses would be likely to prove very difficult to deal with unless I could contrive to make their inclination coincide with my own wishes.

Our appearance—the *Felicidad* being probably the first ship that had ever penetrated so far up the river—created a profound sensation in the town, the inhabitants rushing in and out of their dwellings and about the streets for all the world like an alarmed colony of ants, and finally congregating along the margin of the river to the extent of fully one thousand, most of them being men, every one of whom, so far as I could make out, was armed ; the weapons being spears, bows and arrows, and clubs with heavy knobs on the end. They seemed to be a fine, powerful race, evidently accustomed to warfare, if one might judge by the readiness with which, at the command of an immensely stout and powerful man—whom Lobo declared to be none other than Matadi himself — they formed themselves up into compact and orderly squadrons, and I thought,

ruefully, that if it became necessary to resort to forcible measures for the release of our countrymen, we were likely to have a pretty bad time.

To attempt to open communications with a thousand armed savages, whose evident purpose in mustering on the river bank immediately in front of their town was to resolutely oppose any attempt at landing on our part, was a rather delicate operation ; still, it had to be done, and it was worse than useless to exhibit any sign of trepidation or hesitation. I therefore ordered the gig to be lowered, and with four men, fully armed, at the oars, and Lobo and myself in the stern-sheets, pushed off for the shore. This bold action on our part created a profound sensation upon the savages massed upon the shore, the boat being no sooner under way than they raised their spears above their heads, shook them furiously until the blades clashed upon each other with the sound of a falling torrent of water, and emitted a blood-curdling yell that almost drove poor Lobo out of his senses. We had, however—at Lobo's suggestion—provided ourselves with palm branches, cut on the night before at our previous anchorage, and now, seizing one of these, the Portuguese scrambled forward into the eyes of the boat and stood there, waving the branch violently and pointing it toward the savages. This demonstration had the effect of quelling the tumult, the blacks subsiding into quietude almost instantly, at the command of Matadi ; but it was evident that they had no intention of permitting us to land, for at a second command from the chief they advanced, as steadily as a band of civilized troops, across the short intervening space of greensward between themselves and the water's edge, at which they halted, forming up three deep in a long, compact line along the river margin.

We continued to pull shoreward until we were within easy speaking distance ; when the boat's bows were turned upstream, and while the men continued to paddle gently ahead, using just sufficient strength to enable the boat to stem the current and maintain her position abreast the centre of the line of savages, Lobo opened the palaver by informing Matadi that we were there by command of the Great White Queen to procure the release of the white men held by him as prisoners, and that we were fully prepared to pay a handsome ransom for them; it was only for Matadi to name his price, and it should be cheerfully paid.

To this the chief replied by inquiring what white men we referred to; he knew nothing about white men, and indeed had never seen any except ourselves. And he strongly advised us to lose no time in making our way back down the river again, as his soldiers were very angry at our presumption in invading his territory, and he could not answer for it that he would be able to restrain them should they take into their heads to actively resent our intrusion by attacking the ship.

I knew from this reply, which Lobo duly translated to me, that our friend Matadi was an adept in the art—so peculiarly characteristic of the African savage—of lying, and must be dealt with accordingly. So I said to Lobo—

"Tell him that he is mistaken. Say that the circumstance was doubtless of so trivial a character as to escape the recollection of a great chief like Matadi; but that, nevertheless, we *know* it to be a fact that about six moons ago some thirty or forty white men were sold to him by one Mendouca, a slave-buyer; and that it is those men we are seeking, our instructions being that we are not to return without them, even should we be obliged to destroy Matadi's town with our thunder and lightning in the process of securing them."

My scarcely-veiled threat to destroy his town was received by Matadi with scornful laughter, the savage declaring in set terms that he did not believe in the power of the white men to produce either lightning or thunder; and as to our accomplishing the threatened destruction without those means—why, there were a few of his warriors present who would have a word to say upon that matter. Touching the question of the white men said to have been sold to him, Matadi admitted that he now thought he remembered some transaction of the kind, but had not the remotest idea of what had become of them; he would make inquiries, however, and if we would go away, and return again about the same time next moon he would perhaps be able to give us some news of them. But before troubling himself to make any such inquiries he must be propitiated with a present; and he would also like to know what price we were prepared to pay for each white man, should any be found.

"Tell him," said I, "that this is a case of 'no white man, no present'; but that if the white men are found, I will not only buy them of him at so much per head, but also make him a handsome present into the bargain. Say that the goods to be paid as ransom are aboard the schooner, and that they consist of guns, beads, brass wire, beautiful printed calicoes, suitable for the adornment of any African king's wives; handsome red coats with resplendent brass buttons and gorgeous worsted epaulettes, admirably calculated to set off Matadi's own kingly figure; and superb blankets, red, blue, green—in fact, all the colours of the rainbow. If he and two or three of his chiefs would like to come aboard and see these magnificent articles, I shall be very pleased to exhibit them."

This speech being translated by Lobo, there ensued a long palaver, the result of which was that Matadi declined to go on board the schooner, but had no objection to come off alongside and inspect them from a distance, provided that we would first return and hoist up our own boat. The fact evidently was that the fellow, treacherous himself, suspected everybody else of being the same, and was clearly indisposed to put himself in our power, while he was at the same time devoured with curiosity to see the articles of which I had given such a glowing description. Of course, as I wished above all things to excite his cupidity to the point of determining to possess the goods, even at the cost of having to give up the white men, I readily agreed to his proposal; and at once returned to the schooner and ordered the boat to be hoisted to the davits.

It was evident that my endeavour to excite Matadi's curiosity had been completely successful; for no sooner was the gig out of the water than a large canoe was launched, into which Matadi and three or four other negroes — presumably subordinate chiefs — scrambled, when she was at once shoved off and, paddled by twenty natives, brought to within about twenty yards of the schooner, that being considered, I suppose, about the shortest distance within which it would be safe to approach us. I tried to persuade them to come a little nearer, if not actually on board, but Matadi resolutely refused; and as he seemed half inclined to go back again without even waiting to see what I had to show him, I ordered the steward to open the boxes at once, and forthwith proceeded to exhibit my coils of wire, strings of beads, bandana handkerchiefs, rolls of gaudily-coloured prints, old military uniforms, and muskets, and other odds and ends, the exhibition proving so attractive that before its conclusion the canoe had been gradually sheered nearer and nearer to the schooner until she was brought fairly alongside, and they had even consented to accept a rope's-end to hang on by. Matadi badly wanted us to pass some of the articles down over the side that he might examine them still more minutely, but I would not permit this, thinking it best to still leave some of his curiosity unsatisfied, and at length, after they had been alongside nearly an hour and a half, and had asked for a second and even a third sight of most of the goods, they reluctantly retired, their eyes glistening with cupidity, Matadi promising to institute an immediate inquiry as to the whereabouts of the white men, and to let me know the result as soon as possible.

I was very well satisfied with this interview, for I felt convinced that I had so powerfully excited the covetousness of the savages that they would determine to possess the goods that I had shown them at any cost. And so, as it turned out, I had, although, consequent upon my omission to take into consideration the natural treachery of the savage character, I was wholly mistaken as to the form in which that determination would manifest itself.

It was clear that Matadi still entertained a wholesome, whole-souled distrust of us; for when he landed the troops of warriors were still left drawn up along the river bank, with the evident intention of preventing any attempt on our part to go ashore and satisfy our curiosity by an inspection of his town; we therefore accepted the palpable hint thus conveyed, and stuck to the ship, which, I need scarcely say, had been cleared for action and held ready for any emergency from the moment of our arrival abreast the town.

It was by this time growing late in the afternoon, and as I was anxious to obtain possession of my unfortunate countrymen and leave Matadi's rather dangerous neighbourhood before nightfall, we watched the proceedings in the town narrowly and with a great deal of interest. But although we were enabled with the aid of our telescopes to follow Matadi and his little coterie of chiefs to a large building abutting on the square at the intersection of the cross streets, and which we took to be the "palace," we were unable to detect anything of an unusual character in the appearance or movements of the people until close upon sunset, when we observed a small canoe coming off to the schooner —a craft propelled by four paddlers, with a single individual sitting in the stern. This person we presently recognized as one of the chiefs who had accompanied Matadi alongside earlier in the day; and he brought a message to the effect that the king had ascertained that the white men about whom we had inquired were all safe in a village a day's march distant, and that Matadi would send for them on the morrow, unless we were prepared to make him a present of a musket, five strings of beads, a bandana handkerchief, and a roll of printed calico, in which case he would so far discommode himself as to send off a messenger at once. This was of course very annoying, and I did not at all like the idea of giving these savages anything without a tangible return for it; still, after considering the matter a little, I arrived at the conclusion that to expedite affairs by twelve hours was quite worth the price asked, and the articles were accordingly handed over, not without grave misgivings as to the wisdom of the proceeding. Soon after this it fell dark, the stars sparkled out one after another, lighting up the scene with their soft effulgence, the noises in the town became hushed, save for the occasional barking of a dog here and there, and a deep, solemn hush fell upon us, in which the deep, hoarse, tumbling roar of a whirlpool at no great distance, and the gurgle and rush of the turbid river past the schooner's hull became almost startlingly audible. But as long as we were able to see them the lines of native warriors still stood, silent and motionless, guarding the whole river front of the town. As a matter of precaution, I now ordered the boarding nettings to be triced up all round the ship, the guns to be loaded with grape and canister, the small arms to be prepared for immediate service, a double anchor watch to be kept, and the men to hold themselves ready for any emergency, after the bustle of which preparations the schooner subsided again into silence and darkness, the men for the most part "pricking for a soft plank" on deck, and coiling themselves away thereon in preference to seeking repose in the stifling forecastle. As for Gowland and myself, we paced the deck contemplatively together until about ten o'clock, discussing the chances of getting away on the morrow, and then, everything seeming perfectly quiet and peaceful, we had our mattresses brought on deck, and stretched ourselves out thereon in the small clear space between the companion and the wheel.

I had been asleep about two hours, when I was awakened by a light touch, and, starting up, found that it was one of the anchor watch, who was saying—

"Better go below, sir, I think, because it looks as though it was goin' to rain. And Bill and me, sir, we thinks as you ought to know that we fancies we've heard the dip o' paddles occasionally round about the ship within the last ten minutes."

"The dip of paddles, eh?" exclaimed I, in a whisper. "Where away, Roberts?"

"Well, first here and then there, sir," answered the man, in an equally low and cautious tone of voice; "both ahead and astern of us; sometimes on one side, and then on t'other. But we ain't by no means certain about it; that there whirlipool away off on our port quarter a little ways down stream is makin' such a row that perhaps we're mistaken, and have took the splash of the water in it for the sound of paddles. And it's so dark that there ain't a thing to be seen."

It was as the man had said. It was evident that a heavy thunderstorm was about to break over us, for the heavens had become black with clouds, and the darkness was so profound that it was impossible to see from one side of the deck to the other. I scrambled to my naked feet and went first to the taffrail, then along the port side of the deck forward, returning aft along the starboard side of the deck, listening intently, and I certainly fancied that once or twice I detected a faint sound like that of a paddle stroke, but I could not be certain; and as to seeing anything, that was utterly out of the question.

"Find Warren, and tell him to bring a port-fire on deck, and light it," said I. "It can do no harm to take a look round, just to satisfy ourselves; and it is never safe to trust these savages too much. Look alive, Roberts; moments may be precious if it be as you suspect."

"Ay, ay, sir," answered the man, as he trundled away forward to find the gunner. And meanwhile, as it was evident that a heavy downpour was imminent, I roused up Gowland, and we carried our mattresses below, I repeating to him, as we went, what Roberts had told me.

By the time that we got back on deck again the gunner was aft, waiting for us, with the port-fire all ready in his hand, and I instructed him to go aloft as far as the fore-crosstrees and light it there. A few seconds elapsed, and then, with startling distinctness, came down to us the cry—

"All ready, sir, with the port-fire!"

"Then light it at once," answered I, "and we will see what there is to be seen."

The livid, blue-white glare of the port-fire almost instantly burst forth, shedding its unearthly radiance far across the glassy, swirling surface of the rushing stream, and by its light we saw a startling sight indeed, the schooner being surrounded by a flotilla of at least twenty large canoes, each manned by from thirty to forty dusky warriors, fully armed with spears, bows, and war-clubs. They were about a cable's length from us, and had evidently taken up their positions with the utmost care, so that they might close in upon and reach us simultaneously, as they were now doing. As the brilliant light of the port-fire blazed forth, a shout of astonishment, not very far removed from dismay, burst from the occupants of the canoes, and a momentary tendency to sheer off precipitately became apparent; but this was instantly checked by a loud and authoritative call from the largest canoe—the voice sounding very much like that of Matadi himself—and with an answering yell the savages at once turned the bows of their canoes toward the schooner and began to paddle for dear life.

"Call all hands," shouted I, "and pipe to quarters. Pass the word that the men are not to wait to dress. Another minute and the savages will be upon us!"

The men needed no second order; they had all been sleeping on deck, and had awakened at the gunner's call from aloft, and the glare of the port-fire striking through their closed eyelids, and before the words were well out of my lips they were standing to their guns and awaiting my next order.

"Depress the muzzles of your guns as much as you can, and give the treacherous rascals their contents as you bring them to bear," cried I. "We shall only have time for one round, and if that does not stop them we shall be obliged to fight them hand to hand!"

The whole of the schooner's guns were fired, one after the other, but the port-fire unfortunately burnt out just about that time, so that we were unable to ascertain what effect had been produced, and before another could be found and lighted we heard and felt the light shocks of collision as the canoes dashed alongside, and in a moment found ourselves engaged in attempting to check the onset of a perfect *wall* of savages that hemmed us in on every side, and surged, and struggled, and writhed, and panted as they endeavoured to force a way through the stubborn boarding nettings. It was just the tricing up of those nettings that saved us; but for them the schooner's decks would have been overrun, and we should have been massacred in a moment. As it was, this unexpected obstacle, which of course none of them had observed in the afternoon — the nettings not being then triced up—daunted them, for they could neither displace it nor force a way through it, and while they clung there, like a lot of bees, vainly striving to find or make a passage through it, our men were blazing away with musket and pistol at the black wall of writhing, yelling humanity, and bowling them over by dozens at a time. When at length another port-fire was found and lighted, it disclosed to us an appalling picture of dusky, panting bodies, blazing eyeballs, waving skins and plumes, gleaming spear-points, and upraised war-clubs hemming us in on both sides, from stem to stern, every separate individual glaring at us with demoniac hate and fury as he strove ineffectually to get at us.

The savages fell in scores at a time beneath our close and withering fire, and at length, finding the netting impassable, and themselves being shot down to no purpose, they suddenly abandoned the attack and flung themselves back into their canoes, in which they made off with all speed for the shore, subjected meanwhile to a galling fire of grape and canister from our guns, which I very regretfully allowed to be maintained, believing that our only chance of safety lay in inflicting upon them a severe enough lesson to utterly discourage them from any renewal of the attack. We continued firing until the last canoe had reached the shore, by which time eleven of them had been utterly destroyed and several others badly damaged, resulting in a loss to Matadi of, according to my estimate, not far short of three hundred men. We had just ceased firing, and the men were busy securing the guns again, when the threatened storm burst forth, and our fight terminated with one of the most terrific tempests of thunder, lightning, and rain that I had ever been exposed to. It lasted until about three o'clock the next morning, and then passed off, leaving the heavens calm, clear, and serene once more, and the stars even more brilliant than they had been before the gathering of the storm. Of course, after the attempted surprise of the schooner by the savages, there was no more sleep for me that night, and before dawn I had resolved to send a boat ashore, demanding the surrender of Matadi and his chiefs, as hostages for the good behaviour of their people until the delivery of the English prisoners, the alternative, in case of refusal, being the destruction of the town.

Accordingly, as the rising sun was gilding the hill-tops, I ordered the boat to be lowered, and sent her away in Gowland's charge, with Lobo to act as interpreter, with a message to that effect. The guard of warriors still held the landing-place, and to the chief in command of them the message was given; its receipt, as Gowland subsequently informed me, producing a very considerable amount of consternation. The reply was that Matadi had been very severely wounded in the *accidental* engagement of the previous night, and was believed to be dying; but that the chief to whom the message had been given would communicate with his brother chiefs, and that we should receive their reply on the following morning. And to this Gowland had replied that if the white prisoners were not surrendered, safe and sound, or the whole of the chiefs, Matadi included, on board the schooner when the sun stood over a certain hill-top—which would be in about an hour from that moment — the schooner's guns would open fire upon the town and continue its bombardment until every house in it was razed to the ground. And therewith the gig returned to the ship, and was again hoisted to the davits.

This peremptory message, coupled no doubt with the experiences of the preceding night, had its desired effect ; for while the sun was still a quarter of an hour distant from that part of the heavens that Gowland had indicated, we saw a procession issue from the fetish-house in the centre of the town, which our telescopes enabled us to make out as consisting of a group of white men, closely guarded by a body of some two hundred armed warriors, detailed, it would appear, for the purpose of guarding the whites from the fury of the witch-doctors, or priests, who were thus most unwillingly deprived of their prey, and who accompanied the party right down to the shore, doing their best to instigate the people to attack the escort and recapture the released prisoners. There was a terrific hubbub over the affair, repeated rushes being made at the party ; but the guards appeared to use their clubs with great freedom, and eventually the cortège reached the river, and the whites were safely embarked in three large canoes which, manned by natives, and apparently in charge of some authoritative person, at once shoved off for the schooner.

Upon the arrival of this little flotilla alongside it was found that the white prisoners brought off for surrender numbered twenty-eight, all of whom were in a most wretched plight from sickness and the barbarous neglect with which they had been treated during their long and wearisome captivity. They consisted of the *Sapphire's* late second and third lieutenants, one midshipman, nine marines, and sixteen seamen ; one midshipman, three marines, and two seamen having died of fever during the time that they had been in Matadi's hands. So frightfully were they reduced by suffering and despair, that when the poor little surviving mid — a mere lad of sixteen—was helped up the side to the schooner's low deck his nerve entirely gave way, and he fell upon the planks in a paroxysm of hysterical tears, and wild, incoherent ejaculations of gratitude to God for having delivered him from a living death ; while as for the others, they were too deeply moved and shaken to utter more than a husky word or two for the moment, but the convulsive grip of their emaciated hands, their quivering lips, and the look of almost incredulous delight with which they gazed about them and into our faces, spoke far more eloquently than words. Needless to say, we gave them a most hearty and fraternal welcome, at once and before everything else providing as far as we could for their physical comfort, while Armstrong, our warm-hearted Scotch surgeon, immediately took them in hand with a good-will that promised wonders in the way of speedy restoration to health and strength.

During all this while the three canoes had remained alongside ; and by and by, when I had once more time to think of other matters than those more immediately concerning my guests, Lobo came to me and informed me that the chiefs who had brought off the released white men were waiting for the payment of the promised ransom. I thought this tolerably cool, after the treacherous manner in which they had attacked us during the preceding night ; but I was too greatly rejoiced at the success of my mission to be very severe or retributive in my behaviour just then. I therefore paid the full amount agreed upon, but directed Lobo to say that although I paid it I did not consider that Matadi was entitled to claim a single article, in view of his unprovoked attack upon the schooner, and the miserable condition in which he had delivered up his captives. But I paid it in order that he might practically learn that an Englishman never breaks a promise that he has once made. And having duly impressed this upon them, I gave them further to understand that, should it ever happen that other white men fell into their hands, they would be expected to treat them with the utmost kindness and consideration, upon pain of condign punishment should they fail to do so, and that upon delivering any such whites, safe and sound, to the first warship that might happen to enter the river, they would be handsomely rewarded.

This matter settled, our business with Matadi was at an end, and although there happened to be not a breath of wind stirring, I determined to make a start down the river at once, and get to sea as soon as possible, in order that the rescued men might not be deprived, for one moment longer than was absolutely necessary, of the restorative effects of the pure salt breeze. We accordingly manned the capstan forthwith, hove short, and then proceeded down-stream by the process of navigation known as "dredging"; that is to say, we kept the schooner in the proper channel by means of the anchor and the rudder combined, allowing the anchor to just touch and drag along the ground when it became necessary to sheer the ship away from a danger, and at other times heaving it off the ground a few feet and allowing the craft to drift with the current. And so strong was the rush of the river just then, that by its means alone we accomplished a descent of no less than thirty miles that day before sunset, anchoring for the night in a very snug cove on the northern bank of the river, under the shadow of some high hills. Then, during the night, a light southerly air sprang up, freshening towards morning into a spanking breeze that soon became half a gale of wind, and under its welcome impulse—although we found it rather shy with us in some of the narrowest and most intricate parts of the navigation—we contrived to complete the descent of the remaining portion of the river on our second day out from Matadi's town, arriving off the mouth of Banana Creek about an hour before sunset. Here, in fulfilment of my promise, I released Lobo, who, to do him justice, had served us well when he found that it was to his interest to do so. And I may now dismiss him finally from my story by saying that when one of the ships of our squadron put into the river about three weeks later, it was found that Señor Lobo had profited by my advice to the extent that he had disposed of his factory and other property, just as it stood, to his former manager—the purchase-money being paid three-fourths down, the remainder to be paid by instalments at three and six months' date. And a very excellent bargain he contrived to make, too, so I understood, the unfortunate buyer suffering a heavy loss when the captain of the cruiser made it his first business to destroy the barracoon, which formed a portion of the property, although the aforesaid buyer of course made a point of vowing most emphatically that he had no intention whatever of using the structure for slave-dealing purposes, to which also, as a matter of course, he declared that he had a most righteous aversion.

Having landed Lobo, we proceeded to sea that same night, carrying the southerly breeze with us all through the night, and then falling in with a regular twister from the eastward that carried us right across the Line to about lat. 0·47′ N. From thence we had light and variable breezes to Sierra Leone, despite which we made an excellent passage, arriving in the anchorage in just three days short of a month from the date of our leaving it upon our rescuing expedition; and I am happy to say that when we landed the rescued party they had all so far rallied as to render their perfect recovery merely a matter of time, provided, of course, that the deadly fever of the coast did not carry them off in the meanwhile.

On our arrival in Sierra Leone I was greatly surprised to find the *Barracouta* still in harbour; and I of course lost no time in going on board to report myself and, incidentally, to find out the reason of her prolonged stay in port. But on presenting myself on board I discovered that I had been mistaken in supposing her to have lain there idle during the whole period of my cruise—on the contrary, she had only arrived three days before the *Felicidad*; and after I had told my story and received the compliments of the captain and the rest of the officers upon what they were pleased to term the boldness and judgment with which I had executed my mission, I had to listen in return to a story as gruesome as can well be imagined, although it was told in very few words. It appeared, then, that a day or two after my departure, the *Barracouta* again put to sea with the fixed but unexpressed determination to prosecute a further search for the *Francesca*, the wind and weather having meanwhile been such as to encourage Captain Stopford in the hope that by adopting certain measures he might yet contrive to fall in with her. And he had done so, though by no means in the manner that he had expected, the cruise being without result in the direction in which he had hoped to meet with success. Some days later, however, after the search had been reluctantly abandoned, and while the brig was edging in towards the coast again, hoping to pick up a prize to recompense them in a measure for their disappointment, they had unexpectedly fallen in with the *Francesca* again, and were not long in coming to the conclusion that something was seriously wrong on board her, both her topmasts being carried away close to the caps and hanging suspended by the rigging, with no apparent effort being made to clear away the wreck, although the weather was then quite fine. Sail was of course at once made to close with the dismantled craft, and then another surprise met them, for although the intention of the brig must have been from the first moment unmistakable, no attempt was made to avoid the encounter, which, however, was accounted for a little later by the fact that the *Francesca* appeared to be in an unmanageable condition. Then, as the brig neared her still more closely, it was seen that the sweeps were rigged out but not manned, although the deck was crowded with people, unmistakably blacks. And then it was that for the first time the dreadful surmise dawned upon Captain Stopford's mind—a surmise that soon proved to be true—that the negroes, doubtless goaded to frenzy by their continued ill-treatment, had risen upon and massacred the entire crew and taken possession of the brigantine, which of course they had not the remotest idea how to handle.

The *Barracouta* soon arrived upon the *Francesca's* weather quarter, and the evidences of the fearful deed then became unmistakable, the scuppers still bearing the stains of the ensanguined stream that had poured from them, while among the whole of that crowd of yelling, fiercely gesticulating blacks, not a single white face was to be seen. Boats were at once lowered and a strong crew sent away to take possession of the disabled vessel, but the emancipated slaves, maddened at the thought of again falling into the hands of the hated whites, and, of course, unaware of the fact that the brig's crew were anxious only to render them a service, offered so desperate a resistance to the boarders that Young,

who led the latter, recognizing the impossibility of taking the brigantine without serious loss of life, withdrew to consult with Captain Stopford as to the best course to pursue. Meanwhile, the wind fell away to a calm, of which circumstance the slaves took advantage by manning the sweeps and gradually withdrawing from the vicinity of the *Barracouta*. This was about sunset; and three hours later a bright blaze upon the horizon proclaimed that the notorious *Francesca* had either caught or been set on fire in some inexplicable way. The brig's boats were at once manned and dispatched to the rescue of the unhappy blacks, or as many of them as it might be possible to save; but the brigantine was by this time some nine miles away, the flames burnt with ever-increasing fury, and while the boats were still some three miles distant the doomed ship blew up, and the occupants of the boats saw the bodies of the miserable blacks hurled high in the air in the midst of a dazzling sheet of flame and a cloud of smoke. When the boats arrived upon the scene of the disaster, all that remained of the once gallant but guilty *Francesca* consisted of a few charred timbers and fragments of half-burnt planking, in the midst of which floated some forty or fifty dead bodies of negroes; the rest had vanished—whither?

Such, reader, is the story, and such was the end of the Pirate Slaver, the terrible doom of which, when it became known, caused such a thrill of horror in the breasts of those who had emulated her crew in their career of crime, that from that time forward there was a noticeable falling-off in the number of vessels frequenting the West African rivers in search of slaves; and finally, a year or two later, the appearance of fast steamers in the slave squadron rendered the chances of success so remote that but a few of the most enterprising had heart to continue the pursuit of so risky and unprofitable a business. And when these were one by one captured and their vessels condemned, the infamous trade dwindled more and more, until it finally died out altogether, never, let us hope, to be revived again.

THE END

www.ingramcontent.com/pod-product-compliance
Lightning Source LLC
Chambersburg PA
CBHW020756020726
47495CB00008B/2461